VAPORIZED

VAPORIZED

VICTOR LEVINE

VAPORIZED

VICTOR LEVINE

Spec Time Trilogy
Author's Notes

The **"Spec Time Trilogy"** is a series of books about the conflicted path of an aspiring rock musician, Jon Cells. Equal parts entertainment, historical fiction, and social commentary, the stories, based on an actual character, chronicle three distinct phases of the musician's career and the conditions that helped shape his destiny. Lyrics from each period are woven into the narrative, and the music from those times has been released on separate CDs. "Rocky Heights" music relates to **"Spiritualized"**, "Cracked House" music was recorded during **"Vaporized"**, and "Nobody's Fault" has songs related to **"Immortalized"**.

The first book, **"Spiritualized"** (published in 2015), takes place in and around Boulder, Colorado in 1978. It is framed as a story of growth from one state of awareness to another. The second book, **"Vaporized"** (published in 2011), takes place in Manhattan in 1982 and follows the rough road to glory. The third book, **"Immortalized"**, set in Los Angeles in 1986 (due out in 2017), is about embracing destiny.

The books are interconnected with recurring characters and themes, and each has a procedural mystery that drives the action. All the stories take place over consecutive four-day periods, and characters from the periphery, mystical forces, and relevant subplots broaden the stories of a musician's quest for success into twisted tales with unexpected endings. Some of the Trilogy is based on facts, but all people and events are fictionalized versions of the truth. Lyrics to **actual songs,** most **by Jon Cells** and available on his commercially released CDs, appear in italics.

Acknowledgements

The author is truly grateful for the prescient belief and unwavering commitment of his wife, Kathryn, whose shared karma, love, and support made this book possible.

Additionally, he thanks first readers for their poignant suggestions; savvy editors for their keen-eyed comments; old friends and fellow travelers for sharing parts of their journeys; his sons, Seth, Daniel, and Drew for keeping him and the spirit of the music alive; and all his family members for seeing him through the tough times.

This book is dedicated to John Neulinger,
who, true to his word, "died trying."

"They got a name for the winners in the world.
I want a name when I lose."
   "Deacon Blues" by Steely Dan

MANHATTAN, NEW YORK
THURSDAY, APRIL 15TH, 1982

CHAPTER 1

Jon Cells never filed a tax return, so when the noise woke him up that day, he smacked his hand on the bedside table where his alarm clock lived and tried to go back to sleep. The annoying sounds didn't stop, so he stuck his head and torso out the apartment window and yelled "shut up!" The sidewalk was full of pedestrians but no one looked up. The car alarm stopped by itself, but other cars, jockeying for shortcuts as they inched along the crowded street, drowned out the morning calm with angry beeps and tire squeals. Sneezing on exhaust fumes, Jon forced the window shut. The giant neon clock across the street – the one he actually relied on – blinked through his flimsy curtains. He lit a cigarette and re-arranged his hair, trying to come to grips with reality.

Yesterday's clothes were still on the chair, but he picked up the electric guitar lying next to them instead. Sitting naked on the edge of the bed, he cradled the cool, contoured body against his skin and fingered the neck, mindlessly strumming the song he had been working on the night before: G minor to C minor, then back again. The rhythm crept into his right hand and an early morning dream began to re-materialize. He was performing with his band in front of a packed house at Max's Kansas City. They bounced a heavy pocket off the low ceiling and the crowd pulsed provocatively under its suggestive weight. Lyrics squirmed on his tongue like

1

a live oyster: *"Just my disposition, to do the things I do."* He savored the lines a few times before the taste of inspiration stood him up. Holding the body of the guitar against his waist with his right hand, he rose up bent his knees, one at a time, and marched in place to the rhythm. Then the song took on a life of its own: His left hand stayed with G minor on the third fret while his huge right thumb raked down on the strings and snapped the up-strums. A bass line formed from the hammer-ons and lift-offs. *"A man in my position holds some things to be true,"* he rhymed, repeating the lines until they rode the beat. Weaving some single-note figures between the changes, he felt his free-swinging manhood pulse to life. But just as conviction took shape, his two-dollar alarm clock decided to remind him of the time. Frustrated that he couldn't capture his fresh ideas, he knocked the clock off the table, leaned his guitar back on the chair, and picked up his work clothes. Slipping on the same slinky shirt he'd been wearing all week and wriggling into his skin-tight jeans, he kicked the bedroom door shut with the back of his boot and abandoned songwriting for the day.

Over thirty, in a beaten leather jacket, and determined to keep his dream alive, Jon cruised past the densely packed import boutiques on Canal Street, his field of vision as much occupied by the demons in his head as with the colorful plastic gargoyles hanging from the eaves. Tousling his hair as he passed fragments of his reflection in the store windows, he glanced furtively to see who might be watching. He wasn't sure if anyone was – but that was only half the problem.

Jon wanted it all: recognition, rationalization, notoriety, compensation, adoration, vindication, and relief from the pressures in his head. He wasn't sure how he was going to achieve "it" – what he called "artistic success" – but he knew he was running out of time. Unsettled and dissatisfied, every clack of his heel on the pavement gave him the comforting illusion that even if he was years behind, he was, at least, still firmly on his way. His wiry frame was charged with nervous energy as he twisted through shopkeepers' offerings that protruded onto the sidewalk. With pointed boots, he strode around early morning browsers, groggy homeless sleepers, professional dog walkers, and uniformed school children. He avoided eye contact with the young lovers holding hands, didn't acknowledge the head nods of the local population, and steered clear of all contact that might alter his appointment with destiny. A subliminal soundtrack paced his heels-first tromp. Gibberish, masquerading as words, gurgled between the lyrics he had already settled on.

"Just my disposition,
To do the things I do.
A man in my position,
Holds some things to be true." *1

Moving smoothly across the uneven sidewalks and like a stealthy predator, Jon crossed the side streets as if he had special permission from the traffic gods who regulated the daily migration through the stone canyons. The familiar smells of smoke and coffee eddied around the vortex of his fitful march, and he breathed in the edible vapors deeply enough to satisfy his hunger without breaking stride. People seemed to bounce off his energy field like polarized magnets as he careened through the busy streets of lower Manhattan with the untamed confidence of a distorted whole-tone solo.

Approaching the wide ravine of Broadway, Jon spotted an intriguing ripple in the scattered flock of people ahead of him – a shapely woman walking in the same direction. Almost unconsciously, his pace quickened, and he accelerated through the gauntlet of pedestrians, trying to get closer. But before he could catch up, she sashayed across Broadway and the lights changed, leaving him stuck on the other side. Squinting into the bright clouds of the gray morning that silhouetted the buildings, he waited impatiently at the edge of the swirling river of traffic.

While he was waiting, switching his weight from one foot to the other, a middle-aged man with glasses edged warily away from him. Jon didn't notice him, or the two schoolgirls who were also waiting to cross. The children were too young to understand Jon's kinetic presence, but their bodies reacted violently. One of them stumbled off the curb and into the street. Instinctively, the man with the glasses grabbed her arm and pulled her back to safety just before she was sideswiped by a racing taxicab.

"Watch where you're going!" the man lashed out at both the taxi and Jon.

Jon barely heard him. He had seen the little girl saved from disaster, but it never crossed his mind that he had anything to do with it. Who was that guy talking to? Jon looked around and wasn't sure.

"Watch where you're going!" the man repeated, pointing an admonishing finger at Jon's face.

Jon squinted down and tightened his lips against gritted teeth. Six foot two, vain, and sometimes mistaken for Robert Plant, his shaggy blond mane and bright blue eyes made him believe he was as important as he felt. His resentment circuits began to charge, but before he could retaliate, caution seized his accuser. Ralph Lowell put his arm on the shoulder of the youngster he had rescued, and the girl moved within the aura of his protection. Jon disengaged, and as soon as the walk lights changed, hurried across the street. A few steps behind, Ralph Lowell shepherded the young girls through the intersection and waited until Jon had gone ahead.

The street-corner incident had thrown off Jon's timing, so he slowed down to peek into the buildings, looking for the woman who had caught his eye. He thought he saw her disappear into a corner shop and stopped for a closer look. The bright daylight obscured the store interior, and he had to cup his eyes against the glass to see inside. A man behind the register at the bodega spoke to a customer whose curly hair was cinched in a high ponytail. Jon couldn't see her face, but while he was pressed up against the glass, Sonya Diaz leaned over the counter and kissed her uncle on the cheek as he handed her a small bag. Jon couldn't remember where he had seen her before and crept away before she came out.

Still walking with the schoolgirls a safe distance behind, Ralph Lowell saw the top of Jon's head bobbing through the crowd ahead of them. He accompanied the girls to the gate of their school-yard, then continued another block to his office building on Varick Street. After showing his badge to the guard, he took the elevator to the second floor and settled into his administrative job at the United States Customs Department.

Detective Todd Falin, who was already at work in the Enforcement Division of the Customs Department one floor up from Agent Lowell, had no idea that Jon Cells was even in New York. The file with his picture in it had been sitting on his desk for a week, but there were so many other files related to the same investigation he hadn't looked through it yet. It had been three years since Detective Falin had even thought about Jon Cells, so when he found it later that morning he was surprised to see Jon's picture on his desk again. The memo from the FBI authorizing the stakeout at Laden Imports didn't mention him, and Detective Falin didn't understand Jon's connection to the case. As he shuffled through the stack of reports and surveillance photos, trying to piece together the relationships between his suspects, he remembered the Colorado bust that had put Jon's backers out of business. He never knew if Jon was guilty of anything, because by the time it came to charge somebody, the department decided to concentrate on bigger targets. Jon had slipped off Detective Falin's radar without even knowing he had been on it – and had no idea that the place he was now working at was under surveillance by the same man.

The same bust that had facilitated Detective Falin's promotion to the New York office, had also brought Jon Cells back east. With his freewheeling Colorado friend Duke sidelined and his musical prospects diminished, Jon bought a box van for his equipment and moved back to New York, hoping to continue his career. After several years in the relative isolation of the Rocky Mountains, he was more than ready to embrace the musical zeitgeist that had migrated from London to Manhattan. His band moved with him, and they fit right in with the post-punk music scene that was starting to turn out national acts. Money was tight, but they rented a loft together and scraped by in between gigs. Totally committed, Jon was determined to make a name for himself, and believed he was on the verge of something big. He went midnight bowling with David Byrne and the Talking Heads, visited the eat-out bars and invitation-only clubs with Joey Ramone and other low-life celebrities, shared a love interest with his arch friend from Boulder, Marc Campbell, and was a regular in the crowd at CBGB's and other clubs where Seymour Stein and other music business tastemakers cultivated talent. Jon's group, Cells, played some shows in and around New York, got a little local radio airplay, and was developing a reputation as a contender before they suffered the critical setback they were still trying to recover from.

A late-night altercation with the manager of a rival band resulted in Jon's arrest for possession of a controlled substance, and the punishment – ninety days of supervised release – required him to, among other things, get a job society approved of. Humbled, he found work in the warehouse of a perfume factory at the western end of Canal Street through his father's contact. As the singer, songwriter, and leader of the band, Jon's involuntary removal from the music scene sent his bandmates scrambling, but Jon felt like they were holding him back and he didn't really miss them. He rented a room in a different apartment and planned on lying low for a few months, cutting himself off, using the parole as an excuse to write, rest, and reinvent himself before restarting his career as a solo artist.

Nearing the perfume factory, the sickeningly sweet smells scented the sidewalk for two blocks in all directions, and he held his breath as he went inside for another day's penance. Surprisingly, despite fifteen years of promoting his outsized artistic visions — often at the expense of his health – he was still ruggedly handsome and exceedingly strong. And although his day job could be physically demanding, it wasn't much of a mental challenge, so he was able to keep his internal soundtrack going most of the time. There were only ten more days to go before the terms of his parole were satisfied and he would be free to come out of hiding, quit his day job, and reassume control of his destiny.

CHAPTER 2

Laden Imports was a thoroughly Persian enterprise, with roots that stretched back into the ancient history of perfumery. They had been in the lanolin business for almost 100 years, and most of their commerce was now based on that animal elixir. The viscous yellow oil arrived at the warehouse in the same steel-girdled oak casks used to age whiskey, and these substantial barrels dominated the other, smaller, imported vats, urns, bottles, and boxes that were racked and stacked on the factory floor like the buildings of a miniature city. The gelatinous lanolin still reeked of the musky scent of the animals that had produced it, and that scent was the underlying odor that seeped into every crevice of the building. Originally thought to be a useless bi-product of cleaning wool, lanolin usage had grown exponentially since 1882 when an Englishman first patented an effective process for separating, collecting, and processing the pungent bodily secretions that sheep use to protect their hair and skin, and eventually lanolin production and trade became its own international business that rivaled wool manufacturing. The cleaned wool was spun into threads for blankets and clothing, while the wool grease became the basis of hundreds of products that manufacturers refined into soaps, ointments, and lubricants. Besides lanolin, Laden, whose name was an Anglicized version of a Persian word for flowers, also imported and sold an exotic assortment of organic additives that they and their customers combined with the lanolin to make perfumes, cosmetics, and foods. Using a secret family process, Laden also made their own line of specialty products, but jealous competitors had tipped off law enforcement officials that some of their practices were questionable.

Detective Falin, the Customs Enforcement agent who was leading the Laden Imports investigation, had his own agenda. Too ambitious to be satisfied shuffling papers like the agents on the floor below him, he saw Laden's filing irregularities as a career advancement opportunity. The case was too complicated for his department to handle by themselves, so the FBI had been brought in to oversee what had become a multi-agency operation. Detective Falin was already convinced that Laden was up to something illegal, and the sudden appearance of another onetime suspect, Jon Cells, excited his detective instincts. Swallowing the saliva on the back of his tongue, he leaned back in his swivel chair and called Director Lawson at the FBI to schedule expanded surveillance for the coming weekend.

The anonymity Jon enjoyed on the street was compromised at the workplace, so he entered the front office like a coiled twister and blew directly into the warehouse without speaking to any of the young women at their desks. The wake of his male hormones stirred a flurry of comments, and Rebecca Draper, a pretty twenty-two year old, blushed when he passed behind her. Her workmate, Asalah, the daughter of one of the owners, couldn't control her ear-splitting grin.

"I think he likes you," she teased.

"You do?" Rebecca feigned innocence and ran her hand through her long straight brown hair.

"Oh yeah, I can tell," Asalah chirped. Equally pretty but already married, Asalah lived vicariously through Rebecca's infatuations. She turned up the office radio and sang along to the chorus of the popular Foreigner song. "I've been waiting for a girl like you."

Rebecca hid her smile in her paperwork.

Asalah's father, Saeed Monsouri, was one of the three Monsouri siblings who had moved to the States as young children and now owned Laden Imports. One of his oldest contacts, a wool broker from Prague, had prevailed upon him to help rehabilitate the troubled son of a mutual friend, which is how Jon got the job working in the Laden warehouse. The previous warehouse worker had quit the day before Jon's interview, and so, in spite of his appearance and attitude, they put him to work. To everyone's surprise, including his own, Jon's chitinous rock and roll exterior helped him survive in the pungent environment of the Laden warehouse longer than anyone expected. The physical work was good exercise, and he could remain preoccupied with artistic goals while serving his parole, and he was actually beginning to enjoy his new routine before everything changed.

Inside the warehouse, Colonel Mackenzie, a former Jamaican police officer everyone called Mak, was in charge. He had been with Laden for eight years, and besides his regular job, it was his responsibility to supervise Jon and field the biweekly calls from Jon's parole officer. Mak, half as wide as he was tall, was standing in the locker room buttoning a pressed, heavy canvas work shirt that strained to hold his bulge when Jon entered. "Morning Johnny Soldier. How's the war today?" Mak greeted him in a basso voice that filled the tiny room. His question, full of artificially cheerful island charm, emanated from an oversized square head that was covered with a fuzzy gray carpet of short-cropped curls.

"Morning Mak," Jon answered, completing the ritual exchange with an imitation salute. Uncomfortable in the small room mislabeled "employee lounge," he slipped off his leather jacket and hung it in the crusty metal locker he had been assigned. The driving bass line of his new song, "Disposition", faded, and the emotional intensity of his morning journey dispersed like a bullet fired into a pillow.

Never far from his training, Mak treated all his assistants as conscripts. Watching his charge with watery eyes that rarely blinked, he tested Jon's mettle. "Are we ready for battle today, Jonny Soldier?"

"Ready as I'll ever be," Jon answered, seating himself on a hard wood bench and wrestling out of his pointy boots.

"Ready to honor our history? Carry the flag of our fathers?" Mak probed with Calypso rhetoric.

Jon recoiled at the thought of his father. He slipped his ultra-thin nylon socks into the used work boots he had been given and yanked the laces tight enough to pinch his ankles, searching for a potent response. "Ready to make the sheep stink!" he blurted, standing up and covering his street clothes with a Laden work shirt.

"Always comes back to the sheep," Mak agreed. His proselytizing continued as they went into the main warehouse. "Ready to right the wrongs of this world and the next?"

Jon reverted to adolescent sarcasm as he marched behind in mock formation. "Ready or not, here I come." Making fun of everything made it almost bearable.

Mak retrieved the day's order sheets from a gray metal inbox and spoke aloud as he thumbed through them. "Says we got a few deliveries to get ready for next week, but nothing going out today. We'll brew up some Princess Mist tomorrow."

"Princess Mist," Jon repeated absently, fidgeting with the guitar picks in his pocket. Wrestling the urge to smoke a cigarette, his body twitched and twisted in the slow-motion time, while his disinterest drifted through the dusty rafters. He fixated on squealing exhaust fan bearings that reminded him of feedback, and was halfway through an imaginary solo when Mak summoned his attention again.

"Let's go to the dock and see what the tide washed up."

"Ahoy matey." They shuffled past the organized clutter, Mak trudging purposefully with a clipboard in his hand while Jon, still wired from his morning march, scuffled a solo over the one-and-a- two rhythm of their squeaky shoes against the oil-soaked floor. Working at Laden was like spending the day in a foreign country, and the oily warehouse floor was just an additional hazard in an environment whose signature affront was olfactory. The scented oils, which were mixed with the animal sweat to mask its original unpleasant odor, were also malodorous in their undiluted state. Some of the additive solutions were so old that the earthenware urns they came in had value as antiques, and because their voyages to the factory in the holds of freighters were sometimes disastrous, a special corner of the warehouse was reserved for the cracked, empty, and oozing pottery. Mak saw them as garbage, but Saeed was collecting these relics for resale to antiquity dealers and no one was allowed to disturb his nest eggs. Wooden crates and containers, built by local craftsmen using every available resource to protect the bundles of dried organics from the hazards of temperature and weather, were decorated with enough customs papers, stamps, and seals to keep a small anthropology department busy for years, but identifying the contents was a matter of guesswork for the uninitiated. The United States Customs Department was not comfortable with guesswork, but there weren't even accepted English names for some of the plant materials, so in the interest of expediting the commercial enterprise of well-connected businessmen, some of Laden Imports' paperwork was accepted without verification. Were it not for the Laden labels that listed the contents and customers' names, no one other than the two Monsouri brothers would have known what was inside.

Jon wasn't really curious about anything that Laden did, and only paid attention to what was absolutely necessary. Mak had been able to train him in the variety of techniques for repositioning the unwieldy inventory, and was relieved that he had finally found someone with the intelligence, strength, and stamina to do the job. The hard labor and exposure to noxious fumes claimed the vitality of most hires within a few days, and it had been years since anyone besides Mak had lasted more than six months. Jon's predecessors who had been hired due to fascinations with perfumery, were either unwilling or incapable of doing the physical work, and fit laborers who worked for a few weeks at a time were usually too ill-tempered, dim, or impatient to master the subtleties of handling the delicate inventory.

Some of Jon's abilities were a direct result of his cautious determination to avoid a career ending injury to his hands or fingers. Had he known that Mak was even thinking about grooming him for long-term employment, he would have quit on the spot, because his own plans didn't include spending the rest of his life working at a perfume factory. They stopped to rest every so often and as usual, Jon lit a cigarette and Mak took the opportunity to comfort himself with the sound of his own voice.

"Oh mon, this body ain't getting any younger." Mak said, leaning against a wall and bending over, stretching his arms while they paused.

Although he was sixty pounds lighter, Jon was several inches taller and almost as strong. Flaunting his youth and flexibility, he hopped backwards onto a stack of boxes, inhaled his cigarette, and blew a stream of smoke into the dead air.

"My back's hurting so bad I can't sleep at night," Mak admitted, grimacing as he tried to touch his ankles. "What's been keeping you up at night?"

Jon pressed his thumbnail into the thick calluses on the fingertips of his left hand. "Been playin' a lot."

"Say what have you been playing, Jonny Soldier?"

"Been playing dead, been playing alive." Jon answered enigmatically, then took a long drag on his cigarette.

Mak was not unarmed in a battle of wits. "You keep puffing that smoke stick and you won't be *playing* dead," Jon acknowledged Mak's point with a final drag before coming down off his perch. He ground the butt to death with the toe of his boot and Mak announced a necessary truce. "Come on soldier, we got work to do here."

Mak's experience as a policeman in Kingston had taught him how to handle volatile characters whose only escape from the paradisiacal prison of "island time" was chemical. His steady demeanor had moved him up the ranks to Precinct Captain, and his risky journey to the States, with a wife and child in tow, was undertaken with nothing more than the offer of a job from an indebted Persian businessman whom he had saved from a long jail sentence. Mak didn't see Sattar Monsouri often, but their bond of trust had developed into mutual dependency. Sattar's niece, Homa, ran the business, but there was a lot she didn't know — and no one was in a hurry to tell her. As the chief cook for the past six years, Mak's understanding of perfumery amounted to a highly specialized skill, and he was the first non-family member to be initiated into Laden's proprietary art of odiferous formulation. Curing the premix with the first dilution of alcohol was just the beginning of a process that could take years, and aging brews in various states of readiness lined the shelves of the mixing vault. Keeping track of each batch was more often a matter of judgment than documentation, so Mak had become a highly trusted and integral part of Laden's operation. But although he was basically honest and trustworthy, Mak was not a saint, and since Laden Imports' dependence on him did not earn him all the money he felt entitled to, he had devised an alternate method to exact his just rewards. His employers were unaware of his side business, but the United States Bureau of Arms and Tobacco was not.

Rebecca came into the warehouse to deliver some order forms and watched the men working from a distance. All the office girls were keen to discover Jon's sexual preferences, but had been unsuccessful at warming his cool distance. Jon saw her from across the room and brushed his hair back, lost in dreams of success. His idea of stardom wasn't big houses and fancy friends, and he didn't see himself as a role model with legions of followers, and although he wanted the luxury of money and satisfaction of recognition, he would only accept them on his own terms. Fiercely, he clung to the conceit that anything he did to win that approval would spoil the essence of his artistry.

> *"Just my own convictions,*
> *I'm serving sentence to."* *2

But Jon's defective logic was only one of his problems, and he couldn't avoid the queasiness when a slow whistle would ascend from the base of his neck and spread into his cranium. His vision would blur, and inanimate objects would change in ways he couldn't control or understand. Fighting the sensation of floating above an unseen abyss, he would feel like he was peering over the precipice of sanity. The air would become full of tiny blinking dots of light that drifted like soap bubbles across his retinas. Ordinary sounds would speak to him in incomprehensible chortles. His tongue would go numb and everything would smell rotten. Jon knew he wasn't normal, and characterized his altered states as artistic vision. These visions usually preceded a dizzying nausea which forced him to lie down in a dark room waiting for what doctors had told him was a "migraine" to pass. After the episodes, he questioned whether he was a gifted visionary, or losing his mind, one seizure at a time.

CHAPTER 3

The local radio station masked the grunts and groans of the physical labor, and Jon took mental pleasure in juxtaposing the harsh sounds of survival with the station's commercial inducements, nursery rhyme lyrics, and puerile melodies that cursed his ears.

"Jonny, Jonny Soldier?" Mak's friendly island drawl sounded like part of the song on the radio, and Jon, who had been wandering in the fields of his own fertile imagination, was startled by the interruption to his internal mash-up. Mak was already accustomed to some of Jon's peculiar habits and had learned how to manage them. "Hungry yet? Did you bring lunch today or will you be sharing mine again?" Mak asked, flexing his paternal muscles.

Jon grinned. "Of course I brought lunch; got my hot air-sandwich right here," he mimed, holding an invisible hoagie with both hands and chomping a satisfying bite.

Mak chuckled. "Oh, I expected as much from you. Never mind; you know my Missy K always packs us some extra. We got to keep you strong so I don't have to do everything by myself. Come on, let's break for lunch." They left their burdens in the middle of the floor and set up a makeshift lunchroom among a cluster of empty barrels. Mak opened the plastic containers of jerk chicken and cornbread, and Mak watched his worker share with the satisfaction of a farmer feeding his livestock. Jon devoured the nourishment eagerly, smacking his lips and wiping his hands on his pants with his attitude of a buoyant eight year old. Mak took the opportunity expand his influence. "Missy K wants to know when you're comin' by for dinner. What do I tell her?"

Jon paused to chew on the question. He knew that Mak sometimes just needed to hear himself talk, so he didn't answer.

"She already knows how much you like her cooking," Mak went on. "Why don't you come by and put some meat on that skeleton?"

Jon kept eating. "Sure thing, Mak mon," he responded. Missy K had come by the warehouse a few times, and her empathy made her receptive to Jon's needs. She always sent enough lunch for two, and just as a wild kitten learns to take a bowl of milk, she had tamed Jon with an invisible hand. He thought about the invitation and realized Missy K's kitchen would be a lot nicer than the barren efficiency apartment he shared with a roommate. Jon's usual diet was something wolfed down from one of the ubiquitous street-side eateries in lower Greenwich Village, and "cooking" meant boiling water for tea or coffee on the neglected two-burner gas stove of his apartment. The only food he prepared was toast; everything else came in a container, bag, or a can. Eating was not what excited him. He was too high-strung to be comfortable wasting time feeding himself. He didn't own a TV to fill his idle hours, and sitting around dining was an unfamiliar activity that took place in a social language that he couldn't understand. Usually, he rejected anything that took him away from the one thing in his apartment that dominated his life and filled most of his voids: something that took up not only the vacant space, but the lonely time as well. It was a simple device, but complex at the same time; predictable, but capable of endless variety. The mechanism connected him to the outside world and acted like a cipher for the nameless urges swimming like blind creatures in the turbid waters of his soul. Jon clung to his guitar like a drowning man grasps a lifeline. This was the channel through which the suppressed frustration of the day's indignities escaped like steam from a boiling cauldron, and where, on occasion, denser feelings frothed to the surface. He never wanted to make plans that would separate him from his guitar for too long, but Mak's invitation was tempting. He thought about a hot meal and friendly company. "So when's Missy K makin' her famous salt-fish?" he asked after an unnaturally long silence.

His question startled Mak, who had assumed that the invitation had been rejected as usual. Mak peered cautiously at his unpredictable lunchmate and asked for confirmation. "You say you're comin' by tonight, Jonny Soldier? Comin' to our place for supper?" he added with a touch of surprise.

Jon raised his eyes and nodded yes with half a smile. He couldn't help but like Mak, who was one of the few people he felt he could trust. "Aye, Mak mon. I'm comin' tonight if it's saltfish," he answered in his best Islandese.

"I'll call Missy K now and tell her the good news," Mak confirmed. "Put on the saltfish and let the coco bread rise. Jonny Soldier come marching home." He got up from his lunch seat and went straight to the office to call his wife, reporting the news in a triumphant voice he knew the office girls would hear. Rebecca was surprised and Asalah whispered her secret speculations. They all knew this was the first time Jon had made plans to see anyone from work outside of business hours. Jon was unaware that he was generally liked for his work ethic alone, and he didn't really know how unusual his habit of just showing up and doing his job without complaining was. Everyone could tell that he was headed in his own direction, but they were so wrapped up in their own pilgrimages that they didn't try too hard to understand his path. He didn't intentionally make enemies, and his taciturn manners passed as polite and considerate. The girls in the office liked what little they knew of him, but he was too wrapped up in his own reality to grok their subtle flirtations. He had been invited for coffee, lunch, drinks, and shows, but had declined all invitations with a terse, "I'm busy." His excuses were more transparent than he realized, and speculation about his social life was a lively cluck in the office henhouse. Nothing feeds a mystery more effectively than the lack of information, and in the active fantasy life of his co-workers, Jon had more detectives on his case than he knew.

After lunch, Mak and Jon resumed the inventory wrangling in a noticeably lighter mood; sniffing, poking, and pondering the strange and unknowable contents of the trunks and making jokes at the expense of the long-serving delivery driver, Angel Herrera. Mak waved his hand under his nose. "Whew! This one stinks more than Angel at the end of the week," he joked. "They won't even let him in the office anymore so I have to deliver his time card for him."

"Yeah, Angel can be pretty rough. Good thing we don't see him too often," Jon agreed. "They really don't let him in the office?"

"No sir. Not the way he acts around the ladies. I had to beg Homa not to fire him."

"What did he do?" Jon was actually curious.

"Well let's just say he's no gentleman. Not like you."

"Me? What did I do?" Jon misunderstood.

"You? It's more like what you didn't do."

"I didn't do something I was supposed to?"

"Well, it's not like you were supposed to, but you know how women are."

"Yeah, I guess." Jon had no idea what they were talking about.

Mak had never met anyone so unaware of how they fit into the social politics of the workplace. He revisited the topic throughout their afternoon banter, partly out of curiosity, partly out of sport. The prospect of real food made the barrels more cooperative and the odors seem sweet, and by the time 4:00 rolled around, Jon felt more alive than he had in months.

"So, Jonny, which way you headed?" Mak asked as they stacked the last few small trunks of dried flowers into an unsteady tower.

Jon sneezed from the plant dust. "Across Laight."

"Is that where you're living?"

"No, I just go that way." Jon was never too comfortable sharing personal information. "I live off Canal." He pulled a cigarette from his front pocket and lit up while Mak surveyed the warehouse, looking for anything left undone.

"We stay in Brooklyn, over by Fort Green Park." Mak said. "You can take the IND local and get off at DeKalb." He checked to see if Jon was listening. "Got to give Missy K time to get ready. You come by number 1336 B on Adelphi, say around 6:00?"

"1336 B on Adelphi at 6:00," Jon confirmed, combing the plant residue from his hair with his dirty fingers. The remembered smell of fresh baked muffins from his mother's kitchen wafted through Jon's mind, temporarily overpowering the factory fumes. "You tell Missy K that I'll be there this time," Jon apologized as they entered the unfiltered glare of the locker room. "And tell her she can't make enough to satisfy this hungry." His pale skin and gaunt stare testified.

Mak was finished changing first, and at 4:30 he repeated his address, disappeared into the office, and hurried out the main door. Jon took his time dressing. He used a damp towel to clean the sweat from his neck and torso, wiped his face in the mirror as if he were taking a sponge bath, washed the oils off his hands with the special soap from the dispenser, fluffed the dust from his hair, rinsed his mouth out with gargled water, and blew greenish gray mucous out of his nose. Satisfied that he had regained his enough corporal vanity, he threw his filthy work shirt in the bottom of his locker on top of his work shoes and kicked the metal door shut with the back of his boot. Strutting noticeably, he went into the office to punch out. His friendly goodbye set off another round of cackling, and Rebecca flinched as he passed behind her on his way out the front door.

"He definitely likes you," Asalah teased after he left.

"Oh I don't know," Rebecca blushed, nervously twisting the buttons on her jacket sleeve. She'd had a crush on Jon from the minute she saw him, and even though he only said goodbye, this was his first real hello. She didn't know much about him, but crushes aren't about information. His messy hair, skinny jeans, crooked smile, and animal magnetism gave her a low voltage charge that aroused her feminine instincts. She didn't want the other girls to know the extent of her infatuation, but they all expected her moment would come.

CHAPTER 4

Once outside, Jon gathered the thoughts he had left there in the morning and set off in the general direction of the nearby 8th Avenue subway station. There wasn't any reason to go home and then walk all the way back to the station, and he had less than an hour to kill, so after passing a few blocks of indistinct industrial buildings, he crossed the elevated walkway and ambled past storefronts he had never noticed before. They were selling furniture and vacuum cleaners, beauty and health products, vegetables and groceries – things Jon never bought. He wondered who shopped at these places and what their lives were like. He had grown up in a nominally functional household, but had somehow been denied the essence of the experience. The outsider status of his immigrant parents was a veil through which he saw the world, and even though he lived in the city now and was surrounded by people, he felt that he merely co-existed with them. He lived on the fringe, relegated to the frayed edge outside the seam of society's fabric. In his highest moments, he celebrated his alienation with soaring artistic ambition, but in darker moods, only chemicals relieved his angst.

Jon went into a narrow magazine store to see what everyone else was finding so interesting. He wasn't looking for anything in particular, and his eyes were drawn to the glossy covers of magazines featuring musicians. The Clash and Joan Jett were attracting a lot of attention, and the second British invasion was underway.

The news gave Jon hope. It was the reason he stayed up late at night working on the details of his songs, on the thickness of his calluses, searching for a voice to answer his calling. His early success had been limited to displays of technical dexterity on his Gibson twelve string, a handful of intriguing performances as part of an acid acoustic duo, and several heart-stopping, drug-fueled performances with his electric band. The singles he recorded in Colorado were released on Duke Dunn's custom label, but no one had the focus and commitment to promote them. Jon's appearance in an Andy Warhol film, and collaboration with well-known poet, Anne Waldman, were largely unknown. But since coming back to New York, Jon had established a presence, and everyone who saw him perform knew he had the talent and looks; they figured the rest was just fate.

Jon first picked up a guitar when he was fourteen years old. Both he and his neighbor Nathan got them as Christmas presents one snowy December in 1964. The instruction books showed them how to tune their instruments and where to put their fingers to make chords, and the long nights of that winter were filled with their first crude attempts to make music. A bit older than Jon, Nathan was also a social outcast; the kind of teen whose attention was focused on a reality only he seemed to understand. His gentle nature and offbeat sensibilities were a good balance to Jon's nervous self-confidence, and they formed a musical bond against the brutality of teenage taunts.

Jon's parents were Czechoslovakian refugees from the Bohemian city of Tetschen, a small but strategically located metropolis on the Czechoslavakian side of the river that formed the boundary with Germany. The fertile land had hosted the rise and fall of Celtic, Moravian, Hussite, and Iranian empires, but all the bloodlines were eventually absorbed into the two dominant groups: Germanic and Slavic. During World War II, Jon's father, Kurt, was labeled "mischling" – a pejorative used to describe people who were partially Jewish, and in a cruel twist of geopolitical fate, none of the governmental authorities would grant him citizenship in the land of his birth; the Germans due to his mischling status, and the Czechs due to his German roots. But a few months after the war ended, a box of personal effects and official papers from Kurt's recently deceased father gave him an unexpected opportunity. Kurt's father's legacy included records of business dealings as a supplier of local raw materials, and Kurt reasoned that some of the old customers might be interested in resuming their import activities. He wrote letters to all the old customers, and one company, a cosmetics manufacturer, responded. At their request, Kurt successfully arranged for a shipment of high quality lanolin gleaned from a particular strain of alpine sheep living in the foothills of Bohemia. Mistrustful of his native country, he deposited the commissions from his export business into a bank account in England, and within a few years had enough money to finance his family's emigration. In early 1948, he took his wife and infant daughter to England, settling near the cosmetics factory in the industrial town of Ghoul. None of them ever returned to their native Bohemia.

Bobbi, as Jon's mother Bozina was called, was a thin woman whose coiffed blond hair, pretty face, and stylish cream-colored outfits formed a pleasant veneer that hid her inner turmoil. For her, escape would be much more than a physical journey, because the seeds of continental conflict had been sown at her conception. Her Persian and Moravian blood struggled for control of her psyche, and in battles that roughly mirrored the history of her homeland, she was no more at peace with herself than with her surroundings. She harbored a latent hostility for the world that had persecuted her husband and deprived her of her country, and her unresolved anger eventually worked its way into her physical being, manifesting as psychotic episodes. She would, for no apparent reason, lock her bedroom door, leaving her family helplessly waiting outside, listening to the sounds of her ranting and unraveling. The tense silence between noisy outbursts of thrown objects and screaming was punctuated by her husband's pleading for calm. During these episodes, Jon would retreat to his own room and dull the agonizing hours fretting with his instrument, drowning out the sounds of his mother's emotionally charged breakdowns and his father's distant and impotent response.

"I got a Mental Disorder,
You can look but you cannot touch." *3

No music lessons or encouragement from his parents were necessary. The guitar came at the age when a child's identity begins to take shape, and in the absence of anything else to hang onto, Jon cradled its body and clung to its neck. No one in particular taught him how to play; he devoured a few books that showed him where to put his fingers and figured the rest out himself. He played whatever he thought sounded good and learned tricks from other musicians he ran into at school or at the music store. But his guitar was much more than an instrument to make pleasant sounds with: it was his solace, his muse, and his defense against the misery that made him a prisoner in his own room. It was always there, waiting to pick up the conversation wherever they had left off, and never too tired to continue. His guitar was a dependable friend and cellmate. The rigidity of the neck and firmness of the body were something to hang onto in a world that was always teetering off-kilter. Even the self-inflicted pain of pressing his soft flesh against the thin steel strings made him feel good, and the enormous calluses he developed while honing his skills would last a lifetime. As his worldview formed, his guitar became a weapon and a shield, and his frequent isolation provided the opportunity to develop a mastery born of vengeance. Sensing his growing power, neighborhood ruffians steered clear of his wiry strength, and Jon developed a swagger to match his newly realized advantage. His imagination was filled with dreams of conquest and retribution, and his guitar was an instrument of war in a battle for survival.

Jon's neighbor Nathan was also learning how to play, and the two would trade secrets as they made their first crude attempts to imitate the radio hits of 1964 together in Nathan's bedroom. There wasn't any such thing as electric guitar training in those days, and no one knew that popular music would play a lead role in cultural history, so Nathan's parents steered their son toward a more traditional musical path and bought him an upright bass. Along with the bass came music lessons, and Nathan's adolescent inspirations became guided by traditional music theory. Nathan took to his new discipline with surprising vigor. The upright bass was as big as he was, and the fuzzy low bungs resonated to the innermost recesses of his unusual private reality. The two teens spent a lot of time together exploring new horizons with their instruments, and the musical possibilities multiplied when Jon got a new Fender, and Nathan added a Hagstrom electric bass and Vox amplifier to their collection.

Dedication, practice, and even a dose of competition helped them achieve a musical proficiency, and they soon developed enough skills and confidence to start playing early Beatles songs together, eventually letting their parents and siblings listen to them struggle through renditions of "I Wanna Hold Your Hand" and "She Loves You." With Jon on electric guitar and Nathan on electric bass, they teamed up with another guitar player and a drummer from the local high school and started performing as at the talent shows there. Their choice of popular material guaranteed some level of approval, but the group's performances mostly reinforced Jon's sense of isolation and failure. People clapped and cheered, but never as loud or as enthusiastically as he thought they should have. No one came up to him after the show to acknowledge his self-imagined superiority, or if they did, he didn't accept their compliments. He was as hard on himself as he was on his audience, and replayed all the mistakes of his performances in his head so many times that he couldn't remember what he had done right. Rather than embrace his modest success and build on it, he felt unappreciated, and used his perceived rejection to nurture an already deep-seated mistrust of the world.

"Planning on buying that, or just bending all the pages?" the store clerk asked in a raspy voice strained by city living. "We got a time clock around here and library hours are over."

It took Jon a moment to remember where he was and realize someone was talking to him, but once he did, he stared at the clerk defiantly. Why were strangers always hassling him? He stood, there deliberately thumbing slowly through the magazine as the tension built.

The clerk, a rotund Middle-Eastern man who had spent the last six years crammed behind the counter of his crowded magazine and sundries store, was out of patience. His gun was hidden behind the counter, one grab away, but he had been warned by the police for using it to threaten customers before. His wife couldn't understand why he needed it – she didn't have to stand there all day and deal with the drunks, beggars, and other seedy characters that came into the store to get out of the weather or leaf through the racy magazines at the top of the rack. The shopkeeper, Mahmoud, pretended to not understand when the loiterers talked to themselves, or notice when they spit or trickled urine on the floor. He woke up tired and aggravated every day, carrying on a silent dialog with the beatific Deity whose picture was taped next to the cash register, alternately cursing and praising his God the way a gambler talks to dice. Frustrated at Jon's non-compliance and no longer able to contain his temper, Mahmoud lashed out. "Wassa matta buddy? You deaf or sumthin'?" he gruffed. "Get it or get out!" he commanded as anger swelled his torso. Then he climbed the hidden step behind the counter that he used to make himself look more authoritative while feeling for his weapon. "No speaka da English?"

Jon ignored his commands, and watched with demonic calm as blood filled Mahmoud's neck, flushing his brown face a dull shade of purple.

"Get out! Get out!" Mahmoud barked like an excited watch-dog. "Vamoose! Scram! Get out of here, you...." His eyes popped through flaccid cheeks and bloodshot veins reddened his corneas. His hand felt the heavy lead pipe he kept next to the gun. "Get out!" he yelped, working himself into a frenzy.

Having developed a self-protective layer of indifference that often made matters worse, Jon continued to stand there, pretending to study the magazine, unafraid and somewhat entertained by his un-intimidating adversary's conniption. Inert and uncooperative, he shifted his weight from one leg to the other and breathed in the stale air of resentment. Satisfied that he had not surrendered to orders, he was about to put the magazine down when someone else walked into the store.

She was in a hurry and oblivious to the confrontation taking place. "Hi Mahmoud, Camel filters and Dentyne," the lively customer with a morning-after perm ordered, rummaging through her purse.

"Of course, Miss Margaret," Mahmoud answered politely with only a trace of the rage that had filled him a moment ago.

Agent Margaret wore a dark blue women's dress suit that looked like a uniform, but Jon noticed her uncharacteristically stylish heels when she rose up on her toes to pay. Agent Margaret wasn't young, and didn't look like the rock and roll queen on the cover of the magazine he had been reading, but something about her choice of cigarettes and suggestive pumps aroused Jon's curiosity. She handed the clerk a few bills, and was putting her change and cigarettes in her purse when her eyes met Jon's. Subtly enjoying the attention, she glinted at her admirer, brushing past close enough for him to appreciate her recently applied perfume. The flirtation was not lost on Jon's sense of smell, and momentarily mesmerized, he stuffed the magazine back in the rack and followed her out into the street.

CHAPTER 5

The dwindling daylight expanded his pupils, and by the time he was able to refocus, Agent Margaret was already on the other side of Varick Street. A loud diesel-spewing bus lumbered past in front of him and he lost sight of her before she disappeared into the Customs Office building. Jon glanced around and noticed a large antique clock hanging from a hook on the side of a building ahead of him that read 6:00. How long had he been reading that magazine? Another clock in a display window confirmed the time, and he was jolted into remembering where was and what he was supposed to be doing.

He was late. Mak was expecting him any minute and he wasn't even close to being there. A subway train rumbled somewhere beneath him. Motivated by urgency, he wedged his way between parked cars and angled across the side streets until the steps of the subway station swallowed him whole. Once on the platform, he stood waiting for the train on one leg, his back and foot resting against the neglected tile wall with "Canal Street" spelled out in little blue squares. Breathing through his nose and humming silently, he shared the narrow musty cavern with a scattered collection of multiethnic straphangers. The unnaturally bright glow of mercury vapor lights sizzled with sixty-hertz overtones. Denizens of the underground, slumped or prone in various states of sobriety and consciousness, wallowed in the hot breath of the city's underbelly. Seething broken pipes steamed the odors of human waste and rotting garbage into a putrid bouquet that the commuters pretended not to notice. Approaching cars displaced the trapped tunnel air, misting everyone's face with evaporated mold, and the smells of urine, sweat, and fossil fuels accompanied the deafening clamor of the southbound local as it entered the station and screeched to a noisy pause. The aggressive sensory hostility of the subway platform had an unusually calming effect on Jon, who, impervious to the perils of his environment, felt strangely balanced by the external chaos. He boarded the nearest car and stood, as he always did, wedged into a corner for balance, leaving his arms free to defend himself. Seeing that the sparsely populated cabin offered no obvious threats, Jon's hummed a medley of rhythmically induced rhymes during the twenty-minute ride. The high-pitched clatter rose to a crescendo as the train picked up speed, then coasted to a muted squeal at each station like the verses to a song.

"Standing on the subway,
Listen to the backs sway,
Guess I had my mind made up.
Left down on Eighth Street,
Looking for a backbeat,
*Drinking from a broken cup." *4*

Per Mak's instruction, Jon got off near where DeKalb Avenue passes by the Brooklyn Hospital, and he stopped for some nicotine-induced postulation. What was he doing there? Why had he accepted the invitation? He remembered that Mak said he lived next to the park behind the hospital where Missy K worked, so he crossed over Flatbush and hurried past the massive brick complex. The park, looking overgrown and foreboding behind a chain link fence with fifty years of vines crisscrossing its length, soon appeared on his left. Mak's street, Adelphi, was the first one after the park, but Jon couldn't see the numbers on the row houses that were set back from the street. He worried that Mak had given up expecting him, and like a speedboat that stops too fast, he bobbed precariously in the wake of his own anxiety. The neighborhood toughs hanging around the nearby bus stop looked menacing in the fading dusk. A wave of uncertainty washed over him. The perspiration chilled his neck. A stout, over-bundled, dark-skinned woman wheeling her grocery cart stopped next to him at the corner and noticed his condition. "You okay mister?" she asked with a distinct island accent.

Jon heard her accent. "I'm looking for a Colonel Mackenzie. You know him?" he asked, guessing.

"Mmm maybe." The woman eyed him more carefully. "What do you want with the Colonel?" she asked suspiciously.

"He said his apartment was 1336 Adelphi." Jon said, peering down the darkened block.

"So, what if it is?"

"Well, he's kind of expecting me."

"Expecting you? Why? Are you a friend of his?" She left out the other possible explanations and pulled her large brocade purse closer to her side.

"Well, yeah, kind of, we work together," Jon stammered.

A toothy smile that glinted gold crept over her face. "Oh that's it! You must be the Soldier Boy he was talking about. Missy K's expecting you." She looked at him with fresh eyes. "You're late!"

"You know Mak?"

"Know him! Ha! Missy K and I might as well be sisters."

"Can you tell me which place is theirs'?"

"Of course I can. It's right next door to my own. Just follow me." The woman re-arranged her headscarf and crossed the street, wheeling her basket behind her. Jon followed next to her like a lost puppy as she maneuvered over the uneven sidewalk. "Missy K said you were coming." she mumbled over her shoulder. "You get lost or something?"

"No, not really...." Jon answered, still unable to see any house numbers in the poorly lit neighborhood.

"You sure look lost to me," she chuckled to herself. They crossed a small intersection and went halfway down the next block before she finally stopped. "They stay there." She pointed. "I'll see you later," she added before trundling down the sidewalk.

Jon stood alone and gathered himself. A loud metallic bang from a block away echoed through the evening calm and rattled his nerves. He gravitated toward the entrance he hoped was Mak's and knocked on the substantial wood door. A small voice inside called to its mother. Jon waited, mentally pacing in the disturbed evening atmosphere. A few moments later, the door swung open.

"Well, well, it's about time. Jonny Soldier come off the battlefield," Mak greeted him. "Why are you so late? Where you been?" He searched Jon's face for clues. "Missy K, she.... I've been waiting for you. We were just ready to give up and now here you are. Everything okay out there?" He peered over Jon's shoulder.

"Could be he's hungry," Missy K called from the next room. "Leave your questions and bring him by the kitchen."

"Come on in," Mak welcomed him into their close-knit quarters. "We'll talk later. You met my son Lucius?" Mak introduced the ten-year-old who was peering halfway out the doorway behind him.

Jon related well to children and greeted him with an extended hand. "Well, how do you do, Lucius? What it is, my man?"

Mak prompted his son's reply. "What do you say, Lucius?"

Lucius came all the way into the room. "Nice to meet you, Mister," he recited, timidly slapping Jon five.

Missy K, whose full name was Kiyana, stood over a gas range in a full-length apron decorated with fruit. Her hair was pulled back into a tight bun that showed off the dark, expressive eyes and sculpted cheekbones that defined her beauty. "Welcome, Jonny

Soldier," she said crisply, looking him up and down. "You look hungry. Get him a chair and sit him down," she instructed, clacking her cooking tongs and motioning to Mak. "We need to put some plump on him. Have you eaten anything tonight?" she asked rhetorically.

Jon blinked and took a seat at the empty table where Mak had positioned a chair. Unzipping his jacket to let the warmth of the moist kitchen air seep into his skin, he cradled the hot mug of tea that appeared before him and let the steam flush his face.

Mak peered over Missy K's shoulder to see what was crackling in the skillet. A cloud of aromatic vapor filled the small room. Lucius sat on his knees backwards in a chair across from Jon, his head resting on folded hands, studying the only white person he had ever seen in his kitchen. Self-consciously, Jon brushed the ragged strands from his face and smiled while fidgeting with his calluses under the table. Within minutes, a large plate of steaming food appeared on the table.

"Now don't be shy," Missy K ordered him. "We already ate so it's all for you."

Jon picked up a piece of breaded fish with his fingers and ate it in one bite. He hadn't even swallowed before the next one was on its way into his mouth.

"He sure likes your saltfish," Mak commented as Missy K hovered. "Make sure you try the dippin' sauce; makes the taste complete."

Jon didn't need much encouragement. He held each piece between his thumb and middle finger just long enough for the sauce to drip back to its bowl before disappearing the morsel into his mouth. Relaxed enough to be ravenously hungry, he deconstructed the substantial mound of soft fillets with only token chewing, occasionally dabbing his mouth with a napkin in an effort to appear mannered. His body craved the salt and protein, and his skin reddened as the iodine seeped into the vacuum of his digestive system. Mak's family looked on with thinly veiled astonishment as the whole plate, which had been piled to overflowing, was consumed in less than five minutes. Finally feeling the affects of the food settling in his stomach, Jon pushed back from the table, relieved that the battle for survival was over for the night. He took a noisy slurp of tea and breathed deeply, pushing the air back out through pursed lips like an oboe player forcing a low note. Mak, who had seen Jon's eating habits before, was stoic, but Missy K, who had been trying not to stare, blinked sympathetically. Lucius' eyes widened, and he looked to his parents for a sign that everything was okay. "I'd say he really liked it," Mak observed dryly.

"You ready for seconds?" Missy K asked, only half joking. The urgency of his eating worried her. She had seen that kind of hunger before she came to live in the land of plenty, and didn't need a lesson in manners to know that there was definitely something wrong. She couldn't have explained it scientifically, but she had a mother's intuition that Jon's shaky state of mind and volatile metabolism were somehow connected to his terrible diet. She was right. Coffee and pastry in morning, a slice of pizza or a fast food sandwich during the day, and the same thing or maybe Chinese food at night. Food was always an afterthought for Jon, and his eating was determined by speed, price, and convenience. Though the energy of his youth still masked most of the harmful long-term effects, Jon's obsessive pursuit of his dreams deprived his body of essential nutrients.

Temporarily sated, sitting at the Mackenzie's table, his bodily functions readjusted to almost normal, and he couldn't stifle an involuntary burp that signaled the end of the main course. Lucius' childish giggle celebrated the moment, and peace descended for a brief visit. "I suppose he's had his fill," Mak noted proudly.

"No desert for you?" Missy K asked mischievously, placing a plate of warm pastries on the table. Jon sucked in the fresh coconut gizzada aroma, and tried to act civilized as he delicately plucked a crumby square from the stack and maneuvered it into his cavern-ous maw. A delicate, backhanded wipe of his lips completed the procedure, and the sugary afterglow elevated his corporal satis-faction to new heights. Several more samplings of the tasty cakes were accompanied by a round of potent Jamaican Blue coffee, and in less than one hour Jon had been transformed from lost pilgrim to intrepid explorer. He was so happy – an extremely unusual state for him – that he didn't know how to act. This was uncharted ter-ritory. He breathed normally, grinned for no reason, and felt posi-tively friendly for the first time in a long time. The unfamiliar surroundings of Mak's apartment gave him an added sense of free-dom. Everything was new and unassociated with his old patterns of depression and anxiety. He felt good about himself as he sat at the table across from Lucius, flicking crumpled bits of napkin back and forth in a game of table soccer. A catchy song with an island beat emanated from the next room, and Missy K swayed in her cooking apron as she cleaned up.

"Come on in here, Soldier Boy, come hear what the weather's like down home," Mak summoned from the next room. Jon fol-lowed his voice.

The reggae bass thumped through the furniture and Mak stood smiling next to the controls of an ancient receiver, bending his knees in time to the music. Lucius raced to his father's side and embraced a standing drum almost as big as he was, trying to keep the beat. Mak sung along with the barely intelligible Calypso lyrics, his imagination fully removed from his surroundings. Jon spotted a worn, aqua painted Stratocaster guitar leaning against the wall and gathered it in his right arm. His left hand explored the neck while he thumbed the strings above the bridge. There was no amplifier in sight, and he could hardly hear it over the sound of the stereo, but it seemed to be reasonably in tune. He found some chords that sounded like they belonged, and with an encouraging smile from Mak, he matched the syncopated rhythms with right thumb up-strums. Missy K came shuffling in on the beat and put her hands on Lucius' shoulders as they sang along to the redundant vamp, worshipping in unison.

As the track faded, a baritone-voiced disc jockey broke the spell to remind his listeners that Ja loved them, and so did the Mighty Sparrow, whose song had just finished. The announcer was celebrating the details of the weather in Kingston, pointing out that spring had sprung, when a loud knock at the door shifted everyone's attention. Missy K went to investigate as the radio patter died out under the beginning strains of the next number. Island music is never fast, and the next number, even slower than the last one, barely cut measurable time. An anguished, love-struck crooner pled for his lover's return over a soupy mix of church organ chords that shifted from one minor inversion to the next like an overweight woman getting comfortable in a pew. Lucius tapped fruitlessly on his conga, unable to locate a downbeat, while Mak swayed slowly with one arm outstretched, pining along with his invisible soul mate. Jon added some pentatonic noodling that he was relieved no one could hear. As locked-in as he was on the last song, he couldn't find the key to this one and welcomed the interruption when Missy K came in from the front hallway with two visitors in tow.

"This is my good friend Miss Beatrice," she announced. "I think you already met Mr. Jonny Soldier."

"I have indeed." Miss Beatrice smiled. Jon looked up and recognized the woman who had led him to Mak's apartment.

"And this is her son Robert Maxwell," Missy K continued. "They heard the singing and came to see what all the fuss is about," she explained as they entered the room. Mak turned down the stereo and the two women took seats on the sofa. Robert Maxwell, a rangy teen in fashionably baggy pants, stood leaning against the wall with his folded arms obscuring a silk-screened Reggae t-shirt.

"Come on in here, Robert Maxwell," Mak beckoned the young teen into the men's camp. "Say hello to Jonny Soldier."

Robert inched a bit closer, carefully preserving his teenage cool. Lucius grabbed him around the waist with an uninhibited bear hug and Robert returned the affection with a soft fist to Lucius's back. The two boys separated and exchanged a ritualized hand slap before Lucius pulled the older boy toward Jon for an official greeting. "Nice ta meecha," Robert mumbled, tentatively extending his hand toward the strange looking white man in the middle of otherwise familiar surroundings. He was not prepared for the response.

"What it is?" Jon slapped the outstretched hand crisply. "That's some cool threads you sportin'. Marley or Cliff?" he asked, pointing at Robert's shirt.

"Marley. How'd you know that?" Robert answered suspiciously.

"Marley's the man! He and I go way back, mon," Jon testified and coaxed another hand-slap out of the unsure teen.

"What's your favorite Wailer song?" Robert challenged him.

Jon tucked the guitar under his arm and jerked the backbeat of "No Woman No Cry" across the strings, crowing a chorus in his best Marley imitation. Robert smiled and Mak turned the radio down, beaming with the pride of having brought a troubadour into their midst. Assuming the spotlight, Jon delivered the whole first verse with an authentic accent, and Mak joined him for the chorus the as the energy built. Little Lucius tapped along, transported by the soulful performance. Jerking his guitar in time, Jon marched in place to imaginary drums. The living room filled with the voices of brotherhood as Mak and Robert bent their knees in prayer, singing and swaying along with the siren call. Their voices blended with Jon's hoarse testimony as he stomped out another chorus, drowning out the unplugged guitar completely. The loud singing and wall-shaking rattles from Jon's heavy-footed rhythmic accents made it increasingly difficult for Missy K and Beatrice to carry on their separate conversation, and they were not completely surprised when a teetering floor lamp crashed to the floor, sending a splatter of bulb fragments over the carpet.

"Easy does it, Soldier Boy, we're all just flesh and bone." Missy K interrupted, "The good Lord will hear you without putting your boot through to hell," she added, studying the glass shards. Lucius and Robert quickly withdrew to the pose of innocent bystanders and studied their shoes. Startled and embarrassed, Jon realized he was at someone else's apartment and looked to Mak for guidance.

"He's just feelin it, Mama," Mak suggested. "Don't worry 'bout that old lamp," he told Jon. "Let's have another round. Come on, Lucius, Robert, let's help him out." Mak tried to reprise the chorus. "Nooo Woomaan Noo Cry," but no one joined in. The mood and the lamp were broken.

"We ought to be going now," Miss Beatrice said as she got up. "Robert's got school tomorrow and...." Robert followed her to the door and they let themselves out.

As soon as they left, Missy K ushered Lucius toward his room. "And you too, mister, time to say goodnight." She left Mak and Jon alone in the faded afterglow of Reggae bliss. Jon handed the guitar back to Mak and mentioned something about work tomorrow. Mak just nodded as they reverted back to their taciturn work personalities.

Missy K re-entered the room. "You going now too?" she asked Jon rhetorically. "I'll get your coat from the kitchen." Mak busied himself trying to screw the lamp parts back together until Missy K came back with Jon's coat. She forced a smile, and led Jon toward the exit. "Now don't you worry about that old lamp," she soothed. "We've had it for years, so's was only a matter of time before it got broke. Mak will see you tomorrow and I'll be sure to pack some leftovers." She gave Jon a firm hug and steered him back into the night.

CHAPTER 6

Agent Ralph Lowell looked forward to Thursday nights because his favorite television shows were on. The witty police drama, "Barney Miller", was followed by the monster hit every law enforcement employee in the tri-state area watched, "Hill Street Blues." His wife Clara didn't want their eight-year-old boy to see the violence, and finding no reason to participate in her loveless marriage, she put him to bed before the program began.

Detective Todd Falin had finished dinner at the Irish pub in the village where he often went after work. He was nursing his second beer when, as planned, another Customs Department bachelor, Agent Rudy George, joined him at the bar. Rudy George, pudgy, balding, and in his early fifties, worked downstairs from Detective Falin, next to Ralph Lowell in the "paperwork division," as it was known. He wanted Detective Falin to recommend him for a job in the action-oriented enforcement department upstairs and always looked forward to the opportunity to press his case. They had some Los Angeles background in common and shared a passion for police work, but Detective Falin knew that Rudy was too old and too soft to handle the stress. Still, he tried to include him whenever it was convenient. "What are you doing this weekend?" the detective asked.

Rudy rotated the Port in his snifter. "Nothing, really."

"Good. I've got a job for you. Pay is excellent. Weekend double." "Really?"

"Yeah. I just got clearance to run a stakeout this weekend and we need some extra eyes."

Rudy tried to conceal his excitement. "I'm in. What's the plan?" The detective hesitated. "We start tomorrow. Can you get off early?" "Are you kidding? We're so slow down there they wouldn't miss me if I left for a week."

"Good, but I need two men."

"Well you got me, so now you only need one more."

The detective looked concerned. "Well, it's not quite that simple." "What do you mean?"

"I need someone else we can trust."

Plotlines from the detective stories Rudy liked to read spread out in all directions. "Someone we can trust," he repeated.

"Someone not too experienced," Detective Falin modified the request.

"You don't want to use anyone else in your department?"

"Exactly. My partner, Detective Gillingham, is in on it, but we have to coordinate with some other agencies and I...we need to keep this one quiet."

"I see." Rudy nodded, having no idea what the problem was.

"I was thinking, what about that guy who works next to you. Do you think he would do it?"

"Ralph? You're kidding. He's as adventurous as a house cat."

"Well, he's still a cat, isn't he?"

"I'm not sure. Even if he was, I think he must've been de-clawed by his wife. She's a real bitch. He's got a kid with her so he's stuck. Nice guy, but I feel sorry for him."

"Perfect. Just the kind of guy I'm looking for. Won't ask too many questions and won't understand what's happening."

"So why do you need him?"

"Well, Detective Gillingham and I are going to split up. You'll ride with me and we just need someone to keep him company; department policy."

"Why not get an off-duty cop or someone who knows how to handle a gun?"

Detective Falin caught Rudy's eye in the mirror behind the bar. "I don't want anyone who knows too much, telling me what I can and can't do."

"You mean things might not go according to Department procedure?"

"Exactly. Remember how long it took to get the cooperation of that gentleman in the Bronx?" the detective referenced one of their questionable capers.

Rudy nodded knowingly. "I'll talk to Ralph tomorrow and let you know."

"Talk to him early or I'm going to have to find someone else. I don't want to ask around because as soon as I do, everyone's going to want to know what I'm up to. Then they'll be telling me how to do my job and.... You get it."

Rudy liked being the detective's confidant. "I'll call you as soon as I talk to him. He usually gets in by 9:00. Here's to a profitable weekend." They clinked glasses and talked shop while they finished their nightcaps, then went their separate ways.

CHAPTER 7

Still full from the soul-satisfying meal at Mac's, dizzy from the musical high, and unsettled by the abrupt end to the festivities, Jon stumbled out onto the street. The chill air awakened his nostrils and wended its way up to the base of his brain, where it had the gradual effect of sobering him up. His eyes struggled to adjust to the change in temperature while a row of dim streetlights cast shadow images that wavered in his teary vision. The night echoed with quiet distant sounds of life: a car door closed somewhere; the evening bus passed a few blocks away; a woman called plaintively to her errant cat; a dog barked at a man's voice. Jon stood there listening to the random evening concert, then ambled back up to the park and lit a cigarette. Savoring the taste, he liked the way the smoke singed the inside of his nose as he sucked it in through his flared nostrils. The deep breath of smoke made him giddy, but Jon liked the dizziness as much as he liked sobriety – and he enjoyed going back and forth between the two extremes. Emotionally disconnected from the process, he thought it curious how his consciousness seemed to bounce against the sides of his skull as if he was playing a one-man game of ping-pong with his mind's eye. The woozy game only lasted a few minutes before the smoke and air blended, like hot and cold water delivered through the same spout, into a tepid buzz. The pleasant stimulation wasn't as powerful as it would have been had the cigarette been mixed with weed, but the effect was very similar, and the mild euphoria was Jon's favorite part. It was the reason he smoked: his darkest thoughts and most aggressive feelings emulsified into a harmless vision of nothing in particular. Urgency melted away and he was able to sit on the park bench and enjoy the remainder of his smoke with relative equanimity. He listened more carefully to the sounds of the creatures in the park rustling through the underbrush: a night bird called out to an unknown mate or enemy; the low frequency clamor of the city rumbled in the background. The cool night wrapped around him like a blanket and Jon welcomed the all too infrequent feeling of contentment that is the cornerstone of most people's existence. An old stone Baptist church at the corner of the park chimed the hour. Looking up, he saw it was 9:00.

Jon started walking toward the subway station and noticed an abandoned bike in an alley between two buildings. It started him thinking about his childhood. He hadn't spoken to his parents for several months and had the sudden urge to tell them how great everything was going. He passed a strolling couple and wondered what Donna, his long-time girlfriend, was doing. Their days together in the clear mountain air of Colorado flickered in his memory. The organic smells of Mountain Meadows smoke mix blended with the salty mist of Missy K's kitchen, still smoldering in his mind. What was that song playing on Mak's radio? He tried to figure out the chords on an imaginary guitar as he walked slowly back to the subway station. His only real companions within the stark walls of his bedroom prison were his imagination and his guitar, and he wondered why he always seemed to wind up in his room alone like that.

"The life I lead is frightening,
If I stop and stare.
But luck can change like lightning,
I can taste it in the air." *5

44

The city traffic increased as he hit the busier thoroughfares. No longer rushing, the three-block stroll back to the train revealed sights and sounds he hadn't noticed when he came through earlier: an all-night convenience store blared its neon messages through plate glass windows; patrons laughed out the open door of a passing pub; apartment lights shimmered behind moving curtains; night stragglers, hurrying to the safety of their destinations, passed by without making eye contact. Everyone behaved differently at night, as if they were wrapped in a cloak of mystery that hid the secret reason they were up past their bedtime. During the day, people seemed so plainly confident and full of purpose; going to work, going to school, coming home with groceries and paychecks. But there were only two kinds of people out at night: those that had to be out, and those who chose to be out.

Some people had to work late stocking grocery stores, tending bar, waiting tables, driving cabs, trucks, and buses. Sleepy firemen were on duty, bored policemen were on patrol, security guards were dozing at their posts, and street cleaners were whirring along in vehicles that looked and sounded like slow-moving alien robots. These were the people who had business being out at night, and they blended into the cityscape like the moving parts of the urban machine they were.

But it was the people who chose to be out at night that fueled the mysterious excitement of city life. They were the late-night moviegoers, the rowdy after-concert crowd, the date-night adventurers, the closing-time drinkers, the house escapers, and the thrill seekers. They were the ones who bent the edges of reason to their own unknowable purposes in fits of inspiration and flashes of spontaneity.

Jon had always considered himself a night person, and like most other nightlifers, he lived in the dual reality where his day job was a deal with the Devil who made the world the way it was – a place where you couldn't do whatever you wanted whenever you wanted to. For him, and many others like him, the workday was a time for acquiescence, where rules and rents and rights and wrongs measured and defined every moment. And that made the night much more than a time to rest: it was the time to feel free, to lay down burdens, raise voices, flounder, flourish, and unleash the primeval instincts that limn humans as a species. Artists who had day jobs lived two lives, separated only by dusk and dawn – and there was no question about which reality they preferred. They worshipped the nocturnal God, and every night, along with bored workers and mindless revelers, they jammed the city's nightspots to escape from the tedium of sustenance wages. Following a night out on the town, it was not uncommon for dazed workers to assume their positions the next day like a bouquet of cut flowers, stuck colorfully at their post while their scented beauty evaporated into the gray pollution of commerce.

As it always does, the music of the times reflected this dichotomy, and the quick, shallow, and popular pabulum offered by mainstream acts like Tommy Tutone, Steve Miller, and Rick Springfield didn't satisfy the true-grit instincts of city dwellers. That's where The Clash, The Ramones, Bowie, and in Jon's mind, Cells, took up the cause.

Jon caught the nearly empty train back to Canal Street and emerged into the more familiar surroundings of the lower Village. He continued east, in the direction of his apartment, but he wasn't tired, and his ambivalence about going home gave him an uncharacteristically halting gait.

"Jon? Is that you?"

He thought he heard a voice from behind him, but kept walking, not sure it wasn't coming from inside his own head. "Oh Jonny Soldier," a woman's voice called out more clearly. Another woman's voice laughed, then they called out together in singsong like practiced cheerleaders. "Oh Jonny Soldier, won't you be mine." Unable to ignore them anymore, Jon turned around. Three women fashionably dressed for a night out on the town stood unsteadily high-heels with silly grins and costume jewelry. They looked a little tipsy and hung onto one another for support.

It took Jon a moment to make out their faces, and another for the dawn of recognition to illuminate his memory. Two of the girls he had never seen before, but Rebecca from the Laden office was revealed by a streetlight. The girl next to her started talking to Jon as if they were all old friends. "We just came from The Jasmine Gardens and we're on our way to a club," she said, fidgeting with her blouse as the other girls collected around her. "Bosco Dish is playing and.... And where are *you* going? Want to come with us?" she blurted out. The other girls tittered as Jon approached them.

"Ameeeliah!" Rebecca scolded her unconvincingly.

Ameliah tried to explain. "I was just saying that we were just going somewhere and, well, you know I – " Jon's imposing figure cut off the word supply to her tongue and the effects of the evening's alcohol bubbled in her brain.

"You don't even know him!" Rebecca interjected apologetically. "He must be going somewhere. He's probably tired," she added, hoping he wasn't.

"I do too know him," Ameliah protested. "At least I feel like I know him. You've been talking about him for – " She stopped herself too late.

Rebecca cringed as her escaped cat rubbed its arched back on Jon's pant leg.

"Ameliah!" The other girl moaned in disbelief.

Flattered and amused, Jon smiled. Rebecca rearranged her top and brushed her hair back under the glow of his attention. It had been a long time since Jon's last fling, and this sudden burst of attraction aroused his mating instincts. He was caught off guard and had to work out a response quickly. Shifting to accommodate the diminishing space in his jeans, he realized that the sight of three attractive females asking for his companionship was a distraction worth prolonging. "So *where* are you going?" he asked, still surprised and uncommitted.

"The Black Sheep, you know, on Bleecker Street by NYU," Ameliah answered, suddenly sober.

"The Black Sheep." Jon repeated, as if trying to imagine it. Actually, he knew exactly where it was. He had been there several times – even played a show there once. "Yeah, I know the place," he finally admitted. "Who's playing tonight?"

"We're on the guest list for Bosco Dish," the third girl answered. Then, wrapping her arm through Ameliah's, she added, "Ameliah's kind of, well, you know…. The singer, he likes her a lot."

"We are not dating!" Ameliah protested with mock outrage.

"Well, Freddy really likes you."

They argued like catty friends, but Jon wasn't listening. He and Rebecca exchanged meaningful glances. "Bosco Dish, you say? I hear they're pretty good," Jon lied. Actually, he hated them – especially the lead singer. Jon knew him from his high school years. His real name was… Theodore? Frederick? – Alfred! That was it: Alfred Wanamaker. Jon remembered his geeky face and phony crooning lips. He felt a surge of anger. The recent incident backstage, when he and Freddy's manager exchanged more than insults, made him clench his jaw.

Ameliah saw his reaction. "Oh good, you like him too!" she assumed. "We'll all go to see Freddy's band!" She checked her watch. "Better hurry, they go on in twenty minutes." Locking arms with the other girl, she set off with a purpose, leaving Jon and Rebecca to follow behind. It was an awkward coupling.

Shy even when she wasn't completely sober, the unassuming Rebecca kept far enough apart that touching wasn't possible. She carried herself with quiet confidence, and was gifted with the classic beauty of long dark hair and a symmetrical face. Jon had spied her in the office on the first day of work, but not wanting to subject himself to rejection, had steered clear. Rebecca had misinterpreted

Jon's avoidance as disinterest, so neither of them knew how the other felt.

Rebecca had been with Laden Imports for two years, and her general education and composed demeanor insured her gainful employment for as long as she wanted to work. She was the kind of worker every business looks for: pretty, polite, capable, and honest. She was the pale flower blooming quietly among the fluorescent lights and stacks of paper, and her pleasant mien mitigated the quiet confrontations of office politics. Everyone gravitated toward her non-threatening calm, and in the way neutrons hold the nucleus of an atom together, Rebecca had become an important part of the workplace chemistry. She was the one who was trusted to handle the payables, and she was the one Homa put in charge when she and Asalah went out to lunch.

Rebecca came from a seemingly average family that lived in the suburbs of central New Jersey. Her father was an accountant and her mother stayed at home to raise four children. Rebecca was the oldest, so when the time came for her leave the nest, she was more than ready to shed her roles as first child and assistant mother. She got her degree at the community college, moved into the city with two friends from the area, and got the job at Laden through her father's business connections. Her entire social life was intertwined with her roommates, Monica and Ameliah, and she hadn't had a serious relationship in the first few years on her own. Knowingly, her friends walked ahead.

Self-conscious that he hadn't showered, and out of practice with walking alongside a woman, Jon found it difficult to keep the correct distance from her. Rebecca wasn't sure how to read Jon's mood, so she focused her attention on trying to keep up with her friends. The two didn't really know anything about each other, and neither was naturally very talkative, so the first few blocks were awkward attempts to find a path to common ground. They walked up the east side of Avenue of the Americas where the constant flow of traffic filled some of the uncomfortable void.

Rebecca tried to start a conversation. "So you've been to The Black Sheep before?"

Jon muttered an affirmative as he eyed the evening for danger and clues.

"I've never been there, but Ameliah says it's a cool place," she commented.

Unable to connect to the moment, Jon's reply was non-verbal. Rebecca wondered if the sparkle she saw in his eye was just a reflection of the street lamp playing tricks with her slightly inebriated brain.

"Come on, you guys." Ameliah yelled over the noise of traffic. "Freddy said they were going to start at 10:00 sharp."

Rebecca checked her watch. It was too dark to see clearly, but she thought it said 9:45. Jon soured at the mention of Freddy and wondered what he had gotten himself into. Why was he actually hurrying to see that asshole play? Why was he walking next to this distant siren like an obedient dog? He convinced himself that nothing was ever going to happen between them, so as they turned east on Bleecker, he said "Err, you know, I.... I'm kinda tired."

Rebecca looked directly at him, surprised at how quickly the date was unraveling.

"Me too," she said, disappointed but unruffled.

"We're working tomorrow, right?" Jon continued, sensing an exit.

"Yeah, I am, for sure," she answered noncommittally.

Jon was conflicted. In spite of all his torrid quirks, he could not easily violate the façade of manners he had inherited from his mother, and Rebecca's classic beauty stretched him between his longings and polite behavior. He wanted to be with her, to be debonair and self-assured – he just didn't know how. He wanted to walk next to her in matched gait, his arm around her shoulder on their way to – *that* was the problem! Freddy was the problem! He changed his mind and started to think about how they could ditch her friends and not go to the club. "How long do you think they'll play tonight?" he wondered out loud, trying to cover his indecision.

"I don't know," Rebecca responded, already finished caring. "Hey Ameliah," she called ahead, "what time is the show over?"

"Oh I don't know," Ameliah yelled back. "Why, what does it matter? You've got other plans already?" She elbowed Monica conspiratorially.

"No, not really," Rebecca answered. "It's just that we have work tomorrow and...."

"Oh that's right. Work!" Ameliah replied sarcastically as she and Monica slowed down enough to let the other two catch up. "Yeah, we've got work too," she agreed. "Thank God we're young enough to go out on a week-night and still make it in to work the next day. Monica? What about you? Are you too tired to go to the show tonight? Got to get home early to get your beauty rest?" she teased.

"Oh, Ameliah, you're so naughty! Why do I always have such a good time with you?" Monica giggled. "You're such a bad influence on us, right Rebecca?"

"Oh most definitely. A very bad influence, the worst!" she added with a knowing chuckle.

Jon's was indecisive, and the girls giddy gabbing, moving through the evening in a pack, was an amusing buzz. The lack of pressure for him to speak was a relief, and the high-pitched tone of their friendly chatter was a pleasant counterpoint to his low frequency anxiety. Rebecca looked attractive from a silent distance, so he let himself be swept along in their collective energy as they ventured into the sea of possibilities: Black Sheep, Lone Wolf, Golden Fleece, Lamb Stew. He didn't care where they were going anymore; he was on the boat and it had left the harbor.

Ameliah's garrulous extroversion drowned out the tension, and sensing her role, she rambled on about whatever was on her mind. Unfortunately, Freddy was on her mind, and Jon tried not to grimace at the mention of his name. Walking without speaking, Jon listened to the sounds of the world around him: Ameliah's pointy-heeled strut was a brisk pace for the sidewalk shoe-beat, and her relentless narrative meandered up and down the annoyance scale like a reed instrument playing too many notes. The girls' outfits rustled in time with their steps like the brushed ride cymbal of a drummer, and Jon imagined sustained power chords emphasizing the bass frequency swells of passing vehicles.

The faint perfume of his female companions filtered into his dinosaur brain, and he tried not to stare as Rebecca walked beside him. The street lamps allowed him to size up Rebecca's friends. Although she was vivacious and fully proportioned, he decided that Ameliah was a little too lively for his taste – and she talked so much he could hardly hear his inner demons. Cheerful and inoffensive, Monica was shorter and more reserved than Ameliah. She had shoulder-length curly hair wrapped around a placid face of indecipherable ethnicity, and glided over the pavement like the dancer she was. Jon thought she was cute, but was satisfied that he was paired with the most suitable prospect of the three. Rebecca was the kind of girl Jon dreamed of when he dared to dream that deep. Her natural composure and frozen serenity gave her the overall appearance of being agreeable but mysterious.

"Here we are!" Ameliah announced, pointing to a dimly lit sign across the street. "Not even 10:00 yet." She led the troupe across the last intersection and made a beeline for the half-open door under a flickering neon sign. "Hi, we're on the guest list, I'm

Ameliah and these are my friends," she told the cowboy-hatted hulk at the door.

Jon and Rebecca stood in the back as the doorman counted the quartet with a silent finger. "That'll be $20, ma'am," he informed them with a western twang.

"$20? But we're on the guest list!" Ameliah objected.

"Really? Well, let me check. What's you're name again?" He held a small piece of paper in his hand for reference.

"Ameliah, and these are my friends."

"Ameliah," he repeated, studying the list. "Sorry, I don't see you here. That'll be $20 please." He was polite but unmoved.

Ameliah turned to her friends. "Freddy said he'd put us on the list," she apologized. "I thought that meant we'd get in for free."

"That's all right, I've got five bucks," Monica volunteered.

"Me too," Rebecca added. "Let's just pay and go in."

"Wait a minute," Jon interrupted as he motioned Ameliah aside.

"Let me talk to him. Hey Travis, what's the story here?" he demanded.

The doorman recognized him. "Howdy partner. Didn't see you at first. You with them?"

"No man, they're with me," Jon asserted. "Are you sure she's not on the list?"

"Well, this is the list...." His voice trailed off as he studied the folded paper in his hand and set himself up as an obstacle to their passage.

Jon snatched the paper from him. "Lemme see that.... Here it is!" He pointed indignantly with his finger. "It says Amy right here!" He gave the paper, actually an envelope folded in half, back to Travis.

Travis was unflustered. "Yeah, I see that," he agreed, "but she said her name was Ameliah."

"Oh come on now, Amy, Ameliah, same thing, dude," Jon argued.

"Well, I'm not sure about that. What if someone named Amy comes along? What do I tell her?"

"Oh bullshit man. There's only six names on your damn list and none of the other ones even starts with an A."

Stumped, Travis crossed his arms, set his legs apart, and adjusted his ten-gallon hat as if preparing to defend its place on his head. Jon peered into the empty pasture of his mind and hopped the fence. "Where's Dennis?" he challenged.

Travis stood his ground. "Dennis is inside, but I'm in charge of the door and the list says Amy plus two. I see three of you, so unless you're on the guest list too, someone's got to pay five bucks."

Jon knew Dennis from his Colorado days and resented being treated like a stranger. "Tell Dennis, Cells is at the door."

The girls stood by, unsettled by the mounting aggression.

Travis suspended the confrontation. "Y'all wait here," he instructed them before disappearing into the darkened club. Jon and his companions stood at the entrance, symbolically blocked with a tattered velvet rope stretched between two movable metal posts.

While they were waiting, Ameliah asked, "Who's Dennis? And how do you know him?"

"Dennis is an old friend of mine," Jon answered, patting his pockets, looking for his cigarettes. "He runs this place, sort of."

The girls looked at each other with a mixture of surprise and intrigue. The interaction at the door was unexpected, and there were so many questions they didn't know which to ask first. They had heard that Jon was a musician, and that he played at clubs sometimes, but had no idea he had ever played at this one. They never heard of anyone called Cells, and didn't know if that was his real name, or the name of his band, or his stage name, or all three. His attitude with the doorman was disturbing and they couldn't help but wonder what else they didn't know about him. Why hadn't he told them he knew the people at the club when they first mentioned they were going there? How much could they trust him? What other surprises might he be hiding? The demons of attraction disguised the clues, and Jon milked their attention with a deft gaze into the unknown.

Travis reappeared. "Dennis says to let you all in," he announced in a friendlier tone, gesturing with artificial hospitality as he moved the velvet rope aside. "Here's your tickets, two drink minimum."

CHAPTER 8

The dim atmosphere of The Black Sheep nightclub was lit with tracks of adjustable mood lighting, reducing the black painted ceiling's uneven surface of electrical conduit, air ducts, and a century of modifications to almost invisible. Dark wood wainscoting covered the bottom half of masonry walls with cut glass sconces and framed mirrors. Jon and his female companions seated themselves at a rickety, undersized table with a shiny formica top and tried to get comfortable in the hard wooden chairs crowded around it. Rocking his chair on two unsteady legs, Jon leaned against an outcropping of exposed brick. Monica and Ameliah sat with their seats turned halfway between the table and the stage, looking for signs of the band, and Rebecca situated herself between Jon and her friends. The house music was loud enough that conversation was both difficult and superfluous as they adjusted to the atmosphere of the club. The hurry of arriving on time and the hassle at the front door had raised their collective blood pressure, and they recognized that making the transition to the smoky lighting of the crowded room was a process best facilitated with alcohol. A haggard-looking waitress with streaked hair, a black Danskin top, and a ragged-edged jean miniskirt approached to take their drink orders. Jon ordered a Heineken before she asked, and she nodded silently as the girls ordered margaritas. Ameliah had been to The Black Sheep enough times that she wasn't surprised to see some familiar faces as she scanned the room.

The Black Sheep, owned by a prominent Italian family from Long Island, the Pecorinos, was a crossroads for a lot of rock and roll traffic that passed through Greenwich Village. The Pecorino family's fortune had been made in commercial real estate, and besides the six-story brick apartment building on Bleecker Street whose entire ground floor was The Black Sheep nightclub, they owned an industrial building that housed a recording studio in lower Manhattan. Dante Pecorino, the family's entertainment business provocateur, lived and kept an office in the family's four-story West Village building and held court at The Black Sheep whenever he wasn't otherwise occupied.

At a table near the stage, Sonya Diaz watched the roadies set up the equipment. Sonya, who worked for the band's management company, Pecorino Partners, was there to make sure the show went off as planned, but as the de facto house band, Bosco Dish played there so often that there wasn't much for her to do other than chat with the regulars. Donny DiCalipari, Freddy's high school friend and personal manager, sat at the next table with his girlfriend, boasting about the band's success to whoever would listen. Most of the people near the stage had come to see the act, so there were a lot of people to talk to.

Dennis Strider, who worked for the Pecorinos, operated the sound equipment and was responsible for managing the stage. Roadies moved trapezoid-shaped monitors to strategic locations along the front and sides of the stage and snaked the connecting cables to the equipment behind the side curtains. Then they positioned the microphone stands and stood guitars in front of amplifiers that blinked alive with tiny glowing red lights as they were switched on. An oversized, glittering, purple drum set with a cluster of brass cymbals dominated the center of the small stage on its own riser. Plastic cups, beer bottles, and smoldering ashtrays cluttered the front ledge of the stage as the band got ready in the back room.

Jon hadn't seen Freddy's act in a year, but knew that Bosco Dish had developed a following. A song Freddy recorded had been played on the influential New York FM radio station, WNEW. Jon heard that Pecorinos Partners had rented them a tour bus and were booking them into venues up and down the east coast, and the thought of Freddy Wanamaker being successful infuriated him. Being in a room full of his fans made it worse.

Jon slouched in his chair, sucking his beer like a kid slurps a forbidden milkshake. Freddy appeared on stage in an iridescent purple shirt with greased-back hair and assumed his throne behind the matching purple sparkle drums. The band logo pulsated on the face of the kick drum as he stomped his presence, melodramatically smashing the cymbals to get everyone's attention. After his initial flurry, Freddy gestured to an unseen mixer on the side of the stage and indicated that he wanted to hear more of himself through the monitors. The other band members assumed their positions and adjusted the knobs on their instruments and amplifiers. Random pops, electronic buzzes, and shrill notes mixed with drumming outbursts as the musicians fiddled with their controls until they were ready. Given the signal, the house music stopped and the club murmur quieted to an anticipatory silence. "Please welcome Bosco Dish," Dennis's voice boomed over the PA system.

The band immediately launched into their first number, a brash high-speed rocker. Freddy set the pace with four on the floor against a two-four snare and eight-beat hat. The bass and guitar locked in with the eights and sketched a sixteen-bar blues progression in E. The drums rolled the dominant seventh on the snare and ended every four measures with an obligatory crash. Very tight, they went around twice before backing off the volume as Freddy leaned into the vocal mic for the first verse. The song and lyrics were all stock, but so well executed that the faithful were swaying in their seats and mouthing the words by the first chorus. A quick check of the audience confirmed Jon's worst fears – everyone liked it: Ameliah was bouncing in her seat like a cantering horseback rider, accenting the beat with her arms in the air; Monica was keeping time with her head and shoulders, trying not to be embarrassed by her hyperactive friend; Rebecca smiled pleasantly, clasping her drink with both hands.

Freddy's voice was strong but harsh. After the first song, he shouted out a hoarse "How y'all doin out there?", and the band laid down the quiet, slow, staccato progression that was the intro to the next song as he continued talking. "We're Bosco Dish and we're glad you could be here tonight. Is everybody having a good time? Hey Dennis, how're we sounding out there?"

Dennis gave the thumbs up from the sound booth and friends in the crowd yelled "Right on Freddy! Right on!"

Freddy gathered the enthusiasm and nodded to his bandmates. "Well awwwlll riiight! Let's Dish it, Bosco!" he ordered. The band toned down the treble and dug a deep groove. Keeping time with a heartbeat kick, Freddy delivered the lead vocal part of a jilted lover ballad with the band members adding harmonies to the chorus. The intimate lyrics and sparser drums settled the crowd down to the point where they could communicate with one another.

Desperate to anesthetize himself, Jon got the attention of the waitress and motioned for another beer as the song continued. Ameliah shared her joy with expletives and elbows as Jon gritted his teeth and throttled his second beer in disgust. Her blabbering annoyed him, Rebecca's smile violated his trust, and Freddy's pompous purple drum extravaganza tortured his artistic vision. He didn't bother to excuse himself when he left the table in search of improved surroundings. Intentionally wandering past the sound booth on his way back from the bathroom, he caught Dennis' eye. "Hey man, good to see you," Dennis said, motioning him in. "Whachu binuptu?" he rhymed.

"Been workin the rehab job," Jon answered, waving his odorous sleeve close enough for Dennis to smell.

Dennis gagged. "Phew! You take a shower in that stuff?" Dennis and Jon listened to the blare of the next song from the sound booth, watching the VU meters dance in time with the snare hits. Meaningful conversation was impossible over the din, so their communication was limited to pointing at obscure meter and indicator-light revelations.

Although he learned the finer points of audio engineering at BlueStar Studios, Dennis Strider learned how to mix live sound at Ebbetts Field. That small but well-known club in Denver, Colorado, was a popular stop on the touring circuit. Some of the same acts played The Black Sheep, where Dennis had been house engineer for almost two years. Originally from Long Island, Dennis's career had progressed from playing bass in a rock band to the steadier employment of working with sound equipment. Armed with an electronics trade school degree, he had enough musical training that local acts trusted him to make them sound good, and his steady personality had a lot to do with The Black Sheep's recent success. The Pecorinos relied on Dennis to keep the club running smoothly, and his responsibilities were part managerial. He and the doorman, Travis, coordinated the activities of the club with the rest of Pecorino Partners' business interests. Dennis was the engineer who drove the gravy train and made the decisions when Dante wasn't around, so he earned his perks with tacit approval. "Tootski?" he asked Jon during the break between songs.

Jon hesitated before accepting. "Sure, my ninety days are almost up." Dennis closed the door. Jon bent down and discretely snorted two quick hits from an outstretched coke spoon. "Don't tell my parole officer," he laughed as he stood up. Dennis went next, and they stood without talking for a while, watching the meters and enjoying the effects of the drug. Bosco Dish was already halfway through their set by the time Jon remembered who he had come to the club with. Feeling better, he slapped Dennis five and made his way back to his seat.

In his absence, Rebecca had moved her chair next to Monica's, and barely acknowledged Jon's return. Jon was now on his third beer, and thanks to Dennis's added stimulus, as close to being in a good mood as he could get while Freddy was playing. Emboldened, he slid his chair right next to Rebecca and put his face close to her ear as if he was going to tell her a secret. Startled, Rebecca twisted her head toward him. Their noses touched, and time became a moment. Jon's ironic grin and beaming blue eyes penetrated Rebecca's veneer and their scents whispered seduction. Rebecca wiped the hair from her eyes and asked herself, "Is this the same guy I came here with? Could it be true? Is it possible that he has a gentle side, a sense of humor, a sense of romance?"

Monica turned her head just in time to see Rebecca caught in the swoon and tried to interrupt. "Another drink Becca?" she mimed, touching Rebecca's shoulder. Rebecca moved her head slowly from side to side without taking her eyes off Jon. Monica looked at Jon suspiciously. "Becca, you okay?"

Jon's put his hand on Rebecca's thigh under the table. "I'm great," Rebecca mouthed like a subject under hypnosis.

Monica sensed the intimacy and turned back toward the stage, elbowing Ameliah with the news. Ameliah turned around and smiled salaciously. Rebecca blushed under their scrutiny, and Jon was about to tell Ameliah to mind her own goddam business when a woman up front let out a scream and the band suddenly stopped playing. Everyone stood up to see the commotion near the stage. "Help! Help me, help him!" the woman pleaded. "Somebody call a doctor. Help!" The patrons near the stage made a space around a muscular man sprawled unconsciously on the floor.

"Lift his head!" someone said.

"No! Don't touch him!" another warned.

"Do something, please!" the woman pleaded. "We've got to do something!"

"That's Donny D. He's probably just drunk."

"Maybe he got too high."

Randi, his girlfriend, tried to think. "No, I don't know.... Well, maybe." She pushed on Donny's shoulder and called to him, "Donny, Donny, it's me, Randi. Donny, Donny can you hear me? Are you all right?"

Donny didn't move. His friends in the crowd became anxious.

"Is he breathing?"

"Get him a pillow."

"Something's wrong."

"Is there a doctor in the house?"

The questions turned serious. "Is he on something, you know, some kind of medication?"

Randi got defensive. "How should I know? Who are you anyway?" Wearing four-inch heels and a short mini skirt, she squatted down to touch Donny's forehead, barely keeping her balance with one hand touching the floor. "Donny, Donny baby, wake up it's me, Randi. Pleeease." Donny's eyes blinked open for a moment. "Baby, it's me, can you hear me baby? It's me. Say something." She touched his lips with her fingers and lightly slapped his cheek.

"I think he's coming to," someone observed.

"Ooohh man, what happened?" Donny moaned, waking up.

"Oh oh! Donny! You're back! You're okay!" Randi announced and bent down to kiss him. "Baby, I was so scared."

Donny continued coming around. "I guess I must've passed out. How long was I gone?"

Randi bent down to put her arms around him but lost her balance and landed on the floor next to him. Embarrassed, but thankful for Donny's return, she rolled halfway on top of him. "Oh, I'm so glad you're okay!" She bent down to kiss him. "I was so scared!"

Sonya, who knew them both, tried to restore order. "Forget the doctor, everything's okay," she announced.

Most of the patrons returned to their seats, but the couple remained on the floor and their kissing intensified. "Guess he's feeling better now," someone who was still watching commented.

Enjoying the attention, Randi moved her hips suggestively.

"Do it, do it on the floor!" another friend egged them on. Donny took the cue and put his hands on Randi's rear, drawing her down on top of him as the remaining crowd looked on with a mixture of amusement and lechery.

Randi lost a shoe and pretended to protest as her boyfriend buried his face in the crack of her blouse. "Donny! Dohhhn't!" she cried unconvincingly.

Reggie Whitehead, a Black Sheep regular, led the encouragement that escalated into a multi-voiced chant. "Do it, do it!"

Fully recovered, Donny maneuvered Randi down his torso until both her stockinged knees were on the floor straddling his waist. Her skirt was hiked up far enough to reveal black lace panties, and she kicked off her other shoe for traction. "Donny, don't," she giggled, squirming seductively on top of him. Donny grabbed her breasts with both hands and pumped his pelvis. Aroused, Randi sat up and fixed her hair, scanning the crowd that had re-gathered, unsure of how much further to take the performance.

A loud thud of the bass drum, accompanied by the sudden glare of the house lights, ended it. "Okay folks, show's over. Everyone settle down and let's get back to the music," Dennis announced over the PA. Wisecracking patrons returned to their seats as Randi and Donny got up off the floor and retook their table with gropey hands and guilty grins.

Freddy reclaimed the spotlight. "All righty then! I guess we've got a show to do." He pilloried his snare skin with a long 32nd note roll that ended in a double tom flam, then smashed a few cymbals to make sure he had everyone's attention again. "All's well that ends well, and from what I saw, that ended pretty well!" he said through his microphone.

A few people laughed and a waitress visited Donny and Randi to offer them drinks. Back to full gusto, Donny tried to seize the moment again. "Drinks on me friends, and thanks for all your encouragement!" He put an arm around Randi and grabbed her breast with his other hand to emphasize his point.

She brushed his hand aside. "Donny, don't!" The band was starting their next number and no one was paying attention to them anymore, so he pulled her closer for an unsuccessful apology kiss before settling back into audience status. Sonya waved from the nearby table where she had rejoined Reggie and his friends.

"Here's a little number for you love birds out there." Freddy winked at Donny and Randi. "This one's called 'Love Is,'" he announced in his best Barry White baritone.

A slow pulse of minor keyboard inversions crept over the stage like a rolling fog, and colored lights dimmed to help set the mood. Freddy came down from his riser and leaned the mic stand at an angle while whispering the verses with his lips touching the art deco, SM55 microphone. The bass and guitar played muted quarters and joined him on vocals for the choruses, while the keyboard kept subtle time with a right hand arpeggio. Even Jon fell under the spell, taking advantage of the romantic ambiance to resume his advances.

Timidly, Rebecca put her hand on top of Jon's as it returned to her thigh. She wasn't sure how she felt, and the spectacle with the drunken couple had sobered her up a little. Inherently skittish, Jon sensed her indecision and withdrew. He leaned back in his chair and ran both hands through his hair, trying to find the middle ground between his fitful animal instincts and civilized behavior. A long swig of beer helped settle his nerves and Rebecca used the interlude to check in with her friends. "Did you see that?" Rebecca whispered to them in awe.

"I thought they were going to do it right there on the floor!" Ameliah gushed.

"I know, I thought so too. Isn't that the girl from St. Andrews?" Rebecca asked. "You know, the one who got caught with the married man?"

Monica craned for a better view. "I think so, it looks like her. Who's that guy she's with?"

"I think that's Donny D.," Ameliah said. "He's the one who tried to get me to go to Baltimore with the band." They twisted in their chairs, straining for a better look. "Yeah, that's him," Ameliah confirmed as Donny got up from his seat and headed their way. "He's the band's manager." Donny walked right past them on his way to the bathroom. Ameliah was turned on by his muscular build and confident gait. "Freddy told me about him. He's some hunk, don't you think, Monica?"

"Ewe! Ameliah! He's gross!" Monica disagreed. "Becca? What do you think?"

"Ewe, double ewe! He's a pig, Ameliah!" Rebecca's revulsion earned her points with Jon and she noticed his amused reaction.

Jon had known Donny and Freddy since high school. "He's got a great ass." Jon sniped. "I can see why Freddy likes him." No one grasped the insinuation, but they knew it was a put down.

Ameliah took offense. "What do you mean?"

"Nothin," Jon smirked, relishing his social victory and moving his chair closer. Rebecca and Monica giggled in allegiance.

Humiliated but undaunted, Ameliah turned her attention back to the stage as Freddy introduced the next song. "This one's for the lovely Ameliah," he announced. "Ameliah? You out there? Stand up and say hello to all your friends."

Ameliah rose halfway from her seat to wave, and Donny, on his way back from the bathroom, grabbed her hand. "I've got her over here," he shouted, jerking her the rest of the way out of her chair so that she almost fell. "Come with me sweetheart. We've got great seats up front. Your friend can come too," he added, eyeing Monica.

Ameliah grabbed Monica's hand as Donny led her away. "Come on, Monica," she urged, without letting go. Donny towed them toward the stage through the maze of tables and chairs as the audience clapped lightly.

"Here she is." Freddy pointed as they approached. "Let's hear it for the lovely Ameliah!" Ameliah acknowledged the attention with a wave.

"Freddy is the man!" Donny enthused, seating her and Monica at his table. "What are you ladies drinking tonight? Waitress!" he called out, motioning.

"More margaritas?" the waitress asked. Ameliah moved her head up and down, suddenly speechless.

Donny repeated the order. "Two margaritas for the ladies and another gin fizz for Randi. I'll have another double Jack straight up with a twist – and make sure Suzie knows it's for me." Donny put his heavy arm around Randi and pulled her chair closer. "Randi, this is Freddy's guest, Ameliah, and her friend?"

"Monica," Ameliah answered tentatively. "I'm Ameliah and this is Monica. Nice to meet you Randi."

The women smiled cautiously at one another as the band drowned out further conversation. Donny folded his arms across his chest and followed the band, bobbing his head knowingly as the set progressed. When the guitar player bent down to deliver his solo directly to Donny's table, all the women were duly impressed with his musicianship. Donny gathered their adulation with winks and nods. "Bosco Dish," he shouted, clapping loudly as the last song wound down to a stuttering stop.

"Let's hear it for Bosco Dish!" Dennis shilled over the house monitors. The patrons obliged with a brief burst of clapping that quickly gave way to the noises of clanking glasses and backwards scraping chairs. Mid-tempo house music filled the awkward spaces between sobriety and conversation as customers revisited their drinks, stretched their legs, and checked their watches.

Left alone, Rebecca and Jon tried to adjust to the increased lighting and quieter atmosphere. Jon moved his chair closer and leaned in, trying to bridge the familiarity gap. "Need another drink?" he asked, searching for a point of contact.

Uncertain, Rebecca stared into the distance, holding onto her empty glass with both hands. "Oh, I don't know; I guess," she answered, looking to see what her friends were doing.

Jon was put off at her distraction. "You want to go be with your friends?"

Their eyes met as strangers. "What do *you* want to do?" she asked, not sure she wanted to hear the answer.

Jon's impatience peaked. "Well I certainly don't want to hang around here with Freddy and his band," he said cynically. "Maybe you should go sit with *them*." He pointed.

Rebecca was frustrated. "Maybe I should," she agreed.

Jon's romantic skills weren't up to the challenge. He backed away and stood up abruptly. "Have a nice night then," he grumbled before heading toward the bar.

Startled by his abandonment, Rebecca took a moment to make sure he wasn't coming back before going to join her friends. Ameliah, tipsy and talkative again, greeted her as she approached their table. "Hey Becca! Great show, huh? Pull up a chair and join us. This is Donny and his friend Randi."

"Howya doin'?" Donny greeted her with a nod. "What're you drinking? Waitress!" Donny summoned with a raised arm. "So what're you girls up to tonight?" he asked, leaning forward. They looked confused by his question so he just kept on talking. "I mean tonight after the show. Where you headed? We're having a party back at the hotel, and if you want.... I mean, if you're not doing anything else. It's not that late and, well, I know Ameliah's coming, right? Freddy told me you were."

Ameliah took the cue. "Oh yeah, he told me there was going to be a party after the show. I'm definitely going," she said as if it was planned.

"What about you ladies?" Donny pimped. "The whole band is going to be there, and we've got some party favors, if you know what I mean."

"Come on girls," Ameliah encouraged them. "You're only young once you know. Besides, we came here together and we should all stay together. I'm going to the party and you're both coming with me," she decided for them.

Monica and Rebecca took long sips of their fresh drinks and didn't put up a fight. Donny went in for the close. "We've got a bus outside and you can ride over to the hotel with us."

The plans seemed set but Monica had an afterthought. "What about Jon? Where is he?" She looked at Rebecca. "Do you think he wants to come with us?"

"I don't think he'll want to come," Rebecca answered, squeezing Monica's hand under the table. "I'll tell you later," she mouthed.

Jon stood in a far corner near the bar, holding up a wall with a beer bottle hanging loosely by his side. The mild euphoria of the coke had reversed course and he was descending into depression. He could see Rebecca and her friends making plans at the table with Donny, and his frustration took the form of lyrics.

"I, I know that you're lonely.
But I, I know what to do." *6

A fog of tobacco smoke obscured Rebecca's table as he imagined a tense, backwards guitar part underneath the lyrics. Roadies retook the stage to check the equipment and clear the empty bottles and glasses. The band emerged from the dressing room and filtered into the club to mix with their friends during the break. Dennis came out of the sound booth, had a word with Sonya, and approached Jon, who was lingering near the bar. "Wassup, Slideways?" Dennis said as he approached. "Need some more inspiration?"

"Hey man," Jon answered, still numbly fixated on Rebecca's absence.

"Oh, I see," Dennis commiserated, spying the table of girls in the front row. "Oh yes!" he added as Rebecca stood up and made her way through the crowd. "Is that what's got you all messed up?"

Jon nodded sullenly.

Rebecca's looks were always easy to admire, but dressed for a night out in a tight sweater over snug jeans that disappeared into knee-high boots, her figure was well defined. Without her jacket on, and drunk enough to lose some of her inhibitions, she meandered toward Jon with a purpose. His detached ogling terminated when she brushed her chest against his arm. "Where did you go?" she purred, reaching for his hand.

Completely taken off guard, Jon dropped his beer on the floor, splattering their shoes before rolling under a chair. "Oops!" he apologized, recovering his poise with an embarrassed grin.

Rebecca wasn't flustered. "It's just a few drops of beer," she added seductively, squeezing his hand.

Dennis, who had watched the scene transpire with a tinge of jealousy, winked. "Hey man, got to get back to it. Catch you later, operator," he excused himself.

Jon put his arm around Rebecca and drew her close to his side. The direct physical contact produced a torrent of pheromone that shuddered through their bodies. "Not so fast," Rebecca gasped, pushing away to catch her breath.

Jon's libido seized control of his faculties, and the evening's alcohol consumption helped him lose his grip on manners. His arm around Rebecca tightened, and her objections were drowned out by the background music and commotion at the busy bar.

"Jon, Jon!" she protested, trying to free herself. Acting on impulse, Jon crudely raised his knee between her thighs. "Stop it!" she yelled, digging her heel into the toe of his boot, trying to wrestle out of his clutches. Jon thought she was playing and held her in his powerful arms, puckering his lips in a mock kiss. Flustered and upset, Rebecca concentrated her efforts on escape. She thought about biting his arm, but as she twisted for a better angle, she knocked into a table and sent everything on it crashing to the floor.

The hazard of the broken glass startled them into a pause and sent Jon halfway back to his gentleman persona. They both saw her expensive leather boots coated with sticky shards. "Oh I'm so sorry," he apologized insincerely. "There there, let me clean those off for you," he patronized, squatting while holding her thigh as he wiped her boots with a napkin. "Mustn't muss those lovely boots," he said, attending to the moisture with a flirtatious vertical wipe. Rebecca stood frozen between wanting to get away and being re-energized by his advances. She had never felt such abrupt emotional extremes, and couldn't process the experience in her usual methodical way.

A man who was seated at the bar had been watching them struggle. "You okay?" he asked Rebecca as Jon knelt at her feet.

"I'm fine," she answered covering her breasts from his leer.

Jon finished fussing with her boots and stood up. "Now where were we?" he asked, putting his arm around her shoulders and squeezing her close again.

"Jon!" Rebecca protested and tried to break free.

"What's the matter, baby?" Jon squeezed tighter.

"I'm not ready for this," Rebecca complained, extricating herself from his hold. "I have to visit the ladies' room." She separated, straightened her clothes, and went to find it.

"Nice work partner," the man at the bar commented.

Jon stared him down. "You talking to me?"

The man, with very short hair and a pushed-in nose, sneered.

Jon snapped at him. "What're you lookin' at, buddy?"

"I'm lookin' at a loser," the man answered.

"Oh yeah, that must be you in the mirror behind me, asshole."

The crew cut man rose from his seat. "Did you just call me an asshole?"

Jon ratcheted up the controversy. "What if I did, asshole?"

"Well, I'd have to do something about that, freak. You wanna take this outside?" He moved closer.

"No man, let's take it right here." Jon got close enough to connect.

Travis wedged himself between the combatants. "Whoa, wait a minute guys. Nobody's taking anything anywhere. This is my bar."

"Asshole!" Jon spewed from behind the bouncer.

"Freak!" the man accused. "That girl's way too fine for you, dirtbag."

"Swineface."

Dennis came into the picture. "What's going on here?"

"Got it handled, pardner," Travis informed him. "These guys were just having a lively discussion." He moved the combatants further apart. "Can somebody please clean this mess up?" he asked a passing waitress.

"Everything okay?" Dennis asked Jon with a light touch on the shoulder.

Jon eyed his adversary. "I'm okay, but yaughtabee more selective of who you let in here."

"Okay, Slide. I'll take it into consideration," Dennis calmed him. "Why don't you come join me in the booth?" he added with a twinkle. Jon smirked triumphantly and followed Dennis.

The crew-cut man sat back down at the bar. "Need a refresher, Officer Hemming?" the barmaid asked him.

"Thanks Suzie. Who is that creep?"

Suzie was always a good source of information. "That's Jon Cells. I don't know why they call him that. He's a musician, mostly."

Officer Hemming worked undercover vice for the New York City Police Department and had a nose for intrigue. "Has he ever played here?"

"He and his band did a show last year. A lot of people liked them but I thought they stunk." Suzie pushed a fresh drink toward him then turned her attention to a waitress.

Officer Hemming crushed an ice cube in his back teeth. "Cells," he repeated out loud to himself. "Never heard of him."

Rebecca came back from the ladies room and looked around for Jon. Her eyes met Hemming's.

"He's gone," Officer Hemming answered her unasked question. "You're too good for him anyway. Buy you a drink, honey?"

"No thanks," Rebecca muttered, still looking around.

Monica came up from the darkness. "Rebecca, where have you been? What's all this?" She motioned to the mess on the floor. "You don't look so good. Are you all right?"

Officer Hemming butted in. "Oh, she's fine, now that she got rid of that freak who was bothering her."

Officer Hemming was more interested in women than his job. Years of monitoring the underage drinking and gambling activity in downtown bars had dulled his sense of duty to the force. The information he shared with the Pecorinos helped keep them in business, and once in a while, when he found a willing playmate, he used the hush money the Pecorinos paid him to finance Florida vacation dalliances.

Monica checked with Rebecca to see if she had an explanation for the stranger's attention. Nothing made sense. "C'mon Becca, let's go." She took Rebecca's hand and led her back to their seats.

Donny welcomed them back like an impresario. "There they are!" He waved his arms. "Hey miss beautiful, where you been off to?" he asked Rebecca. Randi gave him a dirty look and puffed her chest out noticeably.

"She ran into an old friend," Monica answered for her.

Ameliah saw that Rebecca was not herself. "Becca, you okay? Who'd you see back there?" Rebecca moved her head side-to-side without speaking. Ameliah guessed it was Jon and sympathized. "Oh I see, well you'll tell me about it later. Do you need another drink before the next set? It's going to start any minute now. Donny's buying, aren't you Donny?" Ameliah added with a flirty smile.

"Sure am, sweetheart. Another round for the girls," Donny broadcast. Randi shifted in her chair and crossed her barely covered legs so that one foot could swing free and rub Donny's leg under the table. Donny got the message. "Would you ladies excuse us for a minute? Randi and I have some business to attend to." He helped Randi climb onto the stage by placing his eager hands around her waist. They disappeared behind the curtains.

Jon followed Dennis into the sound booth and closed the door behind them. Dennis passed him the vial and they discretely snorted a few spoons. Swallowing the numbing nasal drip, Dennis fussed with the settings on the mixer and Jon pulled out a cigarette.

"No man, not in here," Dennis stopped him. "No smoking in the booth: Bad for my asthma, bad for the equipment. Go do that out there – and try not to hurt anybody."

Jon stepped outside the booth and lit up. Taking intentionally long draws, he watched the activity in the club. The busy room was stirring with people, floating at tables and oozing through the crowded spaces like a simmering stew. He couldn't see Rebecca, but figured she was up front with her friends. The coke and nicotine produced a pleasant buzz, and Rebecca's rejection receded into the background.

CHAPTER 9

The lights flickered on and off a few times announcing the start of Bosco Dish's second set. Patrons navigated back to their moorings in the chattering sea of clanking glasses and drunken conversation. The band drifted out onto the stage, and the guitar player, an angular fop with a prominent nose, stood right in front of Donny's table. He gave Ameliah and her friends a knowing wink, then passed the attention to the diminutive bass player, who acknowledged the women with a jerk of his oversized hairy helmet. Sonya chatted with a roadie as the house lights dimmed and Freddy ceremoniously retook his drum-set throne. Donny leaned into Ameliah's hair and whispered, "Freddy's very glad you made it tonight." Ameliah let out a squeal of delight and looked up in time to receive a private pointed finger from the top of Freddy's purple kingdom. "I told him you and your friends would be joining us. The whole band is excited that you're all coming," he said loud enough for Monica and Rebecca to hear.

Freddy twirled his neon-tipped sticks before clicking them together for the count-off. The guitar player grabbed the downbeat with a whole-tone slide, and the keyboard player used his left hand to sketch out a mid-tempo minor-key progression. High octave keyboard string pads, played with his right hand, set the tension, and the bass thump followed Freddy's one and three kicks. The guitarist stabbed upstroke chords along with the snare on two and four, and Freddy let the syncopated energy build before coming in with vocals. A clever three-note, pre-chorus riff, played in unison by the keyboard and guitar, ratcheted up the dramatics. The momentum elevated as Freddy delivered a plaintive lyric about coming home and the audience was sold and delivered. All the small talk stopped as the performers preened, stretching their moments with extended keyboard, bass, and guitar solos. The barrage of inspired playing overwhelmed the defenses of the girls in the front row, and they joined the faithful in rapture. Freddy's drum solo at the seven-minute marked the highlight of the number, and the rest of the shortened set was a meandering coast down from the emotional heights of the opening jam. The audience's energy subsided along with the performers', until everyone was thinking about the time and tomorrow. The last song rocked to a false close with contrived staccato urgency, then revived itself, only to die again a few more times, unconvincingly, like the villain in a bad western. When it was finally over, everyone, including the band, was relieved that it was. The polite clapping was not accompanied by calls for an encore. It was way past time to go and everyone had had enough.

The house lights came on and the musicians extricated themselves from the tangle of cords. Jon stood in the shadows, smoking another cigarette, watching the patrons gather their belongings and bundle up for outside. He noticed several familiar faces pass by on their way to the exit, but none he knew well. Travis, who was saying goodnight at the front door, exchanged a low five with Reggie Whitehead as he left. Officer Hemming, engrossed in conversation with a dyed blond barfly, shuffled past with his prospect. Jon could see the roadies moving equipment and wrapping cable, and when the house had almost cleared, he saw the three girls he had come there with sitting in front with a small group that wasn't going anywhere. He slinked closer for a better look but remained out of sight.

Freddy sat in the middle of the group, one arm around Ameliah and the other animating his storytelling. Monica and Rebecca sat opposite the three other band members, while Randi stroked

Donny and posed in her chair. Drinks were served and no one was in a hurry as Freddy held court. Sonya periodically interrupted the gathering to discuss logistics, and the laughter around the table echoed in the nearly empty club.

Jon couldn't hear what they were talking about and got bored of spying, so he drifted back to the sound booth to visit with Dennis.

"Hey man, you still here?" Dennis greeted him, preoccupied with zeroing out his gear and cleaning his workspace. "Wassup with you?"

"Yeah, I'm still around." Jon said dejectedly.

"Round like a donut, eh?" Dennis replied with his usual light-hearted wordplay. "What was all that at the bar before? Hmm? And where are those girls you came in with?" Dennis noticed Jon's wince and realized he had answered his own question. "Oh I see, always the women. Well, shows t'go-yah...." Dennis continued straightening up and talking. "Hey, you up for some fun tonight?" he asked, changing tone. "I was thinking maybe we head down-town and see a real show. You know the girls there are a lot easier to get next to. Whadya say? It'll be like old times. I can be outta here in like ten minutes."

"Sounds good to me," Jon answered half-heartedly. He was too stoned to be completely upset, and Dennis's plan seemed like a good idea. "Yeah, I'm in. I could use a good time after the day I've had. I'll wait for you, but hurry up, cause I don't know how much longer I'm going to last tonight."

"Oh, we can take care of *that* problem," Dennis said confidently. "Hurry up and wait, story of my life. C'mere." Dennis motioned. "Sounds like you need a few more bullets in your gun." He passed the tiny bottle to him.

Jon drifted off into a corner, sucked in a double dose of inspiration, and returned a few minutes later with a grin.

"Now you're looking alive again," Dennis said encouragingly. "Pass that back over and I'll join you in a few. Wait for me by the door 'cause I got to lock up the booth and tell everyone I'm leaving."

Jon made his way toward the entrance and ran into Travis, who was guarding the night. "Enjoy the show?" Travis asked laconically.

"Not really." Jon answered with equal disinterest. Looking up, he realized that the stragglers making their way toward them were Freddy and his entourage.

"Hey, if it isn't Jon Cells," Freddy condescended as he approached with Ameliah on his arm. "Great show, huh?" He laughed at Jon's non-verbal response.

Ameliah parroted Freddy's attitude, but Monica and Rebecca saw the impending confrontation and positioned themselves in a tight group with the other musicians. Jon searched Rebecca's eyes, but she avoided his gaze. Monica mustered a neutral "Hi Jon, bye Jon" as she passed, pleased with her defense of Rebecca's honor, but otherwise confused.

Donny blurted. "Hey look, it's Jon Cells. When'd they let you out? Sorry about what happened man – *not!*" Donny laughed at his own joke and Randi aped his amusement.

Jon straightened up to full height. "Well well, if it isn't Donny D and his brand new teeth."

"Yeah man, that's right, and don't I look fine!" Donny bared his replacement fangs with pride. "Hey Jonny, my man, we're headed over to the hotel for a little party time, if you know what I mean. Why don't you show your face for old times? Tell us all about your little trip up the river?" He laid down the challenge, patted Randi's ass, and walked out to join the rest of his companions.

Jon and Travis stood near the door watching the Bosco Dish retinue board their bus.

Dennis joined them at the door. "Ready Freddy?" He asked Jon.

"Please don't say that." Jon motioned to the entourage loitering outside. "I've had enough Freddy to last me a lifetime."

"Anything you say, Ray," Dennis quipped. "Let's get outta here. My wheels are around the corner."

Jon and Dennis walked past the roadies who were loading the bus. Rebecca and Monica, seated by a window, saw Jon and Dennis walk by, but the mixed drinks and attentive company masked any real regret. The guitar player sitting across from Rebecca made accidental foot contact for the second time, and she studied him for a moment, assessing how she felt about his advances. Monica and the bass player were ahead of them in the footsie contest, and Ameliah had already disappeared into the curtained back section with Freddy, Donny, and Randi. The roadies got on and sat in front. A middle-aged, uniformed driver closed the door, threw the transmission into reverse, and inched the full-size tour bus backward into the narrow street with a diesel-spewing lurch, barely avoiding the vehicles all around it.

Dennis and Jon were already at the parking lot entrance by the time the bus straightened itself out and chugged past them on its way to the Chelsea Hotel. They wedged themselves into Dennis' red two-seater sports car, which had been built in Japan for much smaller people, and headed downtown. Despite its age, the Mazda RX 7, like all of Dennis's equipment, was in near perfect condition. "Wait till you hear this," Dennis promised, turning up the volume on his custom sound system. A two-chord progression shifted back and forth from A to G, with all the instruments hitting the syncopated accent in unison. Dennis bounced rhythmically in his seat, singing loudly as he steered the car crisply through the empty midnight streets. *"Alligator man donchu come round round my door,"* he repeated the lyrics several times with slight variation. Jon was impressed and lit a cigarette. "Open the window man. You're killing me with that thing," Dennis complained.

Jon obliged and cranked the window down. "When did you record that?"

"That's the mix from last week." Dennis answered, poking the air with outstretched fingers to emphasize the synth line.

Jon took a long drag. "Sounds big. You do that at Heard Tracks?"

"Absatively. They got some new mic pre's and the bottom end has enough punch for an all night party."

"Who engineered?"

"I did. Nigel's been letting me use the studio when it's not booked. It was getting light by the time I locked up."

"That is so cool that Nigel trusts you with the keys. I love that place."

"Yeah, you should come down with me again. I need some of your Jonny Slideways on this track." They listened to the pre chorus. "Right here!" Dennis pointed out as he drove.

"When are you going back in?" Jon asked, always interested in spending time in the studio.

"The studio's open for the whole weekend. Nigel talked to the Pecorinos and we worked out kind of an arrangement." Dennis winked. "They said I could do whatever I wanted just so long as I cleaned up after myself."

"You've got the studio for the whole weekend?" Jon's wheels were turning faster than the whiny engine of the car they were in.

They drove with the windows down in the cool April air, singing Dennis' song at the top of their lungs, which for Dennis was extremely loud. Jon sang some counterpoint slide notes while the tiny car bounced on its suspension. A dark-skinned man with a mustache driving an empty taxi pulled up next to them at an intersection. He looked mistrustfully at the Mazda rocking in place. *"People keep telling me what I've been doing wrong,"* they shouted the lyrics at him. Dennis revved the engine up to full-scale tilt in anticipation of the light change. *"Alligator man!"* he yelled, celebrating the moment with a long tire squeal, leaving the taxi driver frozen at the light. Ten minutes later, they sliced up an alley and parked at a slant between two other cars near the back door of a strip club on the lower east side.

CHAPTER 10

Passing the front door before double parking alongside the curb, the Bosco Dish tour bus pulled up to the Chelsea Hotel on 23rd Street. The roadies got off first and went around the side to open up the outside baggage compartments. They unloaded some stenciled anvil cases and put the guitars onto the hotel's rolling trolley while the musicians and their guests, in no hurry to leave the comforts of the bus, continued socializing. Monica and Rebecca sat around a built-in table, sipping beer with the three band members who were unsuccessfully vying for their mating rights. The guitarist, Rick, seated next to Rebecca, tried to brake through her facade with cleverness, but his words bounced off the wall of her indifference like he was playing a game of handball with himself. The bass player, Bruce, tried holding hands with Monica, but got no response, and the only fluids flowing were beer. Larry, the heady keyboard player with glasses, sat across from the others, pretending to be more interested in an equipment magazine than company. The bus driver went inside and left the motor running so the air-conditioning and electricity could continue working, making the bus into the functional apartment it was designed to simulate.

Donny and Freddy had moved their dates to the private, curtained section at the back of the bus, where they spread out on the plush wrap-around couches. Using his American Express card, Donny chopped up lines of coke on the smoked-glass table in the

middle of the sectional while Freddy and Ameliah explored a long kiss.

"Ah, this is the life," Donny snorted with satisfaction. "I always knew we'd make it big," he gushed, passing the rolled-up $100 bill to Randi. Randi, kneeling on the sofa with her rear end conspicuously elevated, took the makeshift straw and bent over the lines Donny had laid out for her. Positioned with her elbows on the table, she put the index finger from one hand over her nostril and held the tooter with the thumb and forefinger of the other. Inserting the short tube halfway up her nose, she inhaled with a decisive sniff. The numbing went straight to the back of her eyes, and still resting her weight on her elbows, she attempted to maneuver the straw to the other nostril. But as she shifted position, the silk blouse that covered her elbows slipped on the slick glass tabletop and she fell, chin-first, onto the hard surface. Her teeth clamped shut on the back of her tongue, and when she opened her mouth again it was only to scream in pain. In the mad scramble to right herself, she destroyed the remaining neatly spaced lines.

"Whoa, doll." Donny laughed and slapped her protruding bottom. "I know you can see your reflection in there, but it's not really water. We'll do some diving later baby, I promise. Come on over here and let me lick that powder off your face." He helped her sit up, but when he brushed the hair away from her cheeks, he saw she was bleeding. "Whoa, baby. You're all messed up." He sat her back into the folds of the couch and wiped her mouth with his hand. Finding a box of tissues on a ledge behind the sofa, Donny cleaned the blood off his hand and gave a tissue to Randi. She held it against her lips and, slightly dazed, leaned back into the cushions. The other couple was too far away to see exactly what was happening, but every time Randi removed the tissue to check, the blood reappeared. Donny gave her another tissue and straightened out the coke lines.

"I think you'd better sit it out for a minute, honey," he said, helping himself to another long toot. "All right! Damn, that's good!" Donny smacked his lips and tried to share his glee, but Randi had sunk further into the cushions and her eyes were shut. He didn't know if she was just tired or enjoying the numbing effects of the drugs and alcohol, but when she let go of the napkin, blood trickled down her chin. "Here you go," he said, stuffing a pillow under her head and raising her legs onto the couch. He handed her a fresh tissue and she held it to her lips, drawing her legs up into the fetal position. "You just rest," Donny tried to soothe her. "You'll be okay, just hold it here," he told her, putting the tissue firmly over her mouth. Randi tried to hold on, but the tissue slipped off again. Donny stuffed it into one side of her mouth with his finger, which turned him on, and Randi didn't resist as he straightened her blouse and felt her nipples.

Freddy and Ameliah, who were sprawled out on the opposite couch, were too involved in their make-out session to bother with Randi's accident. Turning his attention to them, Donny invited them to partake. "Okay, now it's your turn, but that's gonna be a hard act to follow," he laughed, re-supplying the lines with one hand, while stroking Randi with the other.

After laying out their hits, Donny handed the straw to Freddy. Freddy, who was determined to show his class and style, disengaged from his make-out session and brushed some fallen strands of sticky hair out of his eyes. He sat up with both feet on the floor and leaned over the table for his fix. Holding the rolled up bill to his nose, he descended on his prize. But as he did, the garish amethyst cross he always wore swung out from under his loosened shirt and cracked into the glass, sending the coke flying in all directions. "Shit! I can't believe it. This goddam cross is always falling out at the wrong time," he cursed, tucking it back in his shirt. "Hand me that credit card, Donny."

Donny took another card from his wallet and the two men scraped the powder from the far ends of the table back into the middle, not bothering with the traces that had fallen off and dusted the dark carpet.

"Okay, now let's try that again," Freddy said after re-assembling the lines. "You go first this time." He passed the straw to Ameliah, who had never snorted coke before but wasn't about to admit it.

Ameliah gingerly put the end of the bill beneath her left nostril. and exhaled nervously, destroying the powdery mounds in a puffy burst. "Whoops! I guess I'm not so good at this," she apologized.

Donny was incredulous. He stared at Freddy in disbelief. Freddy patted her thigh. "That's okay, sweetheart, can't be good at everything. Let's line 'em up again, one more time, for good luck."

Donny was losing his patience. His drug high had peaked and was picking up speed in the opposite direction. "Dammit you guys. That stuff costs a lot of money and – "

"Stop with the bullshit man. Just lay it out," Freddy commanded. "You can get some more from Dante tomorrow."

Ameliah felt guilty. "Oh, I'm so sorry I messed up. Maybe I should go. I've got work tomorrow and – "

Freddy put his arm around her waist. "No way baby. The night is young and we're just getting to know each other."

"Oh shit!" Donny interrupted. "Randi's out. Shit. She's still bleeding." Randi's tissue had soaked through and a trickle of blood had started down her neck.

"Maybe we better get a doctor or something," Freddy suggested.

Randi's eyes twitched and she breathed in long gargled inhalations. The two men didn't know what to do.

"Better sit her up," Ameliah suggested.

Donny wiped her mouth and they all watched closely as the blood flow seemed to increase. Donny and Freddy shared a concerned look.

"Hey guys, anyone here?" Freddy called out. "We need some help back here. Guys?"

The keyboard player, Larry, who had taken some pre-med courses in college, poked his head through the curtains. "What's going on in here? Somebody sick?" He answered his own question while he was asking it. Donny was holding Randi up in a sitting position. Her arms rested limply at her sides and her head hung down against her chest.

"She doesn't look like she's having such a good time," Larry noted sardonically, edging in for a closer inspection. "What have you guys been up to back here?" he asked knowingly. He was the straightest member of the band and disapproved of overindulgence. Randi's chest heaved as she struggled to breathe. "Hold her head up before she chokes to death," he instructed Donny. Donny leaned her back against the cushions, supporting the weight of her head with his hand under her chin. A few tense moments passed as they watched a steady flow of blood and drool drip over Donny's hand and into her cleavage, emerging as a wet stain on her blouse.

Feeling embarrassed for her, Ameliah clambered to her side and wiped her chest with a tissue. "Come on, Randi girl. Wake up now, it's okay."

Larry pushed lightly on Randi's shoulders, picked some hair out of her mouth, and forced Randi's eyelid open with his thumb. Her eye was completely dilated and didn't respond to the light. "Get me some water please, someone get some water," he ordered with some urgency. Freddy handed him a glass, and he pinched Randi's nostrils shut, forcing her to suck air through her mouth while he held the glass up to her lips. She wouldn't drink, so he tilted her head back and tipped the glass into her mouth. She gagged, and the water, mixed with bloody drool, streamed down her chin and onto her clothes. Then she shivered and took a few deep breaths. He let go of her nose. "That's it. That's a good girl. Come on

Randi. Come on back," he encouraged. The pace of her breathing increased. "I think she's coming around." He held her wrist and checked her pulse. While he was counting the seconds, Randi's breathing became more rapid, with each breath shorter than the one before it until she seemed to be panting for air. Then, after one breathy gulp, she stopped breathing altogether. Everyone froze as nightmare scenarios raced through their imaginations.

"Randi! RANDI!" They shouted her name as if sheer volume of their calls would reach her, wherever she was. Larry pinched her nose again and then let go. They all stared in disbelief as she sat motionless for what seemed like a very long time. Deprived of oxygen, her eyelids flickered and her throat constricted, and no one knew what to do. Donny, who was still holding her upright, gave her a slap on the back, and to everyone's surprise, she suddenly belched. Then, just as suddenly, she gasped. Her next exhalation was an eruption of vomit that landed mostly on her miniskirt before dripping down her legs. She awoke, but was completely disoriented. A few deep breaths later, she heaved again, and the convulsions continued intermittently for several minutes until there was nothing left in her stomach. Then, trembling, she collapsed into the sofa.

All the men were disgusted, but Ameliah wiped her face and covered her with a throw blanket. Donny continued to support her back with his arm as she came to. Randi's foot began to twitch and she started to cry. "I'm cold. I'm so cold," she sobbed.

"You're going to be okay," Ameliah comforted her. Opening her eyes, Randi saw her legs covered in vomit and burst into tears. Crying, she wiped the fluid trickling down her chin and mumbled incoherently.

The noise and commotion brought the couples in the front of the bus to the scene of the accident. Rebecca and Monica gagged at the vomitus smell, and their eyes met Ameliah's, who was trying to console the shivering Randi while avoiding her excretions. This was definitely not what they all had in mind when they set out for a night on the town, and the roommates silently agreed that it was way past time to go home.

"Okay, show's over, time to get off the bus," Bruce, the bass player called out callously. "We've all seen Randi puke before and she always comes back for more the next day. I'm tired and hungry and could use a hot shower. You guys can stay here as long as you like, but this is way too gross for me."

"Me too," the guitarist, Rick, agreed. "I definitely need something to smoke after seeing this mess. I'll be in our room – and this bud's for you!" he invited, flashing two fat joints that had magically appeared in his hand.

"I'm with you, Rick, my man, you are the dude!" Bruce confirmed. "She'll be okay – and it really stinks in here! Coming ladies? Or would you like to hang around here and help clean up before the cops come?" Bruce and Rick led the retreat. Larry took one last look at Randi, decided that his work was done, and followed Rebecca, Monica, and his band-mates out.

The mention of cops got everyone's attention. Randi was still groggy and bleeding, and Donny knew that if there was something really wrong with her and doctors were called, the cops wouldn't be far behind. He would be able to explain the vomit to the bus driver, who was rented along with the bus and had seen plenty of partying, but an overdose would require a really creative alibi that no one felt up to at the moment.

"Let's get her off the bus," Donny announced, brushing the residual puke from her blouse and skirt. "I'll carry her up to the room and you guys tidy up back here," he added, addressing no one in particular while wiping the splatter from his own clothes.

"Get one of the roadies to clean this mess up," Freddy corrected him. "Tell them they can keep whatever they find." He pointed to the traces of powder on the table. "That should inspire them."

"I'll go with her," Ameliah volunteered, holding Randi's limp hand as Donny carried her up the aisle. "She needs a woman to look after her."

Donny accepted the help. "Okay, but let's hurry. I want to get her up to the room as soon as possible." He swung her dangling calves around the seat backs and tables on their way to the front of the bus. Ameliah held onto Randi with one hand and Freddy with the other as they got off and hurried into the hotel lobby. Rick, Bruce, and Larry, waiting in the lobby with Monica and Rebecca, let them go on ahead.

"Don't you dare leave me here by myself," Ameliah hissed at her friends while being dragged along past them. "I won't be long. You hang out with those guys for a while. I'll come get you." Donny pulled the human chain into an open elevator and shut it as fast as possible.

Waiting for the next elevator, Bruce tried to reassure Monica. "Don't you worry about Randi. She does this all the time." He put an unwelcome arm around Monica's shoulders.

Larry disagreed. "Not like that, man. Didn't you see her face? There was a lot of blood from somewhere; looked pretty serious to me." He saw the bus driver approaching the bus through the lobby window. "We better get out of here before that driver gets a whiff of this and we all get in trouble."

"I agree," Rick said nervously. "Let's get out of here."

Larry had a second thought. "Wait for me," he said. "I'll be right back." He went outside and spoke to one of the roadies who was wrestling an anvil case back into the bus' under-compartment. A uniformed receptionist, barely visible behind the vintage wooden check-in counter, looked up briefly when Larry came back and reunited with the group in front of the elevators. The dull ceiling lights cast a foreboding glow over the worn leather sofas in the neglected lobby. Monica whispered to Rebecca between the hisses and creaks of early morning as they waited. Finally, the elevator's doors opened, and in the imagined privacy of the tiny compartment, the group's collective nerve returned.

Rick was the first to speak at a normal volume. "Phew! That was weird. Did you see the way the guy behind the desk looked at us? I think he must've known something was wrong."

Larry challenged him. "Known what? You sound paranoid."

"Well, maybe he saw Donny carrying Randi in and...I don't know," Bruce speculated.

"Yeah. Maybe he thought Randi was dead or...well, who knows?" Rick said.

"This is our floor," Larry announced. "Let's all just go to our rooms and stay calm. We'll find out what happened in the morning."

"Wanna join us for a smoke?" Rick asked.

"No thanks, I've had enough of this night." Larry said. "I'll see you in the morning – or whenever you get up."

Monica and Rebecca followed Bruce and Rick into the room they shared. With their coats still on, they stood in front of the sliding glass doors that opened onto a balcony. The room was small and crowded with four people in it, so Rick slid the doors open. He and Bruce went outside to look around and the girls followed. Standing behind the wrought-iron railing that faced 23rd Street, they could see the emergency flashers around the top of their tour bus below. Rick lit a joint and passed it to Bruce, trying to regain some altitude. Monica took a toke, but the fresh smoke and night air weren't powerful enough to clear the beer fog and lingering smell of vomit. All the evening's magic had worn off and the girls sat down in grimy plastic chairs, waiting for Ameliah and their release. Rick and Bruce went back inside and turned on the TV.

When they found their room on the sixth floor, Donny handed the room key to Ameliah and waited as she opened the door for him. Freddy put his arm around her. "We're down this way, baby," he said. "Come on, Randi will be okay. This isn't the first time she's been drunk. Donny knows what he's doing." Ameliah wasn't so sure, but she allowed herself to be escorted down the hallway to Freddy's room.

At the end of his strength, Donny kicked the door closed and dropped Randi on the bed like dead weight. She moaned as she fell on the hard mattress. More concerned with himself, Donny left her there and went into the bathroom to wash off. Angry and frustrated, he gnashed his teeth in the mirror and cursed out loud. His coke was almost gone, his nicest shirt stunk from puke, his leather pants were stained with blood, and his $180 dollar Italian leather shoes were covered in slime and probably ruined too. Disgusted, he took everything off, threw it in the corner, and scalded himself in a hot shower.

Randi was lying on her side under the covers naked when he came out of the bathroom in a hotel bathrobe. "I'm sorry baby," she apologized weakly. "I guess I had too much to drink."

Donny opened the curtain and looked out the window before making sure it was all the way closed. He didn't speak.

"I said I was sorry. I have such a headache." Randi's voice was faint. "Are you feeling okay?"

"Okay? I'm pissed. You wasted half my coke, embarrassed me, and ruined all my clothes," Donny spewed. "How do you think I feel?"

"I said I'm sorry, baby. I had too much, that's all." Randi repeated her apology. "Hey, didn't you pass out earlier tonight at the club?" she reminded him. "See, it's not just me."

"That was different." Donny stalked the TV changer. "Why don't you go clean up in the shower?"

"I'm not feeling so good. I don't think I can get up by myself. You may have to help me."

Donny sat down on the bed and slid his arm under the covers. The touch of Randi's skin had an immediate effect on his manhood. He ran his hand up her back, confirming her nudity.

"Mmm, that feels good," Randi encouraged him, glad the subject had changed. "That's helping my headache." She let him rub her a while before feeling her way to his erection. "How can I make it up to you?" she asked, squeezing it. "What can I do?"

Donny lifted the covers and wordlessly slid in next to her. She received him gently and put her hand on his chest. Aggressively, he slid his arm under her torso, rolled her onto her back, and climbed on top. "Not so fast. I'm still dizzy," she said feebly.

Fully aroused, he lay on top of her and forced her legs apart with his feet.

"Donny please wait," she pleaded, "I'm not ready."

Donny was too excited to stop and positioned the tip of his penis against her mound.

"Not yet. Please. Wait!" Randi tried to twist away.

The head of his swollen cock was too big for her opening but he pushed it partially in anyway.

"No, Donny, stop; I'm not wet." Randi protested.

Donny lay the full weight of his body on her and continued to force his way in.

"Donny, please baby, I'm not feeling that good. My head still hurts and you're so heavy I can't breathe." Randi started to panic and tried to push him off.

The mention of her not breathing again caused Donny to rise up onto his elbows so he wasn't crushing her. "Is that better?" he asked, thrusting his hips lasciviously.

"Better, but.... Ouch! Shit!" she screamed as he inserted further. "You're hurting me!" She tried to move but her arms were pinned over her head with his powerful grip and her legs were spread helplessly around his waist. "Dammit, Donny, stop it, please, you're hurting me." Her pleas did nothing to slow him, and she didn't have the breath to complain any further as Donny's thrusting grew more intense. She screamed uncontrollably when he penetrated.

In the anonymity of the infamous hotel, with the sound trapped inside by the closed windows, her screaming excited Donny's bullying instincts. "You're such a little whore," he grunted, relishing the full depth of her vagina. "So you want to make it up to me?" He huffed stale breath in her face and ground her pelvis into the mattress. "Is this how you're gonna make it up to me?" he asked, jerking his hips in short thrusts. "Is this how you're gonna pay for all that coke?" He pounded her harder and squeezed her wrists above her head.

Randi was too weak and traumatized to answer. Groaning, she ceded control of her body. She knew she couldn't stop him, so she lay flat on her back, accepting the abuse in a trembling sweaty stupor.

Finally, after a lustful three-minute rape, Donny roared to a climax in a headboard-banging fit, pinching her nipples viciously as he finished his assault. There were no hugs or kisses when he finally withdrew and rolled onto a dry spot on the other side of the bed. "Now I forgive you," he grunted with satisfaction. His noxious fart poisoned the covers and he was asleep within five minutes.

Randi was afraid to move. She lay motionless on her back, staring at the darkened ceiling, her heart pounding as blood trickled out of her nose and semen trickled down her thighs. She didn't want to excite him again, and lay still until Donny's snores confirmed he was no longer a threat. She ached all over and began to sob. The smells of gas and vomit nauseated her, but she eventually gathered enough strength to quietly slip out of bed. Unsteady on her feet, she went straight to the bathroom to wash up, pee, and assess the damage. She was unprepared for the face that greeted her in the bathroom mirror.

"On no honey what'd you do to your face?" *7

Blood flowed down her chin, and her image was a child's finger painting of mascara, eye shadow, and lipstick. Her stiff teased hair looked like it belonged on a scarecrow that had been left out in a tornado, and one earring dangled through a torn and bloodied lobe. She was sure she had never looked worse, and was too afraid to see the rest of her body before she bathed. Covering up with a towel and holding her bloody nose with a tissue, she filled the tub with steaming water and submerged.

Ameliah and Freddy tried to get romantic, but try as they did, the disturbing images of Randi's emissions made it impossible to rekindle their passion. After an hour of sipping wine from the hotel mini bar and watching television from the couch, they gave up. Freddy was relieved when Ameliah excused herself with the promise to continue at a later date. He walked her out and stopped at Donny's door. Ameliah knocked. "They're probably asleep by now," Freddy suggested when no one answered.

"I don't know, I think I hear the water running," Ameliah whispered in the quiet hallway. "I hope she's okay."

"I'm sure she's fine," Freddy reassured her. "Let's go find your friends and get you a cab home."

They took the elevator down to the fourth floor and knocked on the band's door. Bruce let them in and dove back onto the bed. The room was completely dark except for the television, which cast its flickering blue haze on the bleary-eyed occupants. The air reeked of pot smoke, so Freddy closed the door quickly, hoping to keep the telltale smell out of the hallway. Monica and Rebecca sat side-by-side on one bed with their coats on, while Rick lay perpendicular at their feet. "Come on in and join the party," Bruce invited Freddy. Lying on the bed nearest the door, he was the only one comfortable. "The movie is just getting to the good part."

Freddy made small talk. "Yeah? What movie is it?"

"*Friday the 13th.* You know the one where he – "

"Shush! You're going to spoil it!" Rick stopped him.

Bruce grinned foolishly as the underscore from the movie built to a cheesy tension.

"Ameliah? Are you ready?" Rebecca called from the bed.

"Sshhh; there he is!" Rick pointed to the movie's action.

"Can we go now?" Monica asked.

"No. This is the best part!" Bruce insisted.

"I'm ready if you are," Ameliah answered.

"Dammit, people!" Rick snapped, sitting up abruptly and swatting the television off. "You really know how to ruin a great movie!"

They all stayed in the dark for a few moments until Bruce located the light switch. The two musicians blinked, fighting extreme dilation.

"Thanks for letting us hang out with you," Rebecca said, stretching the truth politely. "We'll have to rent this movie sometime and watch it from the beginning."

Rick agreed. "Yeah, you've got to watch it from the beginning to get the full effect."

"What do you say we get these ladies a cab?" Freddy interjected, motioning his fully baked band-mates out of the way as Monica and Rebecca said goodnight.

"The front desk will get you a cab," Freddy explained, leading the girls down the hall.

The ride down was quiet, but when the elevator opened in the lobby, they were disturbed to see the flashing red lights of an emergency vehicle strobing through the glass front doors.

"Everything okay?" Freddy asked the stoic desk attendant as they approached.

"Everything's a long word," the clerk answered cryptically.

"Can you please call these lovely ladies a cab?" Freddy asked. The girls adjusted their jackets and brushed their hair back while being scrutinized. Satisfied that this was a legitimate request, the clerk accepted his assignment with a head bob. "Thanks, I'll wait with them," Freddy volunteered.

As the quartet stood just inside the front doors, they could see that the flashing lights belonged to an empty police car, idling directly behind their tour bus. Freddy self-consciously buttoned his shirt up all the way as they quietly considered the unfortunate possibilities. The storage compartment door on the side of the bus was open and a uniformed officer was talking to one of the roadies. Freddy's tension elevated when he saw the bus driver lead another policeman onto the bus. The girls nervously whispered amongst themselves while the time past midnight crawled on all fours. The headlights from a car doing a 180-degree turn in the middle of 23rd Street sprayed them blind, and when they could see again, a yellow cab was waiting outside. A small dark man with a mustache was in the driver's seat writing on a pad when Ameliah opened the back door and slid in. Monica and Rebecca shoved in next to her. "Riverside Apartments please, Tenth and Washington."

CHAPTER 11

Dennis gave the doorman of the strip club a low five and headed to his favorite table by the runway. A buxom waitress in a see-through top took their order.

"Two Hineys and two Jacks rocks. Is that all?" she recited, posing long enough to give them an eyeful of her fishnets and garter. "So, where are you gentlemen from?" she asked in a southern drawl, communicating with her breasts.

"We're from around here," Dennis assured her with a studious gaze. "And what's *your* name?"

"Oh, I'm Priscilla, thank you. I just came up from Florida a few weeks ago. Sure gets cold round here." She shifted suggestively.

"Nice to meet you Priscilla. Why don't you fetch us those drinks and maybe we can find a way to warm you up a bit," Dennis suggested with a wink.

"Awl righty, that sounds goood," she exaggerated her drawl and sauntered off in her spiked heels, putting on a show.

Jon shook his head, marveling at Dennis' repartee skills. He hadn't been to a strip club with him in a long time and had forgotten how familiar Dennis was with the drill. "You're something else," he said with awe.

"I'm something else? No, that's something else!" Dennis pointed to Priscilla. "Nothing like fresh talent to start the evening off right."

"True that," Jon agreed as he spotted another waitress serving drinks and eye candy. The music started and Dennis became enthralled with the next performer who directed her gyrations at his obvious attraction. She danced her way around the stage until she was inches away from his unflinching stare and cupped her breasts with her hands in expectation of a tip. Dennis put a folded dollar in her cleavage, and the dancer touched his prematurely balding head before slithering away to her next mark. Other men sat at tables lining the runway, and after midnight on a Thursday, this was one of the busiest places in the downtown part of the city. Priscilla returned with the drinks and placed each one in front of them, like a schoolgirl picking daisies. "That'll be $20, unless you want something else," she solicited.

Dennis took the bait. "What do you have in mind? Hmm?"

"Well, we do have a private lounge." She poured on the southern charm. "And some gentlemen enjoy a little lap dance from time to time." She put her hand on Dennis' muscular chest and raked the back of her fingernails up to his neck.

"That sounds like a great idea." Dennis told her, handing her a twenty. "Maybe I'll take you up on that after a drink or two."

Priscilla looked disappointingly at the twenty. "Didn't y'all like my servin'"?"

Jon reached into his pocket and gave her another five. "There there; all happy now?"

She was a little confused by his sarcasm but thanked him with a tiny curtsey.

After she was gone, Dennis took a swig of beer. "What did you do that for?" he asked.

Jon took a drink "I don't know. I guess I felt sorry for her."

"Sorry for her? Are you kidding? She can get anything she wants with that body."

"Yeah, she's got the body, but that phony southern hoochie-coochie thing is...women like that make me sad," Jon revealed.

Dennis disagreed. "You need to finish that shot, my man. Then let me buy you another one. And if you don't like what you see here after a few drinks, I'm gonna believe what everyone says about you."

"Yeah, what do they say?" Jon asked defensively.

"Oh come on now, I was only joking. Don't pull that tough guy shit with me. Kill that drink for chrissakes. When was the last time you got laid?"

Jon slugged his shot of Jack. "It *has* been a while," he said wistfully, trying to summon desire. Dennis' question triggered memories of how the evening had progressed, and all Jon could think about was how he had felt when he touched Rebecca's thigh. He wondered where she was and what she was doing with those losers from Freddy's band. His blood pressure rose when he remembered how much he hated that stupid purple sparkle drum stock-riff pompous cover bullshit band, and all the shimmying boobs and skimpy negligees couldn't stiffen him up again.

"Who is she?" Dennis asked.

"Who?

"The woman."

"What woman?"

"The woman I saw you with earlier. The one you can't get out of your head."

"How'd you know?"

"You're kidding, right? You're sitting here with three acres of wiggling ass in your face and you're not even paying attention. It's got to be another woman, 'cause I know you're not gay."

Jon puckered his lips as if he was going to kiss him. "I love you, man."

"Get away from me, you pervert," Dennis laughed. "I'm just looking out for you. Buy you a lap dance? Chase away those blues with a big pink stick," he pitched.

Jon declined. "Why don't you have Miss Priscilla rub-a-dub you and I'll guard your drink."

"Suit yourself, loner boner." Dennis flagged down Priscilla, who steered him into the back room for a joy ride.

John tried to concentrate on the dancers, but nothing gelled.

"Baby baby baby don't you tell me no lies Cause I got a little case of terminal thighs." *8

A few songs later Dennis waddled back with a flush smug and ordered another drink. "So whadya say, my man, doing anything fuuuun this weekend?" He leaned in for effect.

"Nah, just working out some parts on my Portastudio." Jon didn't like to blab about his songs until he was ready to present them, and there was too much noise in the club for a detailed discussion.

"Well, why don't you come down to the studio tomorrow and work on some real equipment?" Dennis drained his drink with a straw, noisily sucking up the icy meltwater.

The invitation cut through the competition of loud music and bouncing boobs. "They still got my masters down there, right?"

"That's where you left them. When was the last time we were in?"

"Must've been like six months ago, before everything fell apart." It was a painful memory and Jon lit a cigarette.

"So tell me again what happened," Dennis asked absently, thoroughly distracted by the stage dancer shaking her breasts close enough to demand a response.

Jon was too tired to relive his bad luck story. "Oh, I don't want to go into it now. I'll tell you all about it later." He squirmed in his seat, ready to leave.

Dennis knew Jon's moods and stayed on topic. "Okie smokes. We'll get out of here soon, but I want you to promise to come to the studio and lay down a guitar part for me tomorrow night."

Jon wasn't too excited about staying up all night to work on somebody else's track, but didn't want to pass up the chance to get back in the studio. "What time you get off, like 2 a.m.?"

"Well, seeing as I already have the keys, I was thinking about having my assistant mix the second set and lock up for me. Why don't you come by the club around 9:00 or 10:00, and we'll sneak out the back door and get an early start."

Dennis was very organized, and Jon was starting to like the plan. "We'll sneak it in the back door." Jon repeated, as the next act danced to Rick James.

"Make sure you bring your slide and we'll slide it in slideways," Dennis added suggestively. They stayed for another drink and some more lechery before recognizing the 'time to go' signs of too few customers and too many hovering hooters.

The spring air had cooled considerably since the sun went down, and by 3 a.m. it fogged their breath and refreshed their nasal passages. Wedging themselves back into Dennis's RX 7, they strained to see through the opaque windshield with the defrosters on high. The hissing fan and residual white noise from the club sizzled in their ears, and conversation was superfluous. The streets were even more deserted than they were a few hours ago, and Dennis squinted to see through the steamy windshield and alcohol as he guided the car up to Houston. A mustachioed cabbie with a back seat full of passengers pulled up next to them at the light. It was too dark to see, but Rebecca thought she recognized Jon as the cars separated.

FRIDAY, APRIL 16TH

CHAPTER 12

Homa Monsouri, who had been born in the Kew Gardens section of Queens, wanted as little to do with the ancient customs of her family as possible. She had a fashion streak like her mother, and wore colorful shawls that wrapped her shapely figure in a layer of decency that was an uncomfortable compromise between her Middle Eastern roots and the flowering of her Western personality. Her family legacy manifested in unresolved dreams about her homeland, and her morning dressing ritual was a struggle for inner peace. Lacking any close friends, she expressed herself in creative outbursts on the walls of her bedroom with paint and posters. No one other than her mother knew the depths of her inner conflict, and she assumed a very different persona at work.

With elaborate fingernail designs peeking out from long blousy sleeves, and jet-black hair twisted and tied in an endless variety of tortured styles, Homa spoke in a throaty tone that everyone in the office understood to be the voice of authority. She could be confrontational or cagey, depending on the situation, and the sheer force of her presence was the nucleus around which the business, customers, and employees orbited. The scion of five generations of the Monsouri family, Homa was the hope for their future, and she presided over a Laden Imports office that was a noisy birdcage of activity, with ringing phones, clacking office equipment, and coffee-induced chatter.

As always, she was the first one to work. She put her coffee cup on the window ledge and unlocked the double-bolted door of the industrial building that was home to Laden Imports. As soon as she stepped inside, she recited the family prayer that was also the code for turning off the alarm system. Her faint recollection of a disturbing dream vanished in the bright glow of the hanging fluorescents. Picking her way through the maze of desks and chairs and knickknacks that marked each territory, she touched the Iranian flag poking its head above a cluster of pens and pencils on her cousin Asalah's desk. Only twenty-three, Asalah had already made her life choices, and the framed photo of Homa's young nephew, Amir, made her wonder about her own future. Rebecca's desk, always tidy and pleasant, was next to Homa's old one, and across from Asalah's. Three other desks, only two of which were regularly occupied, sat on the other side of interior partitions.

Every inch of space in the small office served at least one purpose. Dominating an interior wall, steel shelves supported an extensive collection of dusty perfume bottles and packaged products that represented decades of retail offerings from Laden Imports and its customers. Faded posters of exotic destinations were taped to the building's iron support pillars. A light rain of curiously inventive industry advertising materials, hanging from the ceiling on invisible threads, twisted in place as Homa passed beneath them. Large oversized windows that faced the street, partially painted over in the same beige sludge that covered all the other visible surfaces, were reinforced with substantial security bars, leaving only the top row of panes free to communicate with the outside world. A slightly elevated floor allowed people in the office to see the sidewalk if they stood up, but passersby could not see in. The randomly decorated and unnecessarily cramped space was a sweet-smelling prison, but Homa had never known it any other way, and it felt like home to her.

Through the opening to her private office, which was separated from the common area by two steps and an insubstantial sheetrock wall, she could see most of the lower office without leaving her seat. Her flimsy door was usually open and offered only a symbolic isolation from the rest of the staff, but at the instructions of her uncles, Homa dutifully locked it when she wasn't there. All the important documents, along with the telex, answering machines, and an ancient safe were in the private office, guarded by a giant plastic woman's head. Sitting prominently on its own pillar in the corner, the realistically painted head, with unnaturally perfect skin, heavy eye shadow, styled hair, and the word "Princess" written in red glitter on the sparkling tiara it wore, had been giving Homa nightmares since she was a child. The bulb that illuminated its hollow core had burned out years ago, and Homa purposely left it unlit, trying to dim the eerie presence. If her uncles had not insisted that the head stay there, she would have moved it out immediately; she knew that it would never fully be *her* office until she had evicted her grotesquely beautiful companion. She acknowledged The Princess – as everyone called it – with polite resentment, while examining her newly painted fingernails as the first message on the answering machine played.

"Salaam," the message from her uncle Saeed began in Persian. "May the blessings of the prophet be upon you. I am in Beirut now and am very happy to tell you that we have finally shipped the jasmine and cedar oils. You should already have confirmation on the telex. I am still negotiating for the best prices on fenugreek, and hope to have a good supply of pimenta and clove arranged for next month. We have a good lead on fresh willow bark and are enjoying an early spring. Everything else is wonderful here and I still plan on returning some time next month. Please let my sweet Asalah know I've called, and much love to you and your mother. I'll call you Monday at the usual time, God willing."

The next message was from Homa's mother, Samani. "Good morning, my precious. You were sleeping when I came in last night and I didn't want to disturb you. It's very late now and I just want to let you know that Dr. Nouri will be sending Reggie over tomorrow – I mean today – for a check. I'm very tired now and am going to bed. I will see you when you get home tonight. Thanks for taking care of the office, and remember, I love you."

The only other message was from a customer. "Good day, Colin Entwood from Ettinger Rowan here calling to check on our order. We're expecting 120 pounds of strained wool grease for May delivery. Business has been very brisk and we'd like to know the soonest we can receive the shipment. Please give us a call. Thanks."

Homa jotted a note and sipped her morning coffee as she studied the details of a telex she had ripped from its roll. The order was just as her uncle described, except there were three shipments instead of the two she had expected. She didn't like surprises and played the message from her uncle again. Saeed was always even tempered, but something about his overly pleasant report made her uncomfortable.

Saeed Monsouri, along with his brother Sattar and sister Samani, had inherited the business after politically motivated enemies arrested their father, Dadi, eight years ago. Dadi's arrest, incarceration, and presumed death put them at odds with the same authorities who later deposed their political ally, the Shah of Iran, and, in a land whose discords could resonate for centuries, the Monsouri heirs embraced their destiny with the cunning and commitment of orphans' revenge. Deeply connected to the sociopolitical unrest fought on the streets of every major Iranian city, they combined their commercial and social agendas by funding the opposition to the newly formed fundamentalist government. Most of the products Laden imported were grown near or shipped through the Mediterranean, so after their ability to do business in their native country was compromised, they established an office in Beirut and conducted their subversion in relative secrecy. Mild mannered and agreeable, Saeed was the friendly face of the business, while his taller, tense, elder brother Sattar assumed the role of head of the family. A lifelong bachelor, Sattar's dedication to the family's fortunes and traditions knew no bounds, and making friends and enemies along the way, the Monsouris were a silent force in Persian politics. Oversight of the day-to-day operations was left to their younger sister, Samani, who was left with that responsibility when her husband, who was also involved with the family business, disappeared a year after her father went missing. Unskilled in commerce and shaken by the losses, Samani was ineffective and rarely showed up at the perfume factory. Her only daughter, Homa, together with a small group of women including Homa's younger cousin Asalah, did the actual office work. At the instruction of her uncles, Homa had recently moved into the only private office on the premises and assumed the role of functional administrator. She was generally capable, but still had a lot to learn about the family business.

Asalah made a noisy entrance. "Good morning, Homa," she announced melodically. "May peace be upon you," she added in Persian.

"And how is the blessed mother of Amir today?" Homa acknowledged without getting up from her desk.

"Terrible," Asalah answered in her regular voice. "He was up half the night and I am exhausted."

"You poor thing. Why didn't you just stay home?"

Asalah rolled her creaky chair under her desk and began sorting through the scramble of papers strewn on its surface. "I don't want to worry about this mess all weekend."

"You should have stayed home. Don't make yourself sick. Rita will be back from vacation next week," Homa reminded her.

"Your father called from Beirut," she added. "He left a message. Everything's fine and he says to say hello."

"Okay, thanks, I know; he called my mother last night," Asalah reported, preoccupied with finding her favorite station on the office radio. The Friday top forty countdown had already started, and she was hoping "That Girl", by Stevie Wonder, was still number one.

Mak came in a few minutes after Asalah. "Good morning my fair sisters. May the blessings of Ja Lord be upon you," he proclaimed, adapting their greeting to his own faith.

"Good morning, Colonel Mackenzie," they replied in unison like regular parishioners.

Mak poured on the treacle. "Isn't this fine day brighter with you in it?"

"Why are you always so cheerful?" Asalah asked without wanting to know.

"Ras Tafari has blessed me with this day and promised me another," Mak testified as he inserted his time card into the clock. "Ever since the first day when this world was young and the good Lord himself was just a baby – "

"Mak! Stop! Please!" Homa interrupted.

Unfazed, Mak continued without losing his ministerial tone. "The good Lord loves you too, my little sister. And how is the lovely Asalah today?"

"Terrible. Amir kept me up all night and I'm so tired I could fall asleep right now."

"Well, well, that's what the tiny ones do," Mak consoled her. "I was up a little late last night myself." He waited for someone to ask him why, but neither of the women took the bait, so he continued without prompting. "Yes, we had the pleasure of feeding Jonny Soldier last night. Missy K did some special island cooking and we all prayed Reggae together." He cast a juicy comment.

Homa rose to the lure. "Oh that's right; your Soldier Boy actually showed up?"

"Oh yes, and Missy K fed him up good. He'll be a strong one today," Mak predicted as he exited to the warehouse with a swagger.

The Persian bells hanging from a hook on the front door chimed, and Rebecca appeared in the doorway a moment later. "Good morning all," she announced mechanically.

"Good morning, Rebecca," Homa responded without seeing her. Rebecca shuffled in quietly.

"How are you feeling today?" Asalah asked, sensing her low energy.

"Oh I'm fine," Rebecca lied, tossing her jacket on the chair by the side of her desk.

It was hard to hide the truth in such close quarters and Asalah could tell something was wrong. Rebecca's hair was still damp, and her poorly coordinated outfit was well below her standard. "Up late last night?" Asalah pried. Rebecca didn't want to talk, but Asalah didn't have any secrets and didn't get the message. "I was up all night too," she blabbered. "Poor little Amir couldn't stop throwing up and we thought we were going to have to take him to the doctor again."

The mention of vomiting roused Rebecca's visions of the night before. She had been her mother's helper for too long, and the more Asalah talked about Amir, the more certain she was that she never wanted to have to clean up vomit or change another diaper again. "Is he okay now?" she asked.

"He seemed fine when I dropped him off at my mother's this morning. Why are *you* so tired this morning?" Asalah pried.

"I'm not tired," Rebecca said defensively. "Do I look tired?" She brushed her hair away from her face.

"Well, you do look a little under the weather. Maybe you're coming down with a cold or something." Asalah's coffee kept her mouth going. "Amir had one last week. Maybe he gave me the germs and I gave them to you."

"I don't think so." Rebecca checked to see if anyone else was within earshot before making an admission. "You were right the first time. I was up pretty late last night."

Asalah realized that no one else was supposed to hear the conversation and moved her chair closer. She had married young and already had a baby, so hearing about Rebecca's social life was a guilty pleasure. "And what were you *doing* up so late?" She raised her eyebrows. "I thought you and your roommates were just going out to dinner."

Rebecca leaned forward to share her gossip. "Well, Ameliah made plans for us to go to a nightclub after dinner – you remember Ameliah?" Asalah nodded eagerly. "Well this singer she knows has a band who was performing there. He put her name on the guest list and she didn't want to go by herself."

"Ameliah's always up to something," Asalah observed expectantly.

"Exactly, so after dinner we polished off a second bottle of wine and...." Rebecca paused, not sure how much she wanted to share.

Asalah prompted her. "Well, what happened? Did you go?"

"Oh yeah," Rebecca admitted. She wanted to tell her everything but was reluctant to mention the part with Jon.

"Where did you go? Which club was it?"

"The Black Sheep. It's over by NYU," she answered coyly.

"I've heard of that place. I think my uncle goes there once in a while but no one's supposed to know."

"Asalah, you devil! What other secrets are you holding back?"

"Me holding back! You're the one who was out on the town last night and doesn't want to tell me what you did."

"Nothing happened," Rebecca denied unconvincingly.

"Oh sure, and I believe you," Asalah busted her. "It must have been a pretty wild night or else you'd be looking perfect, as usual, trying to make believe it was more exciting than it really was."

"No fair, you know me too well. I can't hide anything from you," Rebecca fibbed.

Homa's summons interrupted them. "Asalah, can you come see me?" she called out.

Asalah gave Rebecca a conspiratorial look. "Coming." She went into Homa's office.

Homa was sitting at her desk, filing her nails "Your father's message was a little confusing," she said as her cousin approached.

"Really? I thought you said he was fine. What did it say? Is something the matter?"

"He *said* he was okay and he loved you and all that, but... I don't know, maybe the way he said it."

"What are you talking about?"

"Your father said that he sent jasmine and cedar oil, but I'm confused because the telex says that we're getting three shipments." Homa showed her the curled telex paper.

Asalah was surprised. She never found the details of office work very exciting. "Is that all? That's what you want to talk to me about?"

"Well, yes." Homa had a nose for business. "This is the third time in a row that uncle Saeed says one thing and the telex says something different." She paused to consider possible explanations. "I thought you might know why. Maybe he's sending something special to you or your mother?"

"Nothing I know about. I really don't see the problem. What does it matter if we get two shipments, or three, or eight? We get what we get, and that's all. I'm sure my father and uncle Sattar know what they're doing."

"Maybe, or maybe there's another explanation." Homa's instincts told her there was.

Losing interest, Asalah wandered over to the sofa and looked at the fashion magazines on the table. "Did you ask your mother? Maybe she knows."

"I mentioned something to my mother the last time it happened and she agreed with you; it's no big deal. Maybe you're both right and I'm just being too picky." Homa put the telex paper aside and changed the subject. "So do you think you'll make it through the day today? It's Friday and there's not much going on."

"I have so much work to do and I don't want to leave it all until next week, so I'll probably stay until three, as usual."

"Rita will be back next week to help you catch up. Why don't you take the day off? I'm the boss now, remember?"

"Oh that's right. My big cousin Homa's my boss now!" They both giggled.

"I can handle the office by myself today." Homa continued. "Dr. Nouri is sending Reggie by later, but Rebecca and Mak are here. Why don't you go home and get some rest?" Homa was being particularly convincing, and Asalah was too tired to win the battle of manners.

"Okay, if you insist. Mother will be happy for me to take Amir off her hands. I'll stay a little while and clean up some loose ends before I go. Thanks for looking out for me – and don't worry so much; it makes you look old," she called on her way back to her desk. "You sure you'll be okay?"

Homa had another reason for wanting her to go. "I'm sure."

CHAPTER 13

Agent Ralph Lowell got to the office early so he could clear his inbox before someone dumped an extra assignment on his desk and ruined his day. Due to the recession, the pile of commercial applications for licenses was mercifully thin, so he took his time sipping coffee and checked the weekend weather in the newspaper before starting his work routine. His boss had invited the senior staff out to his club on Long Island for a round of golf, but the forecast of rain put those plans in jeopardy. His lack of enthusiasm about going out to New Jersey to see his in-laws had already sparked an argument with his wife, so he was looking for an acceptable alternate plan to avoid the punishment of that fate. He cleaned his glasses with his tie and fended off the disturbing ideas emanating from the overweight, buxom young receptionist strutting past as he thumbed through the *New York Post*, searching for an alibi.

Agent Rudy George appeared at the adjacent desk. "Hey, Ralph," Rudy greeted him buoyantly.

Ralph kept his nose to the paper. "Morning, Rudy."

"Looks like rain this weekend," Rudy noted as he put a warm coffee cup on his desk and sat down.

Ralph's sunken chair creaked as he leaned back. "Yeah, so much for golf." He clasped his hands behind his head and stared through the top of his reading glasses at the side of a dull gray building ten feet outside his window. Nothing had changed in the five years he had been sitting there, and he knew every imperfection in the brick and mortar lines that blocked his view of anything else.

Rudy was in a friendly mood and kept talking. "Got any other plans?" he probed.

"Clara wants me to go out to New Jersey and spend the night so Alberto can see his cousins," Ralph recited his sentence and cracked his neck.

"Oh that sounds interesting," Rudy commiserated.

"Yeah, well what do *you* have lined up?"

"Actually, I may have a little excitement this weekend." Rudy tossed a few beans on the floor before spilling.

Ralph was skeptical. "Excitement? I can count the times you've used that word on one hand in all the years I've known you."

Rudy leaned into his paperwork as if the clues were in front of him. "Well, maybe excitement is the wrong word. But it might be intriguing."

Ralph thought he had it figured out. "Okay, you win. Who is she and where are you going for dinner tonight?"

Rudy's professional instincts prevented him from giving up secrets too easily. "No woman is involved, but I'll be dining at the Dashboard Café."

"Where's that? Some new place in Staten Island?" Ralph asked, going along with the guessing game.

"Maybe," Rudy teased him, studying papers on his desk, pretending the conversation was over.

"Maybe? You're going to an exciting restaurant and you don't know where it is?"

"That's right." Rudy licked the tip of his finger and chalked a line on an invisible scoreboard, then went back to his busywork.

Temporarily stumped, Ralph took the top set of completed forms from his pile and used a long straightedge to compare the import license code with the duty revenue report. He didn't care if tariffs were improperly collected because it wasn't his job to notify the licensee or issue a refund, but if he found an instance where the licensee hadn't paid the registration fee to import a particular product, it was his job to note the discrepancy and pass the information along to Rudy. It was boring busywork, but the hours were regular and the pay was good enough to support a family, and the fact that his employer wasn't going out of business made the job that much more tolerable. Ralph fingered the tiny cross he kept on the keychain in his pocket and resigned himself to lining up columns and counting his blessings.

After a few minutes, Rudy broke the silence and restarted the conversation. "Remember Laden Imports?"

Ralph was in charge of all the forms for Manhattan. There weren't that many businesses on their radar that were also in their district, so it was easy to remember the few that were. "I haven't seen anything from them in months."

Rudy laid out a few more clues. "Yeah, well it turns out that the guys upstairs have been watching them for a while."

"Really? What for?"

"It's a long story."

"Does it have something to do with where you're going to eat?"

"Sort of. My buddy up there, Detective Falin, asked me to go along on a surveillance mission."

Ralph knew about Rudy's passion for mystery. Overweight, balding, and a lifelong bachelor, his unrequited ambition was to see himself as a brilliant detective, capable of solving the most complicated crimes, instead of the boring middle-aged government functionary that everyone else knew him to be.

"So are you going?" Ralph humored him.

"Yeah, I think so. It's kind of a stakeout. A lot of long hours in a dark car, waiting and watching." Rudy described it enthusiastically.

He was originally from Los Angeles and had read too much Raymond Chandler.

Ralph raised his eyebrows. "Sounds pretty romantic, you and Detective Falin in a dark car all night. Got something you need to tell me about?"

The innuendo flustered Rudy, so Ralph chalked an imaginary line on his side of their invisible scoreboard.

"It's not what you think." Rudy said seriously. "This could be big." He breathed substance into his fantasy.

Ralph had no real passion for police work. "When is this cookout, I mean stakeout, supposed to happen?"

"This afternoon." Rudy twisted uncomfortably in his chair and looked around the office. "I may be leaving soon."

"Where are you going?" Ralph asked, always interested in the idea of leaving the office early.

"I'm not sure. Maybe here, maybe Brooklyn, maybe Queens."

"Why those other places? The Laden Warehouse is practically around the corner." Ralph pointed out, trying to put the pieces together. "Is that where that restaurant is?"

"You mean the Dashboard Café?" Rudy laughed. "No, that's what the guys upstairs call a stakeout because they always eat in their car." Rudy flaunted his knowledge of detective jargon with another imaginary chalk mark.

"So you're going to spend all weekend eating crappy food in a car with your detective friend and you think New Jersey sounds boring?" Ralph pushed a burst of air through his lips and chalked a crosshatch on his side of their scoreboard.

Rudy acknowledged his points but wasn't finished. "How would you like to join me?"

"Are you crazy? I'd rather spend a weekend at my in-laws watching television. There's a good Mets game on and – what do you and that detective need me for anyway?" Rudy had only been on one stakeout, several years ago, and all that happened was he got indigestion from bad food and a sore neck from sleeping in the car.

"It's overtime plus a weekend double. Forty-eight hours could be over a $1000."

"$1000 and all you do is sit in a car and watch a building?"

"Maybe we take a few pictures if anyone shows up. Only one person needs to be awake, so the other one can sleep. We can put the takeout food on our expense report."

"Why do you want me? Sounds like you've got it all worked out?"

"Well, I don't want you, but I need you. There's more than one location, and they're covering too many cases upstairs. They asked me to ask you if you're available." He fudged the facts.

"Why us? Why not someone from another department who does this surveillance stuff all the time? Couldn't they just get some off-duty cops?"

"Sure they could. But Detective Falin and I are friends and he's trying to throw me one. It's a lot of money but I can't do it alone. We have to work in teams, so they need someone they know and trust. You don't want to make the easy dough?"

Ralph's phone rang. It was his wife wanting to continue the argument they'd had that morning. He held the receiver at an angle to his ear in a futile attempt to keep the words from seeping all the way into his brain and poisoning his mind. The one-sided conversation went on for several minutes, and he occasionally lowered the receiver to bottom half to his mouth to mumble assent. Melanie, the flirty receptionist, brought a stack of documents to Rudy's desk and loitered there, snickering with Rudy at the spectacle of Ralph enduring another of his wife's well known emotional tirades that bled through the receiver like a distant Spanish radio broadcast.

"Being single has its rewards," Rudy needled as Ralph hung up the phone, exasperated.

"How much did you say we could make?" Ralph asked, having second thoughts.

"Over $1000. I would bring Melanie if they let me," He winked at her. "But we probably wouldn't get much spying done." Rudy laughed at his own joke as Melanie slinked back to her post.

"And all we do is sit in a car and watch?" Ralph needed some details before he would commit. "What are we watching for?"

"I've done this lots of times before; it's easy," Rudy exaggerated. "All we do is sit in a car and write down the license plates of all the cars that come and go, even the ones that just drive by slowly. We take pictures of anyone who gets out of their car and goes inside or comes out. They've got new two-way phones in the car and we've got a night vision camera for when it gets dark. It's all very high tech. I don't sleep that well, so you can nod off most of the time and we can take turns making the food runs." Rudy twisted the facts slightly, knowing he would have a better chance of convincing Ralph to come if Ralph thought they'd be riding together. He stopped pitching to let the scent of the easy money entice. Seeing that Ralph was nibbling at the bait, Rudy jiggled it. "Unless of course you'd rather spend the rainy weekend trapped in New Jersey at your in-laws' house fighting with your wife." Ralph had no comeback, so Rudy set the hook. "Alberto will be so busy with his cousins he won't even notice if you're not there."

Ralph swam toward the boat with the hook in his mouth. "Clara will have a better time with her family if I'm not there. We haven't been getting along lately and my in-laws will be relieved that I'm not coming. Making extra money is the perfect excuse! You win this round." He pointed an accusatory finger at Rudy and chalked a line on Rudy's side of the ledger.

"I knew you'd come to your senses. I'll call upstairs and see when they want us for a briefing."

"Briefing?"

"Of course. We've got to know who the bad guys are and what we're supposed to take pictures of. They're not paying us for nothing."

Rudy picked up the phone and spoke to Detective Falin as Ralph concocted the story he was going to tell his wife. "They're ready for us now," Rudy announced as soon as he had hung up.

"But I haven't told Clara yet," Ralph wavered.

"Be a man, Ralph. We're going on an adventure and Clara can take care of herself. You can buy her something special with the extra money – if she ever let's you out of the doghouse."

"Okay, let's go up. I'll call her later. I don't want to have to look at another form until Monday."

CHAPTER 14

Jon woke up late and couldn't believe he had slept through the alarm again. If he left the house immediately he might make it to work on time, so clean clothes, showering, and eating were sacrificed, and he hit the streets at his normal high-speed, agitated gait. Inhaling the delectable odors from his favorite delis, and deliberately avoiding other pedestrians as if he was playing a game of non-contact pinball, he sped down the sidewalk. His work jeans looked like he had worn them all week because he had, and the loose-fitting, mottled nylon shirt he put on again didn't smell any worse than the rest of him. In spite of his complete lack of preparation, he felt as ready as ever.

Having more luck timing the lights and intersections than he was used to, the exercise he got walking elevated his heart rate, which pumped the poisons from his system and steadied his nerves. Recollections of the previous evening's romantic misadventure were obscured by the weekend recording plans he had made with Dennis, and with something to look forward to, he made it all the way to Laden Imports before the first whiffs of work awakened his reality glands. If Mak gave his parole officer a good report he could quit after next week, but then he would have to figure out a new way to make money. He didn't really want to go back moving equipment and dealing, and his 'risk everything' approach had landed him in worse predicaments than the perfume factory, so quitting wasn't as easy a solution as it might have seemed when he was younger. Mak had been good to him, and the steady money more than covered his expenses. And even though his date with Rebecca hadn't gone smoothly, at least they had broken the ice.

The meltwater dripped through his subconscious as he entered the building. Rebecca was sitting alone with her back to the door. Jon's heart rate thudded to a halt as he brushed by her without saying hello, stifling the thump he felt in his chest. She was on the phone and turned around in time to see him pass but didn't interrupt her call to say anything. Homa and Asalah, both in the upper office, waved as Jon punched his time card and quickly disappeared into the warehouse. The cloying sweetness of the factory stuck to his lungs like a suffocating candy coating.

"Bout time you made it in," Mak greeted him looking at his watch. "How's our Jonny Soldier feeling today? All fed up and ready to go?" Mak was always at his best in the morning.

Disturbed about Rebecca, "Morning Mak," was all Jon could muster.

"Morning? That's it? That's all you got to say for yourself after last night?" Mak asked, his feelings hurt.

"I had a great time last night, Mak. Thanks," Jon mumbled, trying to find his emotional footing as he laced up his work shoes.

"We had a fine time," Mak reminded him, "and Missy K made extra lunch today." Mak thought he knew what was important to Jon.

"Always ready for Missy K's cooking," Jon admitted, changing clothes and focus.

"Well, there'll be time for that later. Right now we got some orders to fill." Mak got down to business and led the way through the warehouse. "Being that it's Friday, we'll be stirring up some stink this afternoon," he commented, inspecting the labels wired to some of the inventory. "These go straight to the mixing room for today's batch. I need you to move the rest of the ones with the yellow tags over to the loading dock."

Jon tilted a rough-hewn crate on its end, slipped a four-wheel dolly underneath, and pushed it toward the central mixing room. The door was locked, so he positioned the dolly next to it and retrieved the key from under a nearby barrel. After he undid the heavy padlock, he slid the steel latch bar aside, pulled the solid oak door open and reached inside, feeling for the light switch.

The room was cooler than the rest of the factory and had its own distinct smell. Jon had helped Mak prepare the mixes before, but hadn't spent much time in the chamber by himself. It always seemed like a very strange place, and the intensity of the odors added to the sense of secrecy that hung in the air. A large hollow granite tub that looked like a sacramental basin sat on an iron pedestal in the center of the floor, and a heavy smoked-glass globe light hung over it like a foggy full moon. Bright lights could change the chemical composition of the formulas, so all the activities in the room had to be done in the half-light of ritual remembrance. A six-foot-long rustic wooden ladle, along with other sifting and stirring utensils, stood leaning against the rails of an open-sided box like patient acolytes waiting in a pew for the sermon. Large jugs of rosewater and rectified alcohol were positioned near the mixing basin, dwarfing the smaller urns of infused oils that were gathered in a pre-ceremonial congregation.

Jon deposited his cartage with the other crates of dried plant material that were stacked along the wall. Curious about what was going on in a small room attached to the main one, he opened the door and peaked inside. The interior of the preparation room was completely dark, a condition he corrected with one flip of the light switch. A long oak assembly table with a built-in, stainless-steel sink took up one entire wall. On the opposite wall, a crude iron masher with a sprocketed control arm hovered over a sturdy wooden basin. An asbestos-lined drying kiln sat next to the masher on an elevated brick platform, venting its offerings to the outside world through a series of ducts that extended all the way through the roof. A full- size, gas-fed still, surrounded by large glass containers, took up most of the narrow end of the rectangular space. Under the harsh lighting of the overhead fluorescents, Jon could see decades of dusty sediment that adhered to all the surfaces like a thick layer of crusty paint. Yellowed charts, diagrams, and hand-drawn reminders, mostly in Persian, were tacked to the walls, and the whole room appeared to be decorated with the splatters and blotches of previous mishaps. The unfamiliar setting and strange devices roused unknown fears, and Jon felt like only the voice of God or his counterpart was missing – and he wasn't sure which one he would appear if he stayed too long. Nervously, he turned off the lights, shut the door, and exited as quickly as possible, rejoining Mak in the relative safety of the warehouse.

While Jon and Mak were busy in the warehouse, Asalah tried to wheedle a few more details out of Rebecca. "I'm going home early today, but don't think you're going to get away with not telling me what happened last night," she whispered when she got back from Homa's office.

Rebecca continued to sort through the stack of vendor invoices with a faint smile. Ameliah called on Rebecca's direct line, and in an effort to hide the conversation from Asalah, she pretended it was a business call by resorting to innuendo and code-speak. "Uh huh," she said intermittently. "Mmm hmm, I do," she agreed while readying checks for Homa's signature. Finally, when she thought Asalah wasn't listening, she whispered, "He's here."

"Who's here?" Asalah, who had been eavesdropping, asked.

"Huh?" Rebecca was surprised at being overheard.

"Who's here? I heard you say, 'He's here,'" Asalah insisted.

Rebecca said goodbye and hung up quickly. She wasn't very good at improvising and stared blankly, unable to come up with a misleading answer.

Asalah persisted. "The only men here are Mak and Jon. Who were you talking about?"

Rebecca was stumped, and was just about to tell her too much when Asalah's phone rang. "Yes mother, I'll be there soon," Asalah assured her. "Okay, you tell them I'm coming and I'll stop by on the way there." Another pause later, she added, "Yes, soon; I love you too; Salaam."

Rebecca pretended to have gone back to work, but Asalah wasn't finished. "If this is what I think it is.... Well, maybe you shouldn't tell me, but I guess you're secret's safe for another few days because I have to go now. Don't do anything stupid," she snickered with the delight of imagined naughtiness. "Have a wild weekend and I'll see you Monday." Asalah buttoned her fashionable new nylon coat and sauntered out, humming along to the Earth Wind and Fire song "Let's Groove" on the office radio.

Rebecca dove back into her deskwork and tried to swim through her feelings like an inexperienced snorkeler. She was worried about what would happen if Jon came into the office and she was the only one sitting there. She wondered if she should apologize, but couldn't figure out what she did wrong. Maybe *Jon* should apologize? What would she say if he asked her about where she went last night? There were no markers in the open waters of romance, and she called Ameliah to buoy her. But Ameliah didn't answer, so before drowning in insecurity, Rebecca escaped the emotional riptide by bringing checks that needed signing into Homa's office.

Homa was busy with paperwork. "Just a minute please," she said, lost in concentration.

Rebecca watched as Homa used her extended fingernails like surgical tools to sort through a sheaf of documents bound in an odd-sized ledger.

Looking up when she was done, she studied Rebecca. "I'm glad you came in. I've been meaning to talk to you," she said seriously.

Thinking there might be a problem, and unprepared for a conversation with her boss, Rebecca tensed up.

Homa saw her nervous reaction and eased her fears. "Now that we're here by ourselves, maybe we should order lunch in. Company treat," she said, revealing only part of her agenda. "Are you hungry? I mean if you brought lunch or have other plans I'll understand."

The offer took Rebecca by surprise. "Lunch sounds great." She wasn't particularly hungry, but at least she wouldn't be sitting alone in the office if Jon came in.

"Great. What do you feel like today?" Homa asked.

Rebecca shrugged without preference.

"Well, I could go for some Lebanese food," Homa suggested. "Pita and falafel sound good to me. Is that okay with you? Homa occasionally bought the staff lunch, which they ate together as a group, but they rarely spent any time together that wasn't all business.

Rebecca was a little uncomfortable not knowing what, if anything, was on Homa's mind, but she didn't want to be alone. So even though the Princess, as they all called the sentinel head, gave her the creeps, she was happy to stay in the sanctuary of Homa's office. "Sounds good," she said, and accepted Homa's invitation to sit on the sofa.

Homa phoned their order in to the local restaurant that delivered. "Are these the checks you want me to sign?" she asked, going through the pile Rebecca had put in front of her.

Rebecca nodded.

"Very neat, nice job, Rebecca. Ten percent net ten on this one!" Homa's praise was tinged with a sultry calm.

Rebecca basked in her approval on a stuffed leather chair, browsing through the women's magazines on the sofa table.

When she was done signing the checks, Homa excused herself for a trip to her private bathroom. A few moments later, she emerged with re-applied eyeliner and perfume, and sat with her legs crossed on the sofa near Rebecca. The radio was on in the background, and Olivia Newton John was encouraging everyone to listen to their body talk. Homa tapped her foot in the air to the beat, slowly turning the pages of a magazine while they waited for lunch. "So, what do you do to keep from being bored?" she asked Rebecca innocently. "It's not too exciting around here."

"Oh, I like working here a lot," Rebecca volunteered, feeling energized by the rhythm and sexually suggestive lyrics of the song.

Homa was listening to the lyrics too. "Oh, I know you're happy here. That's not what I meant. We all like it here but, you know, it's not exactly fun, if you know what I mean." She smiled.

"Yeah, I guess not," Rebecca said cautiously. She didn't want to say the wrong thing, and the overstated chorus said too much.

"Let's get physical, physical.
Let me hear your body talk,
Your body talk."

Homa showed her a stylized picture of a model in a swimsuit. "She's very beautiful, don't you think?"

"Mmm hmm," Rebecca agreed politely.

"You're very beautiful too," Homa complimented. "Did you ever want to model? You could, you know."

Rebecca blushed.

"A beautiful girl like you must have many suitors," Homa continued. "Do you have a steady boyfriend? Asalah says you do." she pried.

"No," Rebecca answered uncertainly. Did Homa suspect? How could she know? Had Asalah told her about Jon? She couldn't have said too much. It was only last night. Had Homa known about Jon all along?

Her anxiety showed and Homa noticed. "Did I say something to upset you? I'm sorry. It's none of my business. I just can't imagine you being alone, such a pretty girl...." Homa re-crossed her legs and secured her hair tie.

Rebecca took the cue. "Well, you're quite beautiful yourself. Have *you* ever modeled?

"Me? Well, no, of course not; I couldn't," Homa laughed.

"Why not? You're pretty enough."

"Oh maybe I could if I was back in Persia. But I look, you know, too dark to model here. But thank you for thinking I could. Maybe I should try." She arched her chest.

Rebecca started to relax again. "So do *you* have a boyfriend?" she asked, venturing into uncharted conversational waters.

"Oh, I, I'm not...well, no I don't, at least not right now. I'm single." Homa reddened slightly and shifted her weight to the other hip.

Rebecca didn't notice how far Homa's lips had parted or understand the pregnancy of her stare. The doorbell rang and Homa went to let the delivery boy in. She came back with their lunch in a plastic bag and laid it on the sofa table. They each opened a wax-papered pita and nibbled daintily at the edges, pausing to dab their mouths with napkins and sip orange sodas. Forgetting about the previous night's mischief, Rebecca indulged in the simple pleasure of lunch while Homa inhaled her presence. Wanting the moment to last, Homa ignored the office phone when it rang and let the answering machine do its job. Hearing the message from the Customs Office confirming the appointment for Tuesday ruined her appetite. Rebecca finished eating and went back to her desk. "Thank you so much for lunch," she said on her way out.

"Thank you for the company," Homa replied, conflicted.

The warehouse door swung open and Mak appeared just as Rebecca was settling in at her desk. "Where is everyone?" he asked, looking around.

"Hi Mak. Who are you looking for?" Rebecca answered.

"I'm just here to check on an order, but where are all your friends? You look so lonely in here all by yourself."

"I'm fine. Homa is here with me."

"Where is Asalah?" Mak asked, canvassing the empty desks. "She was here when I came in this morning."

"Oh, she finished early and went home. Rita is off this week and Barbara called in sick." Rebecca gestured at the empty chairs.

"Well, that explains it I guess," Mak replied, looking through some papers on Asalah's desk. "Here it is. I found it." He held one up. "Mr. Entwood would be pretty upset if we left this out of his order."

"Mak, is that you?" Homa called out.

"Yes it is and always will be," Mak patronized.

"Mak, can you come here for a minute?"

Mak bugged his eyes at Rebecca in anticipation of a problem.

"I'll be right there." He rearranged his stack of orders and was about to put them back in his bin when Homa called out again. "And bring the pending orders with you."

Mak tucked them under his arm, shrugged, and reported to the office.

Homa was sitting at her desk with a lit cigarette burning in the ashtray. "Let me see those," she asked, extending her hand to receive the papers. Mak stood in front of her as she examined the order forms. Her hairdo was a marvel of engineering, set off by a dark paisley scarf tied in a convoluted knot that Mak never learned in military training. "I'm trying to figure something out," she said, staring at the papers Mak had handed to her. "Maybe you can help me."

"Of course," Mak responded deferentially. "What can I tell you that the good Lord has left out?"

"Well, Mak," she started slowly, "it seems we have a bit of a mystery on our hands – or at least on our books." She spoke carefully and Mak just listened. "My uncle left a message this morning about some shipments coming."

"Oh good," Mak interrupted, "they must have found the fenugreek."

"Ah yes, probably, but that's not the problem. They said they were sending jasmine and cedar oil, but the telex said we will be receiving three orders." Homa described the inconsistency like a detective.

Mak knew more than he could say. "Maybe he forgot to mention the other one."

"Maybe, but this is the third time in a row that the telex says we'll be getting an extra shipment. Something about the whole thing doesn't seem right. I don't want to pay for something we don't get or don't need, and you know the kind of trouble we've had with customs agents recently."

Mak wondered when Homa would be told the family secrets. "I understand, but what can I do?"

"Well, I thought if we matched these customer orders with what we knew my uncles sent, maybe we could figure out what was coming." Homa didn't realize she was trying to use simple arithmetic to solve calculus.

Mak trod the fine line between telling her too much and being helpful. "Do you want us to do a full inventory?" he offered. "I was going to blend some Princess Mist today, but that can wait."

"No, we're backordered on Mist, so better make some more. We've got all the atomizers we need now and the new boxes look fantastic. I've scheduled a full packaging crew for next week, so let's keep all that on schedule." Homa had another idea. "Can't Jon check the inventory while you make the blend?"

Mak knew it would be problematic. "I don't think so. He won't be able to tell what everything is without my help, and I need him to help me make the Mist."

Homa didn't really know much about what went on in the mix room and was undeterred. "Well, let's give it a try. Jon can just ask you about the inventory if he's got a question, and you've mixed Mist by yourself before."

Mak acquiesced. "Okay, Miss Homa, whatever you say. We'll get right to the inventory after lunch." He left with his new instructions and checked the clock on the way out. He wondered how this was all going to get done before 4:30, and if he should call home to say he might be late. Missy K never worked on Friday night, and he never missed their special Friday night dinner together. He had the keys to the warehouse, and would sometimes stop in on Saturday to finish up anything that needed to be done, and since the office was closed on the weekend, Saturday was also a convenient time to come to the warehouse to attend to his side business.

After dismissing Mak, Homa stacked the order forms on one side of her desk, snuffed out her cigarette, emptied the ashtray, inhaled deeply through the soft cloth she kept in her pocket, and then sawed at her fingernails with an emery board as she contemplated the inconsistencies. Knowing there were still parts of the job she had nothing to do with, and suspicious that the Princess was withholding information, she sneered at the omnipotent head. Her uncles did all the importing and set up most of the foreign distribution, and she knew that, having been born in America, there was no way her language and cultural skills would ever be equal to the task of mastering the subtleties of their international transactions. As an unmarried woman, she had no desire to subject herself to the rigors of travel, so her ambitions didn't venture beyond the metropolitan area. Mak's management of the warehouse operations was an acceptable arrangement for the time being, but for reasons she didn't fully understand, her mother was still in charge of doing the tax returns – and that really bothered her. Samani had become very needy since her father and husband vanished, and wasn't always capable of making good decisions. The family had come to rely on Dr. Nouri to fill the role of family advisor whenever Samani's brothers were away, which was most of the time, and although Dr. Nouri was a relative and her mother's closest friend, Homa never accepted him as the substitute father he tried to be. She looked forward to the day when she could handle all the administration of the business by herself.

CHAPTER 15

The open layout of the enforcement wing of the New York office of the U.S. Customs Bureau misrepresented the secretive prosecutions conducted from there. Unshaded banks of fluorescent fixtures exposed rows of paper-strewn desks, whose surfaces were littered with fragments of truth. Everyone worked in pairs, because the flashes of intuition, gut hunches, and elements of surprise critical to successful police work were too ephemeral to survive the lag-time of filling out detailed reports. The bureau's teamwork policy was maintained to ensure that at least one person would always know the immediate status of an ongoing investigation. Veteran detectives, like Falin and Gillingham, appreciated the practice because it allowed them to spend more time on their investigative missions, and although rigorous compliance with all the rules was an occasional casualty of the policy, the bureau's history of successful interdictions precluded the necessity for drastic change. Only the administrative staff worked normal business hours, and the career bureaucrats who managed the operations wanted to spend as little time as possible sorting though the minutia of each case, so personal relationships and trust were the bonds that held the bureau together. Everyone profited by the laissez-faire arrangement and each took advantage of it in his own way: The agents were free to interpret the rules as the conditions dictated, and the distant, politically appointed bosses, who were too distracted to notice or care, were far enough removed to avoid direct blame for anything that went wrong.

As senior partner, Detective Falin had the authority to assemble his own stakeout crews, and he used the lure of overtime pay to manipulate the subtle benefits that skulked below the line of discretion. His well-known affair with a married secretary at the office was tolerated because everyone else was also keen on bending the rules to their own purposes, and his relationship gave him access to the internal documents and the upper hand in power struggles. He had been with the department, in one capacity or another, since he served with an intelligence-gathering unit based in Vietnam. Originally from Iowa, his all American farm boy appearance had disqualified him from undercover work in Southeast Asia, so he had applied his critical thinking to mastering the administrative system that passed for government oversight. His first assignment back in the states was in Los Angeles, where he used his knowledge of Asian culture to discover illegal shipments from Taiwan. Wanting to be closer to home, he eventually transferred to Denver, Colorado, where he joined the agency's efforts to stop drug trafficking from Mexico and South America. With straight blond hair always neatly parted along the same lines that separated his concepts of right and wrong, he got credit for a high profile bust and was promoted to Detective at the New York. It had taken him three years to understand the intricacies of east coast politics, but now, at age forty-two, he realized that he was at a point in his career where he needed a significant conquest to qualify him for the higher echelons of his department. Acting mostly on instinct, he had decided that the Laden Import investigation was going to be his vehicle.

Although he was shorter, darker, stockier, and rougher than his smooth-talking Adonis counterpart, Detective Gillingham's outgoing personality and uncomplicated personal life made him more popular amongst the office staff. He was married to a Garden City grade school teacher and they were bringing up their only son to carry on the Protestant traditions of work hard, play hard, and wait for God's reward. Several years older and more experienced, Detective Gillingham was eying the retirement clock like a tired footballer waits for the end of regulation, and had no plans to parlay his popularity into advancement. Only one generation gone from his surname's eponymous city, he was happy to submit to his partner's questionable tactics if that left him more time to indulge his passion for watching the English soccer league at his favorite pub.

The two detectives worked stakeouts with the familiarity of an old married couple, but whenever the case demanded more attention than one unit could provide, they split up, each taking a junior partner. Detective Falin liked having Agent Rudy George as his sidekick because they had both lived in Los Angeles, and had, in their younger days, frequented the same nightspots. He drafted Rudy for operations because he knew he could trust him to stand guard while he interrogated the employees of the rock and roll dives, massage parlors, and all night strip clubs.

Agent Ralph Lowell was a stranger among them. He had seen Detectives Falin and Gillingham at interoffice functions over the years, but he didn't know much about them personally. The detectives knew who Ralph was, but seeing him as a boring functionary weighed down by predictable lifestyle choices, never had a reason to talk to him. Unbeknownst to Ralph, the stakeout teams had already been chosen by the time he and Rudy came upstairs.

"Over here," Detective Falin summoned Rudy before he and Ralph were all the way out of the elevator. "We don't have a lot of time, so this is going to be quick." He greeted them with abrupt handshakes. "Detective Gillingham is arranging for surveillance equipment and we're planning on leaving here in an hour. Is that enough time for you?" Detective Falin spoke without looking up as he arranged the papers on his desk.

"We can be ready by then, right Ralph?" Rudy replied for both of them.

Ralph shrugged.

"Good. Meet us downstairs in the parking garage at noon." Detective Falin handed Rudy a file and dismissed them in less than a minute.

"I thought there was going to be an orientation," Ralph said in the elevator on the way back down.

Rudy handed him the file. "Here it is."

Ralph opened up the case folder and leafed through the photographs and descriptions. Even though he worked in the same building, he had never actually examined an active investigation dossier, and was surprised by what he saw. The first thing he noticed was how much of the report described activities in Iran. Many of the photographs looked like they were taken there, and the numerous close-ups of crates and boxes with completely unreadable lettering made him feel like he was protecting the country from foreign invasion. There were also pictures of buildings in Manhattan that looked familiar, and an assortment of faces, some of whom he thought he recognized. Copies of Customs forms were mixed in with reports from the Justice Department, The Bureau of Alcohol and Tobacco, and the FBI. The synopsis of the case against Laden Imports had information gleaned from other blacked-out sources, and the intricate way the facts had been woven into the case excited Ralph's interest in puzzle solving. A glimmer of purpose rekindled the sense of commitment he had once felt, and the scent of the chase aroused some forgotten vigor.

"Almost done? I'm ready to go." Rudy hovered over him as he finished reading. "Did you call your wife yet? You might not have the chance later," he advised.

Ralph had been too engrossed in the case file to envision the logistics of undercover work, and hadn't realized that he might not be able to get to a phone for hours on end. Reluctantly, he dialed home.

The conversation started off badly and went downhill from there. Clara was cleaning the kitchen counter when the phone rang. "What time will you be home?" she asked.

"I'm not coming home." Ralph baited her with a hint of intrigue.

Clara rarely apologized. "No really, I know we had a fight but you still live here."

"I'm not coming home tonight." Ralph enjoyed saying it.

"Why not?" Clara pushed harder on her scrubbing sponge. "You want a divorce?"

Ralph didn't realize how easy it was to restart a full-scale battle. "I don't think so." He was about to explain but she cut him off.

"You don't think so?" She slammed the phone down.

He called her right back. "It's not what you think. Wait."

She picked up the receiver to stop the ringing and hung it up immediately.

He called back again and begged. "Clara, please! I have something to tell you." Silence allowed him to continue. "I'm working tonight."

"Working?" she asked incredulously while bagging up the garbage and unfurling a new plastic liner.

Ralph went right for the hard sell. "Yes, and I'll be making extra money."

"But you're on salary. Since when did they start paying you overtime?" She wiped the faucet suspiciously.

"It's a stakeout," he answered, easing the concept in smoothly.

"A stakeout? You said you would never go on one of those again. Is that what you're really doing? When are you coming home?"

"Like I said, it's a stakeout and I won't be home until Sunday night." Ralph clenched his pen and winced in anticipation of her reaction.

"Sunday? But we had plans to go to New Jersey this weekend. Where is this stakeout anyway? And where are you going to sleep?" Clara's questions increased with urgency as they went on. "You promised Alberto he could see his cousins. My family is expecting us. Are you sure you're going on a stakeout? I don't believe you. You want a divorce. You're still mad about this morning. What time are you coming home? Really. I can keep dinner warm if you're a little late. Ralph, don't do this. Please, for Alberto's sake. Please come home." She attacked and surrendered simultaneously.

"I will come home," he said, trying to calm her. "Sunday night. You take Alberto to New Jersey to see his cousins and I'll buy him something special with the extra money I make." Ralph couldn't believe he got the whole pitch out without further interruption and strained to hear Clara's almost silent reaction.

"Okay," she sobbed. "We can talk about the divorce later." Then she hung up.

Embarrassed, Ralph looked up at Rudy, who had been waiting for him to finish. "Way to go Ralph. That's telling it like it is."

Rudy's sarcasm was unappreciated. "When was the last time *you* had a relationship that lasted more than fifteen minutes?"

"Yeah, can't wait till I find *my* soul mate," Rudy teased him. "Come on, Ralph, they're waiting for us downstairs."

Ralph tidied up his desk, grabbed his coat, and followed Rudy toward the elevator.

"Take messages for us," Rudy called out, winking at Melanie as the doors closed. "We'll be back Monday.

Five floors down they found Detectives Falin and Gillingham standing between two dark Mercury sedans in the lower basement of the building's parking garage.

"Rudy and I will take this one," Detective Falin explained, motioning to one of the identical cars.

Detective Gillingham introduced himself to Ralph. "Monte Gillingham. You're riding with me," he said, extending a soft meaty hand.

Ralph was confused and looked for an explanation, but Rudy had already disappeared into the passenger seat of the other car. "Ralph Lowell, nice to meet you." He shook Detective Gillingham's hand.

"Don't worry about them, mate," the detective reassured him. "You'll see your buddy soon enough. Just get in and we'll catch up with them later."

Rudy chalked a line at Ralph through the closed window as their car pulled out first.

CHAPTER 16

Jon was sitting on a barrel of lanolin, smoking a cigarette when Mak came back from the office. "That doesn't smell like lunch to me," Mak scolded him. "Come on over here. Let's see what Missy K made for us today. Got to be better than that smoke stick." Jon slid down from his perch, threw his butt to the floor and ground it in with his work boot. He followed Mak to the semicircular assembly of empty containers where they usually ate lunch. Mak retrieved his food bag and laid the contents out on the top of an empty barrel. The food was still slightly warm and there was enough for a small feast. Neither of them bothered washing their hands before placing the bite-size morsels of jerk chicken and fresh bread into their mouths with their fingers. They worked through the whole pile in ten minutes and washed it down with the carbonated guava drink that Missy K had also provided. Nothing improved Jon's mood more than real food, and he listened to his new set of instructions like someone watching a movie in another language.

"We've got a special plan for this afternoon," Mak said slowly. "Next week's orders are going to have to wait. We're still going to do some cooking, but we have to do an inventory."

Jon burped and used a flatpick to dislodge a piece of chicken caught between his teeth. "We just did an inventory two weeks ago," Jon reminded him, figuring he may have forgotten.

"Yes, I know, but now we have to do a *full* inventory; orders from the office. Every once in a while something comes up, and this is one of those times."

"What's the difference between a regular inventory and a full one?"

Mak wanted to be patient but didn't have a good answer, so he took the shortcut he was most familiar with: he pulled rank. Calculating the impact of his next directive, Mak got up and re-tucked his shirt. "You need to get to know everything we got here," he said stiffly.

"Uh, huh," Jon agreed to he didn't know what.

Mak tried explaining. "You're going to have to look and see what everything is. You know, like if the barrel says wool grease, then you know its wool grease."

Jon reached in his pocket looking for another cigarette. "Mak, mon, what are you saying?"

"What I'm saying is that you never really know what's in these things unless you look."

"I don't get it. You want me to look inside every single thing in this place?" Jon asked incredulously. "That's what this full inventory you're talking about is?"

"That's it Soldier Boy."

"Are you crazy? How am I supposed to do that? We've got those old giant pitcher things with some kind of oily stuff, and those huge jugs of whatever from someplace, and I have no idea what any of *that* is." Jon pointed, got up, and started pacing.

"You'll figure it out."

"Really? I can't even read these labels, and some of those weird boxes don't even open. We've got barrels stacked on top of each other that I can't budge, and you won't let me move some of your special boxes, let alone open them." He dug his hand in his jeans pocket and pressed a pick into his fingertip until it hurt. "It stinks so much in here I can't tell one smell from the other." The comfort of lunch ebbed as his exasperation flowed.

Mak paused to let Jon calm down. "Homa wants it all done by this afternoon, so just do your best."

"This afternoon!" Jon snapped. "There must be more than 1000 things to check! No way we can do that."

"Just get started and we'll see how far you get. I'll be in the mix room if you need help."

"You're not going to help? This is ridiculous. How am I supposed to even move these things by myself?" Jon's lunch dissolved in stomach acid.

"We all got our orders, so you just be a good Jonny Soldier and start marching."

"This is total bullshit!" Jon complained under his breath, and the idea of working at Laden Imports one minute more than necessary fled.

"Just write down anything that doesn't seem like it is what it says it is. We can look at the list later." He handed Jon a clipboard and went off to the mixing room.

Jon's tension turned to anger, then back into tension again. A wave of nausea washed up his midsection, threatening to drown him in a seizure. The heavy air weighed on his breathing as he sucked in the intoxicating odors that blended into a foul-smelling potion, like too many kinds of liquor in one drink. Unsteady on his feet, he sat back down and tried to reconstruct his assignment. He felt the clipboard and remembered that Mak had told him to write down anything he wasn't sure of, which at that moment was just about everything. He noticed some big barrels of wool grease and realized he had learned a few things in the short time he had been there. Besides the sheep fat, he recognized the giant urns of rosewater from Bulgaria, and some of the oils, like eucalyptus and sandalwood he could identify if he put his nose close enough. He knew what dried sage was, and he could tell the difference between almonds and cloves – but the rest of it? He got up and walked around a grouping of crates, trying to make sense out of the twisted lettering on the official papers glued to them. He wiped the rim of a giant sticky urn, sniffed his finger, and gagged at the overpowering stench. Then he pried open a suspicious box and sneezed as the pungent dust attacked the inside of his throat. Discouraged, he lit a cigarette and tried to stave off another surge of anxiety that was challenging his equilibrium.

The smoke from his cigarette surrounded him like a protective aura, and one particularly desperate drag burned through the anesthetizing layers of scented dust and reactivated his critical thinking. Jon re-examined his predicament and concluded that the idea that *he* should be able to identify everything was utter nonsense. Usually, he and Mak just separated the boxes by the customers' names without bothering to look the contents. Jon wondered if *anyone* really knew what was inside; it seemed like they were always guessing. How many times had Mak raised his shoulders and twisted his mouth as an answer to a question about what was what? If Mak didn't know, how could anyone expect *him* to know? In an epiphanic moment, Jon remembered his friend's Einstein joke and grasped the solution: *"There are only two things in the universe: matter and doesn't matter."* This was a simple case of doesn't matter.

He felt like he had just solved the riddle of Laden's inventory control. There were customer names on almost everything, and it didn't really matter what was in the crates as long as the customers got what they ordered. Then he realized that the fewer items he bothered to write down and ask Mak about, the quicker the inventory job would go. Recovering from his malaise, he waded through the aisles like a beach stroller walks among the curious regurgitations of the sea. He made a few crude drawings, to which he added notes indicating what they possibly were, and decorated the areas to the right of each entry with clusters of lines indicating quantity.

The whole assignment had suddenly become a lot easier, and Jon hummed along to the radio, imagining it was playing his song.

"Seven hundred midgets on the sidewalk
Awful busy talkin'.
When the parks let out
The candles started streaming up the avenue.
Twenty minutes later in a service elevator
I saw you talkin'.
I'm wondering about
Something I'm supposed to do,
About you." *9

Amused by his own indifference, he scuttled through the stacks and rows of inventory, pausing now and then to make useless notes about a particular item whose identity was especially undecipherable, and about an hour later he casually opened the door to the mixing room to report his non-findings to Mak. He was completely unprepared for what he saw.

Mak stood shirtless next to a giant steaming cauldron in the center of the room. The dim light reflected off his sweaty torso. His eyes were closed and he appeared to be in a trance, swaying back and forth as he guided a giant wooden stave through the viscous liquid in the tub. An automatic closer whooshed the door shut, and the only sounds in the chamber were the rhythmic scraping of the stirrer against the stone basin, accompanied by Mak's gentle falsetto humming. Jon stood transfixed as his eyes adjusted to the light and his mind adjusted to the vision. A small gas fire burned underneath the basin and the waves of rising steam blurred the fixed shapes of the room like a Van Gogh hallucination. Jon steadied himself against a wall as intoxicating fumes raced through his respiratory system, distorting his sense of reality.

"Welcome to heaven, Jonny Soldier," Mak greeted him without opening his eyes. "the Princess is glad you're here," he added, continuing to stir and sway.

Jon didn't know if he was supposed to respond, so he just stood there, listening, trying to get his bearings. The granite tub resonated like a bowed cello and Mak's high-pitched humming was eerily pleasant. Jon's appreciation of musical ambiance led him through the gates of imagination.

There was nothing fast or expedient about making potions; only the consistency mattered. Inhaling the oppressive humidity in long deep breaths, he was soon drenched in sweat. Mesmerized, Jon thought he saw a hooded ghost standing next to the cauldron. Lyrics drifted into his head on a diaphanous melody.

"You're my dark guardian angel,
You belong to the night." *10

"Be a good soldier, Jonny, give us another cup of spirits," Mak requested without turning around.

Through the fog, Jon saw a gallon-sized aluminum pitcher sitting on the barrel nearest Mak and touched it.

"Yeah, that's the one," Mak assured him from his trance. "Just fill it up and pour it in here. We're burning a little too slow."

Jon grasped the handle firmly and stuck the pitcher into the mouth of a giant urn until it was submerged. When it was full, he brought it over to the cauldron and poured a clear stream of rectified alcohol into the creamy soup. The potent vapors steamed his face, and Mak continued to stir as the pitcher emptied.

"Ready, steady, round and round, makes the circle in the ground," Mak recited, mashing the remaining chunks against the side of the basin. Time passed. "Just a few left and then we'll be all right," Mak spoke to the darkness. Then, sensing something wrong, he squinted in Jon's direction. Mak knew the strange tricks that the spirits of the conjuring room could play on one's mind, so he wasn't too surprised when he couldn't see Jon through the mist. "Where you hiding, Jonny Soldier?" he called out like a man looking for his invisible friend. He searched the mists without breaking his rhythm. Not seeing him, Mak assumed that Jon had been overcome with fumes and had sought refuge in the side room. He kept the brew circulating, waiting for Jon to reappear, but nothing happened until an unusual smell caught his attention. He let go of his stave and went around the other side of the brew pot to investigate what smelled like something burning. There had been problems with the gas pipe before, but when he reached into the darkness to feel for it, his hand bumped into a solid object that wasn't supposed to be there. At first he thought that a ladle that had fallen into the flame underneath and caught fire, but that turned out to be wishful thinking. Groping in the dimness, his hands grabbed the loose material that he realized was Jon's shirt, and he slid the limp body away from the flames. Dragging him further away, he saw that Jon's shoe was melted and smoldering. Jon was semi-conscious as Mak slipped the burnt shoe off and went into the side room to fetch a cure. By the time he got back, Jon was propped up on his elbows trying to figure out what had happened.

Mak knelt and handed him a moist towel. "Well, hello again my sleepy friend. Did you have a nice rest?"

Jon blinked and wiped his face.

"Talking to the angels again? Just take a few deep breaths," Mak instructed, holding the end of the refreshing towel over Jon's mouth. "Feeling a little better now?"

Jon looked up at Mak's profile, silhouetted against the globe. "I guess I must've just passed out. It's really hot in here."

Mak leaned him up and held a glass to his lips. "Here, have a sip of water and then let's get you out of here before the fires of Hell claim the rest of you." Jon took a sip and regained some composure. Mak helped him to his feet. "Up you go now, soldier."

Unable to put any pressure on his burned foot, Jon limped into the warehouse, leaning on Mak for support. "You sit out here and rest for a while," Mak said, depositing him on a barrel against the wall. "I'll finish up and be out in a bit."

Jon sat in the warehouse, dazed, wiping his face with an oily towel, trying to make sense of his surroundings. He pulled his legs up to his chest to protect himself from hidden enemies disguised as inanimate liquids and powders. The water he continued to sip could not cure the itch in the back of his throat, and his lachrymal gland was unable to supply enough moisture to soothe the sting on his eyeballs. His shoeless foot was black and blistered and throbbing as much as his head. Lunch crept up his throat and he swallowed it back down. He felt greasy and sweaty and dirty and alone, and wondered if his sister would let him in if he showed up at her apartment. Doris was always the stable one: the one his parents were proud of. Jon knew she had a touch of the same artistic insanity as he did, and if anyone in his family would understand, it would be her.

When Mak finally came out of the mix room, his usual avuncular authority had been replaced by the deep distant stare of a warrior returned from battle. "You okay?" he asked without caring too much.

Jon's pride wouldn't let him complain. "I'm okay," he said bravely, squeezing out some confidence.

"Good." Mak toweled off his perspiration and reawakened to this world. "Let's get you out of here. Can you walk?"

Jon tried putting his bare heel down but slipped on the cold oily floor. Light-headed and in pain, he leaned on Mak for support as he limped back to the changing room.

CHAPTER 17

Rebecca was on the phone with Ameliah when Reggie Whitehead let himself in. "Well hello, Miss Rebecca," he startled her from behind. "Here all by yourself today?" he added suggestively.

Rebecca put Ameliah on hold and turned around. "No, Reggie," she said tersely, "Homa's here and she has your check. Mak's in the warehouse." Avoiding further interaction, she went back to her call.

"Thanks doll." Reggie strutted toward the office like he owned the place, spinning the advertising mobiles hanging from ceiling with impertinent swats as he passed. Rebecca watched him disturb the atmosphere and wondered what Reggie actually did. Dr. Nouri, Reggie's boss, was on her vendor list as a consultant, but he never came by the office or sent them a bill. All she knew was that he had some kind of special relationship with the family.

"Hello Reggie," Homa called out as he approached.

"Hello, beautiful," Reggie pandered upon entry. "You look even more sexy than your mother today."

"Nice to see you too Reggie," Homa said sarcastically. "I'm not sure my mother would like to hear that, but thanks anyway. Here's Dr. Nouri's check." She handed it to him without getting up.

"That's it? No 'Hey there, handsome?'" he preened obnoxiously.

Homa sized him up before responding. She didn't know too much about him, but his shimmering polyester suit with the iridescent silk kerchief protruding from the pocket spoke volumes.

"How are you, Reggie?" she asked without wanting an answer. "You must be very excited about the weekend," she guessed.

"As a matter of fact I am. Friends and I got big plans. Gonna be a whole lotta fun. Maybe you want to join us?" Reggie grinned stupidly, posing in his street hustler duds.

Homa was horrified at the thought of spending one moment more than necessary with the low-class thug she considered Reggie to be. She sat up straight and demonstrated her hairdo with a tug on her scarf. "Oh, thank you, Reggie, but I'm very busy myself this weekend."

"Well well, don't you look like trouble?" His squeaky voice cracked with emotion. "Someone's gonna have their hands full with you tonight." He hoisted his trousers and put a hand in his pocket.

"Oh yes, we've got *big* plans," Homa lied convincingly, burying one of her painted claws in her head wrap and filling her chest with air.

"Well, I'll be; missus *all* business getting down *to* business. That, I'd like to see!" Reggie marveled at her exotic pose, lecherously calculating the possibilities. He looked around to see if anyone else was watching, and the sentient Princess stifled further musing. Patting his inner coat pocket to make sure he had what he had come for, he showed a gold tooth and pointed a gotcha finger. "Best be on my way now, Miss Ho-Ma. You have a fine time tonight with Mister Lucky." Then he wheeled around on his heels, as if he were performing to the Earth Wind and Fire song on the radio, and strutted out on the beat. Passing Rebecca, he stroked her hair and winked at her astonished revulsion.

CHAPTER 18

It was early Friday afternoon when Sonya Diaz finally made it into the Pecorino Partners offices. No one else was around, but the coffee pot was hot, so she knew someone had been there. There was a handwritten message from her boss, Nigel, taped to her phone. "Problems with show tonight. Call me at the studio when you get in," was all it said.

With nothing urgent to be done, Sonya stared vacantly at the constant flow of traffic from her second story window. A mist of clouds dimmed the light over the low-rise forest of buildings that was the West Village. It was very different from the crowded Queens neighborhood where she had grown up. One of seven children, Sonya had moved to Manhattan recently and didn't really understand where all the cars, jostling haphazardly down the six- lane chute of 7th Avenue like a stampede, were going. Even though Sonya took cabs once in a while, mostly when she was with Nigel, the people driving their own cars and riding in the back of chauffeured vehicles seemed like privileged strangers. Everyone in her large extended family used public transportation to get to and from work. They would sometimes repurpose a delivery truck for family outings, but keeping a car in the city was a luxury few of her relatives could afford.

She had no special affection for the Pecorino Family, who owned the building and business where she was working, but she did relate to Nigel Acton, the working class Brit who the Pecorinos had hired to manage their music business affairs. His interest in her was not platonic, and they kept the management business running, while the Pecorino brothers, Anthony and Dante, were otherwise occupied. Sonya dialed the number at the studio and Nigel picked up the phone on the third ring.

"Are you there by yourself?" he asked.

"Yes, as far as I know," Sonya answered, looking around for clues. "The coffee pot is going. You were here earlier?"

"Yes. I only came over to the studio an hour ago. Have you seen Dante or Starla?"

"No, I just got here. What's the problem with the show tonight?"

"The roadies got busted at the hotel and half of the band's equipment is locked up with them."

Sonya was used to things going wrong, so she wasn't too surprised. "That sucks."

"Right, and that's not all." Nigel lowered his tone. "You went home last night after the show?"

"Yeah, where was I supposed to go at 1:00 in the morning?"

"You weren't supposed to go anywhere. I just wanted to make sure you didn't go over to the hotel with the band."

"Why not? You miss me?" Sonya searched for some possessiveness.

"Sonya, we've discussed that," Nigel said stiffly.

"I know how to stay out of trouble, if that's all you're worried about."

"I know you do, love, it's just...."

"Just what?"

"Something else happened."

"Something else? What?"

"Donny made a scene when they arrested the roadies. The cops searched his room and found Randi unconscious."

"Randi? Donny was the one who passed out at the club last night."

"Well, they must be snorting some nasty stuff. Donny said he thought Randi was just sleeping."

"What were the cops doing in his room?"

"They asked the roadies where the band's manager was. When Randi wouldn't wake up, the cops called an ambulance and took her to the hospital."

"Shit." Sonya was a casual user, but she hated drug-related problems. Her family didn't approve of the kind of people she'd been hanging around with, and sometimes she wished she had a regular job. "What was the matter with her?"

"Not sure, drugs probably, but she was bleeding in more than one place."

Sonya cringed at the thought. "Donny beat her up again?"

"Don't really know. I got a call from Freddy around 4:00 this morning and he didn't have a lot of answers. I called Anthony and he was going to ask his old man to call the precinct."

"What about the show?"

"We won't know until I get a call back from Anthony."

"What about Randi? What are we supposed to do?"

"Nothing. Just sit tight. I've got some people coming to see the studio in a while, so I've got to stay here. You stay at the office and call me if you hear anything."

"What should I tell Dante if he comes down?"

"Don't tell him anything; the less he knows, the better."

"What if he asks where you are?"

"Tell him I'm at the studio and I'll be back in the office later."

Sonya hung up and stared out the window again. A hodgepodge of pedestrians collected at the corner of West 4th Street, waiting to cross. She thought about asking her uncle for her old job back at the bodega, but remembered why she'd quit: she couldn't bear the thought of keeping track of so many items costing less than a dollar. Anticipating Nigel's return, she rearranged her top in the large entryway mirror so that her cleavage was showing. Even though the excitement of the entertainment business had been dulled by reality, she remained confident that there was a better life waiting for her, maybe with Nigel.

Determined to distance himself from the sooty manufacturing traditions of his family, which had already claimed the life of his uncle at an early age, Nigel Acton first came to London after a short stint in a Birmingham trade school. Gaunt and uncoordinated, with uneven teeth and a reedy voice, he gravitated to the youthful roil of London's nightlife. He didn't play any instruments, but his inherited knowledge of basic engineering principles earned him a regular spot behind the mixer at a local nightclub, where he was able to eke out a living as a self taught audio engineer. Donning the music scene uniform of tight black jeans, thick-soled boots, and randomly attached chains, he immersed himself in the youth culture that was answering the high speed, distorted, white noise calling of his disaffected generation. His strong Protestant sensibilities prevented him from totally losing his identity in the mayhem of alcohol and drug use that claimed the sanity of so many of his peers, and his ability to function in that fractious environment eventually earned him the trust of a club owner who turned the entire live music portion of his business over to the straggly haired, intense survivor.

True to punk tradition, Nigel wielded his hard-won power with callous indifference, graduating from controlling the soundboard to controlling the bands. Stardom and rent money were never easy to come by, so everyone from the Stranglers to the Buzzcocks, had to rely on him to put them on stage and make them sound good, which is how he came to direct traffic at the seedy London nightclub that was an important crossroad of career opportunity. Managers, agents, and record company representatives regularly came to see the acts there, and within a few years of arriving on the scene, Nigel made a lot of contacts. Knowing that friendship in the rock and roll war zone was usually just a matter of convenience and strategy, and that almost no relationships lasted longer than the stimulants and posturing they were based on, he kept an eye out for other opportunities.

Nigel met Dante Pecorino on one of Dante's impulsive jaunts to London. An inveterate New Yorker, Dante had established a reputation in London as a well-known carouser with a sniveling drug habit and a fast checkbook. It was common knowledge that Dante had forced his wealthy family to diversify into the entertainment business to justify his profligate lifestyle, but those on the receiving end of his excesses didn't quibble with motivations. Because the Pecorino's commercial real estate investments included the buildings that housed The Black Sheep nightclub and Heard Tracks recording studio, Dante was able to use the inducement of a New York stage and free studio time as a way to participate in the music business. The family created a management company, Pecorino Partners, to finance Dante's activities, and losses on the management company's books conveniently offset other legitimate profits. Dante was too indulgent to do anything requiring sober concentration, so the actual management of bands, booking of clubs, and operation of the studio was left to hired hands. He recruited Nigel with the lure of a steady job in New York during one of their backroom snorts.

Nigel accepted what he thought was a plum assignment because he had ascended as high up the London food chain as he was likely to get, and wanted to taste the success that some of his compatriots who had gone to the States enjoyed. He knew Dante well enough to know that he came from money, and he had enough of his own to survive for a while, even if a move to New York turned out to be a drug induced fantasy that ended with him using the return portion of the round trip plane ticket he had insisted on. He accepted Dante's invitation and arranged to get his old job back if things didn't work out, but the gamble had paid off, and after a few weeks of crashing on friends' couches, Nigel met with Dante's brother and father, who made him a legitimate offer.

Dante's older brother, Anthony, who operated the purse strings of his younger brother's follies, saw Nigel as an opportunity to relieve himself of some of the burden of keeping track of his troublesome sibling, and convinced his father to hire Nigel full time. They gave him a guaranteed salary and the use of an apartment on the third floor of the building they owned on 7th Avenue, above Pecorino Partners' offices and below Dante's pad. Unbeknownst to Dante, Nigel's responsibilities also included trying to keep Dante out of trouble and the family's losses to a minimum. Besides legitimizing the artist management company, Nigel became the extra big brother and protector that the Pecorino family was looking for, and the position gave him entry into the ownership hierarchy of the New York club scene, where he was often seen in the company of his obnoxious and inept "boss", Dante.

Nigel had an immediate positive impact on the family fortunes. The Black Sheep was already capably managed by another Pecorino Partners hire, Dennis Strider, but with Nigel's help, the popular club's bookings expanded to include touring bands from the United Kingdom. Pecorino Partners took on the U.S. representation of some of British bands, and besides gigs at their own club, the management company set up shows at other venues on the East Coast where they had influence. Nigel took over the day-to-day supervision of the management company and trained their only competent office employee, Sonya Diaz, to help him. Within six months, he was also able to bring the recording studio up to commercial standards. He enjoyed the full support – though not respect – of the Pecorino family.

CHAPTER 19

There was nothing about being twenty-two years old that Monica didn't like. Her job as a dance instructor kept her in great shape, and she still thought of it as a lively career with a flexible schedule. She was usually finished teaching by 5:00 on Friday, and her idea of a good time was going out with friends, having a little too much to drink, and partying till the wheels fell off the pumpkin. She called Ameliah at work to make weekend plans. Ameliah liked to party too, but always with a purpose.

"Again?" Monica asked, disappointed with Ameliah's plan.

"Mmm hmm," Ameliah answered under her breath.

"I know *you* had a good time, but, well, Rebecca and I – "

Ameliah cut her off. "I already spoke to Becca. She's coming."

"Really?" Monica didn't want to start an argument with Ameliah because she always seemed to lose. "When did you talk to her?"

"A while ago. I've got to go now. I'll see you at home in an hour."

Monica's next call was to Rebecca. "I'm not disturbing your work, am I?"

"No, I was just looking over the same stupid papers for the third time. What's up?"

"I just talked to Amy and she said you want to go with her to The Black Sheep again tonight?"

"Yeah, well, that's where *she* wants to go."

"But we just went there last night," Monica protested.

"I know, but it's Friday night and we should go somewhere. What do *you* want to do?"

"I don't know." Monica was a younger sibling and not very independent. "Who's playing there anyway?"

"Who do you think? Freddy's band."

"Ugh! I don't want to see them again. We'll just get stuck with those loser musicians. Maybe you and I should go somewhere by ourselves? Amy doesn't need us to hang out with Freddy. She and that Randi girl seemed to get along fine." Monica remembered being excluded from the private area on the bus and felt resentful.

Rebecca wasn't jealous. "Do you think Randi's okay?" she worried. "I wonder what happened to her?"

"I have no idea; that boyfriend of hers is a pig."

Rebecca heard the hostility in Monica's voice. "Let's just meet back at the apartment and figure out what we're doing then; okay?"

"Okay, see you at home in an hour or so."

Rebecca hung up and let her work persona crossfade into visions of her weekend. Mak and Jon came in from the warehouse and startled her back to the present. She couldn't help notice that something was wrong.

"Where's the first aid kit?" Mak asked her dryly.

"I don't know. I've never seen it. Do we have one?"

Mak searched a dusty cabinet as Jon sat in an empty chair with his injured foot extended. Rebecca saw his red skin, blisters, and blackened toes, and their eyes met in confusion.

"What's going on out there?" Homa called from the office.

"Oh nothing, just looking for the first aid kit," Mak answered. "Have you seen it?"

Homa hurried in at the mention of first aid. "I thought you kept one out in the warehouse?"

"I thought so too, but I couldn't find it out there. Isn't there another one in here?" Mak 's frustration level elevated as he rummaged.

Homa gasped at the sight of Jon's injury. "What happened to him?"

"We had a little accident, nothing to worry about." Mak answered, keeping a lid on his anxiety. "I can't find the bandages." He opened and closed a few more drawers. "Does one of you have an extra sock?"

Rebecca found a ripped stocking in the drawer of an empty desk and handed it to Mak, cringing at the thought of what he had in mind.

"What do you plan on doing with that?" Homa asked, curling her lips with a mixture of disgust and concern.

Mak took a scissors and cut the stocking along its full length, flattening it out on a desk as best he could. "Can someone please get me a roll of toilet paper?" he urged while holding the uncooperative nylon in place.

Rebecca went to the bathroom and hurried back with a fresh roll.

Mak unfurled the roll along the length of the cut nylon, doubling it back and forth several times until it started to actually look like a bandage. "All right, now we're getting somewhere," he said, kneeling in front of Jon. He held the heel of Jon's injured foot in one hand while using the other hand to wrap the makeshift bandage around his instep and toes. He finished the job by wrapping desk tape around until it seemed to hold. "There, good as new," Mak proclaimed,

Homa was skeptical. "Is he going to be okay?"

"Well, I think so. Let's ask him. How you feeling, Jonny Soldier?"

Jon rose from his seat and put some weight on it. "It doesn't feel as bad as I thought it would," he reported tentatively.

"Good. Let's see if we can get that shoe on and get you out of here" Mak said, trying to minimize the drama. Jon's regular boot was too small, so Mak retreated to the changing room to fetch another right shoe. He returned with a large, thoroughly used boot, hoping it would fit over the bandage. Seeing that it didn't, he unhinged a knife from his pocket and cut out the tongue to make room.

"How did this happen, Jon?" Homa asked as Mak prepared the boot.

Jon looked to Mak for guidance, unsure of how much of a description would suffice. "I don't remember," he said stoically.

Homa redirected her questioning with a dose of attitude. "Mak, maybe *you'll* tell me what happened?"

"Oh, Jonny wanted to marry the Princess." Mak said casually. "One of her uncles must not have approved." He spread the cut shoe around Jon's foot.

Homa rolled her eyes in frustration. She hated it when Mak started talking in riddles. "No, Mak, really. I need you to tell me what happened. I have a business to run here."

"Yes, yes," Mak said dismissively, configuring the laces so that they would hold the boot in place without cutting off circulation. "The truth and nothing but the truth," he parroted.

"Mak! Please stop it. Just tell me what happened."

Mak wasn't permitted to share the family secrets. "Your uncle Sattar knows," he deflected, "maybe you should ask him."

"How could my uncle know? He isn't even here! What are you talking about?" Homa's patience was fraying. "Please, Mak, no more nonsense!"

"Okay then, Miss Ho-Ma," Mak agreed with a touch of insubordination. "Jon fell down and burned his foot while we were polishing the Princess's crown."

"Polishing the...? What were you doing?" A glimmering image of the Princess floated through her mind and smiled enigmatically. Homa stopped her inquisition and tried to reconcile the vision in her head with the scene in front of her. "Uncle Sattar knows?" she said in a calmer voice.

Mak nodded knowingly, but Jon and Rebecca were completely confused by the coded conversation.

Homa's attitude changed. "So you're feeling okay?" she asked Jon again. "You think you'll be able to make it home by yourself?"

"He's not going home by himself," Mak told her. "I'm taking him to my place so we can fix him up proper. Right, Jonny?"

"Your place?" Jon reacted with surprise. Mak stared him into submission. He wasn't totally opposed to the idea of being taken care of, and he wiggled his toes in the modified boot. "Hey, I kinda like the way that looks. Maybe we should cut up the other one to match. What do you think Rebecca?" he joked.

Rebecca, relieved by the levity, flashed an approving smile. "Good idea."

Mak helped him to his feet. "Okay, Soldier Boy, let's see if you can walk with that thing on."

Jon stood and tested his sore foot while everyone observed.

"All right, no dancing allowed. I guess we better get to the train station," Mak concluded.

"I don't think so," Homa interjected. "Just a minute; I'm going to make a phone call." She went back to her office as Jon tested his limits of pain and movement, enjoying Rebecca's sympathetic attention.

"I'll go lock up," Mak excused himself and disappeared into the warehouse, leaving Jon and Rebecca alone together.

"How bad does it hurt?" she asked him.

"A little," Jon admitted. They squirmed in silence until the vacuum of anticipation sucked words out of Rebecca's mouth.

"Where'd you go last night?" she blurted, a little hurt.

"Where'd *I* go? Where did *you* go?" Jon countered.

They stared at each other silently, frustrated at their inability to connect through the fence of mutual misunderstanding.

Homa unwittingly diffused the tension when she came back from making arrangements. "I'm having a car come by to pick us up," she began. "I spoke to my mother and she wants me to take

Jon to the doctor. She says his injury is our responsibility because it happened at work, and we don't want it to get any worse." Homa left out the part about getting sued. "Is that okay with you, Jon?" she asked rhetorically.

"Okay, I guess, if you insist," Jon acquiesced.

"Why don't you come with us, Rebecca?" Homa asked, surprising both of them. "I may need your help. I can have the driver drop you off at home afterwards," she explained, adding her own agenda to the arrangements.

"Well, I'd love a ride home, but I don't want you to go out of your way for me," Rebecca answered diplomatically. "Which way are you going?"

"Oh, don't worry about that. You live near the East River, don't you?"

"Who lives by the river?" Mak butted in as he re-entered.

"Rebecca," Homa told him. "She's coming with us. We're going to drop her off at home on the way back."

"Back from where? Who's going to drop her off?"

"Don't worry, Mak. I've got it all worked out. Reggie's coming by with a car and we're taking Jon to Dr. Nouri's office; mother's orders," Homa explained.

Mak took a moment to digest the logistics. "Reggie's coming to pick you up?" he asked incredulously. "Are you sure that's okay?"

"Reggie knows enough to keep his hands to himself," Homa assured him, "he works for Dr. Nouri."

"I better go with you," Mak asserted. He had grown accustomed the role of Homa's unofficial protector since her father disappeared, and knew more about Reggie than she did.

"Okay Mak, if you insist," Homa deferred. "The car will be here soon so we better lock up and get ready."

"I already locked the warehouse." Mak inspected his shoe-carving handiwork. "How's the foot, soldier? Can you feel the toes?" He tapped on them firmly.

"I can feel *that*." Jon winced, flexing his big toe. "But I don't know what all the fuss is about. It's just a little grilled toe," he maintained.

Mak called Missy K to tell her he'd be late.

Rebecca straightened up her desk and didn't answer the call coming into her direct line. Homa wondered why she hadn't picked up. "Maybe that was one of your friends," she commented. "Do you have other plans?"

Rebecca wasn't sure what she wanted to do. "Where is Doctor Nouri's office?" she asked.

"It's in the Old Medical Building down on Broadway."

"Here's Reggie now," Mak announced, looking out the window. "Looks like he brought Dr. Nouri's big Mercedes. I'll sit in front. You three skinny folk can all fit in the back seat."

Detective Falin was parked across the street and took a picture of Reggie sitting in the driver's seat. Rudy found an earlier picture of Reggie in the case folder and pointed it out to his boss.

Proud of his ascension from Harlem street hustler to personal driver, Reggie knew that no one he was picking up respected him, but that only made the fact that there they were, needing him, sweeter. His ego inflated to the bursting point, and he took the opportunity to subtly demean his dependent passengers. "So, how ya'll doin this fine evening?" he mocked as they climbed in.

"Just fine, Reggie," Mak fielded the stealth insult. Jon got in behind the driver, and Homa motioned for Rebecca to slide into the middle next to him.

"Hi Reggie. Thanks for coming to get us," Homa said, sliding into the white leather back seat next to Rebecca.

"No problem, Miss Ho-Ma. Always happy to rescue pretty girls like you," Reggie answered through the rear view mirror as he was pulling out into traffic. "Dr. Nouri didn't tell me that I was going to be *everybody's* chauffeur service. Where you all headed?"

"We're going to Dr. Nouri's office. You'll need to wait for us there because I'm not sure Jon will be able to make it home with that foot. We'll see what Dr. Nouri says."

"Something wrong with his foot?"

"Yes Reggie, that's why Dr. Nouri sent you to pick us up," Home answered. "Jon hurt his foot and my mother wants Dr. Nouri to have a look to make sure it isn't serious. Mak wrapped it up with what we had, but we want Dr. Nouri to bandage it properly."

"Oh, I see. Just checking to make sure Colonel Mackenzie didn't wrap it up in no island herb," Reggie snickered.

"Just drive the car, Reggie. You never know what might happen if you don't pay attention to what you're doing," Mak cautioned.

"Yeah, I guess that's how poor Jonny hurt his foot," Reggie parried. "Not paying attention to what he was s'posed to be doin, right Colonel?"

Mak shot him an unfriendly glare that shut him up for a while. Reggie turned up "Hurts So Good" on the radio and hummed along as the car bucked like a caged ram on its way through the heavy evening traffic. Following a few cars back, Detective Falin let Rudy drive while he read through the case and tried to figure out Jon's connection to Reggie's rap sheet. Inside Dr. Nouri's Mercedes, the back-seat passengers struggled to maintain their equilibrium as the herky-jerky driving bumped them against one another. A nauseating combination of Dr. Nouri's cigar smoke and Reggie's cheap cologne permeated the Mercedes' interior, adding to the discomfort of the penned passengers. Mak wanted to open the window but couldn't figure out how. Reggie observed Mak's efforts in silent amusement as the seat moved but the window stayed shut. "Never been in a Benz before, I guess," Reggie needled him. "Not too many of these where you come from, *mon*. This what you want?" Reggie sniggered, lowering Mak's window from the driver's side.

"That's too much," Homa complained from the back seat as the exhaust fumes billowed in her face. "Turn up the air conditioner."

Reggie twisted the thermostat down and moved the window back up to closed. "That better for you, princess?"

"Thank you, Reggie," Homa said, stifling her annoyance and calculating the time she would be stuck in the car.

Jon was balancing the feelings of his throbbing foot with the tantalizing sensation caused by Rebecca's thigh touching his. Rebecca's left foot and Jon's injured right one shared the same space behind the driver's seat, but the dense traffic and tight quarters muted their intimacy. Homa was miserable being packed in like livestock, but despite the indignity, quietly enjoyed the contact of Rebecca's warm body. They drove on without talking for a few minutes, each chewing their own emotional cud, until Reggie couldn't control his anymore, and spit up again.

"So how'd it happen, Jonny, my man? You try to kick the bucket and miss?" He laughed at his own joke.

"It was just an accident, Reggie. Please watch where you're going," Mak answered for him.

Reggie wouldn't shut up. "Just an accident? What kind of accident?"

"He burned his toe," Mak told him, trying to end the inquiry.

"Burned it? What're you guys doin' in there? I thought it was just some big old stinky warehouse." Reggie knew more than he was supposed to, but that was *his* secret. "Didn't know you were playing with fire."

Mak wasn't sure how much Reggie knew. "No one was playing with anything, Reggie. Some of us work for a living."

"You sayin' I'm not workin' now? Cartin' you losers off to the doctor's office? Maybe I oughta just drop you off right here."

"Both of you stop it already," Homa intervened.

"You sure are making a big stink over all this," Jon weighed in. "The doctor's just gonna wrap my foot up and send me home. I can go see him by myself. Tell them, Mak."

"Tell them what, Jonny? This is all up to the good Lord, and I haven't heard much from him lately," he answered, scowling at Reggie.

"Just be patient, Jon, Dr. Nouri's going to take good care of you." Homa said, trying to maintain control.

A few minutes later they arrived at their destination. "All ashore; here we are," Reggie announced as he pulled into the drop-off spot in front of a substantial old stone building. Reggie stayed put while everyone got out. Jon winced in pain as he tried to put weight on his foot, so Mak lent him a shoulder and helped him through the door.

"What the hell happened to him?" Detective Falin said as he hobbled past slowly.

Rudy noticed Jon's limp. "Looks like he's hurt."

Following Homa and Rebecca, Mak steered Jon into the dimly lit hallway. "Lean on me, Soldier Boy." He pressed the elevator button and they listened to the pulley squeals.

Reggie stayed in the car, bouncing in the driver's seat with the radio blasting a Michael Jackson song against the rolled up windows.

Detective Falin found a spot in front of a fire hydrant down the street and Rudy took some pictures with a telephoto lens. They radioed their position to Detective Gillingham and Ralph, who were still parked near the Laden Imports warehouse.

Homa, Mak, Rebecca, and Jon squeezed into the undersized, ancient elevator and waited forever for the doors to ooze shut. The mirrored walls, musty smell, and lurching upward made Jon dizzy, and standing made his foot throb worse than ever. Fourteen floors up, the elevator opened into a roomy, marble-floored hallway that looked deserted. They shuffled past a few vacant offices until they came to the one with Dr. Nouri's name painted on the opaque glass. The light was on and they let themselves in to the empty waiting area.

"Salaam, hello?" Homa announced their arrival tentatively.

CHAPTER 20

"Hello," a melodic male voice warbled from the back room. "I'll be right there."

Jon settled into an overused leather chair and extended his legs. His bandaged foot became the centerpiece of the small waiting room. Mak sat down next to him, feeling responsible and guilty. Homa stood guard with her arms folded, annoyed at the lack of service. She heard a phone ring and someone answer it, but couldn't hear the conversation. With nowhere to sit, Rebecca stood looking at the framed black and white photographs of a foreign country that covered the walls. The distinct odor of the nearly deserted building brought back vague memories of her own childhood visits to a doctor's office. She forgot where she was for a moment and nearly tripped over Jon's foot, smiling apologetically when she avoided him.

A few minutes later, a buoyant older man with curly graying hair bounded into the room wearing a traditional three-quarter-length white doctor's coat over his dress shirt and frumpy tie. "Welcome, welcome. I'm so sorry you had to wait," Dr. Nouri greeted them as he bustled into the room. "My assistant is already gone for the day and I have a very sick patient back there and...well, these things take time and...well then, let's see, what have we here?" He surveyed the room as he spoke. "My dear child, Homa. I haven't seen you for too long." He embraced her politely. "Your mother tells me everything but how beautiful you are," he complimented. "And this must be the patient." He once-overed Jon, then greeted the others. "Mak, I know, and this lovely lady is?"

"Rebecca. She works with us in the office. Rebecca, this is Dr. Nouri." Homa made the introduction.

"Pleased to meet you, Rebecca." Dr. Nouri nodded as he shook her hand. "Okay then, let's have a look at the patient. Can you walk by yourself?" he asked Jon.

"I think so." Jon stood up and tested his foot cautiously. He grimaced, so Mak got up and offered his arm for support.

"Well, I suppose Mak ought to help you into the examination room. You ladies can wait here. There's some coffee or tea at the end of the hall."

Mak and Jon followed Dr. Nouri into a room with large windows that provided a panoramic view of the city. Jon seated himself in the reclining examination chair. While they were waiting for the doctor, Mak looked over the cityscape, trying to identify landmarks. The Old Medical Building wasn't one of the tallest structures in the area anymore, but Dr. Nouri's top floor view was still commanding, and part of the reason he resisted to moving to more modern quarters. The window openings rested on gray limestone lintels, which formed bands around the dark gneiss blocks that were stacked into a fourteen-story fortress. The pre-deco design was echoed inside with angularly patterned marble hallways, high ceilings, and colored glass fixtures; all rendered in warm, earthy tones. Tenants appreciated the near perfect sonic isolation that the substantial interior oak doors and double thick masonry walls had provided for almost 100 years, and even in the afterglow of its glory years, the building's classic design and superior construction maintained its elegance and dignity.

Dr. Nouri had moved in twenty-five years ago, at a time when he felt fortunate to secure such a prestigious location, and he was now one of the last tenants who kept the faith with the storied edifice, tolerating the outdated ventilation and electrical systems in favor of its womby appeal. Most of the building was vacant, and signs of disrepair blended with faded offerings of long-term leases, but Dr. Nouri and a few other inveterate tenants purchased the property twenty years ago as a long-term investment, and the mortgage payments were small enough that they could afford the privacy of leaving so many of the other offices empty. Over the years, they completed improvements per the original construction plans, and by the time they finished, the building had become much more than just a place to have an office; it was a sanctuary.

Dr. Nouri entered the examination room in a flurry. "Let's get this off," he said quickly, slowing down to remove Jon's modified shoe. "That doesn't hurt?" he inquired, unwrapping Mak's makeshift bandage. Jon didn't complain. "Not bad, Colonel Mackenzie. They trained you well in the service," he complimented.

"Thank you, Dr. Nouri. Is he going to be okay?"

"Well, let's have a closer look." Dr. Nouri focused a light on Jon's foot. He carefully examined the puffy white skin with a cotton-tipped stick, then poked at it with the uncovered wood end. "Does that hurt? That? How about there?"

"Ouch!" Jon reacted to the final jab.

The doctor tested the skin around the adjacent toes before removing his glasses to report his findings. "You're going to be fine in no time." he said confidently. "I know it hurts right now but I'm going to give you something for that. You wait right here and I'll be back with some medicine for the swelling too." He disappeared down the hall to share the news with Homa. Mak breathed a sigh of relief and looked out over the horizon.

Relieved of the burden of fear, Jon wiggled his toes, which already felt better. "I told you it was no big deal," he told Mak.

Dr. Nouri came back a few moments later with a small towel, some capsules, and a bottle of clear fluid. He moistened the towel with the liquid and told Jon to breathe deeply through it. The intense fumes traveled directly into Jon's respiratory system, numbing his sense of touch. Jon downed the pills as instructed, and watched the doctor assemble a tray of small stainless steel surgical instruments with foggy detachment. "What are those for?" he asked.

"Oh, we're just going to clean you up a bit. It shouldn't hurt." Dr. Nouri anesthetized Jon's toes with a poultice and assembled some gauze squares, cotton balls, and white tape while the medicine was taking effect. "Okay, can you feel that?" he asked, gently stabbing Jon's injured toe with tiny scissors.

"Uh huh." Jon grimaced, more in anticipation than from feeling. "But just a little."

"Good. Well, tell me if I'm hurting you." Dr. Nouri folded magnifiers over his regular glasses and cut the swollen toe open with a scalpel. He dabbed the running blood with absorptive pads, trimmed the burned skin with surgical scissors, and removed the separated pieces of skin with tweezers. As brave as he usually was, Jon couldn't stand the sight of his own blood and had to look away.

"You're doing fine," Mak assured him.

"Almost done," Dr. Nouri coddled as he replaced the bloodied cotton with a fresh gauze pad. "There: the right topical and a nice clean bandage and you'll be on your way." He took another potion from his tray, soaked a gauze pad, then pressed it against Jon's toes. "It'll stop stinging in a second," he promised.

Jon winced. "What is that stuff? And why can't I feel my toes?"

"It's a very powerful medicine." Dr. Nouri explained, removing the pad and wrapping his foot with a roll of flexible bandage. "Just keep this on for a day and come back and see me tomorrow." Dr. Nouri taped him up tightly. "I'll go get you a special shoe to keep it clean." He left the room, and Jon wiggled his toes, surprised they didn't hurt.

Homa was on the receptionist's phone to her mother by the time Jon emerged with his new white medical boot. "You're feeling better now?" she noticed, hanging up. "Can you walk by yourself?" Jon was standing without support and demonstrated his ambulatory competence with a few steps. "Excellent! I told you, Dr. Nouri is a wonder worker. Are we all ready to go?" she asked, holding the door open. Jon hobbled through, followed by Mak and Rebecca. They were halfway out when a woman's painful moan escaped from the closing door and drifted down the corridor. "Bye Dr. Nouri," Homa called out, but she didn't get an answer.

"That was creepy," Rebecca whispered inside the elevator.

"Well, I guess visits to the doctor's office hurt sometimes." Homa defended Dr. Nouri.

Rebecca was troubled. "Yeah, but there's something strange about that office."

"I know what you mean," Jon agreed. "Can't he afford any help? There was no nurses, no receptionists – nobody except him. I hope he knows what he's doing." He tested out his toes, amazed that they hardly hurt.

Homa took sides. "Dr. Nouri knows what he's doing, right, Mak?"

"Yeah, he knows, for sure. I'm not sure anyone else knows, but *he* does." Mak endorsed him enigmatically.

"Dr. Nouri said to just keep that boot on and come by tomorrow so he can change the dressing. You'll be better by next week," Homa assured him on the way down.

After drifting slowly down, the elevator clunked to a stop and Jon felt the bumpy landing in his foot. Two casually dressed businessmen were waiting in the lobby when the doors opened. Homa thought they looked familiar, but they moved aside to let the passengers out and didn't make eye contact. Jon was able to walk through the entrance hall by himself, and they exited onto the sidewalk, stopping in front of Reggie's car to discuss logistics.

Homa was concerned. "Jon, I don't think you should try to get home by yourself. Better let Reggie give you a ride."

Mak didn't like that idea. "Why don't you come by my place and let Missy K take care of you?" he offered.

Jon shrugged. He had never experienced so much caring attention and wasn't sure how to handle it. One part of him just wanted to get away from all these well meaning strangers and run back to the safety of his guitar, while another was attracted to the prospect of refuge. Missy K's cooking was always welcome, and Homa and Mak were looking out for him better than his parents ever did. Rebecca's company was starting to feel natural, and even though he was injured, a part of him didn't want the moment to end.

Reggie started the car and rolled the window down. Roberta Flack felt like making love on the radio. They all got in.

"Where are we off to now?" Reggie asked no one in particular.

Jon spoke up. "Well, I don't know about anybody else, but I'm starving,"

"Missy K always makes a special meal on Fridays. We've got plenty of food. Why don't you come for dinner?" Mak invited.

"Sounds good to me," Jon accepted.

Homa had no objections, but her ability to manage was often prescient. "Okay, Mak, tell Reggie where your apartment is, but check with your wife before we leave Jon there."

"I already know where they stayin." Reggie said, swinging the car back into traffic. "Mak and I go way back; maybe too far," he added with a touch of respect.

"Maybe so," Mak agreed.

Reggie took the Brooklyn Bridge and docked the Mercedes on the street in front on Mak's apartment. Detective Falin and Rudy followed them and found a parking spot at the corner of the next block. Everyone waited in the car while Mak went inside. Rudy took a few pictures of the front of Mak's apartment and settled in to read the latest copy of *Detective Magazine*. Detective Falin got out to stretch his legs and peer through the dense growth on the park fence.

Mak heard Missy K in the kitchen. Lucius was sitting on the sofa in the living room, doing his homework in front of the television. Glowing with pride, he rubbed Lucius' head on his way past, and sneaked up on Missy K, nibbling her exposed neck.

"'Bout time you made it home mister," Missy K giggled, "You stop that right now," She twisted in his arms but Mak took another nip. "Stop it before I pinch you with these," she protested, brandishing her cooking tongs.

Mak feigned romance. "Oh please, Mistress Kiyana, I love you so to."

Missy K squirmed in his two-armed bear hug. "Well, maybe later, Mr. Maroon, but dinner's been done for an hour and Lucius and I are hungry." She wriggled free. "Where have you been anyway? What took you so long?"

Mak didn't know where to start but he knew where he wanted to finish. "It's a long story, but I got Jonny Soldier with me and I told him – "

"Jonny Soldier?" she cut him off and looked behind him. "I don't see anyone. You foolin' with me or something?"

"No, Jonny's waiting in the car outside."

"Car outside? What are you talking about? We don't have a car. Those fumes getting to you again?"

Mak reloaded. This was going to take some explaining and there didn't seem to be a shortcut. "Well, you see...."

"Uh oh! Here comes the story." Missy K braced herself sarcastically. "I hope you didn't get into one of those *situations*?"

"No, no; nothing like that." Mak wasn't too convincing. "But we did have an accident at work," he admitted.

"We?" She eyed him up and down. "You don't look hurt."

"No, it wasn't me. Jonny Soldier got hurt."

"And you left him hurt in a car outside? I can't wait to hear *this* story! I sure hope that car is an ambulance."

"No, it's not an ambulance. Reggie gave us a ride here." Mak cringed in anticipation of her response.

"Reggie! Reggie Whitehead? That good for nothing! He's outside my house right now?"

Mak grabbed her. "Now don't get excited." He held her against her will.

"I'm not excited, I'm mad. I'm going straight out to twist that little varmint's nose so he never comes back this way again." She waved her stainless steel tongs and snapped the pointed claws together like a weapon. "What are you doing with a low-life like that? I thought you said your Jonny Soldier had an accident?"

"I did, I mean, he did." Mak couldn't keep up with the questioning. "Reggie just gave us all a ride."

"Us all? There's more of you? This is getting really confusing." They stopped talking when Lucius came in.

"Who's Reggie?" Lucius asked innocently.

"Never you mind, son," Mak told him.

"Oh, never you mind yourself," Missy K corrected him. "We'll be eating in a few minutes so you and go watch TV in the living room while your daddy and I get to the bottom of all this."

"I get to watch TV while I'm eating?" Lucius wandered off happily.

Upset and tired, Missy K put down her cooking utensils and sat glumly at the table. Mak tried to console her but there was no use. He tried to put his hand on hers but she wouldn't let him. "I'm sorry, sweetheart."

"Now you stop that sweet stuff, mister," Missy K objected, pushing his hand away. "Reggie Whitehead, Jonny Soldier, something about an accident...." she talked out loud to herself. "You're all late and now you got a car full of people outside. Mak, you better level with me. What *is* going on?" Her eyebrows pushed together and she wiped the exasperation from her forehead with a dishtowel.

Mak stared at the linoleum tabletop as if the squiggled pattern was a script he could use to explain. "I love you," was all he could say.

Missy K smiled weakly and stared over his shoulder into the void.

"I'll be right back," Mak promised as he exited the kitchen. She heard the front door open and close.

Waiting for Mak to come back out to the car was taking longer than anticipated. Reggie adjusted the radio for better reception. Paul McCartney and Stevie Wonder did their best to integrate opposites while the back seat passengers adjusted to unfamiliar intimacy. Homa was tired of acting like the only responsible adult but was too duty bound to do anything else. The secret warmth she felt being next to Rebecca was dulled by her disgust with Reggie's unspoken crudities, and her sensitive nose felt violated by the overdose of his cheap cologne. Jon squirmed in the undersized back seat, flexing his partially numb foot and choking on his own pent up desire to be home with his muse. The novelty of Rebecca's proximity had worn off and he hoped Mak would come back soon and rescue him from what seemed like another ill-fated date with impossible beauty. Rebecca couldn't figure out how she got trapped in the middle, and wondered what her roommates were doing now.

Mak walked right past the detective's car on his way back to the idling Mercedes. Rudy took a perfect close-up of him, and another when Reggie powered his window down.

Mak leaned over and spoke through the opening. "Sorry for the delay," he apologized.

No one said anything until Reggie spoke up. "What's up, my man? You don't look so good."

Mak knew that some battles are better left unfought. "Little Luke's not feeling too well," he lied. "Guess someone else is going to have to get my soldier off the battlefield. Wouldn't want him to catch whatever caught Luke." He apologized visually to Jon.

"Okay then, that's that." Reggie cut off any possible response by raising the window. "Guess we'll see you later Colonel. Give Missy K my love," he jibed through the glass. "Where to now, Ms. Homa? Your place or mine?" He laughed at his own obnoxious insinuation.

Homa was tired and out of ideas. "Where does Jon want to go?"

"Can't you just drop me off at my place? I really need to get out of this damn car," Jon insisted, rearranging his long legs and kneeing the back of Reggie's seat to reinforce his point.

Homa was relieved at the prospect of being done with the whole ordeal. "Okay, if you think you can take care of yourself. Tell Reggie where you live and he'll get you there."

"I live near Canal and Fifth. I can get out on the corner."

Rebecca announced her escape plans too. "I'll get out when you cross the bridge. There's a subway station right there and my apartment is only three stops away."

"Nonsense, We'll drop you off at your front door after Jon. Let's go, Reggie." Homa ordered.

"Is that an offer, sweetie-pie?" Reggie teased.

Homa finally snapped. "Reggie, you make me sick! I don't know why Dr. Nouri puts up with you."

Reggie changed stations and turned up the radio. They screeched back across the Brooklyn Bridge with a Clash song blaring and the detectives struggling to keep up.

CHAPTER 21

Reggie stopped the car to let Jon out on the corner of Canal and Fifth, and before the detectives could fight through the traffic and get close enough to take a picture, Jon limped to his building and hobbled up the two flights of stairs. He opened the lock, went through the door, and hopping on one foot to the sofa that complained about his sudden flop with a sharp crack. Relieved to be home, Jon smiled to himself and exhaled. There was something about breaking the sofa, one crack at a time, that appealed to him. In fact, he hated it. He hated it because it just sat there in a meaningless, blue cloth stupor, promising comfort it could not deliver. It belonged to his roommate, but Jon didn't care about ruining it because he didn't like his roommate either.

His roommate, Al, appeared. "What was that?"

"What?" Jon feigned innocence.

"That loud noise. It sounded like something broke."

"I don't see anything broken." Jon pretended to look for what had broken, then purposely shifted his weight on the sofa until it creaked. He knew that Al knew what had happened; he enjoyed aggravating him. Al did his best to ignore the obvious. They had argued about the sofa before but Al had been bullied into submission by the bigger, tougher, and thoroughly male adversary. Al's homosexual instincts were frustrated and excited by Jon's aggression, but Jon was not attracted to him. Jon put his feet up on Al's glass sofa table, confident in a dominant role.

Al saw his medical boot. "Careful of the glass. Looks like you already had one accident today. What happened to you?"

"Oh that?" Jon wiggled his toes. "Just a little accident. Doc says I'll be fine."

Al had seen Jon come home injured before, but this wasn't as bad as the time he showed up with bandages wrapped around his head. "What kind of accident?" Al questioned him like a disapproving mother.

"I kind of burned my toes."

"Burned them? How?"

Jon had to think about how he could explain that he passed out from a smell without emasculating himself. "Mak and I were stewing up a potion and we put in too much of one thing..."

"A potion? What kind of potion?"

Princess Mist, what everyone else called it, sounded too gay, so he made up his own name. "Sheep Perfume. That's what it is."

"Sheep Perfume? I thought you worked in a warehouse."

"I do. I told you a million times, I work at Laden Imports over in the warehouse district," Jon said defensively. The apartment was in Al's name. Jon had answered an ad in the newspaper about a room for rent and it turned out that they knew someone in common. They had gotten familiar in the few months they had been living together, but their social lives were completely disconnected.

"So what were you and this Mak character doing mixing up potions?" Al asked, intrigued.

Jon forgot he was being mean. "Well, sometimes we mix stuff together to make something that smells good," Jon answered dismissively. "Is there anything to eat around here?"

"What? First you break my sofa and now you want me to feed you?" Al huffed, easily riled. "I don't know what you've been up to but...."

Jon wasn't up for a fight. "Oh lighten up, man. I burned my toes at work and now I'm hungry."

Al stood with arms akimbo and they stared to a draw. "Okay, but I want to hear what this potion, this Sheep Perfume is all about. It sounds..." He tightened his lips and made a sour face. "Fantastic!"

Jon's mental eyeballs rolled in his head at Al's perverse fantasy, but he didn't want to incite his gayness any further. "Okay, I'll tell you all about it after we eat."

Al sensed romance. "We're eating together?"

"Yeah, just you and me. Whadya say?" Jon knew Al had romantic ideas, and he used that to his advantage.

"Well, there's nothing to make here. I told Sal I'd meet him at the pub and we were going to eat there. You want to come along? You remember my friend Sal?"

"Al and Sal. How could I forget?" Jon chuckled, realizing how easy it would be to rhyme 'Al and Sal' with 'gal and pal.' He started working on a lyric. "Okay, sounds good, but we're going to have to take a cab because I can't walk that far." He moved his foot to attest.

"Are you going to change or wear those same stinky clothes you've had on all week?"

"It's just a pub, right? What do they care if I come in smelling like I work in a perfume factory?" Jon raised his arms and sampled the intensity of his body odor. "I'll just throw on a new shirt, spray a little fresh stink, and I'll be ready to go."

"Okay, but we have to go soon. I told my friends I'd meet them around 7:30. You've got just enough time to clean up – please!"

Jon hopped into his room. "Where are we going?" he called out while he was changing.

"This happening new place in Union Square, Shepherds Tavern."

CHAPTER 22

Monica finished her shower and joined Ameliah in the kitchen of their reasonably priced three-bedroom apartment overlooking the East River.

"Where's Becca?" Monica asked, bending at the waist with a towel on her head.

"I don't know. I thought you talked to her," Ameliah answered, making toast in her fluffy robe and slippers.

"I did, but that was almost two hours ago," Monica said, touching her palms to the floor. "I thought she'd be home by now."

A second child, Monica had learned from the mistakes of her older brother, and her simple goals of looking good and staying in shape were more a matter of preservation than attainment. She made enough money as a dance instructor to afford her modest goals, but her open personality was an invitation to strangers.

Ameliah had always been the wild one, the ringleader, the most ambitious. Her job at a busy law firm gave her the right mix of income and opportunity, and even though she was only a paralegal, she had become an integral part of the office dynamic. Attractive and outgoing, she outshone many of the veteran staffers, whose years of service had left them bleary-eyed and exhausted. The male partners at the firm had difficulty concealing their preference for her assistance, and the other women in the office had difficulty hiding their jealousy.

The three friends from New Jersey had been living together for over two years. Their parents, who had met a few times at school functions, took solace in the knowledge that their "girls" looked out for one another, and regular phone calls to home helped ease their understandable concerns of having daughters living in Manhattan.

Ameliah checked the time on the ridiculous rooster clock her mother had given her as a move-in present. "It's almost 7:30. Maybe Rebecca got out late or something." She crunched her toast and guided the crumbs sticking to her robe back onto the counter. "You're still planning on coming to the show with me tonight?"

"I think so." Monica adjusted her towel and changed stretching poses. "Aren't we going out to eat first? Where do you want to go?"

"I don't care. There's a cool new pub downtown that some of the people from work have been going to. They serve burgers and ribs. We could eat there." Ameliah crackled into her toast and took a sip of coffee. "They have some pool tables and a dance floor. Maybe you could show off a dance move or two?" she said, admiring Monica's limbering exercise.

Monica liked the idea of showing off her body and exaggerated her position in a feat of extreme mobility. "The food's good there?"

"Yeah, I hear the food's excellent." Ameliah already knew where she wanted to go but was trying to lure Monica into thinking she had a choice. "One of the guys I work with knows the owners. He eats there all the time."

The kitchen television was tuned to the weather and both women shifted their attention to its predictable routine. "Unseasonably mild with a chance of precipitation this evening. There's a warm front moving in and it looks like spring rains are right on time," the weather reporter continued. "Better have your umbrella handy tonight."

Monica removed the towel from her head and shook the moisture from her thick, dark, curly hair. "Well the rain won't bother *my* 'do," she said, unconcerned.

"Mine does fine in the rain," Ameliah boasted, primping her styled and tinted light brown set. "Do you want to go now, or should we wait for Rebecca?"

"Where are we going?"

"To Shepherds Tavern. Isn't that what we decided?" Ameliah went back to her bedroom to assemble the rest of her wardrobe.

Monica peered out the window at the thick clouds assembling in the twilight over the river. Her thoughts returned to Rebecca. It wasn't like her not to call. "When was the last time you spoke with Becca?" she called in to Ameliah.

"A few hours ago." Ameliah came back into the living room wearing skin-tight pedal pushers and a blousy top unbuttoned to her cleavage. "You like it?" She spun for Monica's approval.

"You look great. What did she say?"

"I don't remember. I think she said she was coming with us." Ameliah adjusted her hat in the hallway mirror. "Where is she anyway?"

Monica wandered over to the window again to see why the dogs in the downstairs apartment were barking. A big car was stopped in front of the building and someone was getting out.

Rebecca looked up at the apartment and saw Monica's silhouette, but it was too dark outside for Monica to see her. She gave Homa an awkward hug and hurried inside the lobby of their building. Homa got back in Dr. Nouri's car and Reggie pulled into traffic right in front of Detective Falin's cruiser.

"Who lives there?" Rudy, driving, asked as they followed the Mercedes.

Detective Falin checked his paperwork with the visor light. "Draper's kid."

Monica was still staring into the twilight when the sound of Rebecca's keys in the door startled her. "Where have you been?" she asked before Rebecca was all the way inside. "I was so worried about you."

Rebecca was pent up and exhausted. "Thanks for keeping track of me," she said, removing her coat and hanging it in the hall closet. She was the neatest of the three roommates and retained her superior organizational habits even under duress. "It's been quite a night."

"Already? Where have you been?"

Rebecca wasn't prepared to give a full report. "Well, I was at work, and it was almost time to leave when the whole thing started. Is there anything to eat around here?"

"What whole thing started?"

"Becca? Is that you?" Ameliah called out from her room. "What whole thing started?"

"Oh, it was nothing really. It's just that Jon hurt his foot...."

"Jon? The same Jonny Soldier from last night?" Monica asked, hoping for a romance story. "Did you guys make up or have a fight? I was wondering what was going to happen when you saw him at work but I was so busy today I forgot to ask."

Ameliah came in to hear the gossip. "What did you do? You hurt his foot?"

"He didn't try to grab you again, did he?" Monica wanted the details.

"No, no; it was nothing like that." Rebecca had almost forgotten about that incident the night before. "No, I actually had nothing to do with it."

"Then what happened?" they asked in unison.

"Well, he kind of burned his foot while they were...doing something weird out in the warehouse."

"What were they doing? Were you there?"

"No, I was in the office and all of the sudden Mak – you remember I told you about Mak. He's that older guy from Jamaica that kind of runs things in the warehouse. Well, he came in the office looking for a first aid kit and then things just kept getting crazier."

"So, what does all that have to do with why you're late?"

"Well, Homa, you know, my boss. She got involved when Jon came in the office to get his foot bandaged."

"He came in? Did you see him?" Monica was mostly interested in the relationship part of the story.

"Of course I saw him. He sat right across from me while he was getting his foot wrapped."

"And did you talk about what happened last night or say anything or...?"

"We didn't really talk, but we kind of communicated." Rebecca tried to remember exactly what was said, but couldn't. "We just kind of looked at each other and it was... I don't know, kind of strange."

"Strange in a good way or...?"

"Well, it was hard to tell because he was getting his foot worked on and he was sort of in pain."

"And you didn't try to comfort him?" Ameliah snickered.

"No, there were other people around and I didn't want my boss to know I liked him – and I think he was thinking the same thing because afterwards in the car we kind of played footsie and I could tell he was interested but we didn't want anyone else to know so we kind of did it with out anyone noticing."

"What? What did you do without anyone noticing? Whose car were you in?"

"Oh, you guys, I want to tell you all about it but I am so hungry because we didn't have time to eat before we went to see Dr. Nouri."

"Who's Dr. Nouri and why did *you* go to see him? I thought Jon was the one with the hurt foot."

"I am never going to be able to tell you everything that happened without eating first. Is there anything to make around here?" Rebecca rummaged through the fridge. "Can't we all go out and get something? I promise to tell both of you everything."

"That sounds like a great idea. Ameliah and I were just talking about going out for a bite before you came home. We didn't want to make plans without you. Why don't you put on some other clothes and we'll go down to this new place she knows about."

"Yeah, put on some night life." Ameliah encouraged her. "It's Friday night and this place is nice. There's a live band and they serve great food. I've been there before and it's really cool."

"Sounds great, I'll go change." Rebecca exhaled, relieved to be back among friends.

CHAPTER 23

Almost done with his rounds, Reggie pulled into the drop-off spot in front of the elegant Gramercy Park apartment building where Homa lived with her mother. Detective Falin checked the address while they drove by and waited at the corner for Reggie to pass them again.

"Thank Dr. Nouri for me," Homa said, exiting before Reggie could respond. The doorman greeted her at the curb and opened the tall, plate glass doors to the posh lobby of her vintage apartment building. Homa dug in her pocket to retrieve her scented hankie and breathed through it, trying to obliterate the memory of the past few hours. She liberated her tightly twisted hair from its bindings inside the elevator, and was carrying her shoes by the time she reached her eighth floor apartment. Her head hurt, her feet were swollen, and her heart was confused as she stumbled into her mother's care.

"You look awful," Samani greeted her. "Dr. Nouri told me what happened. You must be exhausted. Let me get you some tea." She hugged Homa lightly so as not to disturb her own hair, which was set for the night. "I love you, dear child, and I don't know what I would do without you. Sit down and rest." Samani guided her to the sofa, then padded through the plush white carpeting toward the tidy kitchen. Homa sunk into the frost-colored leather sofa and lay her head on one of the extra soft, fleece pillows. She was almost asleep by the time her mother came back with the tea. Samani set the tray on a gilded rococo table with a heavy glass top.

"Thank you, mama," Homa whispered, in a tiny voice only a mother could hear.

Samani seated herself at the far end of the couch and rubbed her daughter's feet. "You're still my baby."

The television droned inaudibly, and the comforts of home seeped into Homa's subconscious like an opioid. When she opened her eyes twenty minutes later, her mother was gone. "Entertainment Tonight," one of her favorite shows, was flashing, zooming, and tumbling images of grinning celebrities at her like a high school pillow fight. Unhealthfully fascinated with celebrities' personal lives, Homa's dozy meditation was interrupted by a gnawing sensation inside her belly. The turmoil gripped her forcefully, and she drew her legs to her chest to try to relieve the pain. She could see the note from her mother stuck to the edge of the television and knew what it said without looking. Her mother always went out with her friends on Friday night; and Homa usually liked having the apartment to herself – a condition facilitated by her non-existent social life.

As outgoing and confident as she was at work, Homa's personal life was a cloistered truce held together by insecurity and circumstance. The turbulent dreams that interrupted her sleeping patterns had intensified since her father hadn't come home from a business trip abroad, and even though that was seven years ago, her feelings were still raw and unsettled. Artistic outbursts covered the walls of her bedroom, but no one other than her mother, ever saw the graphic depths of her frustration.

The family had done everything in their power to find her father – her uncle Sattar even retraced his steps – but official denials from the Russian, Turkish, and Iraqi governments, and vague stories about his whereabouts from Armenian clans operating in the mountainous region that spanned the three countries, were all that was recovered. After two years of false leads and unfulfilled hopes, the family begrudgingly accepted the official Turkish explanation that Arshan Zemmi had perished in the company of Kurdish rebels on their eastern border. Homa remembered her father clearly, and often wondered what he would be doing if he was alive. She was tired and hungry and missed having a male role model.

After her father's disappearance, her mother's personality completely changed, and the combination of menopause and the prescription drugs she used to manage her mood swings only accounted for some of her erratic behavior. In public, Samani was unflappable, but in the privacy of their apartment, her grief would transform into sudden episodes of vitriolic resentment against the world that had taken her husband and father from her.

Homa sympathized and loved her mother, but her mother was so much of a woman; always worried about womanly things, like her appearance and manners. She always dressed in perfect outfits, with heavy makeup and a plastic smile, as if only the obvious mattered. The all-white furnishings of their apartment made Homa feel like she was living in a blizzard of pretension. Her bedroom was her asylum, and she had taken full advantage of her mother's permission to decorate it any way she wanted. There, she was free to paint and plaster the walls as her artistic urges dictated, and the result was so markedly different from the rest of the monotone apartment that her doorway was more like a passage to another country than the entrance to the next room. The strains of her immigrant parentage, along with a strong personality, prevented her from fitting in socially, so Homa had spent an unhealthy portion of her time alone in her room with unresolved teenage and parental issues. Her father had traveled extensively while she was growing up, and her mother's warmth during those years was tepid and intermittent, and Homa wondered if the absence of a father figure had unmoored her sense of self and allowed her sexual appetites to drift into the breakwater of gender preference.

Homa's stomach pain recalled her from the depths of self-analysis. The wet weather report flashed across the screen as she righted herself, knowing she had to make a dinner plan. She had no expectation of finding food in the rarely used kitchen, and the approaching storm dampened any desire to go out for a meal, so she got up and sorted through the take-out menus in the drawer by the door. Her deliberations between Chinese and Italian delivery were interrupted by a ringing phone, which she answered.

"Mrs. Monsouri?" a man's voice asked.

"No, Mrs. Monsouri is not here. May I take a message?"

"Err, is this her daughter?"

Homa was put off. "Who is this?"

"Uh, this is Rhamin Darius," the caller identified himself. "Are you Homa?" he asked uncertainly.

Homa was surprised. "Who are you? I don't know anyone named Rhamin." She paused, because Darius was a familiar name. "And how do you know my name?"

"Ah yes, very true. I'm so sorry to phone you like this," he said. "I was hoping to talk to your mother first," he added, choosing his words carefully.

Homa's headache and hunger gave her an irritable edge. "Listen, Mr. Darius, or whatever your name is, my mother is not here right now but I will tell her you called." She was in the process of hanging up when the word "first" stuck in her brain and stopped her.

"Wait, please, wait," the caller pled, expecting to hear a dial tone. "It's just a misunderstanding. I'm sorry to have called unannounced. Please forgive me."

Homa wasn't feeling too forgiving at the moment, but held the phone away from her ear and allowed him to continue.

"Are you there? Hello?"

"Yes, I'm here. Now tell me what you want," she asked impatiently.

"Well, I was calling to talk to your mother because Dr. Nouri said that was the proper thing to do."

The mention of Dr. Nouri altered her tone. "Dr. Nouri told you to call?" she asked in disbelief.

"Yes, Dr. Nouri said I should talk to your mother first before speaking with you."

"Speaking with *me*?" Homa was completely flummoxed. She didn't know what to say as the white noise of silence hissed in their ears. Finally, she regained her tongue. "So you were really calling to speak to me and not my mother?"

"No, yes...I'm so sorry," Rhamin stammered.

"Please stop saying you're sorry. I don't know why you're calling me, but if you're a friend of Dr. Nouri's, I will listen to what you have to say."

Rhamin eagerly accepted the opportunity to explain himself. "Yes, yes. Dr. Nouri has been our doctor for many years."

"So why did Dr. Nouri tell you to call my mother if you wanted to talk to me?"

The answer peered over the horizon. "Well, it's difficult; that's why I wanted to talk to your mother first." Rhamin went silent again.

Homa's headache throbbed. "Just a minute please; I'll be right back." She put the phone down and went to the kitchen. She found two aspirin and washed them down with a long gulp of water before returning. Already tired from a very full day, only the vigor of youth gave her enough stamina to continue the conversation. "Hello again Mr. Darius. I have such a headache and I haven't eaten, so please excuse my manners." There was no answer. "Hello. Are you there?"

"I'm here," Rhamin answered softly. "I'm sorry you have a headache. I have disturbed your dinner plans. Please forgive me."

"I forgive you." Homa's stomach gurgled. "Now what's this all about?"

"Perhaps I should call back another time and speak with your mother."

"Perhaps, but my mother doesn't run my life. I am nearly twenty-six years old."

"Yes, I know how old you are."

Homa thought she detected something familiar in the caller's voice. "You're from Persia?"

"Yes, of course."

It all started to make sense. "And you were calling my mother to ask her permission to ask me out for a date?" The name and accent explained everything.

Rhamin was surprised at how quickly he had been revealed. "Err, well, yes, I was. I mean I am, I...."

"That's what I thought," Homa responded with the satisfaction of a puzzle solver.

"So will you?"

Homa hadn't connected to the idea emotionally. "Will I what?"

"Will you please join me for dinner sometime?"

She almost laughed. "That's what you want?" Rhamin's formal manners and overly polite demeanor reminded her of her parents' friends.

"Yes, please. That is what I would very much like."

Homa went on the offensive. "May I ask you a question?"

"Yes, certainly."

"How old are you?"

"Ah yes, of course; that is one of things I had intended speaking with Mrs. Monsouri about. I am thirty-four years old.

"Thirty-four!" Homa toyed with his emotions.

"Yes, but I've never been married," Rhamin said, trying to compensate for his age.

"Oh, I see." Homa said dryly. "But we've never met. Don't you think it might be a little too soon to consider marriage?" she pointed out sarcastically.

"Too soon, perhaps, but we *have* met." he corrected her. "You were young and might not remember, but my father was friends with your father." Rhamin fired his anecdotal weaponry with perfect aim.

Homa retreated. "You knew my father?"

"Yes, I knew him quite well. Perhaps you'd like me to tell you what I remember," he suggested smoothly.

"Yes, I think I'd like that very much," Homa's heart spoke.

"Perhaps over dinner?"

"Perhaps," she answered wistfully. "Dinner sounds nice." Her stomach growled in agreement.

Rhamin, suddenly energized, seized his advantage. "Splendid. How about tonight?"

"Tonight?" Homa glanced in the mirror and brushed the loose hair off her face.

"Well, why not? You said a moment ago that you hadn't eaten. Do you have other dinner plans?"

Homa wasn't prepared for a negotiation. "No, I don't have any plans tonight." She eyed the takeout menus on the table. "Who did you say your father was?"

"My father is Bahram Darius," Rhamin answered clearly. "He was a close friend of your father's."

Homa just listened, so he continued his pitch. "He, my father, I mean we, are Dr. Nouri's real estate partners. We own the Old Medical Building where Dr. Nouri keeps his office."

"You own the Old Medical Building?" Homa latched onto something concrete.

"Well, our company and another company own it, yes." Rhamin was starting to sound like someone Homa could relate to, and before

186

she re-armed her defenses, he fired a direct hit. "Why don't I pick you up in twenty minutes and we'll go to the Lebanese restaurant in Union Square?"

"You have a car?" She didn't realize she had accepted his proposal.

"Of course," Rhamin chuckled. "Is twenty minutes enough time?"

"You know where I live?"

"Yes, I've been to your apartment a few times. Don't worry; I don't bite. You can even call Dr. Nouri to ask him about me. He's still at his office. I can see the lights on."

"You have an office in the Old Medical Building?"

"The rent is very affordable."

"Yes, I'm sure it is." Homa was running out of qualifying questions. "I won't have time to dress up so I hope the restaurant isn't too fancy."

"Its not. Whatever you wear will be perfect," Rhamin assured her, stifling his excitement.

"Are you sure this is a good idea? I mean...I don't even know what you look like."

"I look quite normal, and I know what *you* look like. I'm sure we'll have a lot to talk about, but we can go some other time if that would be better."

Homa considered the possibility but her stomach cut her deliberation short. "Well it might rain, but tonight's as good as any other, I guess."

"Excellent! I have a good feeling about tonight."

"I'll see you outside in twenty minutes?"

"Twenty minutes. I'll be right over."

Rudy and Detective Falin were still following Reggie, so twenty minutes later, when a dark green BMW pulled into the drop off spot in front of Homa's apartment and waited, no one was watching. Rhamin checked his hair in the visor mirror to make sure his short black twists hadn't escaped their greased tonsorial boundaries. He reached in his sport coat pocket and dexterously opened the tiny bottle of scented oil he used for special occasions. He added another few drops to his finger and wiped the residue on his neck before closing the top. It had been a very long time since his last date, and he suffered from the negative effects of both biological repression and social expectation.

Homa had showered quickly, changed her clothes, and assumed the image of a sophisticated, stylish, and assertive business owner. The aspirin had started to work, and she was looking forward to a good meal with some tidbits about her father. She didn't expect the romantic element of this sudden plan to lead anywhere she wanted to go, but was downstairs waiting in the lobby when Rhamin's car pulled in front.

"Mr. Darius?" she asked through the lowered passenger window.

"Yes, yes. I am Rhamin. Please, come in." He opened the door for her from the driver's seat. "I would have gotten out to open the door for you but I – "

"It doesn't matter, I know how to open doors," Homa said, nestling into the impressive European interior of his car. "Nice to meet you," she introduced herself with an outstretched hand.

Rhamin took her hand politely. "Very pleased to see you again," he said, memorizing the touch of her flesh. "You look more beautiful in person than in pictures."

Unaccustomed to male attention, Homa blushed at the compliment. She tried to think of the photos displayed around the apartment but couldn't remember any recent ones. "What pictures have you seen?" she asked.

"Oh, the one I remember most was taken of you in the summer." Rhamin answered, shifting smoothly into traffic. "You were only about sixteen." They both remembered the much-copied family photo that showed off the full bloom of Homa's maturity. "That was before your father – " He stopped himself.

"It's okay, that was a long time ago." Homa controlled her emotions and took the opportunity to study Rhamin's face while he was driving, hoping she might remember meeting him. "So, when is the last time we saw each other?" she wondered out loud.

"Oh, well, maybe at a social function or a restaurant. I don't remember the last time exactly," he said diplomatically. "But I've seen you now and then in passing."

"You have?" Homa was somewhere between flattered and alarmed at the idea that he had seen her but she still couldn't recall ever seeing him.

They didn't speak as Rhamin showed off the torque of his BMW with firm thrusts of the gearshift. Each rise in engine power was accompanied by a jolt of whinnying mechanical horses that pressed Homa firmly into the perforated leather seat. As they raced between stoplights, Homa was impressed with the well-crafted appointments of the passenger compartment, and energized by the contagious excitement that the automotive brand is known to elicit. Although she hadn't considered the possibility that she would actually be attracted to this semi-mysterious caller, the scents of the treated leather, and Rhamin's pungently familiar cologne, blended with the unconscious genetic connection that people from similar bloodlines feel, and all the smells together tested the mettle of her critical thinking. Rhamin was similarly intoxicated by her suggestive patchouli, and so excited at the prospect of untwisting her pomaded hair that he exaggerated his driving showmanship to the point where he forgot what they were talking about.

Homa relocated the fragment of conversation, along the stuttering white lines of 3rd Avenue. "When was the last time you saw me?" she asked again.

"I've seen you around a few times," Rhamin repeated, fully engaged in his vehicular demonstration. "At the Old Medical Building."

The mention of the Old Medical Building sparked her curiosity. They swung around a corner where two provocatively dressed women stood close to the street. The BMW slowed perceptibly as it passed them. Homa was almost as interested in the ladies as Rhamin, and the unspoken microsode made her see him as a man who had eyes for women.

"I saw you earlier today, when you left Dr. Nouri's office," he finally admitted.

Homa was shocked but didn't show it. "Tonight? You saw me earlier tonight?" She tried to remember what she had been wearing and vaguely recalled seeing someone when they got off the elevator. "So you've been spying on me?" she verified, flattered, but uncomfortable with the idea. "You saw me tonight and that's when you decided to call?" she accused him with some conviction. Even in the darkness, she could see that the red on Rhamin's face was not just the reflection of the stoplight where they were waiting.

"I can explain. Please don't be angry with me." Rhamin jerked the shifter around, trying to find first gear, but it was in third when he lifted the clutch.

The bucking motion shook Homa to her senses. "This had better be good," she challenged. Then, remembering their earlier conversation, she dug her nails into the seat. "All that nice talk about seeing my pictures and knowing my father...."

Rhamin retreated and looked for a position he could defend. "I did see your pictures and I did meet your father. I knew I should have spoken with your mother first." The sudden change of atmosphere made it difficult for him to think and drive at the same time. "Dr. Nouri was correct."

"Correct about what? What did Dr. Nouri say?" Homa demanded, advancing her inquisition.

"He said – " Rhamin closed his mouth before inserting his other foot. He gritted his teeth, hoping for the moment to pass; it didn't.

"What did Dr. Nouri say about me?" Homa raised her voice. "Who are you *really* and where are you taking me?" Her objections assumed greater proportion.

Rhamin grasped the wheel tightly with both hands, trying to hang on to reality. The blood drained from his clenched fingers as he stared straight ahead, waiting for what seemed like forever for the next light to turn green. He didn't know which question to answer, and pled for civility. "Please calm yourself. I mean you no harm."

Homa was seething and her accusations lost their polite veneer. "You tried to trick me."

"I did not," Rhamin defended himself.

"Where are you taking me?" she demanded.

"We're going out to dinner at the Lebanese restaurant," he said, exasperated.

A mustachioed cab driver pulled up next to them at the light and smirked at the sight of two upwardly mobile socialites having an argument in their sporty BMW. Rhamin noticed the cab driver watching every time he turned to respond to Homa's challenge, and was so embarrassed, frustrated, and in a hurry to get away, that when the light changed, he ground first gear, then rammed the shifter into third again by mistake. The car lurched to a stall, throwing Homa toward the windshield, then snapping her back into her seat. The cab pulled away first, and as she brushed her loosened hair away from her eyes, she saw the passengers in the back seat of the taxi laughing at her.

"Stop the car," she insisted.

"What? Now?"

"Yes, stop the car. Please, I want to get out."

"Right here?" Rhamin had little experience arguing with women and was at a distinct disadvantage.

"Yes, right here," Homa persisted, reaching for the door latch.

"Wait, please let me pull over." Rhamin maneuvered the car toward the curb and tried to find a place between the parked cars that lined 3rd Avenue.

Homa fidgeted with her overcoat and readied her purse for a speedy escape. But there were no empty spots, and black diesel smoke from a local bus seeped in through the air vents. "Just pull over anywhere," she demanded.

"I'm sorry. I'm trying to find a safe place. I won't be forgiven if something happened to you."

"I won't forgive you if you make me sit in this car one more moment choking on that disgusting smoke from that bus." Homa reached in her coat pocket and covered her face in the silk handkerchief she kept there for such occasions. Rhamin found a side street and turned in, coming to a halt in front of a row of brick apartment buildings. Homa sat, breathing through her scented handkerchief, trying to compose herself, as the first sprinkles of rain dotted the windshield. Rhamin left the motor running, fully expecting her to bolt from the car and slam the door shut, but she didn't move from her seat.

"Is it the rain?" he asked after enough time had passed that an explanation seemed forthcoming.

"Rain?" Homa unburied her face from the handkerchief. He could see that her attitude had changed. He wasn't sure what he was supposed to do or say, so he just sat there, bracing for the next attack. It didn't come.

"Can we still go out to eat?" she asked quietly.

Rhamin hid his shock. "I guess so, if you still want to."

Homa sat up and straightened her headscarf. "My cousin lives around the corner from here. Do you know her too?" she asked, resuming her inquiry more civilly.

Rhamin was extra careful in his reply. "Which cousin is that?"

"Asalah, my cousin Asalah. You probably know her father, my uncle, Saeed too." Homa assumed.

"Yes, of course, your uncle Saeed and your other uncle Sattar. I've met them both several times," he said, trying to sound as familiar as possible again.

"Then you must have *seen* Saeed's beautiful daughter, my cousin Asalah. Were you stalking her too?" Homa insinuated, recovering her edge as the car puttered back into traffic.

Rhamin bristled at the veiled accusation and second-guessed himself. The date that he had long fantasized about was not unfolding according to script. He thought about terminating it ahead of schedule, but vanity and desperation steered the car onto 14th Street toward the restaurant. Then he tried lying. "I don't remember your cousin."

Homa wasn't falling for it. "Oh yes you do. You couldn't know everyone else in my family and not her." Fully recovered, she paused with the satisfaction of regained advantage. "She is the most beautiful Monsouri, so surely you must have noticed her."

"Well, perhaps when she was younger."

"I thought so," she said, sensing his half-truth. "Too bad she's already married and.... I guess that's why you thought maybe I...." She stopped short of overstating the obvious, and they continued driving in silence. The increased rain gave them something to be distracted by until they pulled into a covered parking garage on a side street next to Union Square. A brief scurry through the rain ended at the front door of the restaurant where a maître d' greeted Rhamin by name and seated them by the window.

CHAPTER 24

The rain had increased to a steady drizzle by the time the girls from New Jersey reached Shepherds Tavern. Ameliah was the first one to exit the cab, and she hopped on her toes to avoid the pools of water that had begun to collect on the sidewalk. Rebecca and Monica were right behind her as they entered the already crowded restaurant and joined other patrons waiting to be seated in front of the dark wood reception desk. It was only a few moments before a stylish young woman guided them to a polished aluminum table next to the central dance floor that separated the eating area from the bar. Shepherds Tavern, the recently constructed creation of a well-known restaurant architect with a generous budget, had become the preferred destination of the upwardly mobile in lower Manhattan. All the visible surfaces, from the row of high windows that faced the street to the sandblasted brick walls and artistically considered black ventilation system suspended on rods, had been designed to welcome, excite, and insulate its customers from the concerns of their day jobs. A rustic mountain motif was accomplished with copper light fixtures, wrought iron railings, and museum quality artifacts related to ovine husbandry.

After being seated, Rebecca excused herself and made her way past the pool tables to the ladies room in the back. She brushed herself back to pristine beauty in the bathroom mirror, but the previous night's drama, rain, and strain of the evening's burned foot episode had taken a visible toll on her looks. She splashed some cold water on her face and took a deep breath, searching for her second wind, but a chiseled yuppie pool player, who groaned lecherously as she passed by on her way back to the table, was what actually gave her the jolt of confidence she needed. Ameliah was chatting with someone at the bar, and Monica was guarding their drinks when she returned.

"So what happened to you tonight?" Monica asked her. "Where did you go after work?"

"Oh that, well where do I begin?" Rebecca took a sip of her drink and tried to adjust to the new surroundings.

"How 'bout the part of the story with Jon in it? Remember all the way back till last night when you thought you were in love with him?" Monica prompted.

Rebecca scanned the room. "I thought I was."

"Was? You mean you're not now? What happened?"

"Oh, Monica, I don't know what I think anymore. We have this kind of physical attraction, but everything goes wrong when we get close." Rebecca took another sip of her margarita.

"Every time? I thought last night was the first time?"

"Yeah, well that was the first time outside of work. And then tonight we were sitting right next to each other in the car and we could both feel it, but his foot hurt and there were all these other people around." Her explanation petered out and she watched Ameliah talking intently with a man in a business suit at the bar. Monica noticed them too, and their curiosity was soon satisfied when Ameliah led the man back to their table for an introduction.

"Guys, this is Bradley. Bradley, these are my friends: Monica and Rebecca," Ameliah introduced everyone. "Bradley and I work together. He's the one who told me about this place."

"Nice to finally meet you, ladies. Amy's told me a lot about you." Bradley made eye contact with Rebecca and nodded politely at Monica.

"Why don't you sit down and join us," Ameliah said, motioning to the extra chair.

Bradley sat across from Rebecca with his back to the bar and loosened his tie. His short, curly blond hair was purposely pushed into a low hummock on one side his rectangular head. He was a few drinks ahead of his tablemates and didn't need much encouragement to engage his prospects. "So how do like Shepherds?" He gesticulated proudly. "Some place we've got here. One of our clients is a partner, so let me buy the next round." He winked at Ameliah, who nodded knowingly. A fast-moving waitress took their order and deposited menus on the table before melting back into the crowd. Rebecca picked up a menu and used it to hide from Bradley's curiosity, leaving Monica to manage the conversation.

"The decorations here are great," Monica commented, making small talk. "I love the way they used animal horns to hang things on."

Looking up, Ameliah agreed. "They sure spent a lot of money on the look of this place. Bradley says they have a live music tonight and we can keep these seats after we eat."

"I thought you wanted to go see that other band," Monica reminded her.

"What other band?" Bradley asked.

"We're going to see Bosco Dish after we eat. They're playing at The Black Sheep in the Village," Ameliah informed him. "Have you ever heard them?" she asked.

"Yeah, I've seen them play." Bradley answered. "But I don't think they'll be playing there tonight," he added.

"Why not?" Ameliah asked, surprised.

"I guess you didn't hear." Bradley said soberly. "They got busted last night."

"Busted? How do you know?"

"The owners of the Black Sheep are also clients of ours. Didn't you see Roger at work today?"

"That's what he was yelling about?"

"Yeah, the band was booked for the whole weekend, and now their equipment is locked up and their roadies are in jail. It's a mess."

Ameliah shared a bug-eyed look with her roommates and took a sip of her drink. Scenes of the night before rolled through their collective memory, but no one mentioned their potentially incriminating involvement.

The waitress came back and they ordered dinner, then Bradley picked up where he had left off. "Well, at least you've got seats to *this* show. These guys are terrific." Bradley thought he was in show business. "They play all the hits, and you'll see, by midnight it'll be so packed that you won't be able to move in here. Lots of dancing, and some crazy stuff too." The pitch went on. "There are so many people out of work right now it seems like no one cares about their future. They just want to go out, get lit up, forget about their problems and have a good time. That's why this place is so popular." Bradley crushed the last few ice cubes from his drink with his back teeth and smacked the empty glass down on the table as if he had closed a deal.

CHAPTER 25

Twenty minutes after Rebecca and her friends had gotten there, Jon limped into Shepherds Tavern and followed Al straight back to the pool tables without seeing them. Sal and his friend were standing with drinks while waiting for a table to play on. They greeted Al with looks of approval at what they thought was his rugged new date. Without denying their assumption, Al introduced Jon as his roommate.

"Al always gets the best roommates," Sal greeted Jon, shaking his hand. He noticed Jon's foot. "You already hurt him!" he teased Al.

"You're such an animal!" Sal's friend joined in.

"I didn't have anything to do with that," Al claimed innocence. "But he promised to tell me all about how it happened," he added. "Let's order something while we're waiting to play."

Always able to relate to the disaffected, Jon didn't try to correct their sexual miscalculation. He leaned against a window ledge to take some of the pressure off his foot and ordered a beer and a burger from the circulating waitress. It wasn't his usual type of hang out – lots of white-collar, working-class yuppies airing out their frustrations and hairdos – but he embraced his outsider status with a defiant pose. Al and the other pool players saw him as a potentially formidable opponent, and by the time he'd wolfed down his burger, Jon had assumed the role of mysterious stranger to be reckoned with. After eating, he stood near the back with a cigarette and a beer, watching the Sal and his friend run the table.

The Jersey Girls had finished eating, and Monica didn't see Jon as she passed him on her trip to the ladies room. Jon only figured out who she was after she'd passed, and he moved out of the way before she came through again.

Al saw Jon flinch as she passed. "She's not your type anyway," he teased with beer breath and a playful poke. Sal and his friend giggled at the joke and kissed each other on the mouth. Jon's tolerance strained, and he sucked in nicotine like a desperate diver empties his scuba tank.

"You promised to tell me how you hurt your foot," Al reminded him, motioning his friends closer so they could hear too. "Let's hear about this magic potion you've been making," he cajoled, relishing the expectation of a juicy story.

"Magic potion?" Sal repeated, intrigued.

"What do you call it?" Al prompted him. "Sheep Perfume?"

Sal's friend was unable to resist the allusion. "Oh I *love* sheep!"

Jon stalled with a long swig of beer, and was peering through the crowd, searching for an exit strategy, when Monica saw him on her way back.

"Hey, you! What are you doing here?" she asked Jon, not noticing Al and his friends. Jon looked down at her vaguely familiar cherubic face surrounded by a garland of dark curls and saw his escape.

"Hey!" he greeted her, surprising Al.

"Who's this?" Al demanded.

"Oh, I'm sorry," Monica apologized and looked to Jon for an explanation. Jon couldn't remember her name so he put his arm around her. "She's an old friend of mine."

"Oh, I see," Al said, feeling jilted. Then he turned to Sal, who was confused by the interaction.

Oblivious to the homosexual orientation of Al and his friends, Monica focused all her attention on Jon. "What happened to you last night?" she flirted, mesmerized by his touch and the attention of his electric blue eyes. "Where did you go?"

Lyrics that had been lying dormant in his brain escaped through his mouth. *"I feel like I know you. We've been here before,"* he channeled. *11

"I feel like I know you too," Monica confirmed. Covering her amorous tracks, she added, "Rebecca's here too. We're sitting over there if you want to join us." She pointed in the direction of her table and sauntered away.

After she had gone, Al came closer. "I didn't know how I felt for a long time either," he confided with an elbow to Jon's midsection. "This world is full of false assumptions." He put his arm around Jon, who froze in terror. Al felt him recoil and said, "I see, well maybe some other time."

"We've got a table over here," Sal said. "Come play knock out with us." He placed an arm around Al's shoulder and steered him away from disappointment.

Jon inhaled some more nicotine relief and distanced himself from Al and his friends. A few minutes later, he gimped his way past the stage and arrived at the Jersey Girls' table with a beer and ironic grin. Seeing him approach, Rebecca gasped. The others at her table turned to see what was the matter.

"This guy some friend of yours?" Bradley asked, defending the ladies against the rough looking intruder.

"Yes, we know him," Ameliah assured him. "Bradley, this is Jon, Rebecca's friend." Rebecca blushed but didn't say anything, so Ameliah continued her introduction. "Jon, this is my friend Bradley." The men acknowledged each other as rivals. "Bradley is an attorney. We work together at a law office," she announced proudly. "Jon works with Rebecca at the perfume factory," she added demeaningly, and no one had the friendlies.

Bradley understood Ameliah's derision and noticed Jon's foot. "You look hurt," he said. "Why don't you have a seat and tell us all about it? Never met anyone who worked at a perfume factory before," he condescended. "Seems like a stinky job," he smirked at his own pun.

Bradley's leisure-suit attitude roiled Jon's simmering antipathy. "Why don't you go fuck yourself," he erupted, snarling down at Bradley.

"Excuse me?" Bradley challenged. "You want to take that back, dirtbag?" His pink neck swelled in anger as he rose from his seat and knocked his chair into Jon's injured leg.

Jon pushed him back into his seat and held him there by pressing his full weight on his shoulder. Bradley tried to swat Jon's arm away, but Jon squeezed his neck muscles with a powerful grasp until Bradley cringed in pain. Ameliah rose and aimed a punch, but Jon caught her forearm with his other hand and bent it backwards, until her only relief was to sit back down. With his adversaries subdued, Jon paused to share his indignity with Monica and Rebecca before releasing his victims and hobbling back into the mass of people gathering for the evening's entertainment.

After he was gone, Bradley regained his composure. "Who was that guy?" he asked Rebecca, straightening his jacket and shirt collar. "You work with him? I'd watch out. That guy's trouble," he counseled. Rebecca didn't respond.

"My arm hurts. Are you okay?" Ameliah asked Bradley.

"I'm okay, but what was the matter with that guy?"

"Something happened to his foot," Rebecca said, making an excuse.

"Maybe that's why he was in such a bad mood," Monica suggested.

"Well, I'm ready for another drink," Bradley declared, changing the focus. "It's Friday night and we're supposed to be having a good time. I'll go order us another round and make sure we get that friend of yours out of here before he causes any more problems." He went to fulfill his mission and the girls resumed their conversation.

"That was scary," Ameliah confided. "You were going to tell us what happened at work," she reminded Rebecca. "I thought you said Jon hurt his foot. Are you sure his brain wasn't injured too? Why did he do that? My arm still hurts."

"Well, I thought you and Bradley were kind of rude, didn't you Rebecca?" Monica interrupted, taking sides.

"Yeah, I thought Bradley sounded a little conceited," Rebecca agreed.

Ameliah disagreed. "All he said was that he never met anyone who worked in a perfume factory."

"Yeah, but the *way* he said it, it was like being a lawyer was so much better," Monica challenged.

"Well, isn't it?" Ameliah said, defending her turf.

Loud yelling and a commotion near the bar interrupted their conversation. Bradley returned to the table with an imperious grin. "That friend of yours won't be bothering us any more tonight; I had the bouncers throw him out," he gloated.

"Thank God for that," Ameliah said, shaking her injured wrist. Bradley sat next to her and held her hand the way a noble knight attends his lady, rubbing her wrist with his thumbs affectionately.

Monica stood up and saw Jon through the window. He was standing outside in the rain getting soaked. Rebecca stood up too, and they both watched as Jon limped toward the partial protection of a nearby awning. Their sense of fairness was strained at the sight of him struggling to stand on one leg close enough to the building to avoid the direct downpour.

"What's he doing out there?" Monica whispered to Rebecca.

"I'm not sure," Rebecca said, turning her head so Ameliah couldn't see. "I'm worried about that foot of his."

"We should do something," Monica suggested.

"What can we do? They already threw him out?"

"What are you two looking at?" Ameliah asked.

"We'll be right back," Monica told her as she and Rebecca excused themselves from the table. They were out of Ameliah's sight when they conferred again.

"Do you want to stay here? That guy Bradley keeps making eyes at you," Monica asked.

Rebecca made a sour face. "He's gross and I think he likes Amy anyway. I have the worst luck with guys."

"Bad luck? Every guy you meet wants you!"

"Yeah, but the ones I want...." Rebecca looked out at Jon trying to light a cigarette in the drizzle.

"Maybe we should go help him," Monica suggested.

"Maybe we should."

"Ameliah was the one who wanted to come to this place. Why do we always just follow her around? Let's go tell her we're leaving and she can stay here with her big shot lawyer friend if she wants."

"Sounds good to me," Rebecca agreed. "Look at what she got us into last night."

Ameliah was sitting by herself when they returned to the table to announce their plan. Bradley was socializing with people at the next table, and the band was almost ready to do battle with the alcohol-induced murmur that had risen to a din.

"*Where* are you going?" Ameliah wasn't sure she had heard right.

"I don't know, we'll find someplace where it's not so crowded."

"You don't want to stay *here*?" Ameliah couldn't understand why.

"Not really." Monica shook her head and Rebecca nodded in agreement.

Before they could leave Bradley, arrived back at the table with a friend in tow. "This is Enrique," he introduced. "You know Ameliah from our office, and these are her two highly attractive and *available* friends, Monica and Rebecca," he broadcast, painting pick up lines. "Enrique works for the other side, but we're friends anyway," he announced, elbowing his smartly dressed new companion.

"Pleased to meet you," Enrique said stiffly, seating himself in the chair Bradley had pulled over from the next table.

Bradley got the conversation started. "So Monica, Ameliah tells me you're a dance instructor. You going to show us some moves tonight?" he asked with a wink.

"I wasn't planning on it," Monica fibbed, measuring Enrique's silent attention.

"This band really knows how to get you on the floor," Bradley insinuated.

Enrique took up the cause. "What kind of dancing do you do?"

"I teach modern dance and jazz." Monica answered, enjoying the attention.

"I love jazz." Enrique shimmied his shoulders with his arms extended, revealing a row of shiny white teeth against his pale olive complexion.

Monica didn't like the overt display any more than his perfectly parted, greased hairdo. Her heart wandered back to Jon on the street. "It's getting really smoky in here," she complained. "I need a breath of air. Coming, Becca?" She took her coat and left the table.

Rebecca apologized with a shrug and followed. "That was kind of rude," Rebecca scolded her when she caught up. "Where are we going anyway?" She followed Monica through the crowd toward the front door.

"There he is. Hey!" Monica called out as they pushed their way past the people trying to get in. Jon had found a dry spot under the awning of a storefront a few doors away and acknowledged them with a defeated smile and upturned palms. Refreshed by the weather and giggly from their mischievous escape, Monica and Rebecca skipped through the rain and joined Jon's sidewalk refuge. Energized by his sudden change of circumstance, Jon welcomed them with open arms.

"Does your foot still hurt?" Rebecca asked, snuggling.

"Yeah, what happened to your foot?" Monica asked from his other arm.

"Oh that." Jon extended his wet boot out from beneath his jeans. "Just a couple of burnt toes."

Monica sympathized. "Does it hurt?"

"Not now." Jon pulled both girls closer and squeezed their excitement into his loins. "I bet I can get a cab to stop now that I have such juicy bait," he said, feeling replenished and empowered. "You're coming with me."

"Where are we going?" Rebecca asked.

"The Black Sheep."

Rebecca's alarm went off. "Why do you want to go there?"

"Well, we're not really going there."

"Then where are we going?"

"To the Recording Studio."

"Where's that?"

"Not far; down below Chambers Street."

"Then why are we going to The Black Sheep?"

"To see Dennis."

Monica was getting confused. "Who's he?"

"He's the sound guy at The Black Sheep. Remember last night when we couldn't get in without paying?" Jon reminded her.

"Oh *that* Dennis."

Rebecca never lost her sense of continuity. "Why do we have to go see him if we're going somewhere else?"

"He's got the keys."

"The keys to what?"

"To the studio. We're going to do some recording tonight." Jon said enthusiastically.

"That sounds exciting. Can we come?"

"Wouldn't do it without you!" Jon squeezed his inspirations again and they moved closer to the street to hail a cab. The rain had tapered to a light mist, and traffic around the square was moving slowly, so they walked, Jon leaning on the women for support, to the wide thoroughfare of nearby 14th Street. Union Square was lined with eateries and they passed directly in front of the Lebanese restaurant where Rhamin and Homa were having dinner. Looking through the fogged window, Homa thought she recognized Jon and Rebecca, but couldn't be sure.

As expected, they had no trouble attracting the attention of a cab cruising for fares on 14th Street. The trio wedged themselves into the back seat for the short ride to the West Village.

CHAPTER 26

Detective Gillingham and Ralph were sitting in their car eating fish and chips near the Laden Imports warehouse. They were watching a soccer match through the window of the bar that made their dinner. Detective Falin and Rudy were parked outside a posh apartment building on Park Avenue South waiting for Samani to finish her evening visit with her uptown friends. Detectives Ferguson and Ailes, the two vice detectives who had busted Bosco Dish's roadies, had joined Officer Hemming at The Black Sheep to follow up on their investigation. Cowboy Travis was guarding the door when Jon's cab stopped to let out passengers.

He recognized Jon immediately this time. "Cells, what's happening?"

"Hey, Travis." Jon saw the door wide open and the entry rope missing. "No cover tonight?" Monica and Rebecca stood behind him.

"We don't know if there's going to be a show."

"Who was supposed to go on?"

"Bosco Dish; they got busted."

"No shit?" Jon's mood kept getting better.

"Yeah, the roadies and most of the equipment are at the police station. The Pecorinos are trying to get them out in time to play but we don't know what's going to happen."

Jon stifled a smirk. "Dennis around?"

"Go and see for yourself." Travis tipped his cowboy hat and invited them in. "How you all doing tonight, ladies?" He left his post and followed them.

The atmosphere inside the club was unsettled. The house lights were up and no one was on the stage. Random patrons were talking loudly and milling around the clutter of chairs and tables. Jon escorted his guests to the bar and ordered them drinks before setting off in search of Dennis. Rebecca recognized Officer Hemming, sitting at the end of the bar. She turned her back so he wouldn't see her face. Monica spotted Bosco Dish's manager, Donny, walking in her direction with Bruce, the bass player, in tow. Donny was too preoccupied to notice them and kept walking, but Bruce recognized them and stopped. "Hey, Ladies. Good to see you again. Glad you could make it."

Monica couldn't believe that she had thought he was kind of cute the night before. His annoying, squeaky voice and loose-jawed boyish grin made him look childish, and his head full of bouncy curls was as full as hers. "Oh hi... Bruce? Right?" She distanced herself.

Bruce couldn't remember her name. "That's me! Can't talk now; we're going on soon. Maybe we'll see you after the show? Big party tonight at the hotel if you're around," he lied and escaped into the crowd.

Monica moved closer to Rebecca for protection from Detectives Ferguson and Ailes, who were sizing them up from a few stools down.

"Where's Jon?" Rebecca asked warily, leaning into Monica and looking around for more impending confrontations.

"I can't wait to get out of this place," Monica said as they nursed their drinks and fended off the attention of familiar faces.

Jon found Dennis huddled in the back room with Cowboy Travis, whose pasty skin and sallow eyes made him look like a burly vampire recently escaped from a Dallas cemetery. A baggie of pot lay rolled up on top of an old speaker cabinet, and Dennis was studiously watching as Travis separated a sizable mound of white powder into two even piles on a thick slab of broken glass.

"Just in time, Slide." Dennis greeted Jon. "Cowboy and I are almost finished cutting the cards, so grab a seat and we'll deal you in."

"Thanks, man." Jon leaned up against the wall and waited as Travis carefully guided the white powder into folded paper bindles made from a glossy magazine cover. Travis wiped the residue off the glass with his finger and tasted it, then handed Dennis one of the bindles and a baggie with several thin joints.

Dennis thanked him. "That should last us a while." Salivating, he examined the stash. "Business doing pleasure with you." He fived Travis and held his baggie up to the light where Jon could admire it. "Tonight's a bust, so I'm going to let Richard take over the booth," he told Travis. "We'll be over at the studio if anyone needs me. I don't know where Sonya and Nigel are, but keep a rope on Dante if he shows up. It's your rodeo now, Cowboy."

Travis gathered up his share of the booty and sauntered into the public area like a deputized sheriff. Without the Pecorinos, Dennis or Nigel there, he was next in the line of authority; his own interpretation of frontier justice, which consisted mostly of leaning against the wall with a toothpick in his mouth like a small town sheriff waiting for trouble.

Dennis and Jon stopped by the control room to give Richard a joint and some final instructions, then found Monica and Rebecca huddled together defensively at the bar. Jon's blood pressure rose at the sight of Officer Hemming's porcine face and crew cut, sharing secrets with the bartender. Detectives Ailes and Ferguson, who were seated far enough away from Officer Hemming to preserve their anonymity, heard Donny rant to Dennis about roadies, cops, and equipment rentals without knowing that the cops responsible for the bust were seated right behind him. Donny was too preoccupied with band business to do more than nod to Rebecca and Monica, who, along with Jon, were waiting for him to finish talking to Dennis so they could leave. Sniffling and hassled, Donny hammered out some logistics with Dennis in rock and roll shorthand, and after they finished talking, Donny swung a fake punch in Jon's direction as a way of saying hello. But Jon hadn't been paying attention to the conversation and misinterpreted the gesture as a threat. He tightened his grip on his drink glass, and was ready to use it as a weapon, but Dennis stopped him before he acted. A loud banging from the stage diverted everyone's attention.

Freddy's drum set was still in place from the night before, and Richard smacked the skins a few more times to check for rattles. The crowd took notice, and the possibility that there might be a show increased the murmur. Then Dante Pecorino and his slutty companion, Starla, sleazed in from the doorway and everyone scattered or froze. Dennis led Jon and the New Jersey girls out the back exit before Dante noticed them.

Dante Pecorino headed straight for the stage like he owned the place – because he did. Dante climbed onto the stage, and Starla joined Reggie and Sonya at a table. Donny met up with Dante in front of the drum set. They exchanged a ritualized gumba hand greeting.

"I heard what happened," Dante slurred. "We made some phone calls."

Donny was still furious. "Fucking cops!"

"They're just doing their job, man." Dante wiped his nose with the sleeve of his $800 lambskin jacket and sniffled. "We'll have everything straightened out soon. Wanna get high?" He made a fisted hand gesture.

"Always."

They went behind the curtain at the back of the stage. Dante spooned blasts from his coke vial as they talked.

"Where've you been, man?" Donny asked as he swallowed his hit and wiped his nose.

Dante rounded his lips into a circle and darted his tongue in and out like the devil he was. "Getting my dick sucked. I got your message but I was too busy to listen to the whole thing." During the steady descent of his twenties, Dante's baser instincts had taken over his life. His innocence had been consumed by alcohol, tobacco, sex, and every other drug he could get his hands on; he wasn't very good at separating days into 24-hour periods anymore; and his all night, drug-induced, fuckfest with Starla had lasted well into Friday morning, so by the time he woke up and got to the club, he wasn't sure what day it was. Donny had called him when the ambulance came to pick up Randi the night before, but Dante had been too twisted to pick up the phone. He had heard Donny leave the message about Randi and the hospital and roadies and the police, but didn't care and figured he would get the whole story later.

"Why the hell do I bother calling you?" Donny gruffed, backing away from the foul smell of Dante's rotting teeth.

"Because you need me, asshole." Trash talk was the language they spoke, and friends since high school, their relationship hadn't fundamentally changed.

"A lot of help you are," Donny complained. "My girlfriend's in the hospital and my roadies are in jail. And I need you for what asshole?" Donny was big and tough and full of himself. He viewed the protection of his undersized degenerate friend from a wealthy family as a form of employment, with free drugs as interest payments.

Dante knew his role. "You need me to get you and your little bitch high and your buddies out of the slammer."

"You're full of shit. I called your brother when you didn't answer. Your old man already made a call about the roadies."

"Yeah, I heard," Dante lied. "So why is Randi back in the hospital? What'd you do to her this time?"

"I don't know what's the matter with her this time." He snorted dismissively. "Let's go see what Freddy's up to."

Freddy was standing in a dressing room with his shirt off, applying cologne when they came in. "What's going on with the gear?" he asked Donny through the mirror.

"We've got some borrowed equipment on the way. The guys are at a restaurant around the corner. I'll go get them when the instruments get here."

"What about the crew? They still locked up?"

"Not for long," Dante assured him. "My old man knows the precinct Captain."

"Where's Randi? Is she okay?" Freddy asked Donny.

"The hospital wouldn't let her go. Maybe tomorrow."

Dante lit a cigarette and blew the smoke in Freddy's direction. Freddy objected. "Do you mind?"

"Mind what?"

"Blowing that smoke outside?" Freddy clarified.

"I'll blow it up your ass if I want to," Dante snarled, drawing a long drag. He was about to puff it in Freddy's face but Donny pushed him into the hallway.

"What's the matter with you, man? Freddy's got to sing tonight."

"All the peasants got to sing for their supper," Dante sniggered as Donny closed the dressing room door. "Just make sure he remembers who he's working for," Dante taunted through the door as Donny pushed him away. He and Donny came back out into the club and joined Starla and Sonya at Reggie's table.

It was raining lightly when Rebecca, Monica, and Jon emerged from the alleyway behind the club. Dennis's car was too small for them all to fit, so he drove alone, leaving the other three to catch a cab. There weren't too many empties in that part of town on a wet Friday night, but one conveniently stopped to disgorge its passenger right in front of the club. It was Ameliah, and she was surprised to see her friends standing with Jon in front of her. "I can't believe you just left me there!" she huffed.

"We thought you wanted to stay at the tavern with your lawyer friends," Monica sassed.

The weather discouraged a lengthy conversation. "Well, I would have stayed but Freddy is expecting me here. Have a great time, if that's possible with him," Ameliah sniped, showing her disapproval with a catty smirk before she went inside. Monica, Jon, and Rebecca slid into the back seat of the taxi and gave the driver the address of Heard Tracks.

CHAPTER 27

The short cab ride through Friday night traffic ended in front of a nondescript, dark, metal door in lower Manhattan. Jon pushed the buzzer next to a piece of paper with the handwritten word "studio" taped to the doorjamb. Entry into the exclusive world of multi-track recording was an invitation-only affair, and the location of the doorbell was a carefully guarded secret. Anonymity was a critical element of survival because robbers saw the cache of expensive equipment as an inviting target; clients, some indulging in illegal stimulants, needed to avoid detection; and well known artists who could afford the $1000 a day card rate of fully equipped studios like Heard Tracks sought refuge from the pressures of notoriety in the secretive comforts of a well appointed creative environment.

"Yes?" a barely intelligible voice came through the hidden intercom.

"What it is," Jon spoke the passwords and pushed the buzzing door open. Rebecca and Monica followed. No one was at the substantial, wood-paneled reception desk that guarded the dark office behind it. Jon opened a thick airlock door and they entered a dimly lit hallway with carpeted walls and a wooden bumper rail at waist height. Monica and Rebecca, who had never been inside a studio, shared their excitement with whispers and grins. Jon yanked the oversized handle on the first of two lead-lined, soundproof doors toward him, and stiff-armed the second door open. Their noses were greeted with the distinct smell of burning electronics before they actually set foot in the control room.

Thousands of capacitors, resistors, and op amps sizzled away inside the dozing equipment. Banks of rheostatic ceiling lights, set at twilight, illuminated the comfortable combination living room and cockpit. Three leather chairs on rollers were tucked neatly under the front of the expansive mix desk, which was populated with densely packed rows of buttons and knobs. The control surface extended four feet forward, elevating slightly upwards from the engineer chairs, and was met by a row of vertical meters, running perpendicular to their matched channels at a seventy-five- degree angle. Except for the legs, the whole console was encased in the custom wood frame, and the ten-foot-long, blinking, wood and metal centerpiece took up half the width of the room. It sat in front of an expansive, triple-paned plate glass window that separated the control room from the studio area. Angled walls, covered in a zigzag pattern of wooden slats and carpet, followed the reverse cathedral ceiling whose lowest point was directly over the engineer's seat.

Jon was loved being in the studio. He ensconced his impressionable guests in the stuffed leather couch that sat parallel to the console at the back of the room. "You wait here and I'll go find Dennis," he instructed before leaving.

The girls settled in to the soft Naugahyde sofa, squirming and gushing like backstage guests. "This is so cool!" Monica whispered as she slid to one side and petted the smooth, shiny fabric. Rebecca giggled while trying to make sense out of the strange equipment with hundreds of twinkling lights and meters. The silence was alive with the low frequency humming of invisible motors, accompanied by a barely audible whistle of moving air. Fixated by the static charge of electricity, and intimidated by their unfamiliar surroundings, the girls became self-conscious and stopped talking. Only the sounds of their rustling clothes and nervous breathing interrupted the timeless spell of sensory deprivation. A moving image, refracted in the plate glass window in front of the console, caught their eye and they stood up to see.

As they watched, the colored lights in the studio on the other side of the glass rose like a slow moonrise on an alien planet. A high-ceilinged space, cluttered with movable partitions and a straggly forest of microphone stands, glowed into view. Off to one side, the stout black legs of a grand piano peeked out from a fitted quilt cover that rested on a triple wheeled Colson dolly. An overdub area had been arranged in the center of the room, and Jon was holding a guitar as he and Dennis spoke. Standing right in front of the glass, Monica and Rebecca could see them talking and pointing, but were unable to hear any of the conversation. Like fascinated visitors to an aquarium, their refracted reflections floated in the colored lights on both sides of the glass. Jon put the guitar on a stand and disappeared from view, and a moment later the pneumatic whoosh of the control room door startled them when he re-entered the control room from behind. Tired and disoriented, Rebecca felt lightheaded and sat on the back sofa, while Monica accepted Jon's offer to sit next to him at the console. He pressed a button on the wheeled remote and awakened a huge Studer tape recorder in the corner. Spinning a heavy reel of tape, two inches wide and a half-mile long, the machine whirred to life. Jon, who wasn't that familiar with the console, pressed a few exploratory buttons, which sent a grating screech of high-speed blabber through the speakers. Embarrassed, he frantically pecked at the buttons, twisting knobs back and forth and moving faders up and down, trying to dim the unpleasant noise. Monica cringed and Rebecca covered her ears, and the first thing Dennis did when he hurried back in was to lean over the console and mute the stereo bus.

"Sorry," Jon apologized to Monica, whose level of awake had instantly gone up three notches. Rebecca sank further into the sofa, the victim of sonic abuse and fatigue.

Studio denizens like Dennis were unfazed by the sudden outbursts of extraterrestrial shrieks, explosive cracks, and electrifying buzzes that regularly visit sessions like audible meteor showers. "Got to warm those ears up anyhow. Roll it back to the top," he instructed Jon while making adjustments to the monitoring section in front of him.

"*Never been down to Houston,*" a man's tenor vocal soared as Dennis slid the main attenuators lower to prevent another mishap. Back in control, Dennis plugged two twelve-inch cables into the densely packed 500-point patch bay, checked the settings on a Lexicon signal processor mounted above him in the ceiling, and settled into his captain's chair. He cued Jon to press play again, and the VU meters above each channel strip bobbed into action like a dance team where only some of the members knew the routine. No sound accompanied the jumping needles until Dennis unmuted the channels as the tape spooled forward at a thirty inches-per-second. Satisfied with the setup, Dennis took out his coke bottle and poured a little pile onto the special mirror that lived in the drawer underneath the patch bay.

Jon pecked a few channels off and on to hear snippets of what was recorded on each track; a particularly urgent bass part livened up the room with a fat bouncing thump.

Overly stimulated, Monica's excitement descended below her waist. She swiveled her chair to make eye contact with Rebecca. "You okay?" she mouthed.

The music stopped when the tape recorder went into rewind, and Rebecca, prone and fading, was able to make herself heard. "It's been a long day and I've got a little headache. Is it okay if I just lie down here?" No one objected, so she pulled up her knees, rested her head on the upholstered arm of the sofa, and closed her eyes.

"Tootski?" Dennis asked, passing the small mirror to Jon. Jon quickly snorted two short lines with the rolled up bill. Then he passed the tray to Monica, who checked to make sure Rebecca wasn't watching before she partook.

"Take another breath of hollow air," Jon sang as the coke numbed the back of his throat. "This calls for a smoke." *12

"Outside, my man, you know the rules," Dennis reminded him.

Jon went to the back lounge area to satisfy his nicotine craving. He leafed through the industry magazines strewn on the low table in front of the sofa as he smoked. Recording studios were a cult business and *Mix Magazine* was the only widely read studio publication. In it, boutique manufacturers spent their entire advertising budget on close up photos of anodized studio equipment that touted elevated thresholds, balanced outputs, and minimal harmonic distortion. The glossy ads were interspersed with in-depth interviews of engineers, producers, and artists, and the secrets revealed in those articles were an important source of information for anyone interested in making records. Jon read the articles whenever he got the chance, and the time he spent learning the tricks of the trade and studying how the equipment worked were some of his best moments of clarity. His volatile personality and volcanic urges were perfectly suited for the sonic arts, and he knew that the ability to technically capture those raw emotions defined his career. He was deep in cogitation, devouring audio arcanum, when Monica found him.

"Where's the ladies room?" she asked, giddily shifting her weight in the doorway.

"Over there." Jon pointed, unaware of her emotional state. He went back to his magazine. The air conditioning cycled on, clearing out the cigarette smoke, and by the time Monica returned, her re-applied scent was potent enough to announce her intentions before Jon understood them.

Feeling guilty, she got close enough to see the magazine. "What are you reading?"

"Just some stuff about equipment," Jon answered, still oblivious to her state of mind.

"Wow, what is that?" Monica pointed to a close-up of a fat chromed microphone hanging upside down in a strange wire basket.

"That's a Neumann. It sounds great."

Monica got closer, as if to read the fine print. "What's so special about it?"

"Well, Neumanns – " Jon's explanation was cut short by Monica's knee touching his thigh and he stopped reading. She got closer, and putting her hand on his shoulder for balance, extended one leg in the air as if she was doing a dance exercise. Jon wasn't sure what she was doing when suddenly, using him for balance, she swung her extended leg over his thighs and landed her foot on the other side of where he was sitting. Her new position put her breasts level with Jon's face as she straddled his lap without sitting down.

"Is this okay?" she asked, putting her arms around his head and pulling him closer.

Forgetting everything that a moment ago had seemed so interesting, Jon slid his hands around her waist and inhaled her sexuality. Responding to his grip on her buttocks, Monica pushed her pelvis against his chest and pulled his hair with splayed fingers. Responsively, Jon tilted his head back. She leaned down and indulged a passionate kiss on his mouth. Jon tried to hold her, but a moment later she squirmed away as agilely as she had appeared. She was standing on the other side of the table straightening her shirt before he knew how she got there. "Later," she promised.

Fully aroused and limping, he let himself be led by hand back to the control room, where he was rewarded with another wet kiss just before opening the door. Rebecca was asleep on the couch, and

Dennis was concentrating on the mixing desk, and their romance remained undetected.

"*Never been down to Houston. Never been to outer space,*" the vocal loped through the speakers over a driving bass line. Only when the tape went into rewind was it quiet enough to speak.

"Here's where I need your guitar." Dennis said, pressing play and muting the vocal over the same section they had just heard. Anticipatory keyboard stabs rendered the chords, and Jon's blood returned to his brain as he tried to translate Dennis's arm waving instructions into notes.

The progression had some surprising stops, and it took an entire pass before Jon said, "Got it. I'll go tune up and let's put this to bed." Out in the studio, he took a sunburst Stratocaster from its stand and found A 440 on the nearby piano. He could hear the track playing through the headphones as he plugged into the 100-watt Marshall head next to him. Cranging a chord through the four-by-four cabinet in the isolation booth, he checked his tuning by ear as the tape sped backwards. He was ready to play by the time the red light over the control room window went on, fumbled through the herky-jerky changes the for first few verses, and was on his game by the time the chorus repeated for the second time. The unpredictable stops brought out the minimalist in him. With his glass slide, Jon wailed long tones on the tonic, pausing to make adjustments to the pick-ups until he was satisfied with the distortion level. The track went back into rewind, and when it started again, he stayed with the whole-note feel, adding minor thirds, fifths, and flatted sevenths to the verses. Then, standing with his legs apart and his eyes closed, he dug into the vamp with short bending thrusts. Strong muscular fingers, tipped with permanent calluses, enabled him to strangle an undulating howl out of the Strat and Marshall rig, and he was well into the tag by the time his uncontrollable foot stomp sent a shiver of pain through his injured extremity, reminding his etheric body where his corporal one lived.

"Perfect!" Dennis's voice boomed through the talkback speakers. "Come on in."

Jon limped his way into a rolling swivel chair behind the console. He put his foot up on the arm of the chair Monica was sitting in. "It's bleeding again." She pointed to his newly splotched medical boot. "Does it hurt?"

The playback roared out of the speakers with Jon's solo dominating the room. He rested his injured foot on Monica's thigh, wiggling his bandaged toes as if he were tickling her.

"The doctor told you to take it easy," Rebecca advised from the sofa, missing the romantic signal broadcast.

Dennis was tweaking the invisible parameters of sound when a movement in the small black and white TV monitor below the main speakers caught his eye. He abruptly muted the playback and closed the stash drawer. Moments later, the control room door opened and Nigel, the studio manager, appeared in the doorway with two musicians behind him.

"Hey, Dennis, sorry to interrupt." Nigel announced himself. "I just want to show these guys the room." His quick assessment allowed that the room was presentable, and he entered with a respectful nod to the session in progress. "How's it going, mate?"

"Great, man," Dennis replied succinctly, wanting to keep the visit as short as possible.

The visitors took a cursory inventory of the surroundings, looking carefully at the equipment as Nigel pointed out the highlights in studio shorthand. "MCI 536, eight bus with twenty-four returns, Studer A80, four Drawmers *and* a DBX rack, two 1176's and an LA 2A, H3000, Roland DDLs, Yamaha Rev 5, Lexicon Prime Time, PCM 70 and 224XL, ATR 102, four TAD 15's upstairs actively passed with NS 10's and an awfultone," he recited.

The musicians nodded as if they understood everything while eying the female talent on the back couch.

"Got anything we can hear?" one asked.

Nigel followed protocol. "Dennis?"

"Well, I can play you the wailing solo we just laid down," Dennis volunteered, motioning the guests to the mix center. Jon wheeled his chair to the back of the room near the couch. Dennis knew that part of his job was sales. "Don't I know you?" He addressed the taller of the two longhaired musicians. "You ever play The Black Sheep?" he asked, knowing it was a safe guess and a good way to make small talk.

"Yeah, we played that last year. I thought you looked familiar. You're the sound guy there, right?"

"That's me. I'm Dennis and you are...?"

"Mark, Mark Mason, but everybody calls me Mase. This is my bass player, Rocky." He slapped Dennis five with a crooked grin. "How you been, man?"

"Great, man. What was the name of your group again?"

"Mase and Dixon, only there is no Dixon." Mase chuckled at his own joke with a throaty smoker's rasp.

"Yeah, that's right," Dennis remembered them with an invisible cringe; pressing play before he had to lie about how much he liked them. The track boomed through the mains. Dennis adjusted levels while Nigel sized up his prospects, who were duly impressed, embracing the groove with bobbing shoulders and bending knees. When playback finished, conversation began again.

"Bitchin solo!" Mase complimented. "Who's playing that guitar?"

"Jon Cells. We just laid it down." Dennis pointed to Jon.

"Dude, you got to do some of that on my record."

"No problem, man," Jon accepted. "What'd you say your name was?"

"Mark Mason. Everybody calls me Mase. They call you Cells?"

"Cells, Slide, Jon, whatever."

"How can I get a hold of you? Where you gigging?"

"I'm taking some time off, but Dennis knows how to get a hold of me."

"We're thinking of coming in to record here in a few weeks. Maybe you can stop in. I really dig your playing."

"Sure thing." Jon humored him, never expecting to see him again.

"Okay, let's leave these guys to do their thing," Nigel interjected, wrapping up the visit and escorting Mase and Rocky out of the room. "I'll see you tomorrow," he added before closing the door.

"I think I need to go home," Rebecca yawned. "It's been a long day," she said, staring blearily at Jon's bandaged foot.

Monica was wide-awake. "Well, *I'm* not ready to go yet."

"You're not tired?" Rebecca asked.

"Not really. Maybe we should get you a cab."

Rebecca was upset at the idea of being abandoned by her friend, who seemed to be having a better time than she was. "How am I going to get a cab down here at this hour? It's probably still raining and I don't want to walk to the subway at night by myself."

"We can borrow an umbrella and I'll walk you to the station. It's only a few blocks away." Monica suggested a solution that wouldn't cut her own night short.

Jon volunteered to help. "I'll walk with you, too."

"What about your foot?" Rebecca pointed out. "You shouldn't be walking any more than you have to."

Dennis came up with the solution. "Why don't you drive her? My car can fit three if someone squeezes into the back seat."

"Who's going to drive us?"

"I can drive," Jon offered.

Dennis was anxious to continue the session and tossed Jon the keys. "I'm parked in the lot next door. I'll see you on the monitor when you get back."

Rebecca acquiesced. Monica led the trio down the hall and out the door onto the street. They found Dennis's car and Monica wedged herself sideways in the back. Rebecca took the passenger's seat and Jon maneuvered himself into the driver's. Gingerly, he placed his injured foot on the accelerator.

Rebecca was never too tired to be cautious. "You sure you're going to be able to drive?" she asked warily.

"I don't know, but I'll give it a try." Jon babied the clutch and inched the car out of the cramped spot in reverse. "Where to?" he asked, pointing the car forward.

Monica assumed control from the back seat. "We live in the Riverside Apartments. They're on the east side near 14th Street. Is that too far for you to drive?"

"Looks like we've got enough gas," Jon noted and took off. Living in the city, he hadn't driven a sports car for a while and enjoyed winding the rotary engine up and popping the clutch. The vibration of the shifter in his right hand and Monica's smile from the back seat energized his driving.

Rebecca held on through the turns, trying to keep hers eyes open. "Honestly, I don't know how you guys are still awake," she mumbled, unable to see Jon and Monica exchanging glances through the rear view mirror as they sped their way through the mostly empty, wet streets. Ten minutes later they pulled up in front of the Riverside Apartments. Rebecca got out of the passenger's seat and Monica extricated herself from the back. Standing in a light rain, Monica and gave Rebecca a hug good night.

"Are you sure you're going to be okay?" Rebecca asked, concerned but too tired to argue.

"I'll be home in a while. Jon can drive me," Monica assured her as she slipped into the passenger's seat. "I slept late today and only taught two classes, so don't worry about me. You get some sleep, and I'll see you in the morning."

Rebecca nodded, went inside, and was in bed sleeping within six minutes.

Monica put her hand on Jon's leg as they headed back downtown, their anticipation mounting with each thrust of the shifter. Back at the studio, they re-parked the car, pressed the studio door button, and waved at the hidden camera. Dennis saw them in the monitor and buzzed them back in. Playing pinching games down the hallway, they tasted a long wet kiss before re- entering the control room.

"What was in the air?
It's a Chemical Reaction." *13

Jon's song blared out of the speakers as they entered the control room. He hadn't heard the track for months, and it jolted through his body like a lightning strike. Momentarily forgetting about Monica and his injured foot, he marched in place with a performer's conviction, crowing along with the lyrics. Monica reached through the field of kinetic energy that surrounded him and felt a surge of ungrounded electricity pass through her as she touched his arm. Dennis let the chorus refrain a few times before hitting the rewind button. The babble of backwards chipmunks added to the excitement.

"What did you do to that track?" Jon asked, fiving Dennis his approval.

"Just a tweak here and there," Dennis understated his abilities.

Monica felt the magic. "That sounded great. Whose song is that?"

"Some guy I used to know," Jon answered, brushing aside her compliment. Hearing how close it was to perfection made him feel that much further away.

"Want to do a guitar solo?" Dennis asked. "We're all set up and you're obviously feeling it."

"Feeling it for sure," Jon agreed, cupping Monica's buttocks with his hand as she brushed her breasts against his arm.

"Need another toot?" Dennis opened the stash drawer and handed him the mirror. Four thin lines were already prepared.

"Ladies first." Jon handed the straw to Monica, who erased her lines with two quick snorts before handing it back.

Jon ingested his share and adjusted the angle of excitement growing in his pants. "This is turning out better than I expected," he said, smacking the numb on his lips.

Monica sat next to Dennis at the console as he dialed in an overdub mix. Jon went out to the guitar setup in the studio and put on headphones. The levels were still set from the last track, and Jon knew all the changes in his own song, so there were more than enough guitar licks recorded by the time they had rolled through it twice. He came back into the control room to listen to the play-back while standing behind Monica, massaging her appreciative shoulders as he bent to the uneven, ska-based rhythm.

"Want to work on another track?" Dennis asked during rewind.

"You're too good to me."

"No, you're too good. No telling how far you might go if you can stay out of trouble," Dennis said meaningfully.

Jon flinched. "Don't go killing the vibe, man."

Dennis went to the corner and looked through the row of two-inch masters lined up on the floor. "Which one do you want to work on next?"

"Can we try some lyrics?"

"Sure. Which track do you want me to put up?"

"Let's try the Lonely song. I feel a whole new set of lyrics coming on." His hands slid off Monica's shoulders and onto her chest. She leaned back to look up at him and was greeted by another kiss and groping hands.

"Okay, I've got it here, heads out," Dennis spoke aloud as he lifted the heavy reel and positioned it on the take-up hub. He threaded the tape through the tension arm, across the heads, and onto the pinch roller before tucking the loose end into the empty supply reel. Pressing rewind, the tape started its half-mile journey backward. "I'll go set up a vocal mic while this is going and leave you two love birds alone for a minute. Don't do anything I couldn't do." Dennis winked, enjoying the spectacle of foreplay almost as much as the experience.

After he left, Monica interrupted the fondling session. "What kind of trouble was he talking about?" she asked, pushing Jon's hands away gently.

"Nothing to worry about. Just wrong place wrong time." Jon tried to pinch her.

She stopped him. "What happened?"

Jon wasn't used to talking about his problems. "Me and this guy kinda had a disagreement after a gig and someone called the cops." He tried to squeeze the curiosity out of her but it didn't work.

"Did you get arrested?"

"Well, they arrested him first, but then they found some coke on me, so they got me too."

Monica had a hard time trusting men ever since her older brother got mixed up in a gang. "Is that all?"

Jon gave up trying to be romantic. "Why are we talking about this anyway?"

"All set man," Dennis announced when he came back in. Then he saw that Jon had lost the glint of enthusiasm. "Wassa matter, Soldier Boy; out of ammunition?" Dennis streeted him.

"I was going to ask you about that," Monica interjected. "How did you get that Soldier name? Were you in the army?"

"Yeah, he was in the Army *and* the Leggy. Maybe you should tell her how you got the name Cells while you're at it," Dennis quipped, expanding the diversion.

Jon wasn't amused. "Now there's some real inspiration. Let's play twenty questions and then I'll go out and sing a great vocal."

Jon got up and his foot began to throb again. He shifted his weight with a noticeable wince.

"Oh, I'm sorry." Monica wheeled her chair nearer. "I didn't mean to upset you. Please forgive me." She put her arms around him, squeezing her face into his stomach.

"There there." Jon petted her head like a house-cat.

"Meow meow," she purred affectionately. "All better?"

"That's more like it. I think I'm remembering the lyrics now." Fully prepared for session mood swings, Dennis passed a lit Manhattan Slim to the couple. They each took a potent toke. Dennis reset the counter to zero at the beginning of the track, and the next song sprang to life as he unmuted each channel, one at a time. The first eight strips were all drums, and as he made his way left to right, other instruments joined the beating. A sparse bass line punctuated synths pads playing a suspended minor two-chord swing. Distorted, backward guitar chords, recorded with a highly processed transistor edge, washed over the verse changes. Then the unsteady B section, precariously balanced on top of the dissonant tension, tumbled slowly back into the reassurance of predicable changes like a disturbed child's tricycle falling down a flight of stairs. The progression repeated three times within two minutes and forty-six seconds.

"*I, I know that you're lonely,*" Jon sang along with the only lyrics he was sure of while Dennis worked the sounds into a pulsating, coherent whole that basked them in the super realism rarely heard outside a tuned control room. Elevated by her marijuana intake, Monica lost sight of earth and drifted into the musical atmosphere. Jon scribbled words in the empty area of an advertisement in *Mix Magazine* with a pen he had found. Then he tore out the page and peeled some splicing tape off the roll next to the two track. Operating wordlessly in a routine they had developed over the years, he nodded to Dennis as he went into the studio. A squat, chromed Neumann U67, just like the one he had been admiring in the magazine, was already hanging upside down from a substantial Atlas boom stand.

"Speak to me oh great one," Dennis intoned through the talk-back as Jon adjusted his headphones.

"*Oh I, I know that you're lonely.*" Jon sang the words over and over again in time to the music until he entered a state of vocal readiness.

"A little more for the level devils. Is that as loud as you're going to go, Joe?" Dennis asked, backing down the gain in anticipation of the answer.

Jon moved closer to the mic and delivered his new B section lyrics with a breathy urgency that crept into Monica's panties. "*First I'm gonna pick you up by your lace and squeeze you real hard.*"

"Five fingers, Romeo," Dennis reminded him. Jon put his hand out sideways, with his thumb touching his lips and his pinky touching the pop screen in front of the microphone. He taped the new lyrics to the pop screen stand and stood with his legs apart like a gunslinger at high noon as the intro rolled by. The red record light lit and he fired away.

> "*Oh I, I know that you're lonely.*
> *But I, I know what to do.*
> *And you, you don't want to listen.*
> *But you, you're missin' it too.*"
> *Seven hundred midgets on the sidewalk*
> *Awful busy talking.*
> *When the parks let out*
> *The candles started streaming up the avenue.*
> *Twenty minutes later in a service elevator*
> *I saw you talking.*
> *Wondering about*
> *Something I'm supposed to do,*
> *About you.*

Oh I, I know that you're lonely.
And you, you know that it's true.
First I'm gonna pick you up by your lace
And squeeze you real hard.
Then I'm gonna take you to a different place
And XXXX on your face." *14

Dennis knew it was a keeper halfway through when Jon didn't stumble over the cadent wording. The kissing smacks on the last line clipped just hard enough to activate tape saturation, breaking like a whitecap on top of the moody undulating changes. Jon re-entered the control room, moist with perspiration, like a proud surfer emerging from the barrel of a wave.

He wiped his forehead with his sleeve. "Let me hear that back."

"Oh, you're gonna like it," Dennis assured him.

Monica wheeled her chair in front of Jon. He put his hands on her shoulders and admired his reflection in the control room glass while the satisfying sound waves drenched his ego.

"Ouch!" Monica shrieked as he dug his excited fingers into her shoulder muscles.

Dennis saw Jon's foot bleeding as the rewind whir buzzed through their evening fog. "I think we better quit while we're ahead."

Jon didn't want the moment to end. "You're kidding?" His grip on Monica softened into a rub.

"Too much of a good thing," Dennis explained. "We have the studio all weekend. I told Priscilla I'd be coming by to see her," he added, hoping Jon would remember who Priscilla was.

Monica left for a visit to the ladies room. Jon and Dennis conferred.

"We have the studio all weekend?" Jon confirmed.

"Yeah, I told you we did."

"No one else is going to come in?"

"What do you mean? Why do you want to know?"

"Can I sleep here?" Jon showed off his bandaged foot. "It's rainy and...." A mischievous smirk crept over his lips. "Who's going to know?"

Dennis tried to resist. "I'm going to know, and anyone who shows up here unannounced is going to know. I don't want to get in trouble."

"So that's a yes?" Jon bear hugged him. "I love you man."

Dennis cracked a grin. "I don't want to leave you the keys because I promised Nigel I'd lock up. You'll have to stay here until I get back tomorrow. Deal?"

"Deal. If we need to go out for something, I can send Monica and buzz her back in."

"She's staying too?"

"Well, duh!"

Dennis smiled. "You filthy animal. Don't mess this up. I told Nigel we would have three tracks mixed by Monday."

"Whose tracks? Mine?"

"Of course. How do you think we got the studio time?"

"Huh? What aren't you saying?"

"What I am telling you is that Nigel thinks he can put together a record deal for you and he's specking us the time so that we can get him something to sell."

"I can't believe it! Why didn't you tell me? That's fucking fantastic!"

"What's so fantastic?" Monica asked, rejoining them.

Jon put his arms around her and lifted her off the floor. "Nigel's gonna get us a record deal!"

"Nigel said he was going to try," Dennis corrected him.

"Nigel knows what he's doing. Didn't he have something to do with getting those morons from Queens a deal."

"The Ramones? Yeah, but that was different."

"Whatever."

"I gotta go now. You stay here and I'll see you around noon."

"Wait. Why didn't you tell me this before?"

"I didn't want you to get all jerked up. Thought I'd catch you on the fresh."

"I'll give you some fresh." He slapped Dennis five. "Can you... uh...?" He put his arm around Monica.

"Check the drawer." Dennis said, extending the index and middle fingers from his right hand. "And gimme two." Jon touched the tip of his right index and middle fingers into Dennis' and they fit together like puzzle pieces.

Monica didn't know the plan. "Where's he going?"

"He has a date. He'll be back tomorrow."

"Tomorrow? We're leaving now?"

"No, we're staying."

"Staying? Here?"

"Yep, just you and me." He put his arm around her waist.

"Where are we going to sleep?"

"Who said anything about sleep?" He pinched her rear.

Monica blushed. "I better call home and tell my roommates not to worry."

She used the phone in the front office and was relieved that no one picked up. The rambling message she left about it being too late to catch a cab was as lame as her excuse that it was still raining. The 2 a.m. logic that she would tell them all about it tomorrow resolved most of her guilt.

SATURDAY, APRIL 17TH

CHAPTER 28

Rebecca woke up early and went to the kitchen to make coffee. She enjoyed having the common area to herself and retrieved the newspaper from the front door. She gazed blankly out the west-facing window at the giant domino assembly of buildings, spot-lit with trapezoids of morning sun. Yawning, she checked the blinking messages on their communal answering machine as the coffee pot dripped to life.

The first call was from her mother, who rambled on about siblings and school. Rebecca knew that the details would be repeated during the regular weekend phone call, so she skipped ahead to the next message. On it, Ameliah's melodramatic voice announced her plans to spend the night at the hotel with Freddy. Rebecca wasn't either jealous or impressed. The third message was a hang up, and it wasn't until she heard Monica's voice that her heart kicked into arrhythmia.

"Hi Becca and Amy. I won't be there when you wake up but I don't want you to worry." Monica rambled on unconvincingly about the reasons before saying, "I'll tell you about it later," in a half whisper, then hanging up.

Rebecca couldn't understand everything she said about the weather and cabs, and played the message again, listening for clues. She poured a cup of coffee and opened the door to Monica's room. The confirmation of Monica's empty bed made her feel strange. Scenes of the night before ran through her mind, and she wasn't sure what to think. She got a queasy feeling remembering when Jon hugged them both on the sidewalk in front of Shepherds Tavern, and the feeling germinated, sprouted, and blossomed into perspiration with caffeine fertilizer. Rebecca relived the failed foreplay of the night at The Black Sheep and blamed herself. Feeling guilty, she tried to connect her actions with Jon's injured foot. Then she tried to reinterpret the unspoken dialog in Reggie's car and resolve the attraction she felt pressed next to him in the taxi. Nothing made sense. She entertained the idea that Monica was mixed up in another caper like the time she stayed out all night with her brother's friends, but images of Jon's arm around Monica's waist continued to offer a more disturbing explanation. Coffee cup rings, moistening the newspaper like mushrooms after a rainy day, made reading difficult, so she decided to take a walk, hoping to stop her emotional fungus growth with fresh air. Dressing quickly, she breathed a sigh of relief as soon as she passed through the door to the street.

The air was warm and the rain had washed a layer of fumes and dust from the cityscape. Rebecca's optimistic pink and white tennis shoes squeaked on the dampened pavement as she headed uptown, staying as close to the East River as possible. Although naturally reserved and aloof, she still found comfort in the company of other people, even if they were complete strangers. Walking briskly, she acknowledged her emergent neighbors with a pleasant knowing smile that was the accepted visual currency New York pedestrians exchange. Saturday morning exercisers were walking out their workweek worries, stretching muscles that had cramped from the confinement of office politics and city living. Young mothers pushing strollers smiled proudly as Rebecca admired their charioted offspring. Shopkeepers swept the puddles and litter from in front of their stores, inviting weekend shoppers into arrangements of produce, clothes, and dry goods. The reduced weekend delivery truck, commuter bus, and car traffic flowed more easily through the busy streets that, for once, seemed wide enough to accommodate the population. Saturday morning in the residential areas of Manhattan always had the feel of the morning after a terrible disaster, when the survivors come out of hiding to see who had endured the pressures of the preceding week.

Unable to rid herself of the familiar feelings of alienation that haunt so many city dwellers, Rebecca left her neighborhood and wandered up 1st Avenue, zigzagging down sidewalks she had never traveled. With no particular destination in mind, she eventually wound her way to the oasis of Gramercy Park and stopped for a rest. The sycamore buds were almost open, and green tints poked through last year's dried seedpods in the manicured beds around their blotchy trunks. She sat on one of the park benches near a pigeon-feeding grandmother and longed for the natural world immersion of her suburban childhood. At the other end of the park, Agent Ralph Lowell trudged through the bright daylight like a recently unearthed mole, balancing two cups of coffee and breakfast sandwiches. Detective Gillingham waited nearby in their parked car with the windows down, listening to the news on the radio, trying to stay awake.

Rebecca thought about what her younger siblings would be doing on a beautiful spring day like this and what a surprise visit home might be like. Still pitching between nostalgia and abandonment, she got up and wandered through the northern exit of the park onto 20th Street. A uniformed doorman came out from his foyer to open the passenger door of a white Mercedes Benz. Rebecca had to stop to allow him room to welcome an immaculately dressed middle-aged woman in a casual pants suit, short heels, and wide brimmed hat tied with a scarf. The woman took his hand for balance as she stood a few feet in front of Rebecca.

The woman greeted her as their eyes met. "Rebecca?"

"Mrs. Monsouri?"

"Yes, dear child," she said with throaty smoothness. "How are you? I didn't know you lived close by." Samani was regal in public.

Rebecca was self-conscious and unprepared to run into her boss. "Oh, I don't. I was just out walking."

Detective Gillingham snapped some pictures with his telephoto lens.

"Would you like to come up for tea? Homa has told me how helpful you always are. I'm sure she'd love to see you." Rebecca didn't know what to say. She stood still as Samani adjusted the brim of her hat, reset her sunglasses and dismissed the driver with a queen's wave. The Benz angled back into the street and powered away. "Come now, or do you have another appointment?"

"No, I mean, is it okay? Is Homa here?"

"Yes, of course, come." Samani led Rebecca inside the polished marbled lobby and they waited in front of the elevator. The narrow, filigreed metal doors of the pre-war building opened slowly and they stepped inside. Rebecca had never been in an elevator so small that two people could barely stand without touching, and Samani's potent perfume was stifling inside the confined space. Ancient pulleys creaked and hummed, methodically lowering a counterweight while hoisting them upwards. Rebecca was dizzy from the fumes by the time they reached the eighth floor. She gasped for air as the doors greased open with a muted clack. Stepping into a worn carpeted hallway, she followed Samani's slow-heeled prance to the high-gloss, black lacquer apartment door, where a tiny peephole and two brass locksets stood guard.

"Hold this for me, dear," Samani instructed, handing Rebecca a small zippered brocade bag. Something heavy clunked inside. "Now maybe I can find my keys," she mumbled to herself. Rummaging through a supple oversized leather handbag, she pulled a braided wire ring, full of keys and charms, from the recesses. Like someone who had forgotten their glasses, Samani fumbled one key after another into the locks before the door to the apartment finally pushed opened over a small, tiled foyer floor. A powdery white carpet covered the adjacent living room that was decorated with matching monotone furniture. Shafts of morning sun passing through gossamer curtains, made the whole apartment glow, and an ablated mist of scented dust particles floated in the soft atmosphere. Visible only by refraction, a television mumbled and flashed blue accents from behind the sofa set.

"Homa? I'm home," Samani announced.

"Yes mama," a tired voice called from behind the sofa.

"I've brought a visitor."

"Hello, Doctor Nouri," Homa yawned.

"It's not Doctor Nouri." Samani waited to see if Homa had another guess. "But it's someone you know."

"Mother! I'm not dressed."

"I don't think Rebecca will care."

"Rebecca?" Homa sat up and peered over the back of the sofa.

"Good morning," Rebecca said nervously, standing in the entranceway still holding Samani's bag.

"Why is she here?" Homa asked her mother.

"She was out taking a walk on this beautiful morning. I saw her when Dr. Nouri dropped me off, so I invited her in. I hope that's okay with you. Shall I put up some tea?"

"Yes, please," Homa stuttered awake. "But I need to put on some clothes. Don't you dare look, Rebecca!" she warned, scampering to her bedroom wearing pajamas.

"Please, just put the bag down on that table and make yourself comfortable," Samani instructed, playing hostess as she went into the adjacent kitchen. "I know you've never seen Homa like this, but we are all ladies. You have sisters?"

Rebecca tried to relax in the strange surroundings. "One brother and two sisters. I'm the oldest."

"Then you know what a mother does. How do you take your tea?"

"Milk and sugar, or however you usually make it is fine." Rebecca seated herself at the small white kitchen table as Samani stood by the stove.

The boiling water whistled as Homa entered the kitchen.

"There she is." Samani welcomed her daughter to the tea party with a hug. Without thinking, Homa bent down and put her arm around Rebecca's shoulder, touching cheeks. Rebecca didn't know if the shock she felt was an unintentional part of the traditional Persian greeting, or static electricity from the thick white carpet. Homa straightened up, inhaled sharply, and retied her hair in a tight ponytail that flowed halfway down her back.

"I didn't know your hair was so long," Rebecca said admiringly. "You always wear it up at work.

Homa blushed. "I don't have any makeup on. I feel so naked."

"Don't be so hard on yourself," Samani soothed. "You always look beautiful. Here's your tea." She set a small porcelain pot decorated with tiny colorful flowers on the table, along with two dainty matching cups on saucers. "Sit down," she guided Homa. "You two visit for a while. I'm going to change."

Homa dropped a cube of sugar in each cup and poured the tea. The clinking and scraping of spoons against delicate china filled the conversation void. "Mother says you were out walking?" Homa said. "It's quite a long way from where you live."

"I just felt like taking a walk this morning." Rebecca said cautiously. "I needed some fresh air and it was so nice out after the rain," she explained. "I didn't know where you lived. I just sort of wandered here by accident." She sipped her tea.

Homa sipped hers. "You didn't know we lived here?"

"No. I've never even seen Gramercy Park. It's really nice. All the big trees in the middle of the city."

"Yes, we like it here much better than Queens, although sometimes I miss having a house and back yard." Homa stirred her cup and reflected.

"I miss my house and yard sometimes too," Rebecca agreed, eying the plush arctic landscape of the adjoining living room. "How long have you lived here?"

"We moved here right before my father.... About eight years." Homa shuffled her slippers nervously under the table. "What about you? How long have you been living in the city?"

"A little more than two years. We all moved here right after college."

"That's right, you live with your friends from New Jersey. Where are they today?"

Rebecca shrank noticeably. "I'm not sure."

"What's the matter? Did I say something wrong?"

"No."

"Would you like some more tea?"

Rebecca declined, keeping her eyes down. "No, thank you. I really should be going,"

"I'm sorry I upset you. Would you like to see my room before you go?"

"Okay, but just for a minute."

Homa led her through the living room and into a hallway. They stood at the doorway of Homa's bedroom before entering. It wasn't anything like Rebecca expected. One entire wall was full of glossy posters of television and movie stars, tacked and layered on top of one another at irregular angles so that they seemed to be interacting. The posters were cut out along the lines of their subjects' physical forms, and they were carefully pieced together in a sexually suggestive mosaic reminiscent of a crude ancient bas-relief. Rebecca's eyes bulged as she recognized Warren Beatty's head lying on the bottom half of a bikini worn by Brook Shields, whose lips met Jill Clayburgh, who sat over John Travolta's greased head, whose arm was around Richard Gere, whose hand was on one of Dyan Cannons' breasts while the other one was in Christopher Walken's mouth – and there were too many other recognizable faces and torsos and body parts to concentrate on.

"I did most of that when I was much younger," Homa explained, addressing Rebecca's unspoken shock.

Rebecca didn't know what to say. "It's…"

"It's disgusting," Samani's voice called from down the hall.

"Oh mother, be quiet. I think Rebecca likes it." Homa and Rebecca shared a conspiratorial smirk.

Rebecca pointed to the mural painted on the opposite wall. "What's that?"

Homa swelled with pride. "Persepolis, the ancient city of Iran. My father was obsessed with it."

"It looks beautiful. Did you paint it?"

"Yes. I copied it from some of my father's pictures when we first moved in. He helped me get it started. Do you like it?"

"She's a very good artist, don't you think?" Samani said supportively, coming up behind them.

Scattered assortments of people in native dress, drawn to scale, populated the wall-length mural of the fabled cultural capital of ancient Persia. The rectangular buildings, set on an elevated platform above the desert floor, were decorated with bands of color to simulate the original tile work. Giant stone columns with carved capstones in the shape of two-headed bulls could be seen holding up the three-dimensionally rendered flat roofs. Shadowed steps with ascending figures connected all the densely packed buildings together like an M.C. Escher inspiration. The areas outside the city center were green pastoral expanses, partitioned with tilled fields, roads, and waterways that came from distant mountains. Shepherds with flocks of domesticated animals and clusters of small houses completed the expanse of idyllic pastoral harmony that ended abruptly at the wall's edges.

"That was so long ago. I had a lot of dreams when I was young," Homa rued and withdrew.

"You're still young, my child," her mother said reassuringly. "Why don't you take Rebecca out for a meal? She's been the best worker we've ever had, so I'm sure we owe her at least that. Is that okay with you, Rebecca?"

"Okay, I guess."

"Do you really want to?" Homa searched Rebecca's eyes for confirmation.

"I haven't eaten yet today, so maybe food is a good idea," Rebecca admitted.

"There's a great Middle Eastern place around the corner. Does falafel sound good to you?"

"You always know what to order."

Homa tied her hair up with a scarf and put a light jacket on over her blousy shirt and jeans. Samani retreated to her bedroom.

"I'll see you in a while, Mother," Homa called out, slipping on her sandals near the door. But before leaving, she tossed a verbal grenade and waited for the explosion. "Did I tell you that Rhamin and I are going out tonight again?".

Samani came out in her loose-fitting housedress holding a magazine and glasses. "What? Rhamin – Rhamin Darius? He called you?" Her face was covered in a pasty layer of green skin conditioner.

"Yes, last night – and we went out to dinner." Homa let the information seep through her mother's facade before continuing. Samani's eyes widened. Homa hesitated, not wanting to say too much in front of Rebecca. "Don't worry, nothing happened. He told me some stories about father and is picking me up again to-night. He's taking me somewhere special but won't tell me where."

"That's... wonderful," Samani stammered, untangling her feelings. "The Dariuses have been close to our family for many years."

"So I've heard." Homa twinkled as she shut the apartment door.

Shrugging mischievously at Rebecca's confusion, they went down the cramped elevator without speaking. The doorman anticipated their exit and a gust of fresh air entered the lobby and lifted their spirits.

Rebecca took a deep breath as they hit the sidewalk. "It's so nice this morning. This weather reminds me of New Jersey," she remarked.

Homa's nose twitched in the oxygenated atmosphere and they started walking. "I went to New Jersey a few times with my father when I was young. What town are you from originally?" she asked.

"I grew up near Asbury Park."

"Asbury Park? I think that's near where my family went sometimes," Homa reminisced. "They have some kind of Ferris wheel there?"

"Yes, and a whole amusement park. It's the oldest one in the country. We went there all the time growing up."

"It's by the ocean, right?" Homa confirmed as they walked slowly through the park.

Detective Gillingham and Ralph were on a bench eating lunch in front of expectant pigeons. The birds hopped out of the way to let Homa and Rebecca stroll past.

"Yes, my father has an office practically across the street from the ocean," Rebecca explained. "This weather makes me miss the beach."

"Your father has an office there? I wonder if that's near where we went."

"What do you mean?"

"Well, didn't your father have something to do with you getting a job at Laden?" Homa asked.

"Yes, I think my dad knew someone who knew your family, but I can't remember who." Neither of them was sure.

"I knew I felt connected to you," Homa said, imagining Rebecca and herself as part of the poster montage in her room. "I wonder who our families know in common?" she thought out loud.

"I'll ask my father; I talk to him every weekend."

"I wish I could." Sadness shadowed Homa as they walked in silence for a while.

Rebecca tried to cheer her up by changing the subject. "Where are we going?"

"Oh, just up here a bit. Tell me about your father." Homa imagined her own father as one of the tiny figures in her Persepolis mural.

"Well, he's an accountant, and he's very serious, except when we tickle him. He tries to golf, but he's not very good at it. Mostly, he stays around the house and spends time with the family. My mother and brother and sisters keep him pretty busy."

"That sounds so idyllic, so normal," Homa pined.

"He's working really hard now because it's the tax season," Rebecca added, upholding the family honor.

"Does he have a lot of clients?"

"Not too many, but enough. Mostly he works for local businesses."

"I'd like to visit Asbury Park again someday."

They arrived at the restaurant and sat there for a while, watching the sidewalk parade, chatting about fashion over hummus and pita, until it was time to go.

CHAPTER 29

Her visit with Homa left Rebecca with a fresh appreciation of family life, and the empty apartment she came home to reinforced the urge to connect, so as soon as she put her tennis shoes on the mat next to the door, she called home. Her mother answered while doing the laundry, and most of the conversation was her mother talking and Rebecca listening. Her mother's rambling usually annoyed Rebecca, but in the vacuum of loneliness, she absorbed the trivialities of the life she had left behind with renewed interest. The phone got passed to Rebecca's younger, high-school-age sister, who sought Rebecca's advice on matters academic and social, and Rebecca reprised her role as counselor and protector. Rebecca's two youngest siblings were too busy playing to report anything significant to their older sister. After twenty minutes they had all run out of news to share. Rebecca was ready to hang up when she heard the sound of her father's voice.

"Becca?"

"Hi, Dad. What are you doing home? I thought you'd be busy with tax season and all."

"I am busy, very busy. I just came home to help your mother get the summer boxes out of the attic. Your brother and sister are growing so fast their clothes can't keep up. How are you?"

"I'm all right, I guess." Rebecca exhaled slowly.

Her father's instinct was not dulled by distance. "Oh, I don't like the sound of that. What's the matter?"

"Nothing's the matter," she said unconvincingly.

"Nothing, as in no boyfriend?" he pried.

"Dad!"

Her father reverted to his stump speech. "I just can't understand it – "

"A beautiful girl like you." Rebecca continued his sentence for him.

"Well, I can see this conversation is going nowhere. I've got to get back to work. I have clients coming in from the city this afternoon."

Her father was ready to say goodbye, but Rebecca remembered something she wanted to ask him. "Dad?"

"Yes sweetheart."

"I was talking to my boss today, and we couldn't figure out how I got the job with Laden. Who recommended me? I know it was someone you knew but neither of us could remember."

Her father hesitated. "Why do you want to know that?"

"Does it matter?"

"Well, it might." Her father was rarely cryptic, except when it came to birthday surprises.

"Can't you just tell me?" Rebecca pulled her legs up on the stuffed chair she was nestled in, readying herself for one of her father's long-winded, overly detailed explanations.

"I love you honey," he said in a loud non sequitur. "Mom sends her love too."

"Dad?"

"I'll call you from the office," he whispered and hung up.

Rebecca was still staring out the window, waiting for her father to call back, when Ameliah came home looking tired and disheveled. She collapsed on the living room couch like a jumble of laundry landing at the bottom of the chute. "I am *so* tired," she puffed, wiggling her blouse the rest of the way out of her pants. Smudged eye shadow and tangled hair confirmed her claim.

Rebecca was only mildly sympathetic. "What happened to you? You look awful."

"Well, I *feel* fantastic." Ameliah gamely kicked her shoes in the direction of her room. "Freddy is a fantastic lover," she exaggerated. "What did you two do last night?" she asked, playing 'top this.'

Rebecca put up a fight. "We went to a recording studio with Jon and his friend."

"Oh really! That sounds exciting," she patronized. "Where's Monica?"

"I don't know. She never came home."

"What do you mean? You don't know where she is?" Ameliah asked, alarmed.

"No. I was tired so she and Jon drove me home in his friend's car. I guess she went back to the studio with him." Rebecca cringed at the images conjured up by her story.

"So Monica and Jon drove you home, dropped you off, and then they...." Her verbalization faded into inference. "And you don't know what happened?" She thought the implications were clear.

Rebecca didn't know what to think. "She left a message on the answering machine last night but didn't say where she was. I hope she's okay."

"Serves her right if she's not," Ameliah muttered cattily on her way to her room.

Rebecca tried to keep the peace. "You're not worried about her?"

"You two weren't worried about me when you left me last night – twice!" Ameliah slammed her door shut.

The phone stopped ringing before Rebecca could answer it. "It's your father," Ameliah called through the door.

Rebecca picked it up in the kitchen.

"Sorry I couldn't talk before." Her father sounded hurried. "What's up with you?"

"What do you mean? All I did was ask you – "

"I know what you asked me," he said, cutting her off. "Who have you been talking to?"

Rebecca was confused. "You sound so serious. Did I do something wrong?"

"Maybe. Who wants to know?" Her father was all business.

"Know what? Dad, you're creeping me out. What is going on with you?"

"I can't talk over the phone. When are you coming out here?"

"This is getting weird. I don't know when I'm coming home or what you're talking about."

"Don't talk to anyone," he commanded in a lowered voice. "You never know who may be listening."

"Stop it, Dad. Are you joking? Please stop if you are because this is freaking me out. I'm sorry I asked you. I won't ask you again."

"Becca," he persisted, "listen to me. I'm not joking. I didn't want to tell you before and I can't tell you over the phone. You need to come out here tonight."

"Tonight?"

"Tonight! You have other plans?"

"You're serious?"

"Call me at the office and let me know what bus you'll be on; I'll pick you up at the station. I have to go now. Okay?"

"Okay, I guess." Confused, she put down the phone and sunk into her chair.

CHAPTER 30

The multi-colored, overhead ceiling lights of the studio, dimmed to resemble the firmament, were outshone by the glow from another source across the room. Monica was only half awake when a spark pierced through the gap in her eyelids and lit a quick burning fuse to her reality lamp. She pulled the packing blanket up to her chin and raised her head to see what had interrupted the timeless twilight of the studio. From the darkened drum booth where she and Jon had bedded down for the night she could see someone in the control room. Jon was still asleep, and she didn't want to move for fear of being discovered, so half naked and hiding like a runaway, she lay still and fought off the urge to pee.

As he always did, Nigel brought the control room lights up full and positioned the chairs behind the console in a straight line. He turned the thermostat down, which sent a breeze of cool air into the stale atmosphere of frying electronics. Then he checked the stash drawer for incriminating evidence and sampled the residual traces of the night before by wiping the mirror with his finger and licking it.

During his ten-year music business career, first as a club mixer and then as a studio manager, Nigel had developed an understanding of the relationship between the drugs his clients used and their commercial potential. These were essential skills for keeping clubs and studios booked with paying customers – and he was one of the few people in New York to have mastered the art without being destroyed by it. Almost everyone indulged in some kind of stimulants, and it was up to him to separate the alcohol and drug induced hype from the real business. As a transplanted Brit with roots in the London punk scene, Nigel had his ear to the ground, an eye for talent. He had first blown into New York in 1978 with friends of David Bowie, who introduced him to the city's hoovers and fakirs, and when he came back with Dante Pecorino the next year, it wasn't long before he found a way to parlay his inside knowledge of which acts were on their way up into a permanent position. In an industry that always put a premium on opinions expressed with an British accent, his knowledge of the British music scene and ability to get London gigs for American bands elevated his credibility to the point where, by the spring of 1982, he was a respected figure on the New York music scene.

Nigel usually spent most of his day at the Pecorinos 7th Avenue location, either in his third floor apartment or one floor below at the management company offices, but he was always on call to handle his additional responsibility for the operation of the studio. Located a ten-minute cab ride away below Spring Street, the studio had originally been designed and built by an ambitious architect who had gone broke trying to make it perfect, and the whole building had gone through a bankruptcy before the Pecorinos bought controlling interest and leased it, fully equipped, to the Darius Trust. The Darius Trust only used it sparingly, so in a complicated lease buyout agreement arranged by their mutual attorney, the Pecorinos took over operation of the facility until the lease expired. Nigel's understanding of sound equipment made his assignment of bringing the studio up to commercially viable standards relatively easy. Most of the equipment, which was so expensive that it had helped cause the demise of the original owner, was in pristine condition, so all he needed was a few new microphones and some signal processors. The Pecorinos provided a decorator who redid the lobby and lounge, and independent engineers and producers began buying time and making records as soon as the studio opened for outside business.

Everyone in the music scene wanted to get into a recording studio, but very few had the connections or money to do so. The idea of *owning* a studio was a goal only the wealthy could consider, but successful studios were almost impossible to set up and maintain for more than a few years, and everyone who tried eventually lost money finding out why. Technologically complicated and monstrously expensive, the heating, air conditioning, and wiring installations were worlds unto themselves, and cutting-edge recording equipment was never cheap, particularly reliable, or easy to fix. As popular of an idea as building a studio was, soundproofing in cities like Manhattan was enough of a challenge that it scuttled most plans before they even got off paper. Only big, well-financed record companies like Warner Brothers and Polygram could justify the expense of a truly first class facility, which they used almost exclusively for their own acts. The business of recording unsigned acts was left to a handful of scrappy independent studios like Heard Tracks, who devised numerous strategies to stay in business.

The first of several monumental challenges facing the independents was to create a sonically isolated environment. The wall-piercing rumble of the city's transportation system, emanating from underground trains, truck and bus street traffic, and all the way up to the jet filled sky, could creep into a quiet performance like a distant storm that swelled in volume as it approached. Artists were usually unaware of the interference until it affected them, and engineers eager to capture performances would try to ignore the background noise, hoping the sonic storm would pass before it saturated the tape in a low frequency bath. Total isolation was impossible, and nearby construction activity often sent the sharp cracks of rivet guns and jackhammers through the adjacent masonry and onto tape, killing takes with a spray of midrange sonic bullets. Unsteady electrical currents and sudden voltage spikes could cause the sensitive equipment to slow down or suffer from electronic hiccups, and countless moments of brilliance were lost due to environmental interference.

But external studio problems were not limited to sound pollution and equipment malfunction. Full throttle bands, playing electric guitars, bass, drums, keyboards, and horns, whose vocalists screamed into the early morning hours, weren't good neighbors, so commercial studios had to be located far enough away from human habitat to keep the din of their clients' inculcations from causing disturbed residents to summon the authorities. And keeping the authorities away was always a top priority for chemically induced musicians whose illegal activities risked the career-ending possibility of jail time. But although industrial studio locations were good for social isolation, it made them more susceptible to crime and vandalism. Studios had to remain hidden, because advertising their presence was tantamount to inviting trouble. Unwanted fans, hangers on, rivals, ex lovers, and debt collectors provided further justification for keeping the location of the studio unmarked, undetectable, and available by invitation only. The hidden camera above the buzzer-activated front door helped with security, but every security system is vulnerable, and Heard Tracks had so far been fortunate to escape the enterprise-ending calamities that had doomed some of its competitors.

Even though setting up and operating a studio was a substantial technical and logistical accomplishment, keeping it booked with paying customers was even more difficult. Independent bands that played loud music to crowds of beer-swilling youth rarely had enough money to rent their own apartment, let alone afford the rates of a professionally equipped sound studio. Their best hope for access to recording time – and possible stardom – was to attract the attention of a record company. But the star system was stratified so that record companies, before committing to the expense of signing acts to long term contracts – which included producing a whole album in their own facilities – would pay independent studios to make demos of bands they were interested in. Independent backers of all stripes would also pay for studio time to make recordings of bands they thought had promise, with the hope that their investment would yield rewards commensurate with the extreme risk. The only other real opportunity for bands to get into a good studio was by convincing a studio operator to let them record for free, with the promise of paying them if and when they "made it big."

Narcissistic and ambitious, very few musicians turned down access to free studio time, commonly known in the industry as a "spec time." The concept of "spec time", memorialized by an agreement call a "spec deal", was that the artists would record something good enough to get them a recording contract, and then a major record company would buy the tapes from the studio, either to release them as finished recordings or to tie up the rights to the material. "Spec," a contraction of the word "speculation," was an accurate description of the nature of the agreement, and a reliable indicator of its prospects for success.

As a studio operator, Nigel used his authority to offer spec deals to acts he thought had potential. These inherently simple arrangements were popular with studio operators because they needed to keep their facilities booked. And even though the likelihood of making any money from a spec deal was less than 5%, the cost of operating a studio was constant, and owners realized that it was better to have even a small chance of covering their overhead than none at all. So, when no paying acts were booked, studio operators gambled on artists they thought were most likely to make it.

Spec time was also a good way to do favors, and Nigel had developed a reputation as both an industry player and good judge of talent. Because the Pecorinos also had a management company, the Heard Tracks spec deals included the provision that Pecorino Partners had the right to negotiate contracts with record companies and manage their careers. Management contracts awarded managers at least 20% of the artists' income from record company royalties and advances, live performances, endorsements, merchandising, and publishing, so the potential profits from a successful spec deal were essentially limitless, and the extremely high failure rate was offset by equally high earning potential.

*"It never works out the way that you plan it to be." *14*

Because spec deals amounted to what baseball players call "swinging for the fences," and money was not guaranteed, studios needed regular paying customers to keep the doors open. Nigel represented Heard Tracks in the stiff competition for paying customers, and he was a presence in the local clubs and rehearsal halls where the decisions of where to record were made. He knew most of the local record company A & R representatives, club managers, agents, and sound engineers, and had succeeded in establishing a reputation for Heard Tracks as a place where history could be made. His status within the structure of Pecorino Partners gave him the authority to make whatever studio deals he wanted, and his success was measured not by how much money he brought in, but by how much the parent company had to contribute to cover the overhead of the studio each month. He kept in close contact with Dennis, who ran The Black Sheep, and they directed business each other's way, which is how Jon Cells and Monica came to be sleeping in the drum booth in the darkened room beyond the control room glass.

Nigel took another swipe off the mirror, licked his finger, and rolled his tongue around his mouth like a wine taster. The coke tasted like the usual cut Travis had been supplying. He tapped out a few spoons of the same batch from his own vial and ingested. Over the years he had learned to keep his habit in moderation and had become very selective about who he got stoned with. Experience had taught him that anyone he shared a straw with could turn into an enemy or be a source of infection, and he had stopped doing drugs with Dante, whose big mouth and nose were sources of embarrassment and pollution. Nigel's last bout of bronchitis had left him with a scary wheeze that caused him to curtail his cigarette intake, and in his early thirties, Nigel's body was already feeling the effects of his battles in the trenches of the rock and roll wars.

At Dennis' urging, Nigel had banned cigarette smoke from the control room to protect the equipment, but too many of his clients smoked marijuana to ban that too. It was hard enough to get a good paying session in the door, so he couldn't justify throwing them out because they were behaving like the unruly musicians everyone knew they were. And he couldn't expect vigilance from his assistant engineers because they considered free drugs a job perk, and were also keen to ingratiate themselves to the clientele in the hope that the relationship would spawn career opportunities. Assistant engineers were unlikely to enforce any rules that weren't in their own best interest, so there was no way to know exactly what went on during the all night sessions.

Nigel's morning inspection was a hunt for clues about the status of his staff and customers. He had honed his drug detection skills as a way to hedge his bets, and could tell a lot about the music being recorded by the traces of drugs he found in the morning. He knew that the heavy pot smokers used a lot of special effects, often drowning their message in an ocean of reverb. The tokers rarely played gigs because they were either too stoned to think that it was important to perform, or so convinced of their own genius that they weren't motivated by audience approval. They were also known to indulge themselves in the fantasy that their eventual emergence from their smoky realm would be some kind of cultural watershed, akin to the second coming, where they would be hailed as heroes and adored by minions as they assumed their rightful position atop the pantheon of musical gods. Nigel hated most of their self-indulgent music, but loved having them as clients because they were never finished and ran up big studio bills that were usually settled without much of a fight. Their egos anesthetized, the pot smokers never seemed to mind being bumped from the schedule. They viewed the downtime of scheduling conflicts and technical difficulties as opportunities to smoke, postulate lyric changes, and indulge in the munchies – usually in that order.

Nigel had no control over his customers' musical process; the studio's only obligation was to provide the equipment and atmosphere to facilitate recording—not to give advice. Studio managers were in the business of selling time, and just as a hotel operator isn't responsible for insomnia or the outcome of a romantic evening in the honeymoon suite, Nigel wasn't responsible for which songs the band recorded, what licks would be used for the solo, or how much compression should be applied to the vocal. Although his equipment was more at risk with aggressive customers, Nigel preferred the ones who left traces of cocaine because he interpreted the use of that drug as an indication of market potential. The tooters were the ones whose music was filling the true grit clubs like CBGB's and dance floors of haute couture clubs like Studio 54. Their high-energy music was usually an uptempo wash of piercing treble, comprised of high-speed drumming, distorted guitar chords, and childlike synthesizer lines. Their message was a triumph of style over substance, accomplished with attitudinous lyrics that were rarely sung – the preference being vocals delivered in a falsetto scream or sultry monotone. The day after a session, Nigel could tell how high they were by counting how many beer bottles had been emptied trying to come down. Once in a while, when the cokers were too tired to play fast, someone in the band would write a slow song that sober people could listen to – and that was where they were most likely to encounter success. If Nigel found pot roaches in the ashtrays along with the cigarette butts, it was a clue that the group might have been working on something mellower with intelligible lyrics, and he divined that the traces of cocaine and marijuana, combined with the scarcity of beer bottles, were indicators that there might have been some good music recorded the night before. His interpretation of those signs was: that the band was socially current (cocaine), not too jacked up to play with feeling (few beer or booze empties), and lyrically interesting (roaches).

Alcohol, tobacco, marijuana, coffee, and cocaine were the main drugs that recording clients used, and although most of his clients used these in combination, some dabbled in more exotic stimulants like PCP, snappers, and MDMA. Nigel didn't have to worry about the really hardcore users because heroin addicts didn't like to leave the comfort of their pads unless it was to cop; speed freaks didn't have the patience to sit in a studio long enough to make a record; drunks were too bored with the process; and although occasional trips to the psychedelic vegetable garden were very hard to detect, acid heads were so disoriented that they might not even know who they were, much less remember what they were supposed to be playing.

The telltale traces of drugs were reliable clues to the mental condition of his clients, and he used the information to monitor their progress. Knowing when a booking was about to cancel was essential, because an empty studio was an ongoing expense that had no income potential. Nigel needed to know ahead of time if the ephemeral confluence of emotional and economic factors essential to an extended booking was about to dissipate, because keeping the studio full of spec and paying customers was critical to his own survival. Bands that fought to a standstill amongst themselves, backers who backed away, bounced checks, legal detours, and damaged equipment were all substantial threats to the flow of session money, and Nigel was constantly on the alert for signs of a session's demise.

Nightly reference cassettes full of unedited sections were one of the best predictors of the booking's condition. Mixes featuring guitar or keyboard indicated that the session was in good health and full of expectation. It was easy to imagine the self-congratulatory antics of customers indulging in endless bluesy guitar riffs or meandering keyboard musings. But when the tapes were full of simple repetitive synthesizer lines, it could indicate an expensive coke-induced trance that might be threatening the primacy of the studio budget. If the tapes had a lot of rhythmic breakdowns, it usually meant that some of the band had taken the night off, leaving the engineer and drummer to argue about syncopated triplets while beating their ears into submission. Mixes featuring bass were rare, and always worrisome, because they indicated unsettled differences. As the instrument that connects the rhythm with the chords, experimentation in the bass part often meant that the cohesion within the band was tentative. Bass line experimentation suggested clashes over the musical direction and could be a proxy for bigger issues that could escalate into a booking-ending disagreement.

The unscripted banter between the engineer and performer prior to the take was often left on the reference cassettes, and Nigel was always informed by the telltale small talk. Listening to the jokes, insults, encouragements, admonishments, and expletives was the clearest window into the session, and some of these comments were intentionally left on tape for posterity – or even featured in the final mixdown. Sometimes they revealed the kind of clever spontaneity that was the touchstone of brilliance, and Nigel was always on the alert for signs of rock immortality. Much of the magic that mattered happened in the studio, and capturing the fleeting flashes of genius was the goal of every session. Studios advertised their reputation as a place where recording history could be made, and in keeping with the adage "success has many fathers," the gold records hanging on the walls were used as proof of the paternity test. But, in the same way that every business disingenuously makes sure potential customers know the names of the famous people that have frequented their establishment, studios didn't limit their bragging to legitimate accomplishment, and appropriated the borrowed light of any luminary who had ever worked there, even if it was only for an insignificant moment.

Dennis knew how to operate the equipment and didn't need an assistant engineer, so Nigel couldn't check the studio log that house seconds were required to write in. He checked the cassette machine to see if there were any rough mixes but, as usual, Dennis had put away all the tapes and zeroed out the board, leaving the control room slightly cleaner than he had found it and devoid of obvious clues. Nigel turned on the door camera so he would be able to see when his guests arrived and then went to tidy up the lounge so he could present the studio in its finest light. A crumpled pair of women's panties peeking out from under the couch caused him to redefine his mission.

Were these from last night, or have they been there for days? He picked them up delicately and sniffed. They were moist and pungent. The odor seeped into his canine brain and quickened his pulse like a detective stumbling on a crime scene. He remembered who was there last night and tried to conjure up an image of the panty owner. He knelt down to see if there was anything else hiding under the sofa.

CHAPTER 31

"Good morning," Jon announced, appearing in the doorway. He was barefoot and had his arm around Monica, who was wrapped in a packing blanket with her head shrouded.

"Good afternoon," Nigel replied, eying his guests. His British manners flowered in the presence of cute women. "Dennis didn't tell me it was going to be a sleepover."

"Nigel, this is Monica," Jon boasted with a squeeze. "Nigel runs the studio," he explained.

"Yes, well, pleased to see you again, Monica. I didn't know you'd be spending the night or I would have turned the bed down," he added sarcastically, checking his watch. "I'm glad you've enjoyed your stay but you'd better get dressed now because I have guests coming by to see the studio any minute now. I think these might belong to you?" He handed her the panties.

"Thank you," Monica said, accepting them with a bare arm protruding from her wrap. Embarrassed, she retreated to the bathroom.

Jon followed Nigel back up the hall to plead forgiveness. "Sorry about that, man."

Nigel was much more understanding than Jon worried he would be. "Bollocks. The best parts only come out in the wee hours. Let's just tidy up a bit. We'll tell our guests the session lasted all night," Nigel explained as he raised the studio lights. Jon folded up the packing-blanket bed and gathered up the crumpled tissues while Nigel re-aligned the gobos. "Did you get something down? I mean other than her?" Nigel asked, his vested interest in mind.

"Absatively; some bitchin guitars and an awesome vocal. Wait till you hear it! I wanted to keep going but Dennis had to go," Jon hyped as they headed back to the control room. They met Monica, fully dressed, coming down the hall. All three went back to the booth to wait for Nigel's visitors.

Nigel inhaled Monica's reapplied perfume and tried to stifle his attraction. "So, what do *you* do?" he asked.

Monica's sexual satisfaction glowed. "I'm a dance instructor."

"Lovely." Nigel eyed Jon with a mixture of jealousy and admiration. "Let me know if you need a new dance partner," he said, referencing Jon's foot.

Monica blushed.

"Who's coming?" Jon asked, not looking forward to meeting anybody.

"The other owners are bringing some people by," Nigel said, checking the movement on the screen and buzzing them in. "And there they are." The other owners, a group of Persian businessmen who operated under the moniker Darius Trust, had originally leased the studio to make pop records of traditional Persian music, with ambitions to expand into the creation of politically motivated movies and documentaries, but their interest in media production had waned over the years, and the buyout arrangement with Pecorino Properties was civil and uncontentious. The Darius Trust retained the use of one of the apartments that was part of the studio complex, but refocused their attention on other commercial real estate interests; which included the Laden Imports warehouse, a Middle Eastern restaurant-nightclub in Brooklyn, the Old Medical Building in lower Manhattan, and residential apartments in Queens.

Rhamin Darius led an oddly dressed trio of visitors down the hallway, pausing to show off the gold records, signed publicity photos, and framed studio memorabilia hanging on the walls. They entered the main studio and Rhamin waved through the control room glass as he pointed out the studio features to his guests.

Jon was nervous about being there on spec. "Which one's the owner?"

"The one who waved." Nigel smiled back at the guests while explaining who they were to Jon.

"That guy? I thought Dante owned the place."

"No, not yet, not all the way. Don't worry about all that. I'm the boss here and that's all you need to know." Nigel opened the control room door for the guests.

"Oh, I'm sorry," Rhamin apologized, seeing that Nigel was not alone. "I thought the studio wasn't being used this weekend."

"That's okay. We haven't started yet. Please come in," Nigel maître d'ed. "This is Jon Cells and his friend Monica."

Rhamin gestured with a polite bow, presenting two slender men with neatly trimmed beards. "Hello. I am Rhamin Darius and this is Barbat Chang." They were dressed in matching brocade suits and flanked a sprightly female companion. Stunning, with jet-black hair that descended in a graceful arc below her shoulders, she wore a traditional full-length dress that was trimmed in the same shimmering material as her partners' suits.

"Pleased to meet you," one of the musicians said with an accent, extending his hand. "We have a show tonight so please excuse the costumes."

"They're very famous in Iran," Rhamin bragged. He was dressed like an impresario in a silk shirt with his chest hairs showing. "They're playing all week at our restaurant in Brooklyn. You must come see them."

Jon couldn't resist making a wisecrack. "Which one of you is Barbat and who is Chang?"

"The band takes its name from traditional Persian instruments," the taller of the musicians parried, "but we call her Chang because she plays upon your heart strings like the Persian harp." The female singer moved suggestively to underscore his contention.

Nigel motioned Jon and Monica to the couch. "Why don't you sit down and rest that foot while I show these folks around. Did you bring a tape?" he asked the musicians.

"Yes, of course. We recorded it at the club so the quality is not that good, but that's why they want to come here," Rhamin said, handing Nigel a cassette. The visitors moved to the center of the room, gawking at the profusion of buttons and lights on the console while Nigel cued the cassette. The tape began with the ambient sounds of a busy restaurant, dominated by clanking dishes and unintelligible table conversation. An over-modulated announcement suddenly pegged the meters before someone readjusted the gain to undistorted levels.

"Let's give a warm welcome to Barbat Chang! Salaam," the announcer's voice rang out. Polite audience clapping receded as the band's music sprung to life with a lively hand drum rhythm. The drumming was soon accompanied by the thrumming of a single stringed acoustic instrument. The musicians were impressed at hearing themselves so loud and smiled at one another. Western ears were incapable of detecting the subtle melodic references to well-known Persian songs that on top of the Dorian-playing oud, but Nigel smiled politely. The Westerners were even less connected to the female vocalist's sense of melody as she warbled emotionally charged Persian lyrics in a high tenor, filling the languid stops with pithy glissandos that reached the octave before settling back into what seemed like the verses. Rhamin exchanged cultural pleasantries with the musicians, who swayed to the bouncy dirge and mimed their parts.

"This next one is my favorite," Rhamin declared, trying to share his glee with Nigel, who stood stone-faced, waiting for the punishment to end.

"We've never heard ourselves so clearly," one of the musicians exulted. "Rhamin wasn't lying when he told us how good his studio sounds," The other musicians nodded.

"Then we are agreed?" Rhamin confirmed.

"Of course!" the musicians consented.

Nigel quickly turned the music down to background volume. Chang stretched herself in what looked like a combination floor exercise and traditional dance move. She paused with prayered hands holding the ends of her headscarf above her head.

"Arabesque?" Monica asked, jumping up from the couch to join her. Chang repeated the movement a few times as Monica attempted to imitate her. The men were delighted with the display of feminine agility.

"You must come dance with us," the tall oudist invited. Chang removed her scarf and wrapped it around Monica's shoulder in an expression of sisterhood. Gracefully swaying, she demonstrated some other dance moves that Monica attempted to follow. The mini performance ended with Chang's swipe of the gossamer scarf across Jon's rapt face, and the infused scent had an immediate effect that sent Jon's attention back to his foot and he winced in pain.

"I see Chang's powers have moved you," one of the musicians said, misinterpreting Jon's grimace. Monica sat back down next to Jon, who put his foot on the sofa table for support. "You never did tell me what happened?" Monica said, touching his thigh sympathetically.

Rhamin changed the focus of the room. "So then, Nigel. When is the studio available?"

"How much time do you think you'll need?" Nigel asked the musicians.

"Well, our set lasts about ninety minutes, so how long do you think we'll need?" the tallest musician answered for all three.

Nigel had hoped this would be a quick session because no money was going to change hands, but their minimal demands surpassed even his most modest expectations. "If you just want to record your set, we can do that in an afternoon or evening. Four hours should be plenty of time."

"Will we still be able to overdub?" the drummer asked, referencing the only studio benefit he knew.

"Well, that depends," Nigel answered, trying to limit the studio's exposure to non-cash business.

Rhamin conferred with the band in Persian before addressing Nigel. "Let's start with some time next week, say Tuesday or Wednesday? The band doesn't play on those nights. They will have had time to rest from the weekend so they shouldn't be too tired. Is that okay with you?" he asked Nigel.

"I'll check the schedule. Why don't you give me a call on Monday?"

"Monday is good," Rhamin answered while the band nodded agreement. "Well, thank you for letting us listen." Rhamin shook Nigel's hand as he motioned the band out of the control room. "Please do come to the restaurant and see Chang perform," he said to Monica. "And you go back and see Dr. Nouri." he said, pointing to Jon's foot as he left the control room.

"Dr. Nouri? You know Dr. Nouri?" Nigel asked with astonishment once they were gone.

Jon was confused. "Well, I don't really know him. They took me to see him to get my foot bandaged up." Jon strained to comprehend. "How does that guy know?"

"This is very strange indeed. How do you know Rhamin? And who took you to see Dr. Nouri?" Nigel asked.

"The people I'm working for took me to the doctor. I never saw that Rhamin guy before."

"*Who* are you working for?"

"I guess Dennis didn't tell you. I had to take a day job."

"Right, he mentioned something about that. But that doesn't explain how Rhamin knew you were at Dr. Nouri's office. Where are you working?"

"I got a job at this import place in the West Village where they make perfume."

"I see. I've no idea how all this connects, but now I know why you smell so wonderful," Nigel said, flaring his nostrils. "Or maybe that's because you two haven't had your morning bath yet." His comment made Monica blush.

"That reminds me," Jon said, "I think it's time for a little breakfast." He took a folded paper bindle out of his pocket. The outside camera showed the visitors leaving as he hopped over to the stash drawer. "You hungry, sweetie?" Jon asked, offering Monica a wake up toot.

She saw how bloodied Jon's boot was and hesitated. "Are you sure that's a good idea?"

"Breakfast of champions," he aahhed, snorting two lines.

Monica declined. "I'm going to wait until I eat some real food. We should go see that Dr. Nouri. I know a dancer who hurt her foot and didn't take care of it and now she can't dance anymore. Come on, I'll go with you." Monica was serious.

"I think that might be a good idea," Nigel agreed, noting Jon's blotched brown bootie. "I'll tell Dennis where you went."

"Okay, I guess I'll go see the good doctor, if you both insist," Jon acquiesced, artificially elevated to agreeable. He pinched Monica hard enough to make her squeal. "Last night you were my lover, today you are my mother." He made a note to himself to remember those lines for future lyrics.

"Why don't you go now? I have an appointment later, but Dennis will be here by the time you get back."

"There's just one problem," Jon realized. "I don't know where the doctor's office is."

Monica was surprised. "You don't?"

"The people from work drove me there and I didn't watch where we were going. The office was in some kind of spooky old building between the really big new ones."

"Well, that's helpful," Nigel noted sarcastically.

Monica had an idea. "Didn't Rebecca go there with you? Maybe she remembers where it is? I'll call home and ask her."

Nigel pointed out the control room phone. "Just dial eight to get an outside line."

Monica had a second thought. "Is there somewhere I can talk in private?"

"Sure, you can use the phone up by the front desk."

She went up to the front and made her call from the reception area.

Ameliah answered. "Where are you?"

Monica didn't want to share too much information. "At a recording studio."

"Are you okay?"

"Yes, I'm fine."

"Where did you spend the night?"

"Is Becca there?"

"And who did you spend the night with? Or do you want me to guess?" Ameliah rarely missed an opportunity to meddle.

Monica ignored her probing. "Amy, please, I really need to talk to Becca."

"So do you want me to give her the message that you screwed her boyfriend, or do you want to tell her yourself?"

"He's not her boyfriend. She didn't...I mean...she doesn't...oh just put her on the phone. I need to ask her a question."

"Becca, pick up the phone, it's for you," Ameliah called out.

"Becca," she repeated a little louder. "Hold on, I'll go check and see where she is." Ameliah searched the apartment and returned. "She's not here."

"Where is she?"

"I don't know. We...I went to my room to take a nap and now she's not here."

"She didn't say where she was going, or leave a note? That doesn't sound like Becca."

"Well, her father called her a while ago, so maybe she went back home."

"Okay, tell her I called if you see her."

"Wait. When are you coming back?"

"I don't know. I have to take Jon to the doctor, otherwise he won't go."

"Sounds like an exciting date. Maybe Freddy and I will play doctor again tonight too."

Monica hung up. Dennis was standing in the control by the time she got back from making her phone call. "Good afternoon," he greeted her, still wearing his sunglasses.

"Did you find the doctor's address?" Nigel asked her.

"No, Rebecca wasn't home." She looked at Jon's foot with concern.

"Well maybe Dr. Nouri is in the phonebook."

"Dr. Nouri? What do you want him for?" Dennis asked, joining in.

"He's the one who fixed up Jon's foot. It looks like it needs a new dressing," Nigel explained. "Do you know him?"

"Well, I don't really know him, but...." Dennis hesitated, choosing his words carefully. "His driver comes by the club every so often." Dennis tried to sound matter-of-fact and gave Nigel a knowing eyeball.

"Who's his driver?"

"Guy named Reggie. Comes to the club all the time. He and Travis are friends."

Only Nigel understood Dennis's reference. "I see. Well, maybe Travis knows where the office is then?" Nigel suggested.

"Oh, I know where the office is," Dennis admitted. "I had to drive Travis over there."

Monica saw the solution. "Great. Do you think you can give Jon and me a ride there?"

"Now?" Dennis checked with Nigel.

Monica put on the cute. "Pleeease."

"Could you?" Nigel asked.

"Well, I guess so."

Jon agreed to the plan. "Thanks man, the sooner we go, the sooner we can get back to work."

Nigel approved. "Take the extra keys because I'm leaving too. Mr. P's expecting me at the office. You all go and I'll lock up." Plans were set. Dennis pulled his car out of the studio parking space and Monica climbed into the jump seat. Jon slid the passenger seat back all the way to make room for his legs and realized that his foot was seeping blood.

"That doesn't look too good," Dennis said, noticing the bleeding as he backed out. "The Old Medical Building is practically around the corner so we'll be there in a minute. You could have walked there, if you could walk," he quipped.

They pulled up to the front of the building and stopped behind a big white Mercedes idling in the loading zone. Reggie had the windows up and was blasting "Rock With You" vigorously enough to shake the car.

"You two go up." Dennis said. "There's no good parking so I'll wait here. See you soon I hope." Dennis put a cassette in the stereo and got comfortable.

Rudy wrote down Dennis' license plate number and took a picture of Jon and Monica from the unmarked car parked across the street.

"Yup, that's him alright." Detective Falin put down his binoculars and held up a black and white glossy of Jon from the Colorado file for comparison. "Same guy."

"How do you know him? The one with the limp?" Rudy asked.

"He was mixed up in a case we had in Colorado. We never did pin anything on him."

"What was he doing?"

"I'm not sure, but his friends were some of the most daring smugglers we ever saw. They tricked out small airplanes to fly so low that radar couldn't see them. We lost a good plane and a great agent trying to follow them."

Rudy kept up on Bureau news. "Was that the Boulder bust?"

"You got it."

"So what does that have to do with this case?"

"I haven't figured how this Cells character is mixed up with the Persians, but some guys just seem to turn up wherever there's a problem."

Rudy agreed and jotted some notes in their case folder.

Monica pressed the street level intercom to Dr. Nouri's office and they were immediately buzzed into the lobby. The ancient elevator descended and disgorged an elderly couple. Monica moved out of the way to let them pass and Jon limped inside. Memories of yesterday's visit with Rebecca crowded into the elevator with him. The trip up went slowly, and Jon shuddered at the invisible presence of the conjure-pot ghosts as the doors clunked open on the top floor. They exited into the fourteenth floor hallway and Jon thought he felt a migraine coming on as they entered Dr. Nouri's office. He quickly claimed a chair and tried to fight it off. Monica stood looking at the pictures on the wall of the waiting room, trying to remember where she had smelled the distinctive odor before. A young, bespectacled assistant greeted them with a clipboard.

"Name please," he asked, poised to write them onto the list.

"Jon Cells. I was here yesterday," Jon said, struggling, looking for a place to vomit.

"So I heard," the assistant acknowledged, squatting to check Jon's bloodied boot. "We better get you lying down. Can you walk?"

Jon stood up. "I got this far."

"Come with me." The assistant led them to a small examination room and helped Jon onto the table. "Dr. Nouri will be in to see you," he informed them before exiting.

Jon leaned back on the examination table in obvious discomfort. The coke buzz was wearing off and he didn't know how long he could fight off the migraine.

Monica saw him struggling and was glad she hadn't done any drugs earlier. "You look terrible. Can I get you some water?"

"Please." Jon's face was growing paler as he lay down on his back on the examination table.

Monica went off in search of water. The odor in the hallway was repulsively familiar, and a faint moaning from behind a closed door put her on edge. She found a pot of overcooked mud at the end of the hallway and mixed it with some non-dairy creamer in a Styrofoam cup. Holding her coffee in one hand and water for Jon in the other, she tried not to notice too much on the way back. Jon was drifting deeper into seizure when she arrived.

"Here's your water," she said, trying to hand it to him.

"Just put it on the table," he mumbled with difficulty.

Monica started to get scared and the sips of coffee heightened her nervousness. She stood vigil for several uncomfortable minutes, wondering how she had gotten herself into this situation. Her groin began to throb and the magic of the night before changed faces. What would she do if she had gotten pregnant? She thought about the last time she had been in a strange medical clinic: her brother was being patched up after a street fight. The sounds and smells of the office built into an atmosphere of fear and regret that Dr. Nouri burst when he abruptly entered the room.

"And how's that foot today?" he asked in the practiced parlance of the medical profession with a discernible accent as he touched Jon's foot.

"Oh, that hurts," Jon whined.

"Yes, I'm sure it does." Dr. Nouri doused a thick gauze pad with fluid from a heavy glass bottle. He held it over Jon's mouth and nose. "This will make you feel better. Breathe deeply please," he instructed, adjusting his glasses to study Monica. "You're not the same girl from yesterday," he observed.

Monica cringed with remorse.

Jon sucked the fumes from the gauze as if he were inhaling cannabis and held his breath. The effect was immediate. "Oh shit! What *is* that stuff?" he raved, blowing out hard before sucking in another deep breath.

Dr. Nouri removed the gauze. "Now just breathe normally please." Jon propped up on his elbows, blinking like a discovered cave dweller. Dr. Nouri used a scissors to cut the cloth boot away from his foot. Monica gasped at the swollen purple toes caked in dried blood. "Now you might feel this," Dr. Nouri warned, wiping the toes with a hydrogen peroxide-moistened gauze pad. White foam bubbled everywhere he touched. "Stings a little?" he enquired, checking his patient's eyes.

Jon regained his macho pride. "Not so bad."

"Good. I'll just wrap this up with some medicine again, and please try to stay off your feet this time." The doctor swathed his foot in a pungent poultice and taped it tightly. "My assistant will bring you a new boot to protect that. Come see me again in a few days."

Monica wrinkled her nose after Dr. Nouri had gone. "What is that stuff?" she asked, sniffing the air. "Everything around here smells like my grandfather's bathroom."

Jon wiggled his toes without pain. "I don't know what he uses, but it sure works."

The doctor's assistant came in with a new cloth boot. He fit it over Jon's bandage and tied the laces. "Dr. Nouri said you can use these if the pain comes back," he explained, handing Jon a small pill bottle with several dark gray capsules in it. Jon squinted suspiciously at the small white label with handwritten lettering stuck to the outside. "Dr. Nouri uses a lot of traditional medicines," the assistant explained, addressing Jon's obvious skepticism. "Just follow the directions and you'll be fine," he added before excusing himself.

"Does that mean we can go now?" Monica wondered aloud. "Can you walk, sort of?" she asked.

Jon eased himself off the table and put pressure on his rebandaged foot. "I can hardly feel anything down there," he said with amazement, standing up and letting go of the table. "My headache's gone too. Let's get out of here."

An old woman in traditional middle-eastern dress was already on the elevator, and her young female aide held the door open for Jon and Monica. The elevator stopped on the ninth floor, and a man wearing a dirty baseball cap and sunglasses wedged in for the ride down. The old woman moved behind her assistant for protection from Jon and the unwashed stranger. The man in the cap was breathing deeply as if he had just run up a flight of stairs, and the smell of his perspiration was strong enough to cause a gag reflex. The old woman covered her mouth and nose with a scented handkerchief. The younger passengers simply tried to hold their breath as the elevator car creaked slowly to the ground floor. The winded stranger edged his way out before the doors were open all the way and disappeared. Jon and Monica found Dennis waiting patiently in his car, listening to a cassette. They got in. Reggie's Mercedes was still parked in front of them. The elderly woman and her helper climbed into the back seat of Reggie's car. Detective Falin was dozing, but Rudy snapped pictures of both cars as they rolled past.

CHAPTER 32

Mak took the subway into Manhattan for a Saturday afternoon rendezvous at the warehouse. ATF agents stationed in the building opposite the warehouse watched him disarm the alarm system and go in through the alley door. The delivery drivers weren't due until 4:00, so Mak had enough time to check the progress of Friday's fermentation. The fact that he used his weekend access for legitimate purposes relieved him of some of the guilt he felt for operating a side business out of his employer's premises. The mixing room reeked from yesterday's brewing, so he propped the door open and switched on the venting fans. The base of the cooker was still warm, and he moved the giant slotted spoon that he had left in the mixture to check its consistency. All the chunks had blended into a viscous fluid. As he tasted the mixture from a dab on the end of his finger, a loud knock on the metal roll-up doors demanded his attention. He closed the mixing room door and went to the loading dock to open it. The Laden delivery truck backed into position, and Angel Herrera climbed out of the passenger's seat and onto the platform.

"Buenos dias, mi amigo," Angel greeted him. He had been with the company almost as long as Mak, and they knew each other well. Rough-edged and five feet tall, he used his low center of gravity and street smarts to their full potential. Lacking Mak's immunity to the odors, Angel couldn't stay in the warehouse too long, but his job as the main delivery driver didn't require it.

"Buenos dias," Mak answered. "What do we have today?" Angel's cousin Ramon raised the back door of the truck.

"Chinese crates. They have special flowers in them." Angel said with a wink. Ramon guided one of the crates off the truck and it settled on the loading dock with a loud bang.

Mak inspected the container. It wasn't leaking, and put he put his nose close to the lid for a smell test. A blob of wax, which had been dripped onto the tape that sealed the top of the wooden box, discouraged him from opening it for inspection. He lifted one end a few inches to check its weight. "Must be a lot of flowers in there." Mak observed, easing the heavy crate back down. "How many you got in the truck?"

"Sixteen." Angel said. "They're all about the same. We just loaded them a few hours ago."

"When are you supposed to deliver them?" Mak asked, calculating.

"They could be here for a few months. Mr. Wong said he'd let me know."

"Okay, let's find a place to put them." Mak went off in search of the perfect spot while Angel and Ramon started to unload the truck. Two crates were already stacked on a four-wheel dolly by the time Mak returned, and the three men pushed the cartage to an empty corner of the warehouse.

"Just put the rest of them here and I'll go get the delivery ready." Mak told them before going off in the opposite direction. He climbed the metal stairs that led to a second floor platform and found the long boxes they had stashed there a few months ago. He moved one into the aisle so Angel would be able to find them. Angel had several more of the new crates to move, and Mak knew it would take a while to reload, so he went back to the mix room to check the air quality while Angel and Ramon were wrangling the inventory.

The atmosphere in the mix room had lost its acidity, so he went to the adjoining room to check the progress of other potions. One at a time, he dipped a glass jar into each of the urns of oil that were infused with cedar and sandalwood. Holding the jar up to the light, he checked its color, then passed it under his nose before pouring the contents back into the urn. The sweeter they smelled, the weaker they were, because fully steeped mixtures burned his nostrils with acrid attars. Mak checked the jasmine flowers being absorbed in flat panels of wool grease. They had a pleasant smell while they were first curing, but the growing stench of fermenting sheep fat eventually made these absorptions repugnant too. Then he turned his attention to the macerated seeds from the Red Crown poppy. They were always soaked in their own special heavy glass containers, sealed with a ported rubber stopper, and kept in their own area. Nothing in the warehouse was more valuable than the rare seeds that were the basis for so many of the Laden formulations and responsible for much of the company's commercial success.

Trade in poppy seeds had been going on for thousands of years, and its use as both an ornamental flower and food crop prevented the plant from being classified based solely on the narcotic derivatives it was also known to produce. Laden's license to import plant material for use in aromatic and salubrious formulations gave them permission to buy and sell poppy seeds, and they had used that permission, along with the application of some arcane perfumery know-how, to create products that produced mild euphoria. The company had, until recently, managed to avoid the attention of enforcement authorities by using the seeds of the poppy plant, rather than the sap from its buds, to educe its active ingredients.

The process for extracting analgesics from the Papaver had been pioneered by the Monsouri's ancient ancestors, the Sumerians, whose cuneiform symbol for the species translated into "joy plant", a reference to the effect it had when ingested. Skilled in agriculture, the ancients experimented with various methods for leaching the essences of the plant, and eventually settled on the simple technique of puncturing living seedpods and collecting the sap that seeped out and congealed. That method is still used to produce raw opium in state-run farms and crude mountain laboratories throughout the world, and the preference for this method has as much to do with its simplicity as its effectiveness. Poppies are easy to grow and require no fertilization, irrigation, or insecticides if planted in the proper location, so both authorized growers and subsistence farmers have found it relatively easy to exploit their value as a cash crop.

But buried in the rubble of the ancient Achmaemenid capital, Persepolis, was, among other records pressed into clay cylinders and tablets, the previously unknown formula for using the seeds of the poppy plant, rather than its sap, to impart its euphoric effects. The written relics, along with other mementos of the great city, were salvaged by illiterate nomads who picked through the smoldering ruins after Alexander the Great's army had accomplished their devastating mission a few hundred years after Jesus was crucified. Having no practical use, the itinerant herders who had found the curious but unfathomable pottery stashed them in desert caves where they were eventually forgotten.

The well-preserved gleanings lay hidden for 1400 years until European influence in the region gave rise to a renewed interest in the history of the Persian Empire. Archeological disciplines were introduced and used to catalog and interpret the artifacts that were systematically recovered from numerous locations in the Fertile Crescent. Translation of the rudimentary writing was carried on by a small group of linguistic historians, who spent many decades in the dusty libraries and tents of the Middle East. The curious formula for the transmutation of the "joy plant," rendered in Elamite, wasn't stumbled upon until thousands of other written fragments from Persepolis, most of them accounting records, had been laboriously translated. The researcher who stumbled on the odd text recognized its uniqueness, and hid the news of its existence from his coworkers and employers until he was able to fully decode its meaning. When he finally understood what was written, Professor Cyrus Farsi – the father of Ava Farsi Monsouri, grandfather of Samani, and great great grandfather of Homa – realized the potential significance of his discovery, and kept it secret.

The professor's ancestors had determined that droppings from sheep grazing on the rich irrigated grasslands around Persepolis contained high concentrations of fatty oils, which when used as fertilizer, greatly increased the presence of the intoxicating compounds in the poppy plant's seeds. Cyrus, with the help of his daughter Ava, needed several years of experimentation to narrow down the exact variety of poppy that, when nurtured with the excrement of sheep whose main diet was native plants, produced an abundance of the most potent seeds. The extraction process already in use by the well-established Persian perfume industry had to be only slightly modified to achieve effective results.

Mak was the only non-family member to be trusted with any significant part of the production since the States-based manufacturing had started fifty years ago. His apprenticeship with Sattar had lasted long enough to judge both the integrity of the trainee and their ability to function under the influence of the powerful vapors. Nausea, vomiting, constipation, dizzy spells, dry-mouth, disorientation, dementia, and addiction were all side effects that could disqualify even the most earnest aspirant, so suitable chemists were chosen as much by natural selection as they were by merit.

Satisfied with the progress of his brews, Mak relocked the mixing room vault before returning to check on Angel. All of the sixteen Chinese crates had been neatly stacked with their backs to main walkway so that they opened from behind, the better to discourage a casual inspection. Mak measured the area they took up with a retractable tape and calculated the cubic feet being used. Multiplying by a factor of ten dollars, he wrote down the weekly storage rate in his spiral-bound pocket ledger. Angel and Ramon had already retrieved the other boxes from the second floor and stacked them on the loading dock. The long and narrow heavy oak crates, reinforced with steel banding and secured with metal hasps, were smothered in dark green paint and protected with a sturdy padlock. Mak and Angel re-measured.

"How much do I collect for these, amigo?" Angel asked.

Mak penciled a calculation. "Let's see, they've been here for fourteen weeks. At six and a half cubic feet, they owe us $910 for storage."

Angel frowned. "But they are very heavy, my friend. Ramon and I will have a difficult time with them, no?" he picked up one end to demonstrate.

"We don't have a scale here to charge them by the pound," Mak reminded him. He knew he couldn't prevent Angel from "losing" some of the shipment. Most of Laden's secret storage customers were the same people they normally did business with: shipping agents, customs specialists, truckers, and other warehouse managers. They all understood the difference between "authorized transactions" and "off the books," and none of them were keen to have their gray market enterprise exposed. They preferred being pilfered to being found out, which reduced their motivation to take issue with a few missing pieces, however valuable. Because he was in charge of transportation, Angel was the one who would have to explain the discrepancy between how many boxes were sent for storage and how many were returned, and his petty crime skills had so far kept the enterprise functioning bloodlessly. It was his job to collect the money, so he always kept a gun and muscular assistant in the truck for potentially serious confrontations.

"Okay, my friend. Ramon and I will come back for the truck tomorrow and take them to Long Island," he told Mak. The delivery was four hours away and neither of them wanted to spend Saturday night riding in a truck.

Mak had his own priorities. "I can't come back here tomorrow so you'll have to take the truck now. Do you have a place to park overnight?" Laden had never had an entire truck stolen, but opportunistic New York street thieves couldn't be trusted to leave any inviting target untouched for too long.

"We can park it in front of my uncle's house in Queens. It's on the way to Riverhead anyhow. We'll meet you back here Monday morning. Si?"

"As long as it all gets delivered and paid for. Have you seen your Arab friends recently?" Mak added, always suspicious of new customers.

Angel had a tendency to accept whatever business came through trusted sources and seemed unconcerned. "No, they stopped by my house but I wasn't there."

"Better be careful. Some hombres play by their own rules," Mak warned, having seen what could happen when there was dishonor among thieves.

"I can take care of myself," Angel boasted, showing off the bowie knife tucked against his paunch. "Come on, Ramon, let's get these on the truck and out of here. Don't want to keep the senoritas waiting too long." Ramon took most of the weight as they hoisted the dense wooden crates onto the truck and slid them in. Mak cringed as they crashed against the wall of the truck with a metallic clang.

"Careful, Ramon. Don't want to break the pretty flowers," Angel laughed.

Mak was not amused.

"Don't worry, my friend," Angel assured Mak. "He's just in a hurry to make his movie tonight."

Ramon's physical strength exceeded his mental capacity and he grinned foolishly. His form-fitting T-shirt was stretched over a strapping torso and tucked into tight jeans. His bushy mane bordered a squared face that was unanimated by vacant brown eyes set too far apart to make sense. Much taller and stronger than Angel, Ramon was as loyal, dumb, and obedient as a pet mastiff who knew how to beg and come on command.

Mak waited for them to finish loading and rolled down the alley door after they left. The ATF Agents watching from the building across the alley pushed their telephoto lens through the horizontal blinds and recorded the activity.

CHAPTER 33

Nigel walked the mile-and-a-half from the studio to the restaurant in Little Italy where he was meeting Dante's father,
Dominic, for his usual Saturday afternoon briefing. The refreshing rain of the previous evening had removed a lot of the
pollution from the air, and Nigel worked up a brisk pace, imagining he was a young man dribbling up the pitch with his cousins. Long drafts of low particulate oxygen rushed through his
system, cleansing out layers of tobacco and alcohol-withered
cells. He dug his rock and roll boot-heels into the uneven pavement like a forward uses his spikes. Finally over the winter
cough that would have contradicted any good news he could
have shared, he promised himself to phone home with the fa-
vorable Sunday overseas rates.

Dominic was at a table near the back of Villa Lupi nursing
an espresso when Nigel got there. The waitress sitting with him
got up and went back behind the bar. Dominic offered the seat to
Nigel.

"You look well," Dominic said in perfect English, though his
thoughts were still old country. "And my Dante?" He shifted his
considerable weight in the creaky wooden chair and locked eyes.

"I saw Dante last night," Nigel reported, knowing that was the
only thing Dominic was really interested in. "He looked okay."

"Okay? What does that mean?" Dominic stared through him.

Nigel's British manners were as useless as clipping shears against Dominic's Italian stones. "He was at The Black Sheep. Donny was looking after him." Nigel deflected responsibility.

"You mean Donny and him were getting high in the back room again?"

"I don't know about that," Nigel lied poorly.

Having no patience for posturing, Dominic snorted. "Travis will tell me the truth. He'll be here soon."

Like so many of the restaurants in Little Italy, Villa Lupi was as much an office as it was a place to eat, and Dominic held court there once a month for his unofficial employees and spies. Wishing he were somewhere else, Nigel accepted the cup of espresso that the waitress offered and pushed back from the small round table. Dominic hunched over his empty white demitasse, stirring the grounds with a tiny spoon. His caffeine assisted heart rate pumped anger, guilt, responsibility, and remorse though his bloodstream and into the battlefield of rationalization. He wasn't a particularly religious man – tending to treat Jesus the way he would an under-achieving employee – so his silent curses were more an admission of defeat than an attempt to offend the Almighty.

Dante had been a difficult child since the freezing January day he was born. The ambulance had an accident on the way to pick up Dominic's wife, and their rear-wheel-drive Cadillac almost met the same fate on the late night icy roads. Dante was born jaundiced, hairy, and undersized, which Dominic blamed on his wife's genetics. His other son, Anthony, was married with a baby and a mortgage, living on Long Island. A few years older than Dante, Anthony worked in the main Pecorino Properties office with his father and uncle, managing buildings and providing for a sizable network of dependents. He was skilled at hiding the unsavory parts of his genetic inheritance, and most people saw him as the good-natured, all American, handsome athlete that families hope for – which made the runtish ravings of his younger brother all the more difficult to tolerate. Anthony had earned a degree in law from City College, but bypassed going into practice in favor of donning the mantle of designated successor to the lucrative family business. His limited knowledge of legal matters helped keep his troublesome younger brother's problems from tainting the rest of the Pecorino enterprises, but there was only so much he could do.

Since birth, Dante's redeeming qualities had been an irresistibly impish voice and soft blue eyes that could, and did, charm the pants off many women. But those innocent times were a distant memory, and now, on the other side of thirty, Dante's skills were limited to the cunning of entitlement. The persuasive power of his plaintive voice had been sapped by years of smoking cigarettes and snorting cocaine, and even his mother found it difficult to hear his hoarse laughter and constant chest cough. She could barely remember the few good days of his childhood, which she nourished, bead by bead, every Sunday in church. Dominic had bailed him out of jail, paid off judges, sent him through rehab, and threatened to cut him off – all without being able to alter his son's self destructive agenda. But his parents' pain and frustration – and the collective wisdom of the rest of the civilized world – had no effect on how Dante saw himself.

Dante felt like he was at the pinnacle of his career. Although the management company had very little net income, Pecorino Partners was busy booking live performances for the British bands Nigel had connected them with, and promoting the career of Bosco Dish. Their only office occupied the entire second floor their four-story building in the West Village. Dante's apartment, which had been modernized by the family's interior designer, occupied the top floor. Nigel lived below him in one of the two units on the third floor. The other third floor apartment was used as a crash pad, love nest, and drug den. Dante's main concern was making sure he had enough drugs to keep himself, his girlfriends, and musicians high. Just off 7th Avenue, the building leased the ground floor to a trendy retail boutique whose rent covered the overhead of the property, and whose clientele was a constant source of social interaction and uninvited trouble.

The boutique sold an eclectic collection of clothing and accessories to pierced, tattooed, leathered, chained, and directionless youth in search of permanent cool. Some of them got jobs working at the boutique, and one of them, a chopped-hair, dyed blond everybody called Starla, turned her part-time job downstairs into a full-time occupation on the floors above. An escapee from a repressive Teutonic household in upstate New York whose birth name was Gertrude, Starla's taste for the high life had become insatiable, and overcompensating from her stint as a Tibetan Buddhist, she had dedicated her youth to violating every moral barrier she encountered. Her initial transaction with Dante of sex-for-drugs had progressed into a three-day binge that ended up with her staying in Dante's apartment, and her bedroom skills were so satisfying that Dante gave her a position at the management company office just to keep her available. Sonya Diaz, the other management company assistant, had also come from the boutique, but she had a work ethic and clerical skills. A native New Yorker, she advertised her tantalizing Puerto Rican features in halter tops and skin-tight jeans, and encouraged Nigel to make her extra-curricular training a priority.

Dante rarely came down to the office before the afternoon, and when he did, he spent most of the time smoking at his desk and trying to arrange his next score. Starla wasn't on any particular schedule and concentrated on food, fun, and fashion – which meant that she helped decide what to eat, how they were going to score, and where out-of-towners could buy cool clothes and accessories. She subcontracted most of the visiting bands' requests for female companionship to the girls in the boutique, but serviced the particularly virulent musicians herself in the apartment upstairs when Dante wasn't around.

Dante believed that his main job as manager was to make sure his bands were pumped up and respected in the battle for stage time. He used his endless supply of bullshit and drugs to manipulate the musicians' egos, and the power of his family's name to intimidate his adversaries. Pecorino Partners had teamed up with Dante's hoodlum friend, Donny DiCalipari, to manage Freddy's band, and an independent label run by one of Nigel's United Kingdom friends had released their single. Bosco Dish was developing into a popular regional act, and Dante, Donny, and Freddy believed they were on the verge of greatness. The notoriety of airplay had drawn a steady barrage of tapes and phone calls from other groups hungry for representation, and like anyone who ever put up a shingle claiming access to fortune and fame, the activity gave Pecorino Partners the illusion of being relevant, so in a business predicated on illusion, Pecorino Partners appeared to be as legitimate as anyone else.

By early 1982, the lessons of Dale Carnegie had filtered through all levels of society. There were so many aspiring musicians who believed they could achieve anything with the right amount of effort that their failure was virtually guaranteed. They didn't accept the fact that careers are not built on merit alone, and that the competition for attention wasn't a talent contest. There simply wasn't enough opportunity to go around, but that didn't stop anyone from ignoring the odds any more than lotto players are dissuaded from purchasing tickets. The logic that buying an actual lottery ticket was a safer bet than channeling the vigor of youth into to becoming an all-conquering pop phenomenon was completely lost on tens of thousands of young suburbanites who were enamored with the pop stardom of the Beatles, electrified by the rantings of Led Zeppelin, politicized by the musings of Bob Dylan, carried away on the Allman Brothers express, and justified by the miracle of Woodstock. In the collective mind of America, music had transmuted from a pleasant and sometimes passionate diversion, into a cultural phenomenon that rivaled politics, finance, health, and war. On any given day, moderately accomplished and morally adventurous musicians could exert enough force on society to cause it to re-evaluate itself – or even change direction. The results were sometimes poignant examples of how society could be improved by small groups of determined individuals, whereby ordinary musicians' obvious lack of qualifications only lent credence to the integrity of their message. But almost no one was that lucky or unselfish, and the misinterpretation of the risk-reward formula was distorted into the belief that, besides fame and fortune, the winner's prize included immortality. Sober, methodical, and ambitious pretenders, with only smatterings of creative insight, devoted their lives to the "winner take all" free-for-all they mistook the music business for, and their dreams, often redressed as spiritual callings, were pursued with evangelical zeal. In the face of disappointment and failure, some used drugs to perpetuate their ambition, while others employed the more aggressive strategy of "anything goes" – rules be damned. Access to the promised land of stardom was controlled by record and media companies, whose conduit to talent was fed by a system of nightclubs, managers, agents, and studio operators, and all paths to glory were crowded with the living, the dying, and the dead.

Nigel had the industry knowledge and credibility to make both the management company and studio relevant. More than anyone else, he was the one who put Pecorino Partners in the fame game. Record companies, other managers, talent agents, and musicians visited and maintained contact with the Pecorino Partners office because of Nigel, and he split his time between there and the studio. Dominic had only been to the management office once, and was so aggravated by what he found there that he had kept his vow to never return. He assigned Anthony the job of interfacing with the decadent idiocy of his younger brother, and Anthony kept his father as uninformed as possible. Seeing Dominic wallowing in regrets, Nigel realized that his interview was over. He leaned back in his chair with his arms crossed and indulged his senses in the colorful street life bustling through Little Italy on a bright spring Saturday afternoon. There was plenty to look at, but Travis' entrance was hard to miss.

"Afternoon Nigel, Mr. Pecorino," Travis greeted them in a Texan drawl that thickened when he wasn't working at the club.

"Sit down, Cowboy," Dominic instructed gruffly, and pushed a chair toward him with his leg.

Travis complied with a tip of his black ten-gallon and a nod to Nigel. At six foot two, with broad shoulders and calf-roping arms, Travis was obviously qualified for a job that took physical strength. Along with the hat, the stringy hair hanging down around his face hid the aging that the nightlife had carved into his features. Removing his sunglasses, he squinted noticeably.

"You look a little tired, Travis. Espresso?" Dominic nodded to the attentive waitress. The hard wooden chairs offered Travis no comfort, and he shifted his weight as if he were trying to find a comfortable position in a saddle. Dressed in hand-tooled cowboy boots and tight blue jeans, with a longhorn buckle on his wide leather belt, Travis was always ready to quit his city ways and go back home. He enjoyed looking out-of-place and used his appearance as both a shield against the city and a challenge to New York's unwritten dress codes. He usually dated country girls from out of town who were too drunk to remember, or too kind to report, his sexual underachievement, and maintained his Texas soul with six chords and a cheap steel string guitar he kept in his Brooklyn apartment. At work, Travis hid his musical tastes, because country music was not only unpopular in New York, it was an insult. A few hundred years had done little to erase the common New York perception that the South was a place full of stupid redneck bigots, and playing country music in Manhattan was still akin to singing your fight song in the boot camp of your enemies. The tension and hostility created by Travis' accent and appearance kept him ready for a fight, which was the way he had been trained to deal with adversity. Oblivious to Travis' appearance, Dominic continued his interrogation. "Nigel tells me you saw Dante last night."

Travis checked with Nigel before answering. He knew that the dissemination of information about the activities at the club was potentially self-incriminating, and he could only guess at what Nigel had already told him. Dominic watched their interaction like a detective interviewing partners in crime looks for different versions of the same story. Travis and Nigel had been hired when the Pecorinos took over management of The Black Sheep, and they shared an outsider's status in the mafia-scented hierarchy of the Pecorino companies. They were both trusted – up to a point – but it was no accident that neither of them was from New York or understood a word of Italian. Although they knew that part of their job was to keep tabs on Dante, they were never sure how much Dante knew about their roles or when they were just being tested. Travis picked up his tiny espresso cup with two fingers as if he were handling a baby rattlesnake. He started with the facts. "Dante came in about ten last night."

"And?"

The snake's head twisted in his grip. "He and Donny were working on the roadie situation."

"Working on it? I spoke with the precinct Director and he told me they were going to be released. What was there to work on?"

"The roadies never made it back to the club."

"What about those lazy-ass musicians? Did they make it?"

"Yeah, they played one short set but it wasn't very good."

"Why not? You broke the rules?" Dominic eyed him suspiciously.

"No sir. I didn't give them anything until after they played."

"Then why weren't they any good? Did it have something to do with Dante?" Dominic probed.

"No sir, Freddy was complaining about the sound."

"Well, isn't that Dennis' job?"

Travis had to think of a way to drag Dennis out from under the bus before it ran him over. "Yes, but the roadies usually set up Freddy's monitor mix, and they weren't there. Richard did the best he could but I think Freddy was in a bad mood because of the night before." Travis redirected.

"What happened the night before?"

"Well heck, I thought you knew about the bust and then the hospital and all that."

"The hospital? I didn't hear about that. Who went to the hospital?"

"Donny's girl, Randi," Travis snitched. He and Donny were macho rivals.

Dominic had known Donny since his grade school bully days. "He beat her up again?"

"Oh, I don't know why she was in the hospital." Travis lied.

Dominic's inquiry moved back to its theme. "Where was Dante? Was he involved?"

"With what, sir?"

"The hospital. Did Dante go to the hospital?"

Travis claimed innocence. "I don't rightly know."

"What about you?" Dominic asked Nigel. "Didn't either of you see him last night? How bad was he?" Nigel and Travis shrugged in non-committal unison. The mention of "hospital" raised Dominic's blood pressure. He pushed back from the table and his gaze wandered to a giant pastoral mural painted on the restaurant wall. It showed the rolling hills, vineyards, and villas of his native country, and he recalled simpler times when the family vacationed there. Anthony and Dante were teenagers when they spent a whole magical summer on a relative's farm in the Abruzzo mountains, learning to speak a little of the native tongue and imprinting the culture into their fertile imaginations. Dominic could still see his boys laughing like devils, throwing grapes at one another, slurping up long strings of fat pasta noodles with saucy faces, and running with sticks, chasing sheep through the meadows. It was the highlight of their childhood as far as Dominic was concerned – an opinion that might have changed had he known that Dante had caught up with one of the sheep and lost his virginity. Anthony never told their parents because he didn't want Dante to squeal about the abortion Anthony's sixteen-year-old high school girl-friend had the year before, and these were only two of the secrets harbored by brothers genetically disposed to omerta. Dominic knew that the idyllic mural was just a painting, and the torn Italian flag framed on the wall above the bar reminded him that history has tattered edges. His glazed eyes indicated that the difficult part of the meeting was over.

Nigel broke the silence with a question for Travis. "What time did you close up last night?"

"The band left early but we couldn't get the bar cleared until quitting time."

"Was Officer Hemming still there?" Dominic interjected.

"He left around 1:00 but I took care of him," Travis reported.

Dominic returned to his agony. "What about Dante? When did he leave?"

"He left with Donny right after the show. I reckon they went to the police station or maybe the hospital."

"How much did you give them?"

"I took care of them," was all Travis would admit to. He liked alcohol much more than drugs, and his preferences qualified him as a distributor.

The waitress interrupted. "Call for you at the bar, Mr. P."

Dominic left the table and stood leaning against the counter, watching Travis and Nigel as he spoke in Italian to the caller.

Left alone, the two suspects compared stories. "Where'd you git off to last night?" Travis asked Nigel.

"I went to CBGB's to see some friends of mine. Hunt and Tony Sales sat in with Iggy's band. It was thick and everyone was there."

Nigel hung with his countrymen whenever possible. CBGB's was a dingy, beer-soaked nightclub whose outsized reputation belied its shabby appearance, but Nigel was comfortable in the smoke-filled, crowded atmosphere that reminded him of the London dives where his career began. Famous as a place where punk bands punished their audiences with assaults of sensory-numbing distortion, disaffected teens, rudderless toughs, and androgynous posers reeling from alcohol, snappers, and ecstasy vied for floor space with head-butts, knees, and elbows. Spit was interpreted as a sign of approval, and mayhem was the preferred form of social order. Only the hardiest patrons survived more than a few nights at the legendary club, and in spite of the incorrigible crowd choking on fouled air, every band that played New York wanted to gig there. The tiny stage was un-separated from the open floor by a twelve-inch riser, which gave the anarchic revelers direct access to the performers, who occasionally had to use their instruments to defend their territory. For reasons known only to a few, the club had become a filter for acceptance into the elite world of road-worthy bands with major label backing. The Ramones, Patti Smith, Blondie, and many others earned their fame there, and commanding the stage, controlling the audience, and making it most of the way through their set was a rite of passage that proved that they were tough enough to endure the brutalities of the career they thought they wanted. The gale force hostility of a rowdy audience who encouraged failure was an effective winnow, blowing uncertain motivations and unsure performances off the high-profile platform of lowbrow accomplishment. Record company scouts, talent agents, band managers, club operators, studio owners, equipment company representatives, promoters, and marketers judged the winners and awarded the prizes. Devoted fans, girlfriends, boyfriends, relatives, roadies, drug dealers, and hangers-on lent some sense of restraint to the performances, mixing seamlessly with the social miscreants, narcotic agents, code enforcement officials, collection thugs, libidinous teens, and parents looking for runaways. The fact that this chaotic assemblage of crossed purposes actually recurred with predictable regularity was as much an indicator that marked what many had come to call "the decline of western civilization" as it was a testament to the unfathomable instincts of the human species. Like Woodstock before it, but on a much smaller scale, CBGB's had become a microcosmic convergence of social dichotomies that had mutated into an evolutionary expression. Everyone knew that the culture of excess and the revulsions it precipitated were symbolic of something poignant, they just weren't sure what. Philosophers, sociologists, criminologists, and psychologists exerted their disciplines shoulder to shoulder with writers, videographers, and photojournalists who documented and studied the phenomenon.

Nigel only went to CBGB's when he knew the band that was playing there. He had already earned all the street credibility he needed from participating in the live-music melees of proving-ground clubs in London, and in his veteran years, he had come to prefer the slightly more civil atmosphere of the similar New York club, Max's Kansas City.

Travis had only been to CBGB's once and still suffered from random headaches brought on by the head-butt he had received there. "I can't believe you like that joint," Travis admitted, rubbing his forehead, remembering.

"Who said I like it?" Nigel corrected him.

"Then why do you go there?"

"See friends, hear the word on the street, keep us all in business, mate."

Dominic returned to the table in the middle of the conversation. "You think you're keeping us in business?" he said indignantly.

"Of course not, sir," Nigel corrected himself. "I was only speaking figuratively."

Dominic ignored his reasoning. "I'll tell you what keeps us in business: rent. Rent and the tenants who pay it," he growled. "They make up for the money you two piss away in that studio and nightclub. When are we ever going to see a profit from you?" he challenged. "How much do you need this month?" he added, jabbing a finger at Nigel.

Nigel fielded the accusation smoothly. "For the studio or the management company?" He was in charge of both, or so he thought.

Dominic didn't bother separating Dante's follies in his own calculation. "Combined."

Nigel had been saving a bit of bookkeeping legerdemain precisely for this moment. "Well, the studio doesn't need anything. We've had a good month and expenses are low," he accounted smugly.

"Well, *there's* some good news. What about the management company?"

"You'll have to talk to Anthony about that. He and Dante had quite a row about the checkbook last week, and I'm not sure what they decided," Nigel answered, clearing himself.

Dominic just wanted the meeting over with so he could get Anthony on the phone. "What about you, Cowboy? How much do we owe?"

Travis didn't take responsibility for anyone else's habits. "$1500 for the month," he said blandly.

"$1500? Does that include the door and bar?"

"No sir, that's just for what the door didn't cover." He flared his nostrils like a bridled horse. "Anthony has been keeping track of the bar and the betting." Travis wasn't really qualified to handle drugs *or* money, but he was strong enough to keep from getting robbed, and dumb enough to control.

Dominic returned to his theme. "So where is Dante now? Either of you know?"

Neither hazarded a guess.

CHAPTER 34

Rebecca took the crosstown bus to the West Side. Then, with her soft canvas duffle bag slung across her shoulder for easy movement through the weekend getaway crowd, she took a subway up to Penn Station. Her hair was tied back in a ponytail, and the years melted away as the 3:15 train rumbled out of the city and closer to the scenes of her youth. The clatter of metal wheels was a soundtrack for the montage of rusting construction equipment and soot-spewing factories that blighted the dead zone between New York and New Jersey, but April had sprayed a green mist over the dead stalks in the meadowlands and the barren excavation pits were tainted with signs of life. Rebecca had to wait until the train passed over the mouth of Raritan Bay before full scenes of spring sprouted through the window as the train veered eastward then south, through the lush countryside and coastal towns, on its regular journey down to Atlantic City. Rebecca wasn't sure whether her father had retrieved the message she left on the office answering machine telling him which train she was on, but she was looking forward to the brisk walk along the boardwalk to his office in case he wasn't there when she arrived at the Asbury Park station. The weekend strollers, skaters, and bike riders accompanied her on a leg-stretching stroll in the rumble zone of the crashing surf. It was the last bit of innocent pleasure she would feel for a long time.

Rebecca climbed three flights of stairs up to her father's second-floor office and found the familiar door locked. She couldn't see anything clearly, but a light glowing through the textured glass transom with Herbert Draper Associates painted in gold-trimmed black letters indicated someone was inside. Her knocking resonated in the empty hallway. She heard a phone ring, but then it stopped. She wandered to the big window at the end of the hallway that she used to stand in front of when she was young and savored the fresh air passing through it. The late-day sun sparkled off the smooth surface of the distant ocean, hiding the latent forces of the waves until they crushed the beach in a rhythmic assault. Rebecca clutched her bag, mesmerized by the pink noise symphony.

"Becca?" her father called from behind her. She turned to make sure she was hearing an actual voice and saw him leaning halfway out of his office door. "I thought you were going to call me," he spoke quietly.

"I decided to surprise you. Never know who might be listening in on our plans," she teased.

"I would have picked you up at the bus. You walked all the way?" he said, looking around the hallway to establish that they were alone.

"No, I took the train. I like the trains better; they're more predictable."

"Look at you!" He stepped back, admiring his creation. "Big city girl now. I like your hair tied back like that."

"Thank you, Daddy." She put her arms around him and kissed him on the cheek. "It's great to see you," she exhaled, not really looking.

Herb's paunch was swollen underneath his button-down business shirt. He rarely wore a tie on Saturdays, and his open collar revealed a puffy neck, covered with a day-old stubble field that ended in the underbrush of his chest hairs. "Tax season is killing me," he grumbled, unconsciously brushing short meaty fingers through the stubborn strands of hair that had retreated to the sides of his balding head. "Come on in. I'm doing some prep for a client who's coming in about an hour, but we can talk while I'm working. Helen's not here on Saturdays so you'll have to make your own coffee if you want it."

Helen was Herb's receptionist, secretary, and assistant. A large, pleasant woman with Nordic genes, she had been with Herb for the past eighteen years and there was no confusion about her role. Rebecca sat at Helen's desk in the main reception area while her father worked through a stack of papers in his adjacent office, totaling figures on a calculator with a noisy paper print out. The worn-out swiveling office chair reminded Rebecca of her own desk, and she swung around and peered through the drawn mini-blinds to compare the views. The window overlooked a featureless parking lot, and the chemical smells of ink cartridges, freshly bleached paper, and decaying synthetic furniture reminded her of what she had escaped from: the spacious suite had more filing cabinets than furniture, and was static to the point of oppressive. The office opposite her father's was empty, and her parents still hoped that she would someday tire of the city and join the practice. Rebecca turned on Helen's radio and channeled through the choices, unable to find anything she could enjoy.

"This must be pretty boring for you," her father commiserated from the other room without stopping his tally.

"I'm not bored," Rebecca fibbed.

"I just have a little more work to do, and then we'll talk."

"Okay. I'm in no hurry." Rebecca swiveled her chair in a complete circle and straightened up the papers on Helen's desk. All the Draper children carried the unsettled Sephardic Jewish spirit that had adapted to the political uncertainties, periodic persecutions, and limited opportunities in Europe. Rebecca's parents had met through the social network of the Jewish community in Middlesex County, New Jersey. Her mother, Rina, was sent from Romania to live in America with her aunt when she was six and never saw her parents again. Herb's parents had emigrated from Bucharest a generation earlier and were already established in America by the time Herb and his three siblings were born. They had settled in central New Jersey where, despite the Depression of the '30s, the mix of rolling farmland and industrial manufacturing presented opportunities for immigrants. Herb's father got a job at a local dry goods store, and when they were old enough, Herb and his siblings branched out into professional practices to serve the suburbs growing all around them. His oldest brother became an optometrist, his sister a librarian, and his younger brother went to law school. Herb fulfilled the family need for financial expertise, and his relationship with a distant orphaned cousin, Rina, was as much an arranged marriage as it was a personal relationship. Herb liked rows of numbers and predictable results, and wanted to perpetuate the fortuitous lifestyle he and his wife had created in the challenging postwar environment. He had no interest in mystery, and his modest ambitions didn't depend on risky accounting practices. Were it not for the activities of one client, he would have been free to add and subtract and multiply his children in the relative peace and safety of American suburbia. More than the religious symbols, the large black and white photos of expressive faces plastered to the entryway walls of the Middlesex County Community Jewish Center conveyed the feeling that the spirit of mankind is timeless, universal, and stateless, and more than most cultures, Jews embraced the idea that the human condition is a shared experience. That's why all faiths were welcome in their midst, and that is how Homa's father, Arshan Zemmi, came to be a familiar face at Herb's sanctuary in 1951.

When he first showed up, Arshan was young, single, and broke – which was not unusual for a recent immigrant. He had come of age in the aftermath of World War II and left the rural setting of his childhood in Iran to find his place in the world. His journey had started with a trek to the area capital, Esfahan, and he paid for a long dusty bus ride from there to the Mediterranean port of Beirut with money he borrowed from his uncle. He worked in Lebanon's open-air produce market for a few months and made several lifelong connections before taking a job on a cargo ship headed for America.

One day, Herb's uncle, Morris Draper, stopped by the unemployment office to hire someone to help him take provisions back to his grocery store in South Amboy. He found Arshan treading water in Jersey City's pool of unemployed foreign nationals and gave Arshan a job as a delivery boy. But Arshan's formative years in the Zagros Mountains of Central Iran left him knowing more about milk buckets than milk bottles, and he didn't speak English well enough to make the necessary small talk with the retail customers, so Morris recommended him to someone who needed help on a small dairy farm in the area. Arshan proved to be hard working, reliable, and intelligent, and the farmer soon put him in charge of all the animals. He slept and ate in the barn, but gradually learned enough about his employers' customs to be invited to dinner at their table. They brought him to the Jewish Community Center on Saturdays so he could catch a ride back to Jersey City on his days off, and with a little help from other immigrants, Arshan picked up English and learned to read the newspaper.

Articles and picture books about the recent atrocities of the war in Europe filled the newspaper pages, and Arshan developed a deep sympathy for the people that had taken him in and treated him well. His latent intellectual curiosity blossomed, and numerous political maps expanded his understanding of his own origins, but it wasn't until he found out about Persepolis that Arshan heard his calling. Persepolis had been located a few hours south of where Arshan grew up, but he always thought of it as just another tall tale in a region known for old ruins, myths, and fables. His family came to nearby Esfahan a few times a year to sell the produce they had grown, and Arshan would accompany his father and uncle to the market, riding in the back of his uncle's truck with cloth bags full of wheat and poppy seeds. The salted mutton they also had for sale was wrapped in muslin, and along with bales of wool, attracted flies, so it was Arshan's job to keep the insects off the produce. He was impervious to the strong odors of carrion, but teenagers who lived in the city were repulsed by the stench it left on his clothes and steered clear of his company. Too young to share the hookah with his father and uncle, Arshan preferred the sweet taste of yogurt lassi at the Indian food stall, so his father let him wander off while the men were conducting business. His greatest pleasure was to stand in the alley where the buskers congregated and watch them perform as he sipped his tasty drink. Musicians playing odd stringed instruments, flutes, and hand drums set the mood for dancers in native costumes. Jugglers, magicians, fire-eaters, and animal acts entertained and the audience and solicited donations. The sights and sounds seeped into his soul, but he had little interaction with the performers until one attractive young dancer approached him with her cup. She moved with a snake charmer's sensuous grace and told him her name was Persepolis. Still a virgin, Arshan's serpent awoke, and he gave her the few coins he had left in his pocket. She returned his generosity with the gift of a scented ribbon that he cherished and took back to his mountain home. Using the ribbon to animate her vivid memory, he dreamed of finding her again when he came of age. The fantasy lasted for a few formative years, and though he returned several times to the alleyway where they had met, he never saw her again. Eventually, her memory faded and he didn't think of her for several years – until he saw her name printed on a map in front of him.

Arshan had come to the public library in Jersey City to learn about his adoptive country, but couldn't resist the urge to look up Persepolis in one of the reference books. He was probably just hoping to see a picture of a beautiful girl, but his curiosity opened the doors of his imagination that had been sealed by the busywork of survival. The picture of Persepolis was an artist's rendering of a big square city elevated above the desert floor with numerous stone columns densely packed under the rectangular roofs they supported. Arshan was fascinated and decided to read a little bit of the text, hoping to relight the childhood flame flickering in his memory. He wasn't curious about the ancient kings, Cyrus and Darius, or the story of its destruction by Alexander the Great, but in the artist's interpretation of what the surrounding countryside was thought to look like, Arshan recognized the green hillsides and running water of his youth. Engaged, he read that the ancient Persians were the first to organize the various tribes in the region into cooperative farms, and the city of Persepolis could have never been built or maintained without the constant supply of food that the farmers – his ancient ancestors – produced. Delving into a description of their accomplishments, he read about the religious beliefs of the Zoroastrians, and in stark contrast to what he had experienced in his own lifetime, was intrigued by the explanation that religious tolerance was the basis for their success. His forefathers had understood that only by accepting the beliefs of their neighbors, and allowing them to live according their own principles, could they expect harmony and cooperation. And although the Zoroastrians were capable fighters who had become the dominant tribe in the region, the Achaemenid Empire was built by the application of wisdom, not by the intimidation of force. Subsistence farmers and nomadic herders were attracted to the peaceful bazaars run by the tolerant Zoroastrians, and the miracle of human cooperation in the geologically fortuitous fertile crescent gave rise to what was, in its time, the richest and most civilized city on earth. Inside Persepolis' fortressed walls, the abundance of necessities allowed some people the luxury of time to pursue goals not directly related to their survival, and art, science, and politics were able to develop. The early Persian contributions to the fields of education, writing, commerce, and architecture were a direct result of their "One World" religion that preached peace and tolerance.

Understanding the importance of cooperation, Arshan felt pride and purpose at the discovery that his direct ancestors had built Persepolis on such lofty principles. The notion that the tribes of ancient Persia had many faiths, and that the Jewish people, although a distinct minority, were one of them, also captured his attention. It was impossible to know if a tributary of the tribes of Abraham flowed through his bloodlines, but the knowledge of shared history resonated with his current experience. Armed with his new revelations, he returned to the Middlesex County Jewish Community Center a changed man and took up the cause of restoring peace and sanity to a world recovering from the injuries sustained in its most recent episode of fratricidal madness. His relationship with his Jewish benefactors intensified into a lifelong connection.

Arshan Zemmi met Samani Monsouri in 1955 at a Persian social gathering in New York. Samani, who had come from her family home in Queens with her father and siblings, was attracted to the high-spirited, handsome young man Arshan had become. She accepted her prescribed female role in society without her deceased mother's guidance, and with excited tales of the greatness of ancient Persia, Arshan easily won the approval of Samani's father and brothers. Their traditional wedding was attended by the growing network of interconnected Persian expatriates drawn to the opportunities in the new world. Arshan joined the family business, which benefited from his experience with farming and his Mid East contacts. On Arshan's first trip back to Persia with Saeed, the Monsouri's confirmed their suspicions that some of the Red Crown poppy seeds Laden imported had been supplied by Arshan's family farm, which abutted Monsouri-owned properties already dedicated to that purpose. The Monsouris explained how they were able to grow such potent seeds to Arshan, and Arshan told his family to mimic the planting and grazing patterns of their successful neighbors. Although they didn't understand the relationship of the sheep to the poppies, the Zemmis followed Arshan's instructions and also began to specialize in Red Crown poppy production. Arshan's father and uncle didn't know why their seeds fetched such high prices, but nearby farmers became jealous of the Zemmi family's ascendant fortunes. In an attempt to dim their interest in finding out the whole story, Laden Imports cleverly bought some of the less potent seeds the neighbors produced. But the neighbors still complained to the authorities, and the Monsouri's original perfumery in Esfahan fell under the scrutiny of an egalitarian regime suspicious of successful private enterprise. In 1974, Dadi Monsouri was jailed for passport violations, and the perfumery was raided. The fundamentalists who eventually overthrew Shah Pahlavi had already taken control of parts of the prison system, and Dadi was never seen again. After that, all the significant operations were moved to the Laden warehouse in New York, where Sattar carried on the formulations while the family tried to win Dadi's release.

Importing the raw materials and fabricating the base substances brought the Monsouri heirs in closer contact with Dadi's business partners, Dr. Nouri, and his cousin Bahram Darius. Descendants of the Farsi family, Dr. Nouri and Bahram maintained a minority interest in the perfume side of the business, and together with the Monsouris, operated the real estate holding company, Darius Trust. The two families had some separate business interests, but their common ancestry, real estate, and the perfume business kept them closely knit. Sattar, with Mak's help, continued to make the basic poppy seed formulas in the Laden warehouse that were used for perfumes and bouquets, but the concentrated product manufacturing was moved directly from Esfahan to a secret lab in the Old Medical Building, a few floors below Dr. Nouri's regular offices. Dr. Nouri used his medical training to help Sattar develop new, more potent analgesic formulations, and the relatively harmless enterprise of making mildly opiated perfumes evolved into a lucrative but dangerous side business. Due to Sattar's other responsibilities and travel schedule, Dr. Nouri began to oversee the manufacture of the medicinal strength products, and Bahram's son, Rhamin, took a more active role in their wholesale distribution.

Arshan's long association with the Draper family had provided the level of trust necessary for the disclosure of sensitive financial information, and Draper Associates started doing the accounting for the Darius Trust in 1968. The siblings continued to use Draper Associates even after Arshan disappeared because, by that time, Herb knew more about their finances than they did. Herb had accepted the Monsouri accounting business at a time when he needed the business, and had become a well paid, if uncomfortable, accomplice in their gray market commerce. As their accountant of record for the preceding years, Herb was professionally liable for their previous tax returns, so he chose to continue to be involved as a way of reducing his risk and maintaining his income. His role as accountant expanded into that of money handler, and the company used the inconspicuous location of his office as their drop-off and collection point for their cash-and-carry chemical compound commerce. Couriers would pick up gray market Laden products at Herb's office and leave large cash payments there for Herb to transform into legitimate deposits. Herb knew what Laden did, helped them do it, and he knew what would happen if their activities were uncovered – so he did everything he could to protect them.

But by the time Rebecca came to see him on Saturday, Laden had more problems than even Herb knew about: Saeed's financial support of the Lebanese based expatriates bent on recovering the assets nationalized by the Khomeni revolutionaries had earned him the suspicion of agents for the new Iranian government; Sattar's efforts to form alliances with importers of other illegal substances who were interested in his alchemical skills had attracted the attention of international drug enforcement agencies; United States Customs Agents had been tipped off about the excessive poppy seed importing by a newly appointed Iranian trade minister interested in settling a family feud that dated back forty years; and Mak's off-the-books storage business had been connected with the illegal import of guns and Chinese fireworks. Unaware of his client's other problems, Herb's main concern was how to account for the Darius Trust's large cash deposits that seemed to be increasing in size and frequency. He was a good accountant, but not a magician, and he saw the recent flurry of transactions as signs of an approaching blizzard that would eventually result in a devastating avalanche of irregularities. He made the decision to cooperate with the IRS when they first contacted him six months ago and was worried that his involvement would result in jail time. He couldn't imagine how his family would survive if he were imprisoned, and didn't want to upset his daughter unless he absolutely had to.

Herb continued to work in silence, fending off fears of impending doom. Rebecca thumbed nervously through Helen's *People* magazine collection, waiting for her father to finish. "How much longer?" she finally asked.

Herb could have stopped any time, but he didn't know where to start his "other" conversation, so he continued to shuffle paper and peck at his adding machine, searching for the right moment. "Almost done," he called out.

The phone rang and Rebecca answered it. It was her mother. "Rebecca? Is that you?"

"Yes, mother."

"I didn't know you were coming out this weekend. Why didn't you tell us?"

Rebecca was confused and looked at her father, who was monitoring the conversation. "I thought father told you."

Rina paused before answering. "He didn't."

"Well here I am anyway," Rebecca said cheerfully. Her mother didn't speak. "Is something wrong? Aren't you happy I'm home?"

Herb picked up the extension and butted in. "Of course we're happy," he answered for both of them. "Mom's just tired from all the laundry and house chores. The kids are a lot of work. Maybe we should all go out to dinner tonight and save her from cooking."

Rina was not in the mood for niceties. "I already prepared dinner. What time will you be home?"

Herb kept up a cheerful façade. "We'll be there around 6:00. I'm waiting for clients, and as soon as they leave, we'll come. Can I get you anything on the way home?"

"Did you tell her?" Rina asked.

Rebecca sensed a serious tone in her mother's voice.

"Not yet," Herb said, and hung up without saying goodbye.

Rebecca came into his office and stood in front of the desk. "Tell me what, dad? What's going on around here?"

Herb threw his hands behind his head and rocked back in his squeaky chair. "I have some bad news, Becca," he admitted, grimacing.

"What is it?"

"We're under investigation," Herb informed her quietly.

"For what? You never do anything wrong."

"Illegal stuff. Tax fraud." His fingers tightened into a clasp, and he pulled his head forward, simultaneously preventing it from moving with his neck muscles.

"You committed tax fraud? I don't believe it!"

"Keep your voice down. That's not the worst part."

"There's more?" Rebecca followed her father's silent command and shut the door.

"It's Laden," he whispered.

"What's Laden?"

Herb stuttered out part of the story. "Laden has been doing some fishy things and...the authorities have caught onto it."

"Laden? What does that have to do with you?"

"I'm their accountant. I'm responsible for their tax returns."

"You do the accounting for Laden? Why didn't you tell me? Is that how I got the job there?" Rebecca connected the dots. "I still don't understand why *you* are being investigated if *they* did something wrong."

Herb got up and cracked the mini-blinds open. "I don't have time to explain everything now." He moved away from the window. "My clients are here and I need you to wait here in my office. Don't come out. I'll meet them in the office across the hall and you have to keep completely quiet. No phone calls, no moving, and if you have to go to the bathroom just pee in your pants."

"Dad! This is scary. What's going to happen?"

"Just sit still. They'll only be here for a few minutes and then we'll go home." He shut the door to the office and opened the door to the hallway to wait for his appointment.

A dark green BMW pulled into the parking lot and Rhamin Darius got out. "I'll only be a few minutes," he told his passenger.

"I think I've been here before," Homa said, looking up at the three-story office building.

"Maybe you have. Draper's been the family accountant for a long time. You might have come out here with your father when you were young."

"The name sounds familiar. Maybe I did. Hurry, I can't wait to see the Ferris wheel again!"

Rhamin misinterpreted her excitement. "I'll be right back," he promised, closing the car door and swaggering away with his briefcase.

Neither of them noticed the unmarked Mercury Sable parked in the corner of the lot with the newspaper-reading driver.

"Sorry I'm a little late, Mr. Draper." Rhamin greeted Herb with a loose handshake as he entered. "I have a passenger with me and she delayed our departure."

"Well, it's about time you got a date, my young friend," Herb said, assuming his familial persona. "Let's go in the office and we'll get you back in the driver's seat in a few minutes."

Rhamin followed him into the empty office and put his briefcase on the desk as Herb closed the door. He hinged open the top half of the rectangular black leather carrying case that had been insulated with Styrofoam in the exact shape of the two cylindrical glass bottles that it was designed to transport. Rhamin removed the bottles and stood them up on the desk. Herb unlocked the safe and retrieved two identical bottles, both empty, which Rhamin put back in the briefcase. Then Rhamin delicately placed the full bottles in the safe, flipped the double-sided briefcase over, and opened the flaps. Thee were several clear plastic bags of gray powder, wrapped tightly and taped shut. A wax seal with the image of the Princess was melted over a red string tied around each bag.

"You put them in the safe," Herb instructed. "I don't like to touch that stuff."

"Me neither." Rhamin used a special towel from the briefcase to hold the bags and place them in the safe.

Herb made small talk to ease the tension. "So, how've you been?"

Rhamin took a scented hanky from his pocket and wiped his brow. "Never better, I think I'm in love."

"Great news."

"She's waiting in the car for me, so let's finish up quickly."

Herb took a stack of money from the drawer in the safe and counted out twenty $1000 bundles. "Remember to deposit this slowly, never more than $2000 at a time. Spread it between the three accounts and don't make deposits with the same teller. Citizens just opened up another office in Brooklyn, so rotate the deposits between all the branches."

"What are we coding these as?"

"Rental income."

"Can I use some of the money to pay for studio time?"

"No, that's a separate account. I thought you didn't pay for studio time. What's the arrangement with the Pecorinos now?"

"We're still trying to figure that one out. They want an office in the Old Medical Building and we want them to buy us out of the studio."

"Sounds complicated. Let's just keep the real estate separate from the other stuff for now."

"Okay. Do you have the tax returns ready? I can take them back to the city for everyone to look at and sign."

"Not yet. I filed for extensions this year because we needed time to distribute the cash. Have you come up with any new ideas on how we can hide the income?"

"We're using as much cash as possible to pay the kitchen help and the band, but the restaurant is getting so popular that we're actually making a profit."

"I see."

Rhamin continued. "The Pecorinos are paying for most of the studio now so we can't use cash for that anymore. My father wants to buy another building, but we already have one empty and I don't want to work that hard."

Herb closed the safe and locked it. "Just let me know what you decide."

Rhamin straightened his belt and took the briefcase off the desk. "I'll see you next week?" he said, checking the buttons on his silk shirt to make sure his chest hairs were showing.

"Better make it two weeks. I'm very busy doing returns right now," Herb said, escorting Rhamin to the door. "Good luck on your date." Rhamin left, and Herb went back to the office to turn off the voice-activated tape recorder that was in the desk. Stomach acid roiled through his system and he popped two Tums before turning out the light and closing the door.

Rebecca was standing in front of the window peering through the slats when Herb re-entered. "Get away from there!" Herb scolded her.

"Why? Your guest is gone now."

Herb joined her at the window as the BMW exited the parking lot. Rebecca didn't notice the Mercury follow it out onto Ocean Avenue, but Herb did. "They're gone now," he sighed. "Time to go home for dinner." He put his arm around his daughter but she stiffened.

"I'm not a little girl anymore, dad. What is going on around here?"

I'll tell you all about it in the car. Let's get out of here." He held his finger to his lips and made some eye gestures toward the door.

Rebecca retrieved her duffle and followed him out. "I'm scared," she blurted in the privacy of their car.

Herb didn't answer as he backed their full-size Buick out of parking space.

Rebecca's adult concerns boiled through the surface of her childhood like pimples on a teenager. "What's going to happen?"

"Don't worry. I'm doing everything I can."

"What do you mean? What can you do?"

"I'm cooperating with the authorities," Herb explained. It was a short drive home, so he went slowly, trying to allow enough time for Rebecca to calm down before getting there. "Your mother and I are the only ones who know, so don't mention anything to your brother or sisters."

"Does that mean I'm going to lose my job?"

"Not necessarily; at least not right away. It's important that you act as though you don't know anything. Just show up to work on

Monday and do your job. The Federal agents already know you haven't done anything wrong, so you'll be okay."

"Federal agents have been watching me?" Rebecca gulped. "They know where I live?" She stopped talking as waves of anxiety cut off the air supply to her mouth.

Herb finally got to what was really upsetting him. "It's not the government I'm worried about."

"There's more?" Rebecca barely forced the words from her throat before she started crying. Herb pulled into a parking space and turned the car off so he could comfort her. He hadn't seen his stoic daughter cry since she got hit with a baseball when she was ten, and her tears made her seem like the little girl she once was. "What else is wrong?" she sniffed in between sobs.

Herb hesitated before telling her. "Laden has other enemies besides our government," he said purposefully.

The specter of new threat was a sobering thought. "What do you mean? Who?"

"Let's just say there are some people who would be happy to see them out of business." Herb didn't want her to know too much. "You need to be careful."

"Careful how? What am I supposed to do?"

"Well, for starters, make sure you don't see anyone from work outside of work. I'm not sure who knows what, and there are lots of people watching what goes on there. Just do your job and go home, and when you go out, make sure you are with your friends."

Rebecca couldn't stop a new round of tears. She didn't want to tell her father about Jon or Dr. Nouri's office and was frightened. "Is that it? Are you sure you don't have any more bad news for me?" she sobbed.

"Well, there is one more thing." Herb added. "Nobody should know you're my daughter."

She gasped. "This is the worst day of my life."

"Let's hope so."

CHAPTER 35

Detective Falin and Rudy were still parked outside The Old Medical Building when Detective Gillingham and Ralph checked in. Detective Falin turned the volume of the two-way radio down to prevent the crackly voices from giving them away.

Ralph whispered as Detective Gillingham drove a few cars behind Rhamin's BMW. "Speak up. You don't have to whisper," Detective Gillingham instructed him.

"Roger," Ralph croaked into the handheld with forced confidence.

"What is your location?" Detective Falin asked.

"New Jersey. Somewhere near the ocean."

"*Where* in New Jersey?" Detective Falin asked. "You don't know what town you're in?"

Clueless, Ralph handed the receiver to Detective Gillingham. "We're on Ocean Avenue in Asbury Park; suspects driving slowly, seems like they're looking for a parking space."

"How many suspects?"

"Still just the two of them."

"Good; stay behind. The other agents are in your area following suspects driving a dark blue Cadillac Seville."

"Roger; looking for a dark blue Caddy. Who do we have in the other car?

"Detectives Ailes and Ferguson from Vice."

"Who are the suspects?"

"One of the Pecorinos and someone else."

"We'll let you know if we see them."

"Roger and out."

"Who is Pecorino?" Ralph asked after they had signed off.

"It's complicated," Detective Gillingham said, pulling over as Rhamin found a parking spot ahead of them. "Take a picture and make sure you get the location in it," he specified. Ralph fumbled with the camera until the detective took it from him and got the job done himself. "Didn't you learn anything on your first stake-out?" Detective Gillingham asked. "How'd you get roped into this anyway?"

"Rudy. Rudy and the money." Ralph admitted. "Plus, I didn't want to get stuck at my in-laws house in Elizabeth."

"That's not too far from here. Want to go pay them a visit?" Detective Gillingham needled.

Ralph thought about what they'd be having for dinner about now and considered saying yes. "No thanks," he sighed.

"You sure? I could drop you off and pick you up later?" Detective Gillingham joked.

Ralph, exhausted from sitting in the car for more than a day, weighed that suffering against his wife's verbal abuse. "Really?"

"No. I was just kidding."

"Too bad. I was just thinking...." Ralph's attention drifted.

"Well, would you look at that!" Detective Gillingham startled him, pointing. Rhamin and Homa were holding hands, walking toward the Ferris wheel in the distance. "Looks like our player is about to score a goal."

Nearby, Anthony Pecorino parked his Caddy on the street around the corner from Draper's office. His passenger, a career criminal with burglary skills, got out, swung a small satchel slung over his shoulder, and walked slowly toward the office build-ing. Detectives Ailes and Ferguson stopped two blocks away and watched through binoculars as he made a wide loop around the premises without leaving the sidewalk. Evening courtesy lights lit the front entrance, and only one office in the corner of the ground floor had the interior lights on. The front door was open and the burglar slipped inside and up the stairs to his target. Taking no time to open the locks on the office door of a suburban accountant, Emilio Lugano tongued the back of his remaining teeth, looking forward to the challenge of a tasty safe. Anthony's directions were perfect, and he had no trouble finding his target behind the flimsy metal doors of a vertical filing cabinet in the office on the left side. The double tumbler vault with four-inch-thick sides and interior hinges was built to protect its contents from amateur thieves, but provided little resistance to "Emmy the Key". Two small holes, drilled through the reinforced doors at the precise right spot, were all he needed to disable the dials. The side bolts clunked back to position with a quarter turn of the heavy t-shaped handle. He gently removed the powder bundles he had come for, placing them in the bag he carried with him. Out of curiosity, he lifted one of the two odd-shaped glass bottles and held it up to his flashlight for inspection. It was full of clear liquid. He didn't know what it was but figured that its presence in the safe meant it was valuable, so he made sure the tops were on snugly and placed both bottles into his carrying bag. The bottles made noise when they bumped together, so he put the bags of powder between them and zippered them into the side opposite his tools. He closed the safe door, shut the filing cabinet, and left the office less than ten minutes after he had entered. Returning to the dusk of the street, he walked casually until Anthony pulled the car up alongside him. Emmy got in, and they eased away from the crime scene like a boat observing the harbor speed limit.

"Everything like I told you?" Anthony asked him.

"Just like you said. Piece of cake," Emmy took pride in his profession.

"How many bags were there?"

"Six, and two bottles."

"Bottles? What kind of bottles?"

"Weird looking round ones. Reminded me of the small whiskey bottles they used during prohibition. Want to see one?" He patted his bag.

"You took them?"

"Of course I took them; they were there. I'm a thief, whadya think I was gonna do?"

"Make sure they don't break. They could be dangerous."

"I aint afraid of explosives. We use them for big jobs sometimes."

"I don't think they're explosive, but you never know."

"No? Well, what are they then?"

"Could be some kind of poison or chemical. Those Persians are into all kinds of weird stuff."

"Want me to take them back? Getting in and out was easy."

"Funny. Let's just hang onto them for now. Just put everything in this bag."

"You're the boss." Emmy transferred the booty to Anthony's shoulder tote and they snaked their way back to the Garden State Parkway and up to Manhattan without noticing the detectives following a few cars behind.

CHAPTER 36

Nigel walked back from his afternoon meeting with Dominic slowly. He had been working for the Pecorinos for over a year and it seemed like his career was at a standstill. He knew that Dominic only cared about Dante, and was tired of acting as Dominic's spy and messenger.

Dante's personal life had devolved into a 24-hour cycle of indulgent delusion that made his company unbearable, and Nigel had run out of euphemistic explanations for the no good he was up to. Nobody really liked Dante anymore, and the smell of his money wasn't strong enough to overcome his other body odors. Dante rarely bathed or brushed his teeth, and his attempts at masking his deadly oral vapors with menthol cigarettes and breath mints were futile. Every piece of clothing in his expensive wardrobe was stained or torn, and the haze of drugs slurred both his words and thoughts. Spittle, phlegm, farts, and greasy perspiration emanated from the perversion of his presence, and even his sexmate Starla needed to be fully loaded to tolerate their debaucherous sessions together. Dante's disgusting personal habits were a perfect fit for his obnoxiously repellent ego, but he was oblivious to the fact that no one took him seriously.

Nigel was particularly vexed at Dante's attempts to claim responsibility for the modest success he had brought to the company. The British bands that played The Black Sheep saw through

Dante's bullshit, and Nigel knew he was going to have to do something dramatic to maintain his self-respect and stature in the music business community. He ran through possible scenarios as he walked, measuring cause and effect like the mechanical engineer he had once trained to be. He expected Dante at the studio sometime that evening, so his journey back there was a forced march toward an unpleasant confrontation. He stopped at his local British pub to consult with some pints and countrymen. When he finally got back to the studio, he went directly to his office to search for a way out of the dead end his life had veered into. The phone lit up and he fielded a call from the manager of Max's Kansas City.

Like CBGB's, Max's Kansas City was a well-known destination and home for artists and musicians loitering on the banks of the mainstream. Using mostly the fountain of youth as their water supply, the pooled talent created a previously unknown cultural eddy that eventually became known as the "New York punk scene." Max's differed from CBGB's in that they served food downstairs, and art students, poets, and writers could spend quiet afternoons there before the evening roared to life with amplified fury on the stage upstairs. Nigel preferred the somewhat more civilized atmosphere of Max's to CBGB's and was glad he hadn't fallen so far out of the loop that no one called him for favors anymore.

"Nigel? Arnie here. Is that you, mate?"

"The very same. What's the word?"

"Love is all you need, but this weekend we're going to need a little help from our friends."

"How so?"

"Iggy's got the icky and can't go on, Ramones are out of town, and I don't have enough talent to put on stage for a busy weekend."

"Bit of trouble indeed." Nigel agreed as his wheels started turning.

"Thought you might have some ideas?"

"Right, I'm thinking."

"No doubt, but it's 6:00 and they're filling up the downstairs already. Iggy was booked here for two nights so I'll need someone for tomorrow as well. I've got a few more calls to make, so let me know if you come up with anyone. You've got my number."

"I'll let you know."

"Looking forward to your call. Thanks, mate."

Nigel put the phone down and tried to cut through the dead weight of no good ideas. He wandered down the hallway like a zombie leaving the cemetery, and an offbeat pulse of kick and bass beat against the control room door like a prematurely buried corpse. When Nigel opened the door to the control room, the frantic sonic ghost rushed past him before the closing door cut off the source of its power. Inside the sealed crypt of the control room, the notes were so loud that they took on physical shapes. Dennis, who was bent over the console orchestrating the invisible spirits, barely noticed that Nigel had materialized next to him.

"Nice track," Nigel complimented when the whirr of rewind allowed conversation. "What's this one called?"

"Uh-Oh," Dennis answered.

"Uh-Oh? That's a Cells track?"

"You like it?"

"Let me hear the vocals this time through."

*"Uh-Oh,
Washing my fingers off with snow-oh.
I just want to Uh-Uh-Oh." *15

The clever lyric mirrored Nigel's mood. "Well, that about says it all."

"Simple but to the point," Dennis agreed.

"Where's the Cells genius now?"

Dennis motioned beyond the glass. "He's in the studio getting ready for his guitar overdub." The lights were too dim to see anything clearly, but the intimate movements of the two figures standing near the back wall showed the progress of the preparations.

Nigel leered jealousy. "Musicians; what do women see in them?" He adjusted his balls.

"Musicians. They need us, they feed us," Dennis quipped.

Nigel was still in a bad mood. "What's that supposed to mean?"

"Oh, lighten up, you twisted teabag," Dennis cajoled.

Nigel's other issues crowded into the present. "What do I have to do to get some respect around here?"

"You want respect or a blow job?"

Nigel finally gave in to Dennis's humor. "Both."

"Well, why don't you get this guy a record deal and maybe he'll lend you his girlfriend."

Nigel smiled at the idea.

"Or better yet, you can get your own girlfriend once you get rid of that stinking slimeball you follow around."

His burdens acknowledged, Nigel sat down at the console next to Dennis. "Let me hear that track all the way through."

Dennis obliged, bouncing along in his chair to the aggressive ska pocket that shifted between a relative minor and the tonic before building back to the resolution via the four and five. *"I just want to Uh-Uh-Oh."* The tag lingered during rewind as both men sat watching the silhouettes in the studio demonstrate the possibilities.

A movement in the outside monitor caught their eye. Nigel muttered a curse and buzzed Dante in. Proactively, he got up and opened the control room door as Dante slithered down the hallway toward the light. He had recently showered and was as cogent as he was capable of, but still tripped up the step into the control room and cursed the door handle that he bumped into.

"Too fucking light in here; I almost killed myself," Dante greeted no one in particular.

"Yeah, we like to see what we're doing," Dennis said defensively.

"What's that supposed to mean?" Dante snarled, always looking for a problem.

"Nice weather we're having today," Nigel interrupted, knowing that non-sequiturs seemed like logic to Dante's fractured mind.

Dante rubbed his eyes with the back of his sleeve. "Goddam sunshine almost burned my eyes out today."

Nigel had an inspiration and seized control. "Hey Dennis, crank that track up and we'll burn his ears out too." Turning to Dante, he said, "Have a seat, Demon Breath. Hear your future."

Insults were a form of compliment to Dante's twisted brain. He opened his mouth and hissed as if he were a fume-breathing dragon. Dennis gagged, but Nigel stiffened his upper lip and refused to acknowledge the smell. "Uh Oh" boomed through the speakers and brought a smile to every guilty face. Beaming in the afterglow of sexual release, Jon came into the control room to claim ownership, and animated the listening session by singing along to the track as if he were performing on stage. Using Monica as a prop, he squeezed her rhythmically with the lyric *"I just want to uh uh oh."* Monica blushed, and the other men in the room caught the sexual contagion.

After the music stopped, Dante repeated the tag line, *"I just want to uh-uh-oh,"* grabbing his crotch for emphasis.

"I guess you liked it then?" Nigel confirmed.

"Who doesn't want to uh-oh?" Dante snickered.

"Play him another track, Dennis. I want him to hear how his money's being spent." Nigel directed Jon and Monica to the sofa where, to the delight of the others, they continued their intimacy. Dennis, in keeping with the theme, spooled up a rough mix of "On Your Face." Dante rocked in his chair, feeling the beat, flailing his arms and imitating the drum hits, while watching the heavy petting behind him in the reflection of the control room window.

"I, I know that you're lonely.
But I, I know what to do.
And you, you don't want to listen.
But you, you're missin' it too.
First I'm gonna pick you up by your lace
And squeeze you real hard.
Then I'm gonna take you to a different place
And XXXX on your face." *16

Dennis stopped in the middle of the vamp per Nigel's silent instruction. Nigel leveled a stare that demanded a response at Dante.

Dante accepted the challenge. "Fucking great! I'm in."

"Glad you see it my way," Nigel advised, "but this may cost a little." He winked at Dennis and Jon to stay quiet.

"How much?" Dante asked. "We own the damn studio, so what do we need to pay for?"

"There's always expenses," Nigel reminded him, flexing his nostrils, alluding to the drug budget.

"I've got that covered. Besides that?"

Dennis and Jon had no idea where the conversation was headed. Nigel lowered his voice and took on a serious tone. "We may have to call in some favors," he said, "but it's a fantastic opportunity," he added, allowing for a pregnant silence before inseminating the idea. "Cells is playing Max's Kansas City tomorrow night," he continued, locking eyes with Jon and nodding his head like a hypnotist leading his subject.

"Tell me more." Dante said, sniffling as he reached in his jacket pocket for a cigarette.

Unable to follow the signal path, Dennis stared through the console as if he was too busy visualizing cold solder joints to hear the conversation. Monica didn't know what to think.

"Iggy's band was supposed to be playing but they can't. Everyone in the industry is going to be there," Nigel continued, fleshing out his plan. "Dennis is going to mix the house and I think it's going to be our first major signing," he proclaimed, checking to make sure Dante was following the plot. Dennis' eyes bulged but he didn't say anything. "We've certainly got the goods this time," Nigel bragged. He let Jon's ego off the leash with a nod.

"You got us a gig at Max's tomorrow night!" Jon said enthusiastically, sitting up on the couch. "I've got to call the guys right now. This is fucking awesome!" He stretched his arms and gave Nigel an air kiss.

"Control yourself, mate, you're not doing the Bowie he/she thing are you?" Nigel asked wryly. "Dante, why don't you come see me in the office," he added, hinting at secrecy. "We have some details to discuss. Excuse us, gentlemen; miss."

Dante followed him out into the hallway. "Is this really happening? How'd you get this together? Why didn't you tell me? What's all this going to cost?" he whispered excitedly.

"That's the beauty of it," Nigel boasted. "It's not pay to play. All we have to do is keep everybody high, give the musicians a couple of dollars, pay for cartage, and rent a few pieces of equipment. Max's is giving us the spot."

"Do we have any money in the account, or am I going to have to ask Anthony to kick in?"

"We might need a little help from Anthony, but I'll let you know tomorrow."

"A pre-victory toot for old times?" Dante suggested. Nigel closed the door to his office and put the drug mirror on the desk. Dante laid out light gray lines. "This is a little different from Travis' regular stuff."

"It looks a bit weird. Am I going to get sick?" Nigel asked, looking skeptically at the strange powder.

Dante went first. "I've been doing this off and on for a few months." He sniffled in the chemical traces and swallowed with satisfaction.

"Where'd you get it from?"

"This guy Reggie that Starla knows from the boutique. You may have seen him at the club." He snorted the rest of his lines and offered the silver tooter to Nigel, who opted to use his own instead.

Nigel inhaled. "A bit bitter, but very smooth," he said, impressed. "Got any more of this for tomorrow night?"

"Maybe a lot more. I'll know soon," Dante said, grinning with guilt.

CHAPTER 37

Anthony dropped Emmy off at Penn Station and drove down 7th Avenue to Dante's apartment. He parked in the garage around the corner and climbed the four flights to his brother's funky penthouse carrying a leather shoulder bag. Still following, Detectives Ailes and Ferguson stopped their car in front of a fire hydrant across the street and waited.

Starla answered Anthony's knock in a skimpy robe that barely covered her otherwise naked body. Prominent nipples diverted Anthony's attention from her puffy eyelids smudged with mascara. Yawning as though she had just woken up from a restless nap, she motioned him in. "We've been waiting for you," she welcomed him, rubbing her hands through her permanently messy hairdo and puckering her lips in the hallway mirror, trying to look presentable.

"Where's Dante?" Anthony asked brusquely, gagging in the stuffy atmosphere of an apartment that hadn't been cleaned since the housecleaners were there last month. Empty cups and glasses, randomly left on the dining room table and kitchen countertops, competed for space with plates of remnant food, used napkins, and food-encrusted flatware. Dirty clothes lay crumpled on the floor in the corners of the living room, and the smell of cigarette butts in overflowing ashtrays permeated the stale air.

Starla led her guest to the living room on shaky heels that added an element of suspense to her unguarded sexuality. She sat down on the black leather sofa in front of the television and dangled a shoe from the toes of her crossed leg. "He went out for something," she said, lighting a cigarette.

"When will he be back?" Anthony asked, standing uncomfortably while keeping a wary eye out for rodents and cockroaches.

"I don't know, soon, later," Starla said absently. Her cigarette added to the air pollution while the muted television fascinated what was left of her consciousness.

He didn't want to leave Starla alone with the contents of his satchel, so he brushed some crumpled clothes off a matching stuffed chair across from her and sat down cautiously. "I guess I'll wait for him," he announced. Trying to get comfortable, he slid into the glossy leather cushions, but his gabardine pants stuck to something on the seat. "Shit! What is *that*?" he cursed, pointing to a sticky glob on the edge of the seat. He got up and felt where it had adhered to the back of his dress pants. "Fucking slob! I don't know how you two live like this!"

"Oh, Anthony, don't be mad," Starla deflected. "It's just a little goo." She knew what it was but didn't want to tell him. "Here, turn around and I'll wipe it off you." She put the burning cigarette in an ashtray and took a used napkin from the coffee table. "Closer, I can't reach it." She dabbed the back of his trousers with the napkin.

He twisted his neck trying to see. "Is it coming out?"

"Sort of." Starla dipped the napkin in a glass on the table. She held his baggy pants taut with one hand while she rubbed with the other. "Almost all gone," she said, pushing the material against his butt as he stood in front of her. "Just a little more," she cooed, wiping in slow circles.

Anthony sensed the cleaning part was over. "What are you doing?" He twisted around, trying to see.

Starla feigned innocence. "I'm just making it all better," she said, rubbing more forcefully.

"Starla, stop it!" he protested, fighting arousal.

"Oh Anthony, you're always so uptight; just relax." She continued rubbing, massaging the back of his thighs with her thumbs.

Anthony was confused by the flirtation and didn't know what to say. Ignoring his half-hearted attempts to free himself, Starla slid her hand around to his front side and confirmed the results of her seduction.

"Starla, you shouldn't. What if – " It was too late; Anthony's complaints were cut off by the diverted blood flow.

"Anthony, you're such a bad boy," Starla scolded him, intentionally rubbing his swelling appendage. "What would your little wifey say if she saw you now," she teased, grasping his concealed shaft in her hand.

Anthony couldn't control his hard-on, and gave up trying as she rotated him so that her face was at the same height as his zipper. He tapped the brakes one more time before crashing. "Starla, stop it, please! What if Dante comes home?"

"What if he does?" She pulled him closer and freed his erection. He grumbled a complaint, but her robe fell open, and the sight of her bare breasts sparked him into cardiac fibrillation. She only needed a few hand pumps to coax his orgasm out.

"Are you still mad at us?" she sighed, smiling up at him.

"I can't believe you just did that!" Anthony exclaimed, shocked at himself. He bent over, trying to reach a napkin but Starla wouldn't let go of his penis.

Aroused, she wiped his semen from her breasts to below her navel and stimulated herself. "Is that all you have for me?" she teased, pulling him close enough to reach his personality with her lips. Unsteady on his feet, Anthony used her shoulders to keep his balance while she aroused him again with her tongue. Neither of them heard the key turn in the lock.

Dante heard the quiet commotion in the next room before he said hello. Sneak that he was, he closed the door softly and peeked around the corner for a better view. Still giddy from his last snorts with Nigel, his momentary surge of jealousy was subdued by brotherhood and titillation. Anthony noticed him lingering in the doorway, touching himself, watching. Their eyes met. Sibling rivalry, brotherhood secrets, and forbidden conspiracies passed between them wordlessly. It had been many years since they were teenagers looking at magazines and comparing erections, and Dante grinned maniacally as he stole closer. Standing behind the fellating couple, he held his finger to his lips in a sign to keep quiet and slid his jeans off. Anthony kept Starla's face occupied and guided her to one side of the sofa. Her sexual excitement was startled to the next level when she suddenly felt another body behind her. Anthony grabbed her hair and pulled her mouth firmly over his shaft to prevent her from seeing as Dante thrust inside her readied passageway. The penetration triggered an uncontrollable orgasm, and she held on to reality by digging her fingernails into the flesh of Anthony's back. Neither man could tame her frenzied bucking, and they rifled her frantically from both ends until their shots were fired. Sweating and spent, Anthony removed himself from the action and plopped back down in the chair beside the couch. Dante also withdrew, but angry to have been ambushed and still aroused, Starla turned on her back, reinserted Dante, and dug her heels into the back of his thighs. Her libidinous rage fully unleashed, she punished his pelvic bone with violent hip thrusts as he rode her to a noisy climax like a jockey clinging to a runaway steed. A few cursing screams later, they both collapsed into a leather puddle, spent and dripping. Anthony went to the bathroom to clean up.

Dante was smoking a cigarette with his pants off, rubbing Starla's breasts when Anthony came back from the bathroom. Starla was lying naked without a trace of modesty on the sofa where Dante had finished her off, sharing drags of his lit cigarette through swollen lips.

"Oh that looks good," Dante said, mocking the giant dark water stains where Anthony had tried to clean his fancy pants. "I'm sure Roslyn won't notice."

"I could take them to the cleaners for you," Starla offered. "It's all my fault anyway," she added, inviting blame by lifting her knee flirtatiously.

Dante pawed her leg down, annoyed at her obvious infidelity. "So what happened out in Jersey?" he asked his brother hoarsely.

Married life had dulled Anthony's imagination, and he couldn't take his eyes off Starla's supine form. "Emmy and I took care of business," Anthony assured him absently.

Dante took another drag and stuck the end in Starla's mouth so she could share. "So where is it?" he asked, blowing a stream of smoke at his brother.

Anthony looked at his reflection in the window. His hair was messy, his pants were wet, – and he hadn't felt this sexually satisfied for a long time. "I've got it," he said casually, momentarily jealous of his deviant brother's whoring lifestyle.

Dante had never liked waiting for a score. "So where is it, asshole?"

"I got it right here, asshole." Anthony grabbed his crotch for emphasis.

"What? I let you fuck my girlfriend and now you're going to be an asshole?"

"She started it.... And I didn't actually fuck her."

"So this was your idea?" He smacked Starla's bare thigh with his open hand.

"Ouch, that hurt!" Starla complained as she rolled onto her side.

Dante smacked her exposed ass. "So you had to have my big handsome brother's dick?"

"Ouch! Stop that." She drew her legs up to her chest.

Anthony knew where this could lead. "Stop it, Dante."

Dante tried to slap her face, but she blocked him with a forearm, so he smacked her bottom loudly, leaving a red hand mark.

"Leave her alone asshole." Anthony's raised voice showed some resolve.

"Yeah, I'll leave her alone, just like you left her alone," Dante hissed, taking another half swing. "You couldn't just wait until I got back? You had to have him right in my own living room?" He began to rant.

"I'm sorry, brother," Anthony intervened. "It just happened. It wasn't all her fault."

"That's what I thought. Mr. Wonderful, Mama's perfect Anthony, did something wrong," Dante taunted, as the sibling rivalry heated to a simmer.

"You want to do something about it, little brother?" Anthony challenged him. "Maybe take a swing at me too?" He leaned closer and put his face within striking distance.

Starla tried to get her legs between them. "You two stop it, or I might have to do you both again," she said, offering the only punishment she could think of.

"Sounds good to me," Anthony said smugly.

"Yeah, I'm sure your little wifey Roslyn would like the idea too," Dante sniped. "How long has it been since you've had a good blow job, big brother? I mean before this last one. Guess it must be hard to get it going with the kid around all the time. How's the diet working for Roslyn? Is she down to a size fourteen yet?"

"Shut the fuck up, you little asshole," Anthony seethed, ready to strangle Dante's mouth shut. "Why don't you go snort some more drugs? You probably haven't had any for at least an hour."

"Well, that's the best suggestion I've heard all night. What have you got?"

"Your shit is in the bag," Anthony snapped, "but there's a problem."

"Oh?"

Anthony retrieved his leather satchel from the floor and cleared space for it on the coffee table. "Isn't there anywhere that's clean in this hell hole?" he groused, wiping wet puddles off the table with a dirty shirt from the floor.

"Shut up, you neat freak," Dante snapped back. "What's the fucking problem with the score?"

"Emmy." Anthony set the bag down on the table and they all heard the contents knock against the glass tabletop.

Dante sat up. "What the hell's in there? That doesn't sound like blow."

"That's the problem: Emmy got a little carried away." Anthony undid the fastener on the folded flap and took out Emmy's zippered cloth pouch. Removing the plastic bags one at a time, he lined them up on the table with the wax seals showing. Dante leaned forward for closer look and Starla sat up and put her chemise back on.

"Holy shit! That's way more than I expected." Dante gawked as he handled a bag of powder and tried to make sense of the wax seal. "What *is* that thing?" he wondered aloud.

"Some kind of special mark. These guys are proud of their shit," Anthony assessed.

Starla was fascinated. "It looks like a woman wearing a crown," she observed.

"How many are there?" Dante asked while counting. "Six?" he said out loud just to make sure he wasn't dreaming.

Starla was getting excited. "Let's try some!"

"Not so fast." Dante was an experienced addict. "This stuff looks pretty pure," he said, examining one of them.

"Yeah, and wait 'til you see these," Anthony said, removing the two custom glass bottles and ceremoniously standing them up on the table.

Dante picked one up and looked through the clear liquid inside it. "What the hell is in *there*?"

"I'm not sure. They were in the safe and Emmy just grabbed them."

Dante started to wiggle the heavy rubber stopper out.

"Be careful; that shit might explode," Anthony cautioned, looking around for lit candles. "Better put out that cigarette. I don't want any surprises."

"It might blow us up?" Starla asked as she ground the smoldering butt to death. After it was completely extinguished, Anthony and Starla moved slightly away and watched as Dante twisted the rubber plug out of the bottle and put his nose to the opening. The slight whiff watered his eyes and his grip on the bottle loosened. Anthony grabbed the bottle before he completely let go, and Dante slumped back into the sofa in a daze. Holding the bottle as far away from himself as possible, Anthony became dizzy as he struggled to keep it upright while replacing the stopper. Starla, who had been furthest away from the fumes, leaned in and finished putting the stopper all the way back before Anthony let go. The brothers melted into their seats, trying to regain control of all their faculties and left Starla holding the curious cylindrical bottle. She studied it closely and noticed the same face etched on the glass that she had seen on the wax seals.

"Holy shit. What *was* that?" Dante mumbled like a sleep talker with his head lying limply in the couch cushions. Anthony slacked in his chair and rubbed his eyes, speechless. Starla continued to study the Princess's head as the Pecorino brothers drifted in and out of consciousness. A strange calm came over her as she sat on the edge of the sofa, fascinated with the odd-shaped bottles, humming a song she remembered from childhood.

CHAPTER 38

The neon sign on the 10th Avenue New York Diner was only partially lit, and the chromed outside hadn't been cleaned up to a shine in more than a decade. Nobody famous ever ate there, and its procession of owners had eked out a living for sixty years by grilling short-order food and flavoring hot and cold water. Taking advantage of the 24-hour service, unwashed patrons occasionally fell asleep on the caved-in cushions of railroad booths that hadn't been recovered since the restaurant was built, and the few customers unlucky enough to make the diner their Saturday night destination were too concerned with their own problems to care about anybody else's. It was a perfect place for undercover cops to meet.

Detective Gillingham, the largest of the men, ordered six coffees from a haggard middle-aged woman with no discernible waistline. Ralph was squeezed against the inside wall next to him. Detectives Ailes and Ferguson, both with average builds, sat across from them and were equally uncomfortable in the stiff-backed booth. Detective Falin and Rudy sat on swivel stools at the counter opposite the table with their feet in the aisle. It wasn't the most private seating arrangement for a secretive meeting, but there was no one close enough to eavesdrop, and they were all happy to be out of their cars, so they talked as freely as if they were at their desks.

Detective Falin led the discussion. "So where are we?"

"At Delmonico's Steak House. Don't you recognize the atmosphere?" Detective Ferguson, the wise guy among them, quipped.

"Yeah, I'll have the sirloin tip," his longtime partner, Detective Ailes, chuckled with him.

"And you, Detective Gillingham? What will you be having tonight?" Detective Falin asked with a phony British accent, going along with the joke.

"Bangers and mash will do it for me. Is that on the menu?"

Rudy joined in the sport. "I'll have the baked halibut with corn fritters."

"I'll have that sexy young waitress," Detective Falin said, referring to the bedraggled server disappearing through the swinging doors of the kitchen. "And you sir, Agent Lowell?" he asked, finishing role call.

Ralph was hungry. "Can I order a steak here?"

"No," Ferguson deadpanned, "you can't have a steak out on a stakeout – department rules."

Everyone was still laughing by the time the waitress arrived at the table with a few menus under her arm, balancing six cups with two hands as if she were competing in an event at the church picnic. She put them down together in the center of the table with only minor spillage, then retrieved her order pad from her apron, her pencil from her ear, and her charm from a construction site.

Detective Gillingham pushed a cup toward Ralph. "I believe you ordered the medium rare?" They enjoyed another round of guffaws.

The waitress was unaffected by their levity. "You gentlemen need menus?" She held them out.

"Sure, thank you ma'am." Detective Ailes accepted and distributed them.

Seeing that no one was eager to order, the server excused herself. "I'll be back."

After she had shuffled away, Detective Falin picked up the thread of purpose again. "So let's get down to business. Where are our suspects?"

Detective Ferguson was the first to respond. "We've got the Pecorino brothers at Dante's apartment in the Village. God knows what they're up to but he didn't tell me," he cracked. "Looks like they know more about the Persians than we suspected."

"What do you mean?" Detective Falin asked.

"Well, we knew they were partners in that real estate deal with the recording studio, but we never made the drug connection between the two," he explained.

"Are you sure the Pecorinos were after drugs and not money?"

"No," Detective Ailes volunteered. "All we know is that they hired Emmy the Key and that means that they knew there was a safe to break into."

"I guess we'll have to see how that one plays out. You're going back to the 7th Avenue location after this?"

Detective Ailes nodded affirmatively. "We'll either be there or at The Black Sheep," Detective Ferguson corrected. "Whichever has better beer."

Detective Falin ignored his wisecrack and threw to his partner. "What else have we got?"

Detective Gillingham filled in some detail. "Draper took his daughter home for the night. We're not sure what *she* knows, but *he* doesn't know about the robbery yet. The New Jersey agents have the overnight. Darius junior was playing Romeo on a Ferris wheel or merry-go-round somewhere out there, but he's probably back in the city by now. We've got someone watching the Gramercy Park apartment?"

Detective Falin flipped through his spiral-bound pocket notepad looking for the answer. "A couple of New York's finest, if that's any comfort," he grumbled.

"Oh great, that gives me a lot of confidence. Maybe we should bring them some coffee so they stay awake this time," Detective Gillingham suggested sarcastically.

"I don't think much is going to happen there before tomorrow, so let's just move on," Detective Falin continued. "Fortunately, the guys from ATF have eyes on the Laden warehouse and The Old Medical Building locations, so those should be secure until we relieve them." The detective ticked off his list, put his pad away and sipped his coffee. "Now all we need to do is wait."

"Wait for what?" Ralph asked innocently.

"The green light," Detective Gillingham explained patiently. "That's got to come from Operations."

"Yeah, Operations gives the signal and then we bust out the revolvers and storm the place." Detective Ferguson's comedic timing got them laughing again, but Ralph was too tired to get the joke.

Detective Ferguson kept it going. "They didn't give you a gun?"

"Oh, leave him alone," Rudy said. "As boring as this is, it's still better than the weekend at his in-laws we rescued him from."

"Ooh, weekend with the in-laws, arguing with your wife, saying you're sorry and making excuses. Good choice, Ralph. I'll drink to that!" Detective Ferguson raised his mug and motioned the waitress for a refill.

Ralph was not amused and looked out the window. On a warm Saturday night, everyone who could afford to get out of town was already there, and he toyed with the idea of going home to enjoy a peaceful night alone in front of the television.

The agents ordered mystery-meat burgers and loitered at the diner as long as possible before returning to their cars. As they dispersed, Detective Falin radioed an update to Director Lawson's office.

CHAPTER 39

Dennis already had the drums set up and miked by the time Marco and Frankie got to the studio for rehearsals. Jon saw them in the monitor and went down the hallway with only the slightest limp to let them in. They hadn't been to Heard Tracks in six months, and hadn't played together for four, so there was a lot of catching up to do to be ready for a performance the next night. Monica had gone back to her apartment, expecting Jon to join her there after rehearsal.

"Hey man," Jon greeted the other musicians warmly.

"Hey Cells, how you been man?" Marco, with his Fender bass slung over his shoulder in a soft carrying bag, gave him a one-arm hug and they headed down the hall. "I was worried about you," he admitted, blue eyes peering out from his shaggy blond mullet.

"Thanks, man. Like I told you on the phone, I'm really okay. Got some good writing done, and getting to bed at a reasonable hour hasn't hurt. What about you? You still playing with those guys from Brooklyn?"

"Nah; they're losers. I've been working for my cousin during the day. You know, the one who has the stereo store."

"Cool. Well, it's good you're around cause this is going to be big." Jon cranked up the hype.

Frankie, the drummer, was a few steps behind them and always needed to know where "one" was. "What's this all about man?" he asked, opening his jacket to show off his Keith Moon T-shirt and muscles. "I had some other plans for tonight, so I hope you're not just bullshitting."

"Lighten up, Frankie boy; and welcome to the big time." Jon led them through the control room door like a maître d'.

The lights were up full and the arsenal of equipment bristled like a munitions depot. Marco was impressed. "Holy shit. This is a lot nicer than I remembered it."

Frankie saw the drums set up in the studio through the window and went around the console for a better look. "Whose drums are those?" he asked, gaping at the six-piece red and chrome set with four cymbals on a low riser in the middle of the room.

Jon stoked his enthusiasm. "They're yours tonight."

"Awesome, I always wanted to play on a Gretsch. That looks like a Blackhawk II. Can I go out there now?"

"Go get em, Frankie. We'll be out shortly," Jon encouraged.

Marco had a fascination with electronic equipment and was studying the console. "So what's the plan?" he asked Jon after Frankie had gone to check out the drums.

"Like I told you. We're playing Max's tomorrow night."

"I know that, but what are we playing?"

Jon hadn't thought about the set list. "Our usual stuff."

"You mean *your* usual stuff," Marco observed.

"Well, what else is there?"

Marco was prepared for that question. "I've got some new songs. Maybe we should play *them*."

Jon didn't usually like Marco's songs but needed to keep him excited. "Can we learn them in one night?"

"Frankie and I already know two of them. All they need is a couple of guitar parts and some lyrics."

Jon didn't want to point out how ridiculous it was to say you wrote a song when it didn't have any chords or lyrics. "Okay, I'll see what I can come up with and we can try them," he hedged. "We all set up?" he asked Dennis.

"I'll be ready before you are." Dennis answered.

"Come on, let's see how much we remember." Jon suggested, leading Marco out to the studio and into the ruckus of Frankie's drumming. Marco set his bass bag down on the piano and unzipped it, reverentially removing his creamy white Fender instrument. Jon's guitar was already plugged in and waiting for him on a stand. Marco plugged in and got signal. Unable to tune or get a tone he liked over Frankie's drumming, Marco turned up the studio's double fifteen Ampeg loud enough to be heard. Frankie got the message and quieted down so they could talk.

Jon was ready to go, but Marco fiddled with his new electronic tuner and checked the intonation with harmonics. "I didn't bring any charts. Is there some paper around here?" he asked studiously.

Jon remembered what he didn't like about playing with Marco. "Let's just play something we know, okay? That good with you, Frankie?"

Frankie crashed his reply. "I'm a drummer. Who needs paper?"

Jon's sunburst Fender Strat was already tuned and wired through a distortion stomp box, so he and Marco only had to make minor tonal adjustments in between Frankie's disruptive cymbal hits before they had a sound they could live with. The drums were miked, and the amps were baffled to reduce bleed-through and split with a direct box feed. The vocal mics were wired through the console and fed to the musicians through headphones with the submix. Jon started off with the B minor backbeat of their first single, "Uh Oh," as Dennis responded to the musicians' headphone level requests.

"More vocals," Jon sang.

"More me too," Marco requested.

"Yaaahhh, *hey*!" Frankie screamed into his vocal mic while maintaining a tight snare roll that ended in a crash. Dennis doubled the compression ratio on his mic input, dialed the threshold down, and adjusted the levels of the vocals being sent to tape as they stumbled through a warm-up version of the song.

"Well that sucked," Marco complained as soon as they finished.

Frankie bashed a few drums, still trying to get used to the set. "What do you expect? We haven't played together in months. I'll tell you what though, these Zildjians sizzle!" he celebrated the sound of his ride with a stiff stick and let it ring.

Jon dug into the repertoire. "Let's try 'Terminal Thighs,'" he suggested, grinding the rhythm on the bottom strings. The mid-tempo, straight eights were easier to cop, and they were all locked in by the time they hit the five-chord build.

"Come on baby donchu tell me no lies
Cause I got a little case of terminal thighs." *17

Jon shouted the lyrics like he was yelling at someone across the street, then launched a pithy solo over the B section. Frankie flammed the build and pedaled fours with the hat while waiting for the second verse. Chemistry reestablished, the trio stretched verse-two into an all-out jam that whet their appetite for more.

"Well, that's more like it," Jon said. "Let's do 'Don't Change Your Mind'. Count us off, Frankie."

Frankie held his sticks over his head and clacked them. "One, two, one two three four."

"Don't change your mind...
It happens all the time.
Time's up!" *18

The two-four pocket bounced like a teenager on a pogo stick, and it took a few tries for them all to jump on the stops cleanly. Jon weaved the rhymes in between the changes. Dennis rolled the tape.

*"With your punk rock boots,
And your hula-hoops,
It's no substitute,
For a gun that shoots." *19*

The song was over before they were tired of it, and Marco let loose a descending bass line that ended with a trill. "It's all coming back to me now," he admitted. "Damn, I miss playing live."

Dennis' voice came through the talkback monitors. "Sounding good in here. Why don't you take a break and come on in."

Jon and Marco untangled themselves from their headphones and went into the control room, exchanging low fives. Frankie was right behind them when they opened the door and bathed themselves in the glory of the fat sounds blaring out of the mains.

Jon voiced his elation. "That's fucking incredible!"

Marco was amazed. "I didn't even know you were recording all that."

Dennis liked what he heard too. "You guys sound pretty good for not playing together for a while. Play like that tomorrow night and it's deal time," he added with uncharacteristic confidence.

Marco caught the fever. "Let's go run through the whole set. I can't believe we're sounding so good. What time do we go on tomorrow?"

"Midnight. Nigel got us the midnight spot," Jon said like he had an appointment with destiny.

"That's fucking awesome; I can't wait." Marco celebrated with five for Frankie. "See, I told you this was going to work out."

"Come on guys," Jon said, "let's go through a few more songs."

"How long do we have tonight?" Marco asked. He had a lot of ideas he wanted to try out.

"Another hour or so," Jon answered. "We're sounding pretty good already and I think Dennis has other plans."

"You guys are only playing for a half hour," Dennis interjected, "so you'll only have time for five or six songs. Nigel's coming by with some people at 9:00 so we should be outta here by then."

The musicians returned to the studio and played through a shortened set. They worked out some new guitar parts, practiced their harmony vocals, and inserted a few dramatic stops before they were satisfied that they could put on a good show. Stoked and tired, they went out for a band meal at a pizza pub before going their separate ways. Jon headed straight to Monica's apartment.

CHAPTER 40

Monica was home with Ameliah, who was primping for another night out with Freddy. Tensions muted, they stayed out of each other's way in the kitchen and barely spoke while rotating in front of the bathroom mirror. Neither of them had talked with Rebecca all day, and all her note said was that she was at her folks' house in New Jersey and would be back sometime Sunday.

When Ameliah was ready to leave she forced a conversation. "Where do you plan on sleeping tonight?"

"I'm not sure. What about you?"

"I'll probably spend the night at the hotel again." Ameliah glamorized the idea but Monica didn't respond. "You can have the apartment all to yourself," Ameliah continued. "I hope you're not too lonely," she baited.

"I'll be fine," Monica replied, covering her excitement with blasé.

"Well, don't make too much of a mess if you have company," Ameliah insinuated. "You know our house rules."

"I know," Monica answered, annoyed.

Ameliah changed her tone as she paused in the doorway, on her way out. "Monica?"

"What?"

"Promise me you won't bring that Jonny Soldier guy here. He creeps me out."

Monica crossed her fingers. "I promise."

"I'm sure Becca wouldn't like the idea either," she called from the hallway as she left.

CHAPTER 41

After a memorable evening at Asbury Park, Rhamin dropped Homa off in front of her apartment and went back to his office in The Old Medical Building. The building looked deserted, but at the request of the FBI, the precinct had stationed an agent in the basement. The front lobby was locked, so Rhamin used his keys to get in and operate the elevator. He got off on the tenth floor and walked casually through the perpetual twilight of the interior hallway to the office suite he shared with his father. The office was dark but he didn't bother turning on the lights, preferring the twinkling illumination of the city blinking through his windows. Placing his briefcase on the desk, Rhamin leaned back in his leather chair with his hands behind his head, enjoying the light show and basking in the afterglow of a successful date. Homa's hand still tingled in his palm, and he ran his fingers beneath his nose to smell the traces of her company. In his imagination, he saw her as a white-robed bride twirling to echoey flute music in an open field. He thought about the words he would speak at their wedding and how proud his father and kin would be. It would be a marriage of equals: two powerful families united again to strengthen the bonds that sustained them. He fantasized that Arshan would miraculously appear at the ceremony and confer his blessings, and he saw his own father sitting with Homa's grandfather, Dadi, at the reception. Their pairing would produce children who would add to the richness of their successful lives together and they would support homeland freedom and charitable causes with their accumulated wealth.

The idea of money connected him back to his briefcase and the bundles of cash in it. He slid the briefcase forward and turned on his desk lamp without noticing the red light blinking on his answering machine. There was no telling who might be behind the darkened windows that looked across urban ravines, so he got up and drew the blinds before removing the cash that he needed to count. His mind was elsewhere as he recited the tedium of numbers that added to his family's fortunes, and after finishing the second pile of twenties and tens, he removed his glasses, cleaned them with his pocket hankie, and wiped the grime of commerce off his hands. The persistent blinking red light caught his attention, and he pushed play to listen to the message on the machine.

Herb Draper sounded composed but nervous. "Rhamin, I have bad news. Please call me."

It was a very short message and he played it again to make sure he recognized the caller. Rhamin checked his watch and wondered if it was too late to call Herb at home. It was only 10:00, and he knew Herb would probably still be up, but they had a long-standing agreement to keep their business and family lives separate. It had only been six hours since they saw each other, and the mention of "bad news" had a sobering effect that clouded the idyllic vistas of his imagination. Reality sneak-attacked his solar plexus with a sharp jab. Suddenly, he found himself sitting in an office with wads of secret cash stacked in front of him. Fear chased the last guests from his imaginary reception, and he realized that Herb wouldn't have called him if it wasn't important. He knew he needed to call him back immediately.

Herb answered during the first ring. "Hello."

Rhamin was always careful on the phone. "I got your message," was all he said.

"There's been a robbery," Herb said quietly.

"Robbery? Where?"

"My office."

Silence passed between them. Rhamin flinched. "Your office? Did they...?"

"Yes."

"How do you know?"

"I went back to the office to get something after dinner," Herb lied.

"I see." Rhamin struggled to get the words out of his mouth. He didn't know what to do. "I need to speak with my father. How late can we call you?"

"Call me tomorrow. We can't do anything about it tonight."

"Did you file a police report?"

"Of course not."

"They didn't take anything else?"

"Nothing. They knew what they were looking for."

"Then it's someone who...."

"Exactly."

"They got everything?"

"Everything you brought." Herb clarified his role for the agents who were listening to the call.

"They opened the safe?"

"Yes."

"How? Wasn't it locked?" Rhamin was more naïve than mistrustful.

"They drilled some holes in the door."

"This is awful."

"Very bad."

"Who would do this?"

"I don't know." Herb took the opportunity to distance himself further. "They're your customers."

"Perhaps." Rhamin didn't know who to trust. "We'll call you tomorrow. Noon is okay?"

"I'll be at the office."

"Speak to you then."

"Good night."

Rhamin sat stunned for moment before dialing his father.

CHAPTER 42

Nigel was standing at The Black Sheep bar when Dante showed up, glowing with confidence. It was 11:30, and Starla teetered next to him in four-inch heels and a low-cut blouse that was an effective distraction from her poorly applied eye shadow and makeup. They were much happier than usual and Nigel was surprised to see them holding hands. Suzie had their drinks ready before they asked, and Officer Hemming nodded hello, keeping his covert distance at the end of the bar.

Donny came to greet them in the lull between Bosco Dish's sets. "Looking good tonight, Starla." Donny complimented, visually molesting her as they talked business.

Dante flashed a trace of his boyhood charm and raised his glass. "Feeling good, aint we honey?" He put his arm around Starla's waist and showed her off. "You got your own squeeze back yet?"

"They're supposed to let her out tomorrow," Donny huffed.

"How's Freddy doing?" Dante chitchatted.

"Real good. He thinks he's in love again. You know Freddy."

"Figures. Either of you seen Travis?"

"He's in the back," Nigel answered, jerking his head in that direction.

Suzie approached them from her side of the bar and delivered a quiet message to Dante. "Officer Hemming wants a word with you." Dante excused himself, leaving Starla with Donny and Nigel as he took a seat next to Officer Hemming where the bar doglegged.

The officer spoke without making eye contact. "They're onto you," he said into his drink glass.

"Yeah, so, that's why we have you," Dante snorted, unfazed.

"It's not my area."

"What's not your area?"

"Narcotics."

"I thought you were Vice?"

"I am, but what you're doing is out of my area."

"Narcotics aren't a vice? Hallefuckingluyah. Now I can get high and not break the law," Dante said a little too loudly, laughing at his own joke.

Officer Hemming sipped his drink through clenched teeth. "Don't be stupid. That's not what I'm talking about."

"What are you talking about?"

"What were you doing tonight?"

"What do you mean?" Starla noticed his guilty smile from thirty feet away.

"Earlier, with your brother at the apartment."

Dante couldn't believe his ears. "What? Now the cops want to tell me how I can screw?"

"Nobody cares about that. What did Anthony bring to the party?"

"Jeeze, you guys are nosey. My own brother can't visit me without someone having a problem?"

"Anthony did something he shouldn't have."

"Anthony? My perfect all-American-married-with-kids-mama's-boy did something bad?" Dante loved the taste of misbehavior. "Maybe you should ask my girlfriend what he did; but I'm not sure she would file a complaint."

Losing patience, Officer Hemming took another sip. "Look, do you want me to tell you what your father pays me to tell you, or do you want to sit here and be an asshole?"

"So serious. I'm in too good of a mood for bad news."

"Okay, suit yourself, but don't say I didn't warn you."

"Warn me about what? I thought you said Anthony's the one who did something bad."

"It's your problem too."

"Yeah, why?"

"Because they know."

"Who knows? What do they know? You goddam cops all talk in riddles."

Officer Hemming turned to face him. "You want it straight?"

"Give it to me...straight up, bartender," Dante challenged him.

"The cops know about the robbery."

Dante blinked. "So, the cops know about everything."

"And so do the people who got robbed."

"They know they got robbed or who did it?"

"If they don't know who did it already, they will soon."

"Why? Who's going to tell them? The cops?"

"You think I'm the only cop with special friends?"

Dante downed the rest of his drink and let the warm glow settle his nerves before he got up and went back to his own business. Donny had taken his spot at the bar and was feeding his libido with Starla's emanations. Dante slapped her on the back of her skintight mini skirt and sat between her and Nigel. Leaning close enough to Nigel to share his poison breath, he hissed, "We have to talk."

"Now?"

Dante leaned into Starla's hair. "Be right back, honey. You keep Donny entertained."

Starla welcomed the attention.

Dante mouthed her an air tongue as he and Nigel retreated to the private office. They found Travis there, looking through a *Playboy* magazine spread featuring a model with a straw hat and red cowboy boots.

"Mmm nice; wishing you were back home?" Nigel asked, poking fun.

Travis covered his embarrassment with bravado. "Yi ha! Ride 'em high. What's up? Another stray out there needs to be roped in?"

Dante got right down to business. "Close the door."

"You guys dry?" Travis asked, opening the desk drawer to get out his stash.

"No. I've got a little present for *you* this time." Dante pulled a packet of gray powder from his pocket and laid it on Travis' desk.

Travis held the clear plastic baggie in his hand and felt its weight. "What the hell is this?" It was still taped, and the wax seal was unbroken. "This must weigh a couple of ounces," he estimated, putting it on the scale. "Three point two," he read the needle, impressed.

"Wait till you try it," Dante touted.

Nigel took his turn ogling the bounty. "Is that the same stuff we had at the studio?"

"Same stuff." Dante picked it up and broke the seal, then unwrapped the outer baggie.

"Careful partner," Travis cautioned, placing a tray underneath the bag.

Nigel was uncomfortable with where they were headed. "We really shouldn't be doing this during business hours."

"Fuck business hours," Dante exulted, sticking a long-handled teaspoon inside the bag. He filled it to overflowing and dumped its contents on the tray like a pile of gray sugar.

Travis looked at it with the magnifying loop he kept on the tray. "What kind of shit *is* this?"

"Who the hell knows, but wait till you taste it." Dante partitioned a tiny mound with the spoon. Travis touched it with his fingertip and moistened the residue with his tongue. The bitter taste sent an involuntary surge of saliva through his mouth. Dante saw Travis' pained expression. "It's better when you snort it."

"I'm still working," Travis declined. "I'll try some later."

"Good, because I'm leaving this with you to sell."

Travis protested. "What? I don't even know what it is."

"Doesn't matter. Just let your regular supplier taste a sample and he'll buy everything you've got," Dante instructed, revealing his plan.

Travis balked. "Why don't you just sell it yourself?"

Dante glinted mischievously. "I've got too much to sell already."

Nigel knew Dante was up to something. "There's more of this?" he questioned suspiciously.

"A lot more," Dante bragged.

Nigel took a closer look and considered the possibilities. "Where'd you get it?"

"Never mind that; just get rid of this for me. I figure it's got to be worth at least a couple of grand. We got a deal cowboy?"

Travis looked to Nigel for direction. "I'll try," he said warily.

Nigel shared his concern, but they had both worked for the Pecorinos long enough to know when to stop asking questions. "It really is quite pleasant once you get past the taste," Nigel encouraged with a shrug.

After they had gone, Travis put the bag in the stash drawer and returned the prep tray to its hiding place, wondering how much he should tell Officer Hemming. The background in the Playboy photos looked like where he had grown up, and comparing that to his immediate surroundings, he thought about how far he had strayed.

Reggie Whitehead and Sonya were talking with Donny and Starla at the bar when Nigel and Dante returned. Dante grabbed Reggie's sleeve and pulled him aside. "We gotta talk," he whispered with a cockeyed smirk.

CHAPTER 43

Dr. Nouri usually fell asleep with the TV on, so when the phone woke him up and he saw Jonny Carson interviewing a guest, he knew it had to be past 11:30. The program went to a dramatic clip of Anthony Newman's latest movie, "The Verdict," as he picked up the receiver and said hello.

"Sorry to disturb you," Bahram apologized. "Are you alone?"

"Yes, of course. I was sleeping."

"We have a problem." Bahram's serious tone matched the mood of the clip on TV.

"Yes?" Dr. Nouri was a light sleeper so it didn't take much to return him to full clarity.

"There's been a robbery."

"Robbery?" He patted his bedside table until his hand landed on his glasses. "Who's been robbed?"

"We have."

The pronoun "we" had worrisome implications. "Was anybody hurt?"

"No, it was just a robbery."

"Thank God. Where are you?"

"Home," Bahram answered from his comfortable study overlooking a quiet street in Queens.

"Your office got robbed?"

"No, thank God."

"Where did it happen? The restaurant?"

"No, much worse."

"The laboratory? The warehouse?"

"Someone broke into Draper's office and took everything Rhamin brought there today," Bahram said, looking sympathetically at Rhamin, who was sitting across from him, dumbfounded.

Dr. Nouri gulped. "Everything?" Neither spoke as the information compiled. Dr. Nouri used the remote to turn the television sound down and broke the silence in a hushed voice. "This is very bad news." He took a sip of water from his bedside.

"Very bad news."

"I'm sure they don't know what they have." Dr. Nouri had prepared the bottles himself.

Bahram twisted toward the wall to hide his worry. "It could ruin us all," he whispered, tugging on the good luck charm around his neck.

"We've got to get them back," Dr. Nouri said, overstating the obvious.

"Of course. Do you think we should we call our policeman friends?"

"Not just yet. Tell me all you know."

"I'll put Rhamin on the phone. He's the one who told me."

He handed the receiver to Rhamin. "Good evening, Dr. Nouri. I'm sorry to bother you so late." Rhamin's respect for his elders masked his lack of confidence.

"Nonsense; just tell me what happened."

"Well, I delivered our usual shipment to Draper's office around 4:00 today. Everything was as it always is. I left the merchandise, took the proceeds, and came back to the city."

"Was anybody with you?"

"Why, yes...." Rhamin hesitated, embarrassed. "Homa came along for the ride and we went to the Ferris wheel afterwards."

"I see," Dr. Nouri said, knowing Rhamin's intentions. "Did she come in the office with you?"

"Of course not. She waited in the car. I didn't tell her anything."

"Good. The less she knows, the safer it is for her. Did you tell anyone you were taking a drive? See anybody before you left? Run into anyone accidentally along the way?"

"No, only Homa; I can think of nothing else." Rhamin's mind ended at his heart.

Dr. Nouri continued his questioning. "And how did you find out about this robbery?"

"Draper called me."

"When?"

"Just a while ago."

"What did he say?"

"He said he had to go back to the office after dinner to retrieve something. The safe was and open and there was nothing in it."

"Do you think he's lying?"

Rhamin had never considered the possibility. "No, I don't think so."

"Do you think he took the merchandise and said someone else stole it?"

"No, why would he do that?"

"Why does anybody steal? What was he wearing?"

"Who?"

"Draper."

"A shirt, pants, why? I don't know; I don't pay attention to such things."

"I want you to remember if there was anything unusual. Anything about your visit there that might give us a clue. Think, Rhamin, was anybody else in the office when you went there?"

"I don't think so; I didn't see anyone else. His other office door was closed." A slight nausea roiled his stomach and he grew pale. Dr. Nouri didn't speak. Bahram took the receiver back.

"Rhamin doesn't know anything and we can't do anything tonight. We should meet for breakfast in the morning."

"We need to tell the Monsouris. I'll call Samani."

"At this hour? Is that such a good idea? She gets upset so easily. Maybe it would be better to wait until the morning."

"Do you know where Sattar is? Can we reach him? He would want us to contact him immediately."

"I think he's still in Miami. I'll try the last number he left me."

"Okay, but don't say too much over the phone. There's no telling who might be watching him."

"Agreed."

"What about Saeed?"

"He's still in Beirut."

"That's too far away to be helpful but I'll place a call. Early breakfast?"

"8:00, usual place."

Bahram hung up the phone and looked deeply into Rhamin's tearful eyes. "Trust the Princess. She will find a way home," he said soothingly.

Dr. Nouri went to his desk and scribbled down some ideas.

SUNDAY, APRIL 18TH

CHAPTER 44

The restaurant at the corner of Fulton and Pearl was down the street from The Old Medical Building and always open by 6:00 a.m.. Sensing that Dr. Nouri was not his usual buoyant self, the waiter with a twelve-word English vocabulary followed him holding a coffee pot. Shuffling his sandals on the way to his usual booth, the doctor carried the aches and pains of sixty-five years favoring his left side. News of the robbery had kept him up most of the night, and he hadn't bothered disciplining his gray curls, which, failing to reestablish themselves atop his head, had wandered over his ears and burrowed down to the safety of his collar. His thick reading glasses were smudged from too much handling, and the napkin he used to clean them only spread the finger grease. He put them on the table next to the list he had compiled and stared blankly at the sparse Sunday morning traffic while waiting for Bahram.

A neighborhood fixture, the Ruda Coffee Shop was home to a wide assortment of New York transplants. Catering to their clientele, a mixture of simply prepared Eastern European dishes and standard American fare was served. No one stumbled into Ruda – except an occasional drunk, who was promptly shown the door – and the out-of-town diners were usually relatives of regular customers. The weatherworn sign and half closed window blinds helped keep the curious away, and the muted murmur of multiple languages translated into privacy. A cluster of bells attached to the front door announced arrivals and departures, and the sturdy spring on the inside hinge made sure that those interruptions were minimally disturbing to the ruminant customers. It was an ideal place to plan out the day, and Dr. Nouri was not the only one there wrestling with problems.

When Bahram finally arrived, he wedged his pudgy torso between the table and bench seat, and signaled to the waiter in the universally understood coffee hand-gesture. A few years older than his cousin and cohort, he was equally disturbed but less disheveled. His tailored shirt, open two buttons, revealed a red agate amulet nestled in a profusion of graying chest hairs, and he held the pendant in silent prayer, pulling unconsciously on the gold chain around his thick neck. The men acknowledged each other, but neither of them spoke out loud until the waiter arrived with Bahram's caffeine. Their conversation was mostly in Persian.

"Salaam."

"You are well?" Dr. Nouri asked.

"As well as can be expected." Bahram didn't let go of his good luck charm.

"And your family?"

"Rhamin blames himself."

"Nonsense," Dr. Nouri said, wiping his glasses.

"Sattar is coming," Bahram blurted.

"You found him?"

"Yes. He was still in Miami. He'll be landing at LaGuardia this evening."

"You told him?"

"Of course. As much as I could over the phone." The men sipped their cups and smiled blandly, masking the seriousness of their conversation.

"And Saeed?"

"It was morning in Beirut when I spoke to him."

"What does he think?"

"He doesn't know who did it, of course, but he said he wasn't surprised."

"Really?"

"Yes. You know he doesn't like this part of the business. Too dangerous."

"He is angry with us?"

"More worried than angry. He asked me to have Sattar call him if I spoke to him first."

Dr. Nouri pushed his handwritten paper to Bahram's side of the table. "I've made a list."

Bahram studied the paper. "A list of what?"

"Friends, enemies, others." The list wasn't very long.

"You made this last night?"

"I couldn't sleep."

"What do you propose we do? We are not detectives."

"I'm not sure. I have no experience in this sort of thing," the doctor admitted, rubbing his eyes.

"Neither do I, but it's a very short list." Bahram said, studying it. "I think Sattar will have some ideas too," he reasoned.

"Let's hope so," Dr. Nouri agreed. "We're going to need some help."

Bahram read the list. "What about Reggie? Maybe he knows something?"

"I've thought of that. He usually has the weekends off. I'm sure he doesn't get up early on Sunday morning. I will phone him later."

"Good. We have a fellow at the restaurant that takes care of a few things for us. I will have Rhamin contact him and see what he can find out." Bahram made some notes with the golf pencil he found in his jacket pocket. "Maybe Mak will have some good ideas too. Didn't he used to work as a policeman in Jamaica?"

"Yes, but we should let Sattar talk to him; they know each other well," Dr. Nouri reminded him.

"Agreed," Bahram said, looking at the paper. "What about Draper?"

"What about him? I was never in favor of using him," Dr. Nouri revisited an earlier conversation.

"I've never liked him either," Bahram admitted, stirring lines in the mud at the bottom of his cup.

"Do you think he can be trusted? Maybe he had something to do with the robbery?"

"I don't know. The Monsouris haven't been the same since Arshan disappeared. Saeed and Sattar are always traveling, and Samani doesn't go to the office anymore. Other than Rhamin, who ever sees Draper besides the couriers?"

"You think he's been unfaithful?"

Bahram maintained contact with their Persian customers through intermediaries. "I doubt it; we would have heard if there was a problem."

"I don't know, something about Draper seems unhealthy."

"But why would he steal from us? He is well paid – and if there is a problem it will surely be bad for his business."

"Yes, and if the Princess Tears are discovered, the police might get involved – and that will be bad for him too."

"Perhaps Draper had nothing to do with it."

"Perhaps, but who could have done this?"

Bahram checked the list for some more ideas. "Only someone who knew what was in the safe. Rhamin had just dropped off the merchandise, so maybe he was followed?" Bahram's stomach growl escaped from his mouth.

Dr. Nouri imparted medical advice. "You should eat something. We should order."

Bahram signaled for the waiter, who appeared at their booth with the coffee pot and vacant smile. Unable to communicate verbally, Bahram pointed to number six on the grimy menu he had retrieved from its permanent home next to the sugar dispenser. He held up two fingers. The waiter retreated, and like two old wrestlers struggling to finish a round, the men leaned on folded arms and drew long breaths through their noses while pondering their mystery. Their meals arrived, and they cleared most of the food off their plates before the nourishment revived the conversation.

"Who could have known?" Dr. Nouri asked, nibbling his last piece of toast.

Bahram dabbed his mouth with a napkin, covering a burp. "Enemies of our cause."

"In New York? You think they have agents in America?"

"I wouldn't be surprised. It's been a few years since they took over, and maybe they're more friendly with the CIA than they admit." Bahram soaked the remnants of his eggs with toast and continued. "Or maybe the Americans don't even know there are foreign agents working here. I wonder how many countries have agents in New York? Certainly not just Iran."

The breakfast food absorbed the stomach acid, but had no effect on Dr. Nouri's bitter memories. "You think it might be the revolutionaries?"

"Maybe, but why would they just *steal* from us? Why not do us more harm than that? Burn our buildings or run us over with their taxis?" Bahram paused to consider the possibility before answering his own question. "I suppose that might be too obvious; the local police would get involved. Their spies might be revealed. It would make more sense to just put us out of business," he concluded.

"They've tried to do that before. A prayer for Dadi." Dr. Nouri made a hand sign and invoked the Holy Spirit. The men bowed in remembrance before continuing.

Bahram looked at the list again. "So who else could have done this? Someone who knows our business," he postulated. "They know we can't go to the police."

Breakfast was eaten and the waiter cleared their plates, and neither of them had a hunch.

"Our customers in Los Angeles are satisfied?" Dr. Nouri sought confirmation.

"I heard from them last week and there was no indication of trouble."

"When are they expecting the next delivery?"

"This week. Their man is going to stop by Draper's Monday or Tuesday."

"Do you plan on telling them?"

"Unless you can make another batch quickly, I'll have to."

"Impossible. Mak only mixed the ingredients Friday."

"You don't have enough to make a partial order?"

"I have some premix left but it takes time to complete the process," Dr. Nouri explained. "I'm not sure we should tell them about the robbery. It might scare them and disrupt operations."

"We should talk to Sattar about that."

"Agreed. Sattar will have to make some decisions."

The old men parted company and made plans to meet later.

CHAPTER 45

Detective Gillingham was reading the paper while Ralph was dozing in the underground parking lot at 10:30 a.m.. Rudy and Detective Falin rolled in and stopped next to them. Ferguson and Ailes came ten minutes later, and by 11:00 seven cars, twelve men, and one woman associated with the investigation had converged for a meeting. Director Lawson was already upstairs in the fourth-floor conference room of the building on Varick Street that was the nerve center of the New York Customs Bureau. They all headed straight for the coffee pot and joined the assembled support personnel jabbering themselves awake under the painfully bright glow of fluorescent lighting. Everyone eventually found spots in the semicircle of metal folding chairs.

"Good morning. Men, ma'am," Director Lawson began the meeting. "I hope you all got plenty of rest 'cause it looks like it's going to be a long day."

His welcome was greeted by the collective groan of agents who had spent the last two nights trying to catch a few winks in the discomfort of state-issued blue sedans.

"I'm still sleeping, so wake me up when today starts," Detective Ferguson mouthed off, unafraid of rank.

"Today has officially begun, Detective Ferguson, and seeing as the government is paying you double for Sunday, we've decided to squeeze forty-eight hours of labor out of you. Any other questions or comments?" Director Lawson snapped, demonstrating a pre-emptive display of authority.

"I have a question," one of the agents from ATF said. "Why can't we just bust in, seize the evidence, arrest everyone, and be home in time for dinner?"

A murmur of approval echoed the popularity of the suggestion.

"Well, Agent Arthur, I must say I appreciate your enthusiasm," Director Lawson answered. "If only police work was that easy."

"With all due respect sir, what are we waiting for?" Agent Arthur's partner asked.

"Thank you for asking, Agent Margaret. As soon as you all stop asking questions I might actually be able to tell you what's going on," the Director answered sharply. The chatter abated. "Now that I seem to have your attention, I want to tell you why you're here this morning. There have been some important developments in the Laden case, and we think that things may come to a head tonight. Certain individuals not officially associated with the United States government – "

"You mean spies?" someone interrupted. It was an unruly crowd for a Sunday morning.

"Gentlemen, please. Our sources tell us that the man we've been looking for is on his way to New York as we speak. Now, before anyone asks why we don't just go to the airport and pick him up there, let me fill you all in on why he's coming here."

"He's coming to see the Empire State Building?" Detective Ferguson japed, unable keep his mouth shut.

Director Lawson stayed on point. "I don't think that will be his first priority. There's been a robbery and he's not very happy about it. As Detective Ailes will explain in a moment, the Darius Trust experienced an acute loss yesterday."

"The shepherds got sheared?"

"Something like that, and we have reason to believe they will attempt to rescue their stolen property from the wolves that took it as soon as possible – maybe even tonight." Director Lawson nodded to Detective Falin. "You can all use the lunchtime lull to relax and check in with your loved ones, because everyone will be on call and in position by 1600 hours. As I said, it's going to be a long night, so rest up. My assistant, Special Agent Farmer, will hand out your assignments in a little while, but I want you to listen to what Detective Ailes from Vice has to say, because he is our expert on the Pecorinos."

"Pecorinos? I thought we were after the Monsouris. I must be in the wrong briefing," someone noted, only half joking.

"Thank you for that distinction," Detective Ailes responded. "I am here to tell you how those two families are connected."

"Oh please great leader, connect the dots for us."

Director Lawson conferred his authority. "Come on guys, let the man speak. Your safety may depend on what he has to say."

Detective Ailes continued. "As I was saying, the Pecorinos and the Monsouris are connected in several ways." He listed his points on the left side of a dry ink board as he spoke. "They own real estate together, they share an interest in a recording studio, they have been known to use the same attorneys, and their biggest customers use the same bookie."

"Wow! That sounds positively evil! Let's go get em, boys!"

"Wait, there's more." Detective Ailes drew some horizontal lines across the board.

"Let's hope so."

He drew a downward line that separated the board in half. "Both of these families are into drugs and money laundering."

"Now we're getting somewhere."

"Correct. We've known about the Pecorinos' side businesses for a long time. We have an informer who handles their party favors, and an agent who keeps an eye on the numbers operation at their main location." Detective Ailes wrote "The Black Sheep" on the right half of the board. "Their entertainment company is a front, and we have to include it too." He wrote "Pecorino Partners" on the right side too. Then he drew a horizontal line under the two names on the right side and continued. "The Laden warehouse is Monsouri's main location." He listed it below the line. "Nothing much goes on at the recording studio or at the other nightclubs, but, as we all know, the Old Medical Building is a hot spot." He listed that under the Laden warehouse.

"Is that where the drugs are?"

"We're pretty sure; that's where the Darius Trust operates from. The doctor's office and laboratory are there too, and we'll get to that later, but now we need to get to the scene of the crime."

"An actual crime? Hallelujah!"

"Draper's office in New Jersey." Detective Ailes listed it under the Old Medical Building.

"Isn't that out of our jurisdiction?"

Director Lawson weighed in. "We have that worked out; say hello to the Jersey agents working with us." The New Jersey agents waved dismissively.

Detective Ailes went on. "Draper is under investigation by the IRS and has been cooperating. A lot of what we know about the Monsouris comes through him, and his help will be critical to making our case, so it is important not to blow his cover. You all know what that means." No one mouthed off so Detective Ailes kept talking. "The Pecorinos have been operating a legitimate real estate business for quite some time, staying away from the major action in gambling and drugs that the mob controls, but unfortunately for them, Dante Pecorino, who you all know from briefings, has a nose for trouble."

"Yeah, he's got a nose all right. Maybe we should call him 'Elephant Man,'" someone who had just seen the Anthony Hopkins movie interjected.

"Let's just stick with Dante, though I think his mother must be second guessing her choice of Christian names by now. Anyhow, the Pecorinos have been able to insulate themselves from most of Dante's shenanigans up until recently. They have known about his drug habit for a long time, and have taken an active role in controlling it by limiting his access to family money. His brother Anthony controls the purse strings, and Dante gets most of his drug fixes from the family's supplier at the club. Anthony and Dante's other babysitters report to the old man, who, from what we understand, wants nothing to do with the entertainment business. Dante's mother goes to church three times a week and still thinks her son can be saved."

"Can I get an Amen?" someone jived. There were no takers but a few people cleared their throats.

The detective continued. "This arrangement has worked very effectively for the past few years, or even longer, we're not sure," he explained.

"So the family gives the kid drugs to keep him from being a drug addict?"

"Brilliant!" The absurdity roused a collective chuckle from the detectives.

"Strange as it seems, that's how they decided to deal with it," Detective Ailes confirmed.

"Why didn't my parents think of that?" Detective Ferguson asked. "I could have saved a fortune on beer!"

The room burst out laughing.

"All right, gentleman, ladies." Director Lawson said, stifling his laugh. "Let's let Detective Ailes finish his story."

"Thank you, Director." Detective Ailes maintained his focus. "As I was about to say, Dante's habit has grown over time, and he now supports his girlfriend's habit as well as his own. He also uses drugs to impress his so-called friends in the music industry, and from what we hear he's been having trouble maintaining his big-shot image with the meager stipend from his family. And that is why we're all here this morning." Detective Ailes paused to make sure everyone was following. "Any questions so far?"

"I thought the Pecorinos were millionaires. Why don't they just give him the money and let him do his thing until he kills himself?"

"Or someone else."

"These cases always seem to have a few dead bodies lying in them."

"It's just a matter of time before someone doesn't wake up from one of those drug binges."

"Or someone doesn't pay their bill and wakes up dead."

"Can't these Pecorinos just buy their way out of their problems?"

Detective Ailes resumed his presentation. "Maybe they could, but even rich families have their limitations: Dante's management company has cost them a lot in unsuccessful ventures, the studio operates at a loss, and their nightclub barely breaks even. Their development project on Long Island has hit some snags, and one of their key political operatives lost the last election in Nassau County. To be blunt, we think they're running out of money *and* patience. Dante has tried to convince his family that his music business empire is going to be so successful that they won't need to bother with real estate anymore, but no one takes him seriously. The family has tried to keep him on a short leash, but his ambitions keep growing and his habits keep getting more expensive."

"Maybe they need to teach the kid a lesson?"

"Don't think they haven't thought about it."

"How much do a couple of broken fingers cost these days?"

Director Lawson reined them in. "Gentlemen, let's leave the crime to the criminals."

"As I was saying," Detective Ailes continued, "Dante is a dangerous character with a lot of expenses. We think that's why he set up the robbery." Detective Ailes wrote Dante's name on top of the vertical line that separated the two sides of the ink board.

"What did they steal?"

"Well, that's another issue; we're not exactly sure. I think that Detective Falin from Customs is going to take over from here and try to answer that."

Detective Falin stood up and took the marker pen. "For those of you too busy to read my briefing, I'll give you a recap," he condescended, living up to his reputation. "Laden Imports has been operating in this country for almost fifty years. Most of the stuff they import is harmless and legitimate, and they've been pretty good at filling out the paperwork and following the rules. We really didn't know too much about them until recently. They sell raw materials to perfume and soap makers, but they also make a few of their own products – and that's where it gets interesting. We didn't know we had a problem with them until a couple of years ago when everything changed over in Iran. That's when we got a tip about their secret side business."

"There's always a side business."

"Exactly. We see a lot of illegal shipments in the New York office, and we've busted people smuggling everything from baby animals to bales of pot, but most of the time we catch them because we know what the illegal stuff is. What makes this case so special is the raw materials. These characters are really clever." Detective Falin wallowed in undivided attention before making his announcement. "These people have figured out how to make heroin into perfume," he stated emphatically, pausing for effect and imagining another stripe on his uniform. "No dirty needles or bloody noses, just a whiff of a scented handkerchief or a drop on the skin. That's all their customers need to get high."

"Holy shit!"

"Heroin perfume?"

"What a fucking gold mine!" The room took on its own buzz.

"Who are these people?"

"How did they figure that out?"

"How come no one ever thought of this before?"

"In all my years, I never heard of that!"

"I thought my wife was a little too excited about that new "Opium" perfume I bought her."

Detective Falin enjoyed his moment of authority. "This isn't anything like the stuff Yves Saint Laurent makes. They just call that stuff "Opium"; this is the real thing. You can't buy it in the local drug store."

"Where *can* you buy it?" Agent Margaret, spoke up. She was the highest-ranking female officer in the room, and even though she dressed conservatively, she had an active social life that she enjoyed reminding the men about.

"Maybe we should send Agent Margaret undercover to score?" Rudy suggested.

Detective Falin liked the idea of working closely with her. "Now there's an intriguing idea."

Detective Gillingham redirected. "Maybe we should concentrate on the facts. This meeting is cutting into my lunch hour." He had an English soccer match he was anxious to see, but the other agents weren't done thinking about the intoxicating possibilities.

"Do they make it into a soft drink too?"

"Now *there's* a way to spike the punch!"

"I wouldn't want to be at that party!"

"I'll have a vodka nod, bartender."

"Make that a double shot." The puns and murmurs continued.

Annoyed, Detective Falin erased everything on the ink board with a few swipes. "As I was saying, the Monsouri family is in the drug business, which is why this is not just a U.S. Customs problem." He started another list, drawing as he talked. "We tried to handle this ourselves, but had to contact Vice when we discovered their street business and laboratory; that's why we're working with Detectives Ferguson and Ailes. We needed the help of ATF to go over state lines to follow the distribution, and that's how *they* got here." Agents Arthur and Margaret raised their hands. "The FBI took over communications between the departments, and Director Lawson got us clearance from the Justice Department. The FBI also got the IRS involved, and that's how we were able to get the accountant in New Jersey to cooperate. The CIA, who gave us the original customs tip, is still in touch with our overseas sources. Officer Casey is here to coordinate our efforts with NYPD." He stopped writing, turned around, and folded his arms smugly.

"Anyone have an aspirin? I have a headache."

"No but you can sniff my hankie for a dollar."

"That's disgusting!"

Director Lawson took over again. "I hope the detectives' history lessons have helped fill in some blanks."

"More than I ever wanted to know."

"The crooks are getting too smart for me. Can I have my old desk job back?"

"Nothing more satisfying than catching, cuffing, and hauling the bad guys down to the station," one of Officer Casey's men observed.

"You may have a chance to do that before the day is over," Director Lawson said cryptically.

The idea registered with Ralph. "Really?" he asked.

"Yes," Director Lawson confirmed. "As I said, we think something's going to go down tonight. The head of the Monsouri family is flying in and he's not in a good mood. This is now an FBI operation and I will let Detective Falin finish his part of the story before I explain our plan."

He gave the floor back to Detective Falin. "I don't need to bore you with everything we know about the suspects, but here are the important facts: We received our first tip more than two years ago, and have been closely monitoring their activity for about six months. They have been using their accountant's office in New Jersey as a distribution point, and we were watching the office yesterday, trying to pick up a tail on their customers from California, when something unexpected happened. Detective Ailes and Ferguson, who were monitoring Anthony Pecorino because one of their bands got busted, got a tip that he had picked up Emilio Lugano, a career safe-cracking criminal. Detectives Ailes and Ferguson had a hunch something was about to happen and tailed them out to New Jersey. While they were watching, Anthony sent the professional in to clean out the safe in the Monsouri accountant's office. We didn't know that the Pecorinos knew about the Monsouri's side business, and still aren't sure if they were after cash or drugs, but the Monsouris already know about the robbery and we don't expect them to take it lying down.'

"So the Italians robbed the Persians? Sounds biblical."

"There could be another holy war, right here in New York."

"I don't think there's enough soldiers for an all-out war," Director Lawson weighed in. "But we do expect a confrontation. Let Detective Falin finish, because I want you all to understand what he is about to say."

"We don't think the Pecorinos really know what they have," Detective Falin explained seriously. "The Monsouris make a powder with a high narcotic content that their customers dust on scarves and pillows, then inhale the odors to get high. The Pecorinos probably know the powder they took is potent stuff, and it's enough like the other powders on the street that they'll figure out what to do with it – someone is probably shooting or snorting

371

it right now. We think that's what they were after, and we know that's what they got. But, if our source is correct, the Pecorinos may have also taken two bottles of a much more powerful liquid that is used to make the heroin perfume. This concentrate is so strong that, supposedly, a few drops can knock someone out in a matter of minutes." He stopped talking and everyone took a mental gulp.

"What is it? It sounds like some kind of biological weapon."

"Sort of, not really, but you could call it that," Detective Falin stammered at the end of his knowledge.

"Maybe we should get the HazMat people involved?" Agent Arthur suggested.

"Now we've got poison gas to worry about?"

"Where does this end?"

"We're hoping this ends tonight." Director Lawson answered. "Here's what you need to know: The Pecorinos – Dante Pecorino, to be exact – has the stolen drugs in his apartment not far from here." He paused for effect. "And you all should know he is a reckless drug addict capable of enormous stupidity. The good news is, he's probably still sleeping. But there's a show tonight at a club called Max's Kansas City and we're sure he's going to be there."

"We're chasing these guys to Kansas?"

"No, the club's right here in Manhattan on 19th Street. The New York cops know all about that place. Right, Officer Casey?"

"Got that right. We go fishing for collars there all the time," Officer Casey confirmed.

"Anyway," Detective Lawson continued, "we hear the show is real important to Pecorino Partners, and Dante will definitely be there, showing off."

"Dante's going on stage? What's his act?"

"A freak show!"

"No, some band they manage is going to perform. They're trying to get the group signed to a major record deal or something like that. Dante thinks they're going to make millions and he won't have to depend on his family money anymore. Our staff psychologist, who has been advising on this case, thinks he's trying to prove to his family that he's not a failure. I don't know how all that fame and redemption stuff works, but here's what I do know: Dante has a lot of money and pride at stake, and we should be prepared for anything."

"You're losing us, Director. What's this got to do with drugs and robbery? Who are we supposed to arrest? Musicians?"

"No, the musicians are just sheep. All they know about drugs is how to use them." Detective Falin pointed out the obvious.

"I could use some drugs myself about now," someone joked.

"Listen, we don't know what to expect, but Dante has a gun and a lot of dangerous drugs, and the situation may get out of hand when the Persians find out who robbed them."

"How are they going to find out?"

"Bad news is hard to keep secret, and once they find out, it's not going to be difficult for them to find the culprits because the whole damn music industry knows about the show tonight." Director Lawson made his point.

"But I thought the Pecorinos and Monsouris were partners?"

"Partners are not always friendly."

"Maybe they don't want to be partners anymore."

"Robbery has been known kill a friendship."

"So what are we supposed to do, Director?"

"Special Agent Farmer is making out your assignments now. We'll pick up a tail on Sattar Monsouri when he lands at LaGuardia. He's the head of the Monsouri family now, so he'll probably make the decisions on how they plan to get their merchandise back." The agents discussed the facts amongst themselves.

"One more thing," Director Lawson raised his voice. "For those of you who don't know, this Sattar is no pushover. He is the oldest, and by far the toughest, Monsouri. He should be considered armed and dangerous." Everybody got quiet again. "Keep in mind that his father and brother-in-law both disappeared and were probably murdered by his enemies in Iran, so he is battle hardened. Lately, he has been in Miami meeting with South American drug gangs who want to take advantage of his import license, and we know for certain that he has experimented with ways to make perfume from marijuana and cocaine. We think Sattar will lead us to whatever action is going to happen, and we're hoping to catch him red-handed. We're going to have agents watching the Laden Imports warehouse, the Old Medical Building, and some of the apartments around the city to see if the Persians mobilize. One team will keep an eye on Dante and the stolen merchandise, and the rest of us will be stationed in and around the club where we think Dante will show up tonight. Special Agent Farmer will stay in touch with Officer Casey, and NYPD will back us up." Director Lawson wrapped it up and the men started to gather around Special Agent Farmer.

"So what's the name of the band?" Agent Ferguson asked irreverently.

Rudy had read the brief. "I think they're called Cells."

"Perfect name for an arresting night."

"Do you think the bad guys will show up?"

"That place is full of bad guys." Officer Casey shared.

"I bet there's going to be some freaky little girls there too." Detective Falin whispered to Rudy.

"I hope I can stay awake," Ralph wondered out loud what he had gotten himself into.

CHAPTER 46

Reggie heard the phone ringing from the shower. He slipped on the tile floor as he ran, soaking wet, to answer it. His barely-legal overnight guest giggled from under the covers at the sight of his exposed genitals flopping freely and pulled the sheets up to her chin. Sudsy water collected on the oval rag rug next to the dresser where Reggie stood with the phone to his ear. A warm breeze through an open window raised goose bumps on his exposed skin. His bed guest cast an admiring glance at his well-proportioned, muscular torso, and he shook his flaccid member at her with a goofy smile, holding the receiver in his other hand, trying to concentrate on the phone call.

"Good morning to you," he answered the caller, pretending his penis was a talking puppet.

"Reggie, this is Dr. Nouri."

"Yes, I know." His visitor revealed a momentary breast.

"Are you busy?"

"Sort of." The flirtations were having an effect.

"Reggie, I need your help," Dr. Nouri said earnestly.

"Okay, boss, sure thing," Reggie said mechanically, getting close enough to the bed to make contact with his guest.

"Can you come by the office today?"

"It's Sunday," Reggie pointed out. "Can't this wait until tomorrow?" he asked, pre-occupied with foreplay.

"No, I'm afraid not. This is important. I'll pay you overtime of course."

Reggie's vocabulary was limited by diverted blood flow. "Mmm hmm."

Dr. Nouri sensed he didn't have Reggie's full attention. "When can you come?"

"Ooh!" Reggie squealed, reacting to the oral stimulation of his bedguest.

"Are you in pain? Is everything all right? Reggie?" The alarm in Dr. Nouri's voice caused Reggie to withdraw his participation.

"I'm okay," he said, aching. "You need me today? What time?"

Professionally capable of interpreting patient moans, Dr. Nouri guessed what Reggie was up to. "Is 3:00 too soon?" he asked sympathetically.

"Okay doc, see you at the office at 3:00," Reggie forced an answer and threw the receiver on the bed.

CHAPTER 47

Dr. Nouri's next call was harder. Samani rarely got out of bed before 11:00 a.m. and was never in a hurry to embrace news from the outside world. Her morning routine consisted of strong coffee and plain toast, which she enjoyed from the comfort of her generously pillowed, queen-sized bed. Soft pastels and rococo-influenced furniture insulated her from the distractions of modern living, and her ever-present perfumed scarves coated her isolation into an almost impenetrable barrier. She had stopped wearing feminine sleeping attire since Arshan disappeared, and the thick flowered nightgown she slept in doubled as her housedress. Everything in her bedroom – with the exception of the telephone – belonged to a different era, and even that was a pink and white antique recreation with a built-in clock whose muted bell struck at one-hour intervals. Spending more time in bed than anywhere else, it was both her office and sanctuary. She picked up Dr. Nouri's call with her usual disconnected complacency.

"Yes."

"Did I wake you?" Dr. Nouri asked with his best bedside manners.

"No," Samani answered disinterestedly.

He could hear the distance in her voice. "Have you had your coffee yet?"

"Yes," she said dreamily, ensconced in her pillows, watching the cloud patterns on her window shades.

Dr. Nouri guessed her condition and decided to be blunt. "Samani, I have some bad news."

"Oh?" she acknowledged without urgency.

"Yes, we've been robbed," he said plainly, getting right to the point.

"Oh?" Samani wondered how warm it was outside. The caffeine and residual narcotics in her bloodstream had blended together, inducing a state of alert tranquility usually reserved for the extremely pious or seriously hung over.

"Samani, dear, this is serious. Your brother is coming in tonight."

"My brother? Oh good. It will be nice to see him. Who is coming? Saeed?"

"No, Sattar. He is flying in from Miami."

"I love Miami. How long has he been there?"

"I don't know; it doesn't matter." Dr. Nouri was frustrated but went on being nice. "Will you be getting out today? It's very pleasant outside."

A shaft of direct sunlight ignited her curtains. "Yes, I see that."

"Sattar's plane lands at 6:00 tonight. Rhamin will meet him at the airport."

"How is Rhamin? Did you know he and Homa...?" Her voice trailed off before she finished the sentence.

"Yes, I heard they were together. Let us pray it is their destiny."

"He is such a fine young man; if only my Homa sees it." Samani sighed at the alter of fate.

"God willing." Dr. Nouri gave up trying to talk sense. "Sattar will stay with me as usual. I'm sure he will call you tonight."

"Sattar is coming?"

"Yes, tonight."

"Why?"

"Because of the robbery."

"Robbery? He was robbed?"

"Yes, we all were. I told you a moment ago."

"I was robbed?" Samani looked around her room to see if anything was missing.

"What did they take?"

"Princess Powder and Princess Tears."

"That's terrible." She checked her nightstand to make sure her dowsing bottle was still there. "What shall we do?"

"We're making a plan right now. Nothing will be decided until Sattar arrives."

"My brother will be very upset." Fear of her older brother stimulated her metabolism. Sattar had been jealous of all the attention his parents lavished on his younger sister and took sport in teasing her with an acute but misguided intellect. "Will Saeed be coming as well?" Saeed, the middle sibling, had always acted as a buffer between Samani and Sattar.

"No, he is still in Lebanon and we're not sure of his plans yet."

Samani got out of bed and peered out the window. "When did this happen?"

"Yesterday. Last night."

She examined the buildings near hers, looking for clues. "Where did it happen?"

"In New Jersey. The shipment was stolen from Draper's office."

"New Jersey?" Her journey to sobriety continued. "The accountant is in New Jersey."

"Yes, I know." Dr. Nouri was relieved that she was getting it. He took his glasses off and rocked back in his office chair.

"How did this happen?"

"We don't know."

"What will we do?"

"We will wait for Sattar and then decide."

"Was anybody hurt?" She tried to remember if she had heard Homa come in last night.

"No, it was only a robbery, thank God."

"Does Bahram know?"

"Of course, he's the one who told me."

"And Rhamin is okay?"

"Everyone is okay for now. We will call you when Sattar gets here."

"I will tell Homa."

"Are you sure that's a good idea? She doesn't know everything about The Princess yet. Maybe it would be better if she didn't know too much?"

"I will talk to her; it is time she knew. She is a grown woman now."

"Be careful what you say, Samani dearest. We are all in this together." Dr. Nouri had never married and had no children of his own, but descendants of the Farsis and Monsouris had intermarried so many times that it was impossible to calculate the exact relationships anymore, and he treated Homa like daughter.

Samani's hope and faith fused together.

"Homa is older and wiser than we know. She is her father's daughter and carries Ava's spirit. She will help us."

CHAPTER 48

Samani put on her robe and padded down the hallway to her daughter's room. It was almost 11:00 and Homa was still asleep. Her mother knocked lightly and creaked the door open wide enough to see her in bed.

Homa heard her and spoke without opening her eyes. "Good morning mother."

"Good morning child," she said haltingly.

Homa heard the uncertainty in her voice. "What's the matter?"

"Oh nothing." Samani didn't know where to begin. "We'll talk when you're awake."

"I am awake." Homa sat up in bed. "What's the matter?" she repeated.

"Do you want coffee?"

"Is it father?" Homa asked, always hopeful for his miraculous return.

"No dear."

Homa slumped back against her pillows and stared at her mural. "What then?"

"I will make your coffee and bring it to you." Samani went to the kitchen.

Homa focused on a small painted figure in her mural that she often designated as her father, and spoke to him with her heart. He never looked at her directly, but she knew he could hear her. He was standing in a hilly green field outside the city, surrounded by puffy white sheep in dots of red poppies. The image soothed her nerves with promises of pastoral peace. Lost in reverie, she heard the high-pitched bells of animals grazing in the mountain meadow and her father's voice humming a shepherd's lament. But the vision faded as the bells turned into the clanking dishes of the breakfast tray, and her father's faint song was lost in the low frequency oscillation of city traffic.

Samani placed the tray carefully on Homa's nightstand. She added a lump of sugar to the coffee and stirred. "Just the way you like it," she sighed.

Homa picked up the saucer with one hand and grasped the delicate china handle with the other. She leaned back into her pillow mass. "What is it mother?" she asked, sipping herself awake. Samani dusted a shelf with her sleeve and smiled painfully. "Mother, I am talking to you! I know you have something to tell me. Please, I promise not to be angry."

"It's not that child."

"Well, what then? Are you sick again?"

"No, I feel well." She didn't sound too convincing.

Homa sat up cross-legged. "Mother, please tell me what you came to tell me."

Samani stopped dusting and her face drooped. A tear welled in her eye as she sat on the edge of the bed. "Oh Homa, darling, we need you," she sobbed.

"Who needs me? Needs me for what?" Homa put the coffee down and placed her hand on her mother's hand. "I hate to see you upset."

"I'm sorry. I'm just so scared." Samani fought back tears.

"Shall I get your handkerchief?"

"No, that won't help us now."

"Okay mother, now you're worrying me. You need to tell me what the problem is," Homa insisted.

"Something's been taken," Samani gasped.

"You've taken pills? Do you need me to take you to the hospital?"

"No, someone's taken our...our...property."

"Someone's stolen from us? There's been a robbery?"

"Yes."

Homa looked around her room suspiciously. "Where did this happen?"

"Not here."

"At the warehouse? I knew I couldn't trust the delivery drivers. I will call Mak."

"No, not yet. It wasn't there." Samani said weakly.

"Are you going to tell me or do I have to guess?"

Samani heaved a sigh. "It's a long story. Your father made me promise not to tell you until you were old enough to understand."

"How could father know about a robbery that just happened?"

"He couldn't. It's...just...that.... Homa, darling, I know you think you know everything about the business, but there are some things we haven't told you."

Homa was a bit offended. "Like what?"

"Like how we make our special perfumes."

"I wanted to learn how to use the mix room, but Sattar and father wouldn't let me. They said it was too dangerous."

"It *is* dangerous, and that is why we kept you from it. Did you not see what happened to the worker on Friday?"

"That was an accident. Mak said he got too close to...." Homa remembered Mak's steady gaze and changed tone. "What is it about the perfume that makes it so special? I'm old enough to know now."

"Yes, child. You're a grown woman now."

"Does this mean you're going to teach me how to make the Princess Mist?"

"No, the conjure pot is a job for men. But you need to know a few things about the process."

"Do *you* know?"

"Yes."

"Have you known all along?"

"Yes, since before you were born."

"Please tell me."

"It's a very long story. It goes back 150 years...even longer if you go back to the beginning."

"Should we get dressed and go somewhere. Maybe for lunch?"

"No, I prefer to tell you right here on the edge of Persepolis where your father can see us." Samani waved her hand in front of the mural and prayed for guidance. Homa eased back into her pillows as the story began.

"A long time ago, my great grandfather was a professor in Iran. He was not an important professor or the head of anything, but he knew Persian languages and taught at a University in Esfahan. One day, British archeologists who were interested in our history hired him to translate ancient writings that had been discovered in the region. It was a good way to make some extra money and he enjoyed the challenging work. He worked for the archeologists for many years and became a specialist in Elamite and other languages that had been lost with the ages. No one spoke those words anymore, but he was able to understand most of what was written. One day he came across some writing that had an odd translation. He wasn't sure what it said and didn't want to disappoint his employers with his failure, so he never told them about it. He kept the cylinder – the letters were pressed into soft clay and then rolled up to dry – for many years, trying to unlock its mystery, mostly out of curiosity. Eventually, after he had stopped working for the British, he discovered that the words were a formula for making a special kind of perfume."

"I think I've heard some of this story before. Is there more?"

"Much more. As you know, our ancestors were the originators of perfume making. They made many kinds, some of which we still use today. But the formula my great grandfather found was for a kind of perfume that made people feel happy, especially when they were in pain. The ancients thought of the perfume as a kind of medicine. It was very complicated to make; there were many steps and some very special ingredients. The people of Persepolis, where the relic was from, were very skilled, and this medicine was one of their most important products."

Having built up to her favorite part of the story, Samani took a deep breath and patted her eyes with a tissue. "Our ancestors were very advanced in many ways. Besides perfume making, they were able to build the beautiful fortress you and your father have painted on the wall. Persepolis was the richest and most beautiful city in the world for a long time." Samani glowed in the reflection of accomplishment. "Most of our ancestor's success was based on the idea that people should live in peace. Many different peoples lived in the area around Persepolis, and they all had different customs, different religions, and even different languages. Our ancestors were the strongest and most powerful, but they were also wise. They were able to unite the tribes, and together they built canals to bring water from the mountains so crops could be grown in the desert and animals could be raised. She showed Homa the places on the mural. Our ancestors wanted everyone's life to be happy – not just for no reason – but because happy subjects were easier to rule. The formula your great great grandfather discovered was for the medicine to make people feel good. It was the recipe for a happiness medicine." Samani sparkled with pride.

"There is a recipe for happiness?"

"Yes, at least that's what the ancients thought." Samani reached in her robe pocket for her handkerchief.

Homa's imagination wandered the buildings of her mural. "What did the professor do? Was he able to make the medicine?"

"Not at first. Just because he found the recipe didn't mean he could follow it. Making perfume is not simple, and he was a professor of language, not a chemist. He didn't know where to get the proper ingredients or how to mix them together."

"What was his name?"

"Cyrus Farsi."

"So what did he do?"

"Well, he was a professor, and like many in our family, he was very smart. He didn't want to share his secret, so he studied perfume making on his own. There was a lot of information available to him at the university library, and with the help of books and a few innocent questions he figured out how to set up a small laboratory in a spare room of his house."

"Where did he get the special bottles and plastic tubes? They didn't have those back then."

"They didn't use the same things we use today, but perfume making has been around for thousands of years. There are many ways to withdraw beauty from nature, and Cyrus learned some of these methods."

Homa sat up. "Was he able to make the happiness perfume?"

Samani was relieved that Homa was paying close attention and continued her story. "Well yes...and no. He was able to make small quantities, but it was very weak. He was still learning how to do it before he began running out of money and time. After a year or so, his standing at the university began to decline because he had been neglecting his students. He had very little to show for his efforts and his wife became frustrated. She wanted him to pay more attention to her and their young daughter, and one day while he was out, she destroyed his laboratory and threw all his equipment away."

"That's terrible!"

"Yes, and he was very upset. But he accepted his failure and went back to being a full time professor and father."

"That doesn't sound like the end of the story," Homa said, fully awake and leaning forward.

"It's not. Some years later, when their daughter got older – "

"What was her name?"

"Ava."

"Your grandmother Ava? The one you've told me about?"

"Yes. When Ava became old enough to marry, her mother found her a suitor from a wealthy family and made wedding plans. Ava was very smart, just like her father, and not just a pretty girl." Samani stroked her daughter's hair. "Ava didn't like the boy, but agreed to do as her mother wished. I'm sure she would have gone through with it, but her mother became ill and died before the wedding could be arranged. Naturally, the wedding plans fell apart. In their grief, Ava and her father became very close, and Ava remembered the happy times of her early childhood when she would sit and watch her father in his laboratory. She asked her father what he was working on all that time, and when she heard about his efforts to make a happiness formula, she convinced him to set up another laboratory and show her what he had been doing. Happiness was something they both desperately needed, and the experiments excited her and gave them both a reason to go on with their lives. Ava became intrigued with the idea of making a happiness perfume and studied the books her father brought home from the library."

"Why didn't she go to the university to study?"

"Women weren't allowed at the university back then. They were just supposed to make babies and take care of the children and the house."

"Even the smart ones?"

"Smart women like Ava suffered the most, so the time she spent learning perfumery was a labor of love and freedom. But first, she had to master the basics. After a time she got good enough to make fragrances that other women wanted, and that's how my grandmother started: selling pomades and tinctures and powders. Her father, who had gone back to his language studies, supported her in every way, and Ava was so successful making and selling regular products that she didn't bother trying to recreate the ancient happiness formula for several years."

"So your grandmother started the family business," Homa repeated, understanding the family lore she had grown up with more completely.

"Yes, that's right." Passing on the family's oral tradition filled Samani with renewed purpose. She sat on the edge of the bed, took one of Homa's elastic ties, and cinched her hair up. Her handsomely rounded face glowed like the Princess head in the office, and she was more cogent than Homa had seen in years. "Then, one day," Samani went on, "while researching the ancient languages, Professor Farsi discovered that one of the Elamite letters used in the formula had many meanings. It was a very crude language, and many of the symbols we call letters today could stand for more than one thing. When Cyrus translated the original happiness formula with his new understanding, he discovered how the ancients used certain sheep to make their medicine stronger. He shared his findings with his daughter, and together, the two of them set out to make the happiness recipe again."

"And did they succeed this time?"

"Oh yes, dear child. You and I are the living proof."

"I don't understand."

"It is a very long story, but it is important that you know it because we still use some of the knowledge in our business."

Homa's attention elevated at the mention of business. "We do?"

"Yes. The Professor realized that the secret to making the happiness formula was the special seeds – Red Crown seeds."

"Red Crown seeds? The same kind we use for the Princess Mist? Is that why the Princess wears a red crown?" Homa began to understand.

"Yes, and the secret of the seeds was that they had to be grown in special soil."

"What kind of soil?"

"The world is full of hidden connections, dear child. The poppy seeds we use are only grown in southern Persia. They must be made healthy by the droppings of a certain kind of sheep that have been fed on the ancient grasses growing there."

Homa digested the information before she asked her next question. "How could the Professor get these seeds? Persepolis was gone and no one was growing them anymore; we're they?"

"No. But even though Professor Farsi was not wealthy, his family still owned a small farm in the Zagros Mountains that had been theirs longer than anyone could remember. Although it took years to raise a small flock of the right kind of sheep, he was able to grow enough poppy plants there to make some of the formula."

"Is that where we get our seeds from?"

"A few, but it is a very small farm and there isn't much room to grow."

"So where do the rest come from? We use so many."

"That is all part of the story. I am so relieved that I am finally telling you." Samani squeezed her daughter's hand tightly and closed her eyes. They sat quietly for a few minutes before she finally continued. "Fate smiled upon Professor Farsi. A wealthy family with much land nearby agreed to plant some fields according to his instructions. The Professor told them that the reason they should plant the poppies was because it would make the sheep's milk taste better, and even though he was deceiving them, the sheep did make better milk. The meat of the sheep also had a special quality everyone seemed to enjoy, and of course the wool from the sheep was also very useful. The wealthy neighbors profited from the arrangement and converted all of their grazing land to specialize in Merino sheep. Your great great grandfather was too old to harvest the seeds by himself, but the neighbors let Ava collect the poppy seeds after they bloomed. One day, when Ava was in the fields harvesting by herself, she met a man tending the sheep and they fell in love."

"In love?" Homa giggled. "What was his name?"

"Farid Monsouri"

"Monsouri! Is that...?"

"Yes. The Farsi's neighbors were the Monsouris. Ava and Farid married and the perfume business became very successful. She gave birth to my father, Dadi, and they started our business. You and I would not be who we are if not for them."

"Did you ever meet them?"

"Farid died before I was born, but Ava was still alive...very alive," Samani rhapsodized.

Homa was moved by her mother's devotion. "She must have been a very powerful woman. Did you ever meet her?"

"Only a few times. I was very young and she was very old, but I can still remember the fire in her eyes."

"What did she look like in person? I've only seen pictures."

Samani had been waiting for this question. "Her eyes were violet and her body was old, but other than that, you are made in her image." She stroked her daughter's hair and lost herself in reflection.

"What a wonderful story. I feel so lucky." Homa returned her mother's affection with a gentle hand. "Why are you so upset?"

Samani welled with emotion. "I am scared."

"What are you scared of mother? I will protect you."

"I hope you can." She hung her head despondently.

"You promised to tell me what was wrong. I haven't heard anything about a robbery or what kind of danger we might be in. How can I help if I don't know?"

"It's the happiness secret."

"Someone's stolen our secret?"

"No, but they stole some of our most potent mixture."

"Well, can't we just make more?"

"Yes, probably, but there are other problems."

"What other problems? The business has plenty of money."

"We have enemies."

"Everyone has enemies."

"Yes, but our enemies are the government."

"Which government? Iran or the United States?"

"Both. The Ayatollah's henchmen have turned this country against us."

"But the Americans hate the Ayatollah."

"Yes, but they both hate our success."

"Why do they hate us? What did we do wrong?"

"They think we broke the law."

"Whose law? Did we do something illegal?"

"It didn't used to be illegal, but now the government thinks it is."

"Is it our happiness formula? Is that what they think is illegal?"

"Yes. They think it is some kind of illegal drug." Samani exhaled the burdensome truth and wilted. Unconsciously, she rubbed her fingers through her scalp and pulled her hair knot apart. The elastic tie snapped and her hair fell around her face.

Homa's body stiffened. "That's horrible! Why do they think that?"

Samani regained some of her composure. "Because we use the Red Crown poppy seeds."

Homa saw the danger. "And poppies are also used to make heroin! They think we're making drugs? I can't believe it!" Samani didn't correct her. "But isn't morphine also made from poppies? All the hospitals use it," Homa reasoned. "Who makes that?"

"Some people have a license to make medicine out of poppies, but we don't."

"Can't we get a license?"

Samani struggled under the weight of truth. "There are no licenses to make this kind of perfume."

Homa stroked her arm sympathetically. "Maybe we should get dressed and go for a walk. The fresh air might make us feel better,"

Homa said softly, trying to console her. Tears welled in Samani's eyes and her jaw trembled. Fearing she might collapse, Homa got out of bed and held her with both arms. "It's all right mother," she consoled. "It will all work out," she hoped aloud, looking over her mother's shoulder at the mural.

Samani held her tears. "I'll go put some outside clothes on now." She went back to her room and changed while Homa got dressed. A few minutes later, they met in the living room and embraced again. They descended to the ground floor and were ushered into the open air by a uniformed doorman. Gramercy Park was peaceful, and they continued talking while the agents watching them kept their distance.

Homa had dressed for spring in light cotton pants and a loose fitting shirt. "It is such a beautiful day outside. Let's not be sad today mother," she said, holding her mother's hand.

Samani, wearing a three-quarter jacket and a silk scarf, wobbled as she sat on the edge of the bench with her knees together. "I'll try."

Homa tried to steady her. "Do you see any enemies here in the park?" she asked soothingly.

Samani squinted behind dark, oversized Chanel sunglasses. "No, but that doesn't mean they're not here."

Homa looked suspiciously at the people around her. Pickpockets, gropers, and even muggers were criminals that every city dweller had to be aware of, but she had never considered the possibility that there might be hidden forces aligned against her. The familiar peace of her neighborhood park suddenly seemed precariously balanced between the routine and the unpredictable. The sweet organic smells of flowers and fertilizer mixed with the acrid acids of dog urine and bus fumes. The innocent casualness of Sunday morning submerged under the flood of unasked and unanswered questions. For the first time as an adult, Homa saw nameless fears in strangers' faces. Her mother sat quietly next to her, watching her grow up.

"Are we in danger now?" Homa asked with newly acquired vigilance.

"Not here, not now," Samani told a white lie through deep red lipstick.

Homa guessed the truth anyway. "Is the government watching us?"

"Perhaps." Samani didn't want to believe it and put her tiny scented pillow to her nose to dull reality.

"You look a little pale, mother. Shall we walk? The exercise might be good for you."

"No, I didn't wear the right shoes. Let's just sit here for a moment and enjoy the spring weather."

Neither of them did.

CHAPTER 49

The late night phone call from Bahram came just after Sattar returned to his room. His meeting in the Miami hotel bar with a representative of a Columbian drug cartel had gone well, but his excitement from receiving the first big order for chemicals needed to liquefy their products bubbled away more quickly than the alcoholic buzz from his Shiraz nightcap. Bahram didn't give him too many details over the phone, but the coded mention of Princess Tears was enough to convey the severity of the problem. Sattar contacted the airline, booked a flight home, and called Bahram back with the arrival information within thirty minutes. Sleep was impossible as his mind raced through twisted paranoid scenarios of betrayal and retribution. He finally got out of bed at 7:00 a.m., showered, packed, checked out, and took a taxi to the airport to see if he could get on an earlier flight.

The airport terminal was crowded with spring vacationers wheeling suitcases packed with dirty clothes and mementos. Sattar sat as far away as he could from the obnoxious children fighting in T-shirts that identified their holiday highlights. He got a seat on an early 10:00 a.m. flight to LaGuardia and tried to read the Sunday paper while he was waiting. The customs agents seated across the aisle appeared to be business travelers heading to New York for the week. Sattar didn't trust anyone he didn't know, and didn't care what they, or anyone else, did, as long as it didn't interfere with his plans. The agents had been shadowing him for two weeks and were ready to act, but Sattar gave them no actionable cause. Happy to see him leave their jurisdiction, they called the New York office before he boarded the plane and went back to the Miami office to fill out their report after his flight took off.

The call from Bahram was disquieting, but not wholly unexpected. Sattar had left the path of innocent assumption a long time ago and was ready for battle. He owned more than one gun, and he carried his favorite pearl-handled Derringer in his luggage. So far, his superior negotiating skills had allowed him to advance his agenda without killing anybody, but he assumed it was only a matter of time before a confrontation elevated into an armed conflict.

The weekend receptionist at the Customs Bureau who answered the phone call from the Miami agents just took a message, so by the time Director Lawson got it, Sattar had already landed and was headed to his hideaway upstairs from the recording studio. As part of their lease agreement with Pecorino Partners, the Monsouris had retained the use of one of the two apartments designed to house overnight customers of Heard Tracks, and Sattar used it as a place to stay when he needed to disappear. There was no phone or mailbox, and only his brother, Bahram, Rhamin, and Dr. Nouri knew about the arrangement. They all respected his privacy, and the police couldn't figure out where Sattar vanished to on occasion. His official residence was the spare bedroom in Dr. Nouri's apartment, and all the members of the Persian community assumed he lived with Dr. Nouri when he wasn't traveling. The cab from the airport dropped him off on the corner of Spring Street and he used the back entrance to access his fourth floor retreat. He didn't call anyone to say he had arrived, because his first council of war was a ritual with the disembodied.

CHAPTER 50

Roslyn was annoyed at having to manage the kids by herself all morning while Anthony slept. When his father called at 11:15 Sunday morning, she tucked the wireless receiver under Anthony's ear and stood next to the bed in her robe with their squirmy toddler straddling her hip. "Get up now, lazy boy. Your father's on the phone," she whined in a nasal Long Island accent that was as disruptive as a smoke alarm.

Startled from his dreams and lying on his stomach, Anthony talked into his pillow without realizing his father could hear him. "My father? It's Sunday morning. What does he want?"

"Why don't you just ask him yourself?" She shifted the toddler to the other hip and repositioned the phone against his face.

"Get up!" Dominic's angry directive sizzled through the fog in Anthony's brain.

"Good morning, father," he said calmly, rolling onto his back without opening his eyes.

"What's so fucking good about it?" Dominic spewed.

Anthony was more even-tempered than his father and accustomed to his outbursts. "You sound upset. What's the matter?"

"Don't give me that old boy-scout bullshit," Dominic snarled. "What have you and your good-for-nothing brother been up to?"

"What do you mean?" Anthony maintained his innocence while peeking to see if his wife was listening.

396

"I said, don't bullshit me, asshole. I got a call this morning from a detective at the precinct."

"Oh? What did he say?" Anthony cleared his throat and sat up, nodding pleasantly to Roslyn as she took the baby to the next room.

"They picked up a friend of yours, Emmy, last night."

Anthony gulped silently. "Why did they call *you*? He needed to post bail?"

"No. They're not going to let him go so easy." Dominic took a full breath and delivered the bad news. "You know, Emmy's been in trouble before. When they leaned on him, he squealed."

Anthony felt a wave of anxiety bounce off the pit of his stomach and slosh halfway up his throat. "Just a minute," he said, reaching for the glass of water he always kept on his night table. "What did he tell them?" he asked cautiously.

"The detective wouldn't tell me everything."

"What *did* he tell you?"

"He said he was calling as a friend. He and I go way back. He wanted me to know that my good-for-nothing kids opened a can of worms," Dominic said bitterly.

"He told you we were going fishing?"

"Don't be a wiseass. You know what you did."

"What else did he say?"

"He told me I was going to have to call in some major favors to fix this, and he couldn't help me. That's not like him. Whatever you two got your hooks into is way too heavy for the fucking flounder rigs you've got in the garage."

"I'll take care of it, dad, promise." Anthony wanted to say more but Roslyn came back in holding their diapered toddler. "Roslyn needs some help with the baby so I'll call you a little later," he said cheerfully, putting the phone down and shifting into daddy mode. Roslyn handed the baby to him and went to fetch a clean diaper.

She came back to the bed and spread the new diaper on their comforter as Anthony held his son Raphael up. Roslyn undid the poop-filled pad, wiped Raphael's bottom with a clean corner, and rolled up the excrement with a well-practiced maneuver.

"Baby's got a stinky butt," Roslyn sang, holding Raphael's tiny hands.

Anthony gagged at the smell. "What have you been feeding him?"

"Daddy doesn't like Raphy's poopy," she teased. "Hold him for a minute while I throw this in the garbage." She disposed of it in the adjoining bathroom.

"Daddy loves his little man," Anthony said, holding Raphael upright and burying his chin into the folds of his neck. He snortled a sloppy wet kiss against Raphael's delicate skin. Eighteen months old, Raphael giggled at his father's attention, then suddenly shrieked in his ear and burst out crying.

Roslyn came back and took Raphael out of his arms. "What did you do?"

"Nothing. All I did was give him a snuggle and he started whining."

"You must have scratched him with your beard," she said, soothing the redness she saw on Raphael's neck. "When was the last time you shaved?" she scolded. "I told you that you can't go near him with that stubble. He has very sensitive skin."

Anthony felt his stubble. "I shaved on Friday."

"Well, it's Sunday morning, mister, and you're too hairy to go without shaving. Where were you last night anyway?"

"I was with my brother at the club," Anthony said, dismissing the question as he stood up. He pretended to be looking out the window to check the weather. "Nice day out," he said absently.

"I thought you were with your brother *Friday* night?" Roslyn sensed the half-truth. "You two sure have been spending a lot of time together lately." She wasn't too wrapped up in motherhood to be suspicious. "What mischief has Dante been up to this week?" she pried, bobbing the baby on her hip.

Anthony didn't answer. His head didn't feel right and his father's call had put him on edge. Wearing only his underpants, he walked toward the bathroom, but Roslyn's alarm stopped him.

"What's that?" she gasped.

"What?" Anthony couldn't see it.

"That." Roslyn pointed at him. "What happened to your back?" Still holding Raphael, she came closer. Anthony twisted in front of the bedroom mirror and saw the fingernail marks Starla had left on his lower back. His heart pumped a surge of blood through his system, trying to stimulate his brain into coming up with a believable explanation.

"Oh that, I fell on the golf course," he said nonchalantly, edging toward the safety of the bathroom.

"Not so fast, mister." Roslyn held him by his shorts with her free hand and came closer for an inspection. "That doesn't look like a fall – unless you fell in a sticker bush and someone had to drag you out." She traced her fingers along the scratch lines and fell silent. "It looks like you were in a fight...or...."

Anthony's elevated heart rate reddened the wounds that advertised his guilt. He tried to cover them with his hand as he pulled away and escaped to the bathroom and locked the door. A long hot shower gave him time to think, but he didn't have any good ideas. He examined his scratches while drying off. The baby's diaper rash cream didn't help, and he was bleeding from the scabs that had the hot water had loosened. The large Band-Aid he found in the medicine cabinet wouldn't stick to his oily skin, so he used a towel to try to stop the bleeding. Unable to see clearly, he used the towel to wipe the mirror, smearing his naked reflection with blood. The stink from his son's diaper filled the steamy room and activated the residual effects of the previous night's drug poisoning. Feeling dizzy, he held on to a towel rack for support as he saw his blood-smeared image in the mirror. Standing naked, he had his first glimpse of Hell.

Roslyn was on the bed, sobbing, with Raphael on her stomach when Anthony came out of the bathroom and entered Purgatory.

CHAPTER 51

Jon woke up in a great mood late Sunday morning. Monica's spacious apartment had an elevated view of Manhattan that made him feel like he was on top of the world. Their nighttime intimacy had transcended sexuality, and for the first time in a long time, he felt like he was in love. Everything seemed to be going his way. Rehearsals had gone better than he had expected, and Nigel was confident that this would be the turning point in his career. Dennis had made all the arrangements with the club, and Dante had left him a stash of the best blow he had ever tasted. It was almost too good to be true. His muscular body tingled with hot tea and optimism. Satisfied, smitten, and standing behind him in a full- length silk robe, Monica put her arms around his midsection as he gazed out over his newly conquered kingdom.

"How do you feel?" Monica already knew the answer.

"I feel great!"

"Are you hungry?"

"Only for you." He pinched her.

"I love you." The words came out of her mouth before she could stop them.

He pinched her again and patted her behind. "I love you, too."

Her open hands slid up his chest and through the dark blond curls that covered it. Hugging him from behind, she nuzzled her face against his upper back. Jon shifted the weight off his injured foot and reached behind to feel the contours of her sides. They held their embrace in front of the window until the affection produced a bulge in Jon's tight fitting jockey shorts. He turned to face her, but the ringing phone disrupted their foreplay.

"I better answer that," Monica complained. "It might be one of my roommates."

Jon limped to her bedroom to wait for her while she talked on the phone.

Rebecca wasn't sure which of her roommates had answered. "Monica?"

"Yes, it's me. Hi, Becca. Where are you?" Monica asked, hoping she was still in New Jersey.

"I'm at my folks' house."

"Oh nice. It must be pretty out there today?"

"Yes, very. A little cloudy, but it's warm."

"Same here."

"Is Amy home?"

"No, I think she spent the night with Freddy again."

"Are you alone?"

"Yes, just little old me." Monica felt bad for lying. "When are you coming home?"

"Oh, I don't know, sometime tonight I guess." Rebecca was still in shock from her father's revelations. "What are you doing tonight?"

"I don't know. I might go out, I might not," Monica fibbed. She didn't want to mention her plans with Jon.

"Well, I don't know what I feel like doing either. Maybe I'll see you later. I'll leave a message if I decide to stay in New Jersey."

"Don't you have work tomorrow?"

"I think so, I'm not sure."

"Not sure? Did you get fired or something?"

"No. I...I can't really talk right now. I'll see you later." Rebecca wanted to get off the phone without saying too much and forgot to ask Monica about the night she didn't come home.

"Okay," Monica said, relieved she didn't ask. She hung up, but Jon wasn't in the bedroom waiting for her. "Jon?" she called out.

"I'm in here." His voice came from the bathroom. Monica sat on the bed rubbing lotion on her hands as she waited for him. Too much time elapsed so she called out again. "Are you okay in there?"

Jon didn't answer immediately. "I'm okay but I don't feel so good." His voice sounded strained.

"What's the matter? Is it your foot?"

"I don't know, maybe it's the medicine." He had swallowed two of Dr. Nouri's tablets with his tea.

More time passed in silence and Monica started to get concerned. "Can I get you anything? Aspirin or something?"

"Yeah, maybe aspirin would help. My head is killing me."

"Your head hurts? You have a headache?"

Jon opened the bathroom door and came out in a loosely buttoned shirt. His face was pale and his hair looked like he had just escaped from a helicopter.

"You look awful. What happened?" Monica asked, alarmed.

"I...I think I'm getting a migraine," he said meekly as he dove into the bed. "Turn off the lights, please," he begged, lying on his stomach with a pillow over his head.

"Here's some aspirin." Monica extended her hand but Jon didn't budge. "Do you want some water to take this with?"

"Coffee. I need some coffee," Jon pled into the pillow and rolled onto his side. He tried open his eyes but the room started to spin and Monica's outstretched hand became a moving target. Nausea set in, and he felt like was going to vomit. Monica tried to sooth him by putting her hand on his head, but he brushed her away and twisted onto his other side, coiling the covers around him.

Monica got worried. "What can I do?"

"Nothing. Leave me alone!" Jon bleated in agony. Then, suddenly, he sat up and grabbed the aspirin from her hand. "Coffee. I need some coffee. Quick!" he urged. "And close those shades...

please!" He flopped back down again and started moaning, writhing on the mattress as if he were wrestling with an unseen foe. His bloodied boot left traces of red on the sheets, which had wrapped around his legs.

Monica was frightened. She put her hair up with an elastic band, tied her robe snugly, closed the shades, and went to the kitchen to make some coffee. The magnetized card with emergency numbers that Rebecca had stuck to the refrigerator when they first moved in was suddenly comforting. Listening to Jon's groans through the closed door, she wondered what she had gotten herself into.

CHAPTER 52

The morning meeting lasted until 1:00, and by that time all the detectives were more concerned with lunch than logistics. Ralph and Rudy, who had worked at the Varick Street location longer than anyone else, recommended dining options to the agents from other departments as they filtered down to the basement parking garage. Director Lawson and Special Agent Farmer sent an assistant to fetch some sandwiches and stayed behind in the situation room they had set up on the fourth floor. A written phone message, one of several left in Director Lawson's box by the weekend secretary, said that Sattar's flight had been changed. She was new on the job, and Director Lawson only realized the significance of the message when a fallen blob of his chicken salad sandwich highlighted the "urgent" box that had been checked at the Florida agent's request. He stuffed the remainder of the sandwich into his mouth and picked up the message to study it.

"When did this come in?" he called out to the receptionist sitting on the opposite side of the partition.

She came in and examined her handwriting. "A few hours ago. I wrote the time down, see?"

Food residue had blurred the number. "Is that an eleven or a one?"

"I think it was this morning," she answered, walking back to her desk. She liked the weekend shift because there wasn't much to do and she could catch up on her magazines.

"Farmer, look at this." Director Lawson showed him the message.

"Shit! I thought he wasn't coming until tonight." Farmer checked his watch. "If that's an eleven, he must be here already."

Director Lawson agreed with the assessment. "But where?"

"We've got all his locations covered. I'll call the field officers and update them." Farmer pulled his list and started dialing. Director Lawson put a call in to the Florida office to try to glean some details, and was too deep in conversation to overhear Farmer talking in code to Rhamin Darius.

"Mr. Darius?"

"Yes. Who is this?"

"The sky is cloudy today." Farmer gave the clue.

Rhamin knew who it was. "Yes, very bad weather. Do you know the forecast?"

"Rain tonight. Someplace out west. Loud music."

"Music playing?"

"Yes, they expect a big audience."

"Who?"

Farmer pretended to check his watch. "Your enemies," he said, in a barely audible whisper.

Director Lawson heard the sibilance and looked over at him.

Farmer covered himself with police jargon. "Roger that. All available units in the area of 17th and Park at 2100 hours." He hung up, leaving Rhamin mostly confused.

"Who was that?" Director Lawson asked.

"NYPD operations manager."

CHAPTER 53

On Sunday afternoon, Nigel woke up to the distinctive sound of the freight elevator closing in the echoey hallway outside his door. He had stayed up past dawn, sipping port and sniffing drugs with an old friend from London and her date. The stash Dante had left him was much mellower than the usual speed-cut coke, and listening to music through the $20,000 monitoring system in the control room was a connoisseur's experience that helped them stay awake. Too tired to make it back home, Jennifer and her boyfriend took the bedroom in the upstairs apartment, and Nigel had slept, fully clothed, on the couch. He sat up and listened to footsteps pass his door and go into the apartment next to him. The residual effects of the previous night's binge leaned him back into the support of the cushions. He rarely stayed overnight in the studio crash pad, and everything looked unfamiliar through the fog of his hangover. He knew that the Monsouris used the other unit that took up the rest of the fourth floor, but he had never seen anyone in it. The activity there aroused his curiosity, so he struggled to his feet and wobbled to the window, hoping to catch a glimpse of the occupant reflected in the dark glass of the modern building across the alley. Squinting, he saw a man with a beard come to the window and look outside before closing the blinds. Unable to see anything else, Nigel closed his own blinds and retreated back to the couch with a headache.

A little while later, Jennifer came out of the bedroom in a bathrobe, wide-eyed and cheerful. "Gooood afternoon, Nigel. Lovely day, mate." Jennifer announced.

Nigel didn't even try to match her energy. "Afternoon."

"A bit too much for you last night, sport?" she teased him with voluble British patter while looking through the efficiency cabinets in the barren kitchen.

"Maybe a bit." Nigel rubbed his head, in awe of her metabolism.

"Suppose there's any jo in this place, love?" Jennifer worked at a big record company and knew all the jargon.

"If you can find it," Nigel said with his eyes closed.

Jennifer studied the blinking numbers on the microwave. "Can this clock be right? What time do you have?"

Groping, Nigel found his watch on the sofa table and held it to his face. "I've got 2:30."

"Really? I feel fabulous! I haven't slept this late since I was in my early twenties," she exulted. "That was really something special last night. Anything left for this evening?"

Jennifer was Nigel's best music industry connection. "As much as you want, love," he assured her.

"What time is the show tonight?" she asked, running her fingers through stringy brown hair that was going to need some work to look good.

"Supposed to go on at midnight, but you know how that goes." Nigel pushed his thumbs in his eye sockets to relieve the pain.

"There's absolutely nothing edible in this entire kitchen," Jennifer concluded after looking through all the cabinets. "Doesn't anyone ever stay here?"

Nigel couldn't remember the last time he rented it out. "Not really. We only use it when we can charge the clients for cleaning and the like. It's not a hotel, so the bands prefer to stay where's there's service."

"Well, I suppose I'll have to rouse Bradley so we can fetch something to eat. Will you be joining us?" she invited, heading back to the bedroom.

"No thanks. I'll stay here and tidy up." Nigel lay with his palms on his forehead, trying to reconstruct the shape of his brain. He heard the shower cycle on and off, and a short time after that, Jennifer and Bradley came out dressed and ready to go. Fashion plate that she was, Jennifer's hair was tied tightly back under a stylish tam, and she wore glossy knee-high boots that stopped six inches short of her skirt bottom. A flowing plaid cape covered her form-fitting top and midsection. Bradley's wet blond curls were freshly parted, and his wrinkle-free leisure suit lived up to its reputation.

"Sure you won't join us?" Jennifer asked, posing.

"Thanks," Nigel declined without getting up. "Where are you headed?"

"Bradley's taking me to his restaurant on Union Square; wants me to hear their house band tonight before your show." She shared her skepticism about Bradley's band with a knowing wink. "I'm on Cells' list, right?"

"Cells, right."

The name sounded familiar to Bradley, but he didn't make the connection.

"Really excited to see them live. I hope they look the part. We'll be very interested if they sound like what you played me last night."

"You're plus three?"

"Yes, Simon and Dave will be with us."

Bradley got restless and opened the door to leave.

"Excellent. See you there," Nigel said goodbye.

"With your inspiration? You know Simon," Jennifer called as the door shut. "Midnight?"

"Midnight, rock and roll time," Nigel answered as he lay back down on the couch and reviewed the guest list in his mind. A quiet commotion in the next-door apartment distracted him, but he fell asleep for another hour and didn't get back to his own apartment until late that afternoon. Sonya's note from the night before saying she would see him tomorrow had been slid under his door.

CHAPTER 54

Missy K had the whole day planned. The family outing started with a social walk to the church with friends and neighbors. Her large Jamaican community was evenly split between Pentacostals, Baptists, and The Church of God, but strolling on the sidewalk in their Sunday best, they all belonged to the same faith. Lucius' and his friends made no distinction between congregations, and chased each other in and out of the unorganized, slow moving procession. Inside the small stone church situated at the edge of the park, the youngsters were mostly interested in the behavior of the adults, and nothing was funnier than a nodding parishioner teetering in his seat – except the occasional noisy gaseous emission during a particularly inspired sermon. None of the kids understood the devotional mumbo jumbo, but their participation in the hallelujahs and amens grew more fervent as the service went on, in the hope that God would let them go out to play if he heard how loud they were. Most of the congregants empathized, and discipline was minimal.

To Missy K, the struggles of her enslaved ancestors were more vivid than the sufferings of Jesus, and church was much more about community than communion. A direct descendant of a celebrated Maroon, Missy K was a fierce defender of personal freedom, which is how she justified her marriage to Mak, whose Scottish ancestry was on the other side of the slavery fight. But Mak's African roots were nurtured in the soil of their native continent, so, between the two of them, the Mackenzies embodied most of the traditions of their Jamaican homeland.

Services were over in time for lunch, and in the spring weather, the street became a commotion of resurrected congregants celebrating their own, less than perfect, lives. Darting children in unbuttoned shirts chased one another around their parents' leisurely procession like gnats annoying slow-moving targets. Older teens and young lovers walked in loosely defined packs on the opposite side of the street as the adults and senior citizens kept one another company, nursing their infirmities back to comfortable chairs and sofas. The regular Sunday afternoon get- together was an extension of sacred family time, and everyone was expected at the moveable potluck feast that was Miss Beatrice's turn to host. Missy K went straight to Beatrice's house to help set up, sending Mak home to fetch the food she had prepared.

Mak thought she was calling to tell him what not to forget when he answered the phone. He didn't recognize Sattar's voice at first. "Excuse me. I think you have the wrong number," he told the caller.

"Colonel Mackenzie," Sattar made his gravelly voice unmistakable. "I need to see you."

"I...it's Sunday. Where are you?"

"I'm here." Sattar confounded the eavesdroppers with ambiguity.

"Can't this wait until tomorrow?" Mak asked.

"No, I must see you today. Something's happened to the Princess." Sattar spoke the code words.

Mak counted the covered dishes on the table and calculated how many trips next door he would have to make to bring them all over. "I have some arrangements to make," he huffed, reluctant to drop his family plans.

"I expect so," Sattar said tersely. "What time can we meet?"

"Sometime later this evening?" Mak asked, pushing the envelope.

"I'm afraid that's too late. This is an emergency."

"Emergency? I don't like the sound of that."

"You'll like the details even less."

"What can *I* do?" Mak protested, resisting his policeman's mentality. "I'll tell you when I see you. Is 5:00 okay?"

Mak was relieved it wasn't sooner. "5:00 will work," he sighed.

"At the warehouse?"

"No, the lab."

Mak flinched. "5:00 this evening, see you there." Meetings at the lab were very infrequent and never casual. The strange customs and proximity to extremely illegal concoctions made Mak uncomfortable. He knew he would have to put on a happy face for the rest of the afternoon and went back to Beatrice's with two hot casseroles and a heavy heart. His friends tried to get him to sing along with the radio, but his spirit was earthbound. A few beers helped his general mood, but Missy K didn't approve of or appreciate his early departure, and he left the gathering under orders to provide a full explanation when he came back.

CHAPTER 55

The dial tone resonated in Rhamin's ear like a swarm of angry bees. His blood pressure rose and he wanted to call back, but knew that was impossible because the arrangement with Special Agent Farmer was very specific: the only time they could talk privately was in the steam room at the gym. He wasn't due to see him until their usual Monday workout, so he could only guess why Farmer had called him. He called his father, and the two of them sorted through the clues.

"The agent called you at home?" Bahram confirmed with surprise.

"Yes. I think he must have been at his office because he hung up quickly."

"What did he say?"

"I'm not sure; something about music and our enemies. Then he started talking like a policeman, but I don't know if that had anything to do with us."

"What did he say about our enemies? What does music have to do with it?"

"I don't know. I wasn't expecting his call, and he hung up before I had a chance to ask him for details."

"But why would he call you at home and not just wait until tomorrow?" Bahram postulated, trying to put the pieces together. "What exactly did he say about tonight?"

"It sounded like he was giving orders to other policemen to be somewhere on Park Avenue at 9:00 tonight." Rhamin remembered that much.

"I wonder if this has anything to do with the robbery?" The white noise of silence whispered nameless fears until Bahram spoke again. "What time are you leaving to pick up Sattar?"

Rhamin looked at his watch. "Not for three hours."

"Bring him straight to the lab. We'll wait for you there."

Rhamin hung up, but the phone rang as soon as he put it back in the cradle.

"Why didn't you tell me?" Homa asked, agitated.

"Homa?"

"Of course. *What* is going on? What are we going to *do*?" She was almost frantic. "Mother told me everything – at least I think it was everything. What other secrets are there? I can't believe you've kept all this from me. I didn't even know you existed until two days ago, and now it's like we're related." She paused to reload.

"Slow down. Let me explain."

"You better. Mother is so upset she's gone back to bed and I don't know what to do. My head is exploding with— where are you?"

"At my apartment; where you called me."

"Where is that? Is it near here?"

"No, I told you yesterday, I live in Queens."

"What are you going to do? What am I going to do?"

"About what?"

"The robbery. The agents. The business. Don't play stupid with me. I know everything now," she railed.

"Everything?"

Homa paused at the edge of horror. "What else is there?"

Rhamin paused before answering her. "Maybe you should meet us at Dr. Nouri's laboratory."

"Dr. Nouri's office?"

"No, the lab. And don't use the front door," Rhamin added seriously.

"Where is it?"

"On the tenth floor."

"The tenth floor where?"

"The Old Medical Building, a few floors below Dr. Nouri's office. I thought you knew everything."

Homa gulped. "Maybe I don't. When are you going?"

"I am picking up your uncle at the airport in a few hours. We should be there by 7:00 or 8:00."

"That's too long. My uncle? Which one? I don't know what to do with myself.

Rhamin put on a brave face. "Take care of your mother and pray. The family has been through tough times before."

Homa put the phone down and went back to her room. She knelt in front of her mural and spoke with her heart. Tears welled in her eyes for the first time since she had accepted the consensus that her father wouldn't be coming back. She put on the traditional robe her father had brought back from one of his business trips and buried her nose in the special scented pillow her mother had given her for comfort.

Rhamin turned on the television to keep him company but was interrupted by another phone call.

"I'm here," Sattar announced in a low whisper. "Don't speak my name."

Rhamin turned down the volume on the TV.

"Meet me at the lab in two hours." Sattar instructed.

"I'll be there," Rhamin promised. His next call was to his father. "I just heard from him. He's here already."

"Where?"

"I don't know. He wants us to meet at the lab in two hours."

"Okay. Call me when you're leaving, then bring the car around and I'll meet you downstairs." Bahram lived in his own apartment nearby.

CHAPTER 56

Dr. Nouri sat in the back seat of his car as Reggie drove him to his Queens apartment. There was a specially fitted suitcase in the trunk filled with bottles of liquids and the recipe book. He had also packed several small boxes of special chemicals used to make the Princess Powder and Princess Tears. It was impossible to save everything, but he wanted to move the essential ingredients in case the laboratory was raided. Reggie waited with the motor running while the doctor moved the incriminating evidence and supplies into hiding. When he returned a few minutes later, they got back onto Astoria Boulevard and wended their way across the Queensboro Bridge and down 2nd Avenue, until they got near the Old Medical Building in lower Manhattan. As planned, Reggie parked in the indoor lot a few streets away, and they walked right past the tired agents who were on the lookout for their Mercedes. They entered through a side door that was usually locked, and it was 5:00 as Reggie took up a position near the tenth floor window that looked down over the darkening street. Dr. Nouri retreated to the attached laboratory to rearrange what remained there.

Dr. Nouri's lab was much different than the mix room at the Laden warehouse. There were no barrels or crates, and a large ceiling fan kept the air cool and circulating. The door was modified to prevent the noxious odors from escaping into the rest of the building, and the tenth floor was far enough over the pavement that there was little danger of being able to trace the distinctive fumes to the open window that allowed for fresh air. Ample fluorescent lighting illuminated the clean and organized workspace that was no bigger than a regular office – which is what it appeared to be from the outside. No one but Dr. Nouri and Sattar knew how to use the array of flasks, gas-fueled burners, and condensation tubes that usually occupied the central worktable, and although Dr. Nouri had removed most of them, a few partially processed mixtures, identified with dates and symbols in a language only the initiated understood, sat aging on shelves. Ava had written all the important information, including the procedures for making the various dilutions, into only two books, and used a mathematical code to frustrate anyone who might try to steal the formulas. The keys to unlocking the mysterious curly lines of classic Farsi were passed on verbally. Dr. Nouri had removed the instruction manual that was usually kept in the office, and the other was hidden in a family-owned property in southern Iran.

Detective Falin was on duty, and a little while after Dr. Nouri had arrived, he recognized Mak approaching the Old Medical Building. He elbowed Rudy to get the camera and radioed the information to Director Lawson's van.

"Looks like they're having their meeting," Detective Falin reported. "How many so far?" Director Lawson asked.

"Just two or three."

"You're not sure?"

"NYPD's got someone inside watching the back stairs, but we haven't heard from him for a while."

"Keep me posted."

An old man in a ragged overcoat limped his way past the stake-out car, using a cane to steady himself. A floppy hat covered the part of his face that wasn't bearded, and he when he stumbled into the doorway of the Old Medical Building, the agents assumed he was a bum looking for an empty stoop. Once inside, Sattar shed his disguise, unlocked the service elevator, and took it up to the tenth floor. Hearing the coded knock, Mak opened the door to the large office attached to the lab.

Dispensing with the pleasantries, Sattar asked, "Where's Nouri?"

Mak motioned to the lab room. "In there."

Sattar tapped on the door and entered in one motion.

Reggie stood by the window while Mak stayed on the opposite side of the room, trying to avoid a conversation. It was futile. "They pay you extra for Sundays?" Reggie agitated.

"Of course not," Mak answered, displaying his stature.

"They payin' me. I'm making double today!" he bragged. "You oughta ask 'em. They makin' plenty off you."

"Shut up, Reggie. You don't know shit."

"Yeah? Well I know a lot more than you think." Reggie smirked. "I got my own secrets. I don't need yours."

Mak considered chemistry more important than gossip and was unimpressed.

Reggie couldn't keep his mouth shut normally, and the tension of the moment only made it worse. "You may know how to mix some of that shit together, but I know who buys it," he boasted.

Mak was surprised they would trust him. "They got you selling?"

"Sure 'nuff. I've been riding the choo-choo for a while now." Reggie showed off his locomotion shoes.

A light knock interrupted them. Mak was closest to the door and opened it to let Rhamin and his father in. Bahram was still dressed in his golfing casuals, his messy hair and puffy neck the only clues to his mental anguish. Knowing he would be seeing Homa, Rhamin had donned gabardine pants and high gloss loafers, looking like he was on his way out to dinner at a nice restaurant.

Sattar heard them come in and came out of the lab to say hello. Thin and just under six feet tall, Sattar wore dark pants and a zippered black nylon pullover shirt. His full, graying beard and errant strands of salt and pepper hair blended into his bushy black eyebrows, giving him the overall appearance of a caveman who had just come back from a shopping trip to a men's store. Worlds collided between the slow blinks of his intense, deep-set eyes. "Salaam," He greeted his partners in a throaty tone, clutching each man by the forearms while observing the traditional three cheek Persian ritual. "Let me see you." He pushed back from Rhamin and admired his tailored taste. "You look well." He kept his hands on Rhamin's shoulders and stared into his soul. "The family is most fortunate," he complimented Bahram.

Dr. Nouri emerged from his lab and joined the growing council of war. The men sat in wood-armed chairs between matching antique side tables. A worn Persian rug covered the entire floor of the room that had been designed as a spacious office. High ceilings with wide crown molding were painted the same off-white as the walls, and the perfect geometry of the old construction was evident in the straight lines and even surfaces that had maintained their shape for 100 years. The original two-inch-thick oak office doors, paned with heavy plated glass, opened and closed on oiled hinges with the slightest coaxing, and the huge, double-hung windows still slid easily in their tracks. Everything about the construction quality of Old Medical Building reflected a time when craftsmen were given time to practice their art, and the Darius Trust felt secure in their inner sanctum.

A round central table, covered with a small dark carpet, supported an ornate, brightly painted metal hookah, whose coiled arms attached to its bulbous base like nesting snakes. Sattar moved his chair closer to the table and loaded the hookah bowl with moist tobacco pinched from a woven silver bag in his pocket. He lit the bowl with a lighter that had been passed down through the generations along with the hookah, and everyone except Mak took a turn sucking through one of the hoses. Dr. Nouri turned the ceiling fan on its lowest speed and opened a window to aerate the opiated smoke that was filling the room. Bahram closed his eyes and gurgled his portion slowly, pulling on his chained amulet and muttering a prayer only he could hear. Rhamin sipped his portion as if it were a cognac and exhaled as quickly as possible, his face flushed with fear of the ancient ritual he had only participated in a few times. Reggie inhaled a thick column of smoke as if he were smoking special hydroponic pot, and needed all his strength to keep from coughing. Dr. Nouri was immune to the papaver extracts, but in spite of the hookah oil's soothing effect, his lungs cringed from the acrid tobacco smoke. Only Sattar thoroughly enjoyed the intoxicating effects of the mixed stimulants, which transported him to oracular consciousness.

The humming started soon after the second round, with Sattar leading a Hijaz chant in long low tones emanating from the depths of his abdominal cavity. His compatriots joined the mournful prayer with measured exhalations of breath that depleted the flow of oxygen to their brains and made them even more lightheaded. Reggie had never participated in the Persian smoking ritual before, and he felt like his head was being crushed into the size of a pea. Spittle foamed on his lips, his eyes bugged out, and for a moment, he teetered on the edge of consciousness. Dr. Nouri noticed his condition, and without interrupting his own meditation, held a cloth dampened with the antidote over Reggie's nose. Only partially recovered, Reggie's body attempted to rid itself of the poisons with a deep sputtering cough. As he wilted in his chair, the spinning room slowed and his focus fixed on Mak's mistrustful glare. Thirty minutes after they had started smoking, all their prayers were finished and they got down to the business at hand.

Sattar started the meeting formally. "In the eyes of our ancestors, we convene this council of the Darius Trust," he began. "May our decisions be guided by Allah and wisdom. Who will answer my prayer?"

"I will," Rhamin coughed out the ritualized response.

"Rhamin Darius answers for us all. Let us begin," Sattar proclaimed before switching to a more conversational tone. "Rhamin, tell us the last time you saw the Princess Tears."

"Draper placed the bottles in his office safe."

"Did you see him lock the safe?"

"I can't remember."

"Did he place the Powder there too?"

"I placed it there myself."

"Was there anyone else in the office?"

"I didn't see anyone."

"Was Draper his usual self?"

"I think so. I was in a hurry so I didn't stay long."

"Why were you in a hurry?" Rhamin took a deep breath. "Someone was waiting for me in the car."

"You took someone to Draper's office?" Sattar frowned at the unsettling detail.

"Yes, but it was Homa." Rhamin blushed.

"Homa?"

Each of the men had a different reaction.

Bahram spoke up in his son's defense. "They were on a date."

"A date? I thought you had agreed to stay out of her life," Sattar reminded him, disturbed by the news. "We've gone to great lengths to protect her. Why would you tell her our business?"

"I didn't tell her anything. She just sat in the car and waited for me."

"How long have you been seeing her?" Sattar questioned him as a father would.

"That was only the second time. We went to dinner the night before."

"And now you two are...?"

"I love her but I'm not sure she feels the same."

"You may be right," Mak interjected. "I'm not sure she's the marrying type."

"Why not?"

Mak saw her more frequently than anyone else in the room. "Has she ever had a boyfriend?" he insinuated.

Reggie, who was feeling better, had no trouble following this part of the story. "You mean...maybe she's not into boys? Imagine that! Pretty little thing like that. What a waste!"

"Neither of you know Persian women," Bahram said, defending her. "Dr. Nouri and I gave Rhamin permission to contact her."

"Yes, but we told him to speak with Samani first," Dr. Nouri pointed out.

"I asked to speak with her when I called, but Homa answered the phone and...." Rhamin knew his explanation was lame.

"Samani is not the same as the last time you saw her," Bahram said, addressing Sattar. "She cannot go more than a little while without her handkerchief."

"I see." Sattar took another pinch of opiated tobacco and re-loaded the pipe. No one else joined him in another round. Reggie stuck his head out the window to avoid the smoke and thought he saw a man on the sidewalk looking up at him. Mak sat by the door, guarding them from intruders. Bahram and Nouri shared 60 years of wordless thoughts, and Rhamin squirmed in his seat, unaccustomed to Sattar's peculiar demeanor and paternal scrutiny.

After a deliberate exhalation, Sattar resumed his questioning. "You say Homa doesn't know what you were doing there? Why does she think you went to New Jersey?"

"I told her I would take her to the Ferris wheel. She remembered the Ferris wheel from when Arshan took her there and I thought it would.... We held hands. The robbery happened after that," Rhamin answered, feeling exonerated.

Bahram defended his son. "Homa didn't steal anything. What does any of this matter?"

"She may have been followed," Sattar replied, sharing the reason for his concern.

Rhamin gasped. "I told her we were meeting tonight."

"You asked her to come?" Bahram confirmed, a little surprised.

"She was very upset so I told her she could. I hope that's all right?" Rhamin answered.

"Homa is welcome," Sattar decreed. "I just hope she's not followed."

"Followed? By whom?"

"Our enemies."

"Who are our enemies? The Ayatollah's men?"

"Yes, and maybe their American friends."

"The Americans know our business now?"

"Yes, I think so." Sattar didn't want to tell them everything he knew.

"Are you saying the Americans robbed us?" Bahram asked.

"Perhaps," Sattar said enigmatically.

"Why would they do that?" Mak asked. "Policemen want to catch you red-handed."

"Who else could it be?"

The council fell silent as they pondered the possibilities.

"Reggie, any ideas?" Dr. Nouri asked. "What about your customers?"

Sattar was surprised. "Reggie has customers?"

Bahram, who was in charge of sales, explained. "You've been away for a long time. We decided to let Reggie market some of the weaker Princess Powder. He's doing quite well with it."

Sattar sensed the danger. "Who are his customers?"

"I only have a few," Reggie answered for himself. "That was what they told me. Only two or three customers."

Bahram tried to justify his decision. "He's only been doing it for a few months. We only give him one packet at a time. It's the same customers he had customers from before."

"From before? Who are these customers?" Sattar insisted, knowing a rat when he smelled one.

"One is a guy from Jamaica. I've known him half my life. I think Mak knows him too."

Mak nodded but didn't blink.

"And the other is...." Reggie stopped himself. "I don't think you know him. He's a very rich Italian guy. Always pays up front"

"Where do you know him from?"

"I met him at a club his family owns, The Black Sheep. It's in the Village."

"I've heard of that club," Rhamin noted. "I think the Pecorinos own it."

Bahram hadn't put the pieces together. "Who are they again?"

"They're the ones who own the recording studio building," Rhamin reminded his father. "We talked to them about an office here. Don't you remember showing them around the building?"

"That was last year. There were two of them, right?"

"That's right. They really liked the privacy."

Sattar digested the facts as the squeaky fan cleared the last of the smoke from the room. "The Pecorinos know our business? Who is this customer of yours?" he asked Reggie. "What's his name?"

"Dante. Dante Pecorino." Reggie stammered out the truth and everyone felt it.

"And this Dante, what kind of man is he?" Sattar asked.

"He is scum," Rhamin interjected. "He's the one who came here with his brother, I think. I saw him recently at the studio."

"He would do something like this?" Bahram verified. No one defended the idea.

"The truth needs no introduction," Sattar said in Persian. "Where is this thief? Do you know where he lives, Reggie?"

"Yes, not far from here." Reggie said tentatively.

"But how can we be sure it was him?" Rhamin asked cautiously.

"Maybe you should ask your friend at the FBI if he knows something about this Pecorino," Dr. Nouri suggested.

"Maybe that's why he called you," Bahram added.

Sattar's radar blipped. "The FBI called you?"

"I told father; our informant called earlier today. We only spoke for a few moments before he hung up. I wasn't sure what he was trying to say."

"What *did* he say?"

"Something about our enemies and music. Then he sounded like he was talking to someone else about a police operation tonight. I think he said Park Avenue and 17th Street."

"He must have been calling for a reason," Bahram pointed out.

"Very strange. Enemies and music," Dr. Nouri muttered, wiping his glasses with a tissue.

"This is very complicated, and it seems there's a lot more to talk about." Sattar shifted in his chair. "Shall we order dinner?"

No one was really hungry but they welcomed the opportunity to stop playing detective. Bahram found the takeout menus and they settled on Chinese food. Rhamin circled everyone's choices and called the order into their usual restaurant. As Dr. Nouri's assistant with knowledge of the neighborhood, Reggie was volunteered for the job of fetching dinner. The smoke and drama had overwhelmed caution, and when he left the building, he thoughtlessly went out the front door. Detective Gillingham and Ralph saw him and immediately radioed Director Lawson for instructions. Reggie was already a known criminal, so they figured they had a good excuse to pick him up for questioning.

Detective Gillingham drove around the corner and got out of the car in front of where Reggie was headed. "Whoa there, Reggie, my man."

"Excuse me. Do I know you?"

Detective Gillingham wasn't in a uniform so he flashed his badge. "No, but we know you."

Reggie noticed an NYPD patrol car approaching. "What did I do?"

"Nothing we know about. We just want to talk to you."

Reggie was uncomfortable around police. "About what?" He cocked his shoulders back and set his legs, preparing for a physical confrontation.

"Easy does it, mate. No one's going to hurt you," Detective Gillingham said. "We just want to know about why you're working for that doctor friend of yours on a Sunday night. Awfully late for business hours."

Reggie flared his nostrils and whinnied like a bridled horse. "The economy isn't bad enough? A man can't work when he needs to?"

"How much you making for weekend hours?" the detective spurred him.

Reggie bucked. "That's my business – enough. How much *you guys* makin?"

Detective Gillingham didn't like being thrown. "Always got a smart answer, eh Reggie?" He moved close enough to intimidate.

"Always got a dumb question, Mr. *po*-leese-man. Now what else you want to talk about?" Reggie challenged him.

The detective shifted tactics. "Is it just the doctor in there with you? Sounds pretty cozy," he insinuated, raising his eyebrows.

"I aint no homo, man. There's a bunch of them...." Reggie didn't realize he'd been baited.

"That's what we thought." Detective Gillingham nodded the other cops closer.

Reggie felt outnumbered as the beat officers joined the detective on the street. "What exactly do you guys want to know?"

The detective got close enough to put his hand on Reggie's shoulder. "Where are you off to now?"

Reggie recoiled at contact. "On my way to pick up food. All right?"

Detective Gillingham got to the point. "Is Sattar in there with them?"

"Who?" Reggie's expression told them what his words didn't.

"Thanks, Reggie. You be careful tonight." He backed off. "We don't want to have to ID you later at the morgue."

Reggie blanched and the cops stood aside and let him pass.

Detective Gillingham reported his findings to Director Lawson, who spread the information to the rest of the agents in the field. No longer concerned with secrecy, Reggie walked right past the unmarked patrol car and nodded to the officers as he returned a little while later carrying two white plastic bags with red Chinese characters. A taxi stopped right in front of the building just as he was approaching, and Homa got out. Her hair and face were completely covered by a headscarf and her body disappeared within a shapeless garment. Reggie didn't recognize her until they were inside the building and they rode up the elevator together without talking. Homa stared at the floor and Reggie's impertinence was muzzled by her strange costume and the seriousness of the moment.

Arriving on the 10th floor, Homa opened the laboratory office door and startled the gathering with a simple "Salaam." Her hoarse voice emanated from a dark colored hijab. No one had ever seen her wear traditional Persian women's clothes.

Rhamin rose to greet her. "Homa?"

Homa nodded. "Uncle." She bowed slightly in Sattar's direction.

"Welcome, child. I am Bahram, Rhamin's father," Bahram introduced himself.

Homa acknowledged him and studied the room with twitching nostrils. The familiar looking Persian decor was steeped in the residual smell of smoke. Reggie put the food bags on a side table and tried to ignore Mak's intense scrutiny.

"Please, Homa, come in, join us," Dr. Nouri welcomed, motioning to a chair, trying to lighten the mood. "You took a taxi?"

"Yes. I hope I'm not disturbing you," Homa apologized.

"Nonsense. I told you to come," Rhamin assured everyone. "Your mother is feeling better?"

"No. She is more upset than ever," Homa said, looking at the hookah suspiciously.

"We are all very upset," Bahram agreed.

Sattar was shocked to see her in a chador. "You look wonderful...very beautiful.... You are Ava reborn, truly." He embraced her by the forearms and bent his head. "Come and join our council. Your father's seat has been empty too long," he invited, pulling a chair next to him.

Homa struggled to find a comfortable seating position with the unfamiliar folds of material draped around her. Rhamin positioned his chair next to her, leaving Bahram and Dr. Nouri on the other side of the hookah table. Mak kept his distance while Reggie opened a container and picked at the food with chopsticks.

"What is in *there*?" Homa pointed to the opaque glass in the door to the other room.

"That is our laboratory," Sattar explained.

"May I see?"

"Dr. Nouri will show you later. Right now we need your help."

Homa was surprised. "What can I do?"

"We need you to pray with us."

Homa looked fearfully at Rhamin. "What has been decided?" she asked.

"Nothing yet," Sattar said. "We need a sign."

"Don't be frightened," Rhamin assured her. "You are one of us." He grasped her hand.

Sattar loaded the hookah again and drew the first smoke. His eyes bulged at the peak of inhalation and he and handed a hose to Homa. She had never smoked hookah before, but knew about the ritual. She drew her breath bravely and held the air, imploring Mak to participate with pleading eyes while holding a lungful. Mak got the message and joined her around the pipe. He put the hose to his lips and gurgled smoke into his mouth, allowing it to billow his cheeks before releasing it in a steady vent. Rhamin didn't want to smoke anymore, but wanted to show solidarity. He, Dr. Nouri, and Bahram sipped their portions ritually, out of respect. Only Reggie sat out, preferring to gnaw on spare ribs and calculate the points he could earn with the police by turning them all in. Conversation was asphyxiated in the rarified atmosphere, and the rhythmic squeals of the ceiling fan hypnotized time. The intoxicants released Homa from the physical plane, and her spirit returned to the land of her dreams. Sattar studied his niece's breathing and could tell from the twitching of her closed eyelids that she had entered into another dimension. She began to rock in her chair and speak in a low, distorted voice, only vaguely reminiscent of her natural one.

"There is a place," her spirit spoke. "Where joy is eternal and no one is in pain," she mumbled the lamentation and fell silent. The fan turned many times before another word was spoken. "Bathe the children in Princess Tears. It is our destiny," Homa channeled, swaying slowly back and forth. Rhamin came closer to steady her but was prevented by Sattar's outstretched arm.

"She will find her own way back when she is ready," Sattar said softly.

Homa continued to rock in her chair, muttering indistinguishably in a low rasp for several minutes. Then, as the effects of the drugs released their hold on her mind, her eyelids began to flicker open and shut. She bent forward and held her head to her knees for another few moments before sitting upright, fully conscious again.

CHAPTER 57

Jon had spent most of the afternoon curled up on Monica's bed, wrestling with his migraine monsters. They always seemed to attack suddenly, and once they established a chokehold, it could be hours, or even days before he could breathe normally again. Other people had headaches that they *called* migraines, but those were only faint facsimiles of what Jon experienced. Besides the intense pain, which was immune to less than eight extra-strength Excedrin, Jon's migraines made him so nauseated that vomiting provided only partial relief. Once he had thrown up everything inside his stomach, whatever that was in the process of being digested came rushing out his other end in a gusher fueled by several cups of black coffee. The hallucinations, phantoms, and bizarre fantasies accompanying his physical spasms, pushed him to the brink of insanity, and the only thing that saved him from going completely mad – and scaring the hell out of whoever was around – was the fact that he knew the seizure would eventually end. Just as unpredictably as it appeared, the relatively weak migraine that assaulted him in Monica's apartment subsided after a few tortuous hours. Reclaiming his sanity, Jon bolted upright at 4:00 and sought the refuge of a hot shower. After toweling dry, he wriggled back into his clothes, gave Monica a hurried kiss, and caught a city bus back to his apartment.

Monica stripped and remade her bed after Jon left, and had just finished cleaning up the bathroom before Ameliah got home.

Ameliah knew Monica had had a visitor by the number of cups in the kitchen sink, and announced her displeasure through Monica's closed door. Monica didn't answer her complaint, so she retreated to her own room and closed her door too.

The final tune-up for the band was scheduled for 5:00 at the studio, so as soon as Jon got back to his apartment, he changed into his trusty leather pants and body-fitting stage shirt and hobbled over to the subway with only one of his leather boots on. Frankie and Marco were standing on the street looking for the buzzer to the studio door when Jon arrived.

"You going to be able to stand up and play tonight?" Marco asked, looking skeptically at Jon's un-shoed foot.

"Absatively," Jon said confidently as he pressed the buzzer.

The door vibrated and Frankie grabbed the handle before it stopped. "It's about time. We've been out here for ten minutes," he complained.

"How long do we have?" Marco, carrying his bass, asked as they entered the studio.

"They're sending a truck over around 7:00 to pick up our gear," Jon explained as they neared the control room.

"They're sending a truck? We don't have to move our own stuff?" Frankie asked, impressed. "Is someone going to help us carry it too?"

"That's the plan." Dennis answered, welcoming them into the control room.

"Holy shit! Who's paying for all this?" Marco asked.

Dennis was authorized to brag. "Nigel's company is paying for everything."

"Everything? How much are *we* getting paid?" Marco asked.

"$100 for yesterday, $250 for tonight – and that doesn't include beer and refreshments."

Frankie liked the arrangements. "That's awesome!"

"How long do we have to play for?" Marco asked.

Jon deferred to Dennis. "We're only doing six songs, right?"

"That's what Nigel said," Dennis confirmed.

"Six songs, shit, we can nail that!" Frankie was pumped.

Jon led the band back into the studio. "Let's go through the show one more time before we break down. The truck won't be here until 7:00." No one had touched their setup, so all they had to do was plug in and tune up. They started out with their underground hit from the Boulder days, "Uh Oh," and whittled the set down to six of their best songs. The loud music chased away the residual effects of Jon's migraine, and they were tight and inspired by the time they finished. "That's as ready as we'll ever be," Jon declared, ending rehearsal.

"So what are we going to end with?" Marco asked as they put their guitars away.

"Yeah, and what order did we decide on?" Frankie chimed in.

"We'll just have to feel it, guys. You know how it goes. Performing's like visiting another country where they don't speak your language. We'll just have to see what's working and go with it." Jon said enigmatically. Marco and Frankie exchanged shrugs and followed Jon into the control room to listen to the playback of what Dennis had just recorded. It sounded better than they had ever heard themselves, which boosted their confidence to peak levels.

The cartage truck showed up on time at 7:00. Two roadies packed up and loaded the drum cases and amplifiers in a few minutes. "What time do you guys go on?" one of the roadies asked.

"Midnight," Jon told him.

"Okay, your stuff will be backstage by the time you're ready. We're picking up for the band that goes on before you, so we should have it all there by ten."

The roadies left, and Dennis tidied up the studio as the band sat in the control room enjoying the playback of their rehearsal. Jon shared a few tastes of his stash and their collective enthusiasm elevated accordingly. When he was done, Dennis locked up the equipment closet and shop door, turned off the work lights, and ushered the band out the front door. Jon and Marco carried their own guitars, and Dennis went with them to eat at the neighborhood pizza pub.

"So you think we're really going to pull it off this time?" Marco asked his bandmates, sliding into the booth.

"You keep pulling *anything* long enough and it's gonna come off," Frankie jibed, elbowing him as they sandwiched in. "That's what *my* mother told me."

"Pipe down you two. Tell them what you told me," Jon cued Dennis.

"Listen guys, like I said, Nigel's got some serious people coming tonight. He said was that they already like the stuff they heard and just want to see you do it live before they sign you."

Jon beamed, and the focus shifted to eating, drinking, and flirting with the waitress. After dinner, Dennis stood up and stretched. "I've got to be there early; see you later." He left them at the restaurant and went to his car. Jon, Marco, and Frankie psyched up for the show before leaving to hail a cab up to the club. They got to Max's Kansas City a little before 10:00 p.m..

CHAPTER 58

Dante didn't get up until sundown. Starla was lounging in a bathtub full of hissing bubbles when he came into the bathroom to urinate. They were still high from the night before, and Dante's aim was so bad that only half his piss made it into the toilet. Starla poked a sleek leg through the mound of bubbles and used her painted toenails to wave. "Come on in," she invited, blowing suds into the air.

"Not now, sweetheart," Dante answered, steadying himself against the sink. "I've got to make some calls." Wearing only a loose fitting shirt, he shuffled through the dirty towels and clothes on the floor, back to his spot on the living room sofa. Stabbing the open bag of Princess Powder on the table with his pocketknife, he licked the sharp side of the blade. A trickle of blood mixed with the finely granulated powder and he tongued his lips, savoring the mixture. Then he lifted the greasy phone receiver to his ear and pushed the grimy numbers he hoped were Nigel's. He could hear Nigel's phone ringing through the floor and felt the footsteps going to answer it.

"Hello," Nigel answered, already annoyed.

"What time is it?" Dante slurred.

"Don't you have a bloody clock up there?"

"Yeah, but it doesn't work," Dante droned, slicing random lines in the spilled powder that dusted the table.

"It's 6:30. What's up?" Nigel snapped.

"We're all set for tonight?"

"The truck is on the way to pick up the equipment at the studio. I just got off the phone and everyone from Jennifer's label is planning on showing up."

"Good. Did Donny get a hold of you?"

"Donny? No, why?"

"I told him to call you."

"Why?"

"He came over last night and we...I told him Freddy could showcase before the other band."

"What? Why did you do that?" Nigel asked, horrified. "No one is planning on that."

"Like you said, everyone's going to be there."

"But they're not coming to see Bosco Dish."

"They are now."

"We only have the stage for an hour, and that includes setup."

"The other band can go on after Freddy's finished."

"There's not enough time for that. How will their equipment get there?"

"Donny left a message for the cartage guys last night."

"We haven't cleared it with the club."

"I'll take care of your friend Arnie when I see him."

"Yes, but the stage and door need to know ahead of time." Nigel was running out of objections.

"That's your job, man. That's why I'm calling you."

"Does Freddy know about this?"

"I'm sure Donny told him."

"Let me know for sure, because there's a lot of preparations to make if this is really going to happen."

"It's going to happen." Dante licked the knife again. "See you at the club."

"Fuck you!" Nigel screamed and hung up. His frustration pieced the floorboards and twisted into a smug smile on Dante's face.

Dante's phone rang as soon as he put in back in the cradle. "Asshole," his brother said.

"What do *you* want, asshole?"

"Dad knows."

"Dad knows what?"

"He knows about last night."

"He knows you did my girlfriend?"

"No, stupid, he knows what went down in New Jersey."

"How does he know that? You told him?"

"No, he got a call from a friend of his at the precinct. They picked up our guy Emmy.

"So?"

"Emmy talked."

"What did he tell them?"

"I'm not sure, but they've still got him."

"Too bad for him."

"No, you dumb ass, too bad for us!"

"Why?"

"They'll go easy on Emmy if he tells them who he was working for. That's the way this shit works."

"Shit. What are we going to do? Can't dad fix it?"

"Maybe, but not right away."

"Just a minute." Dante put the phone down and snorted lines he had made.

Anthony heard him. "What are you doing?"

"What do you think? I needed that."

"You're going to need something else too." "What?"

"A gun."

"Why? Are we going to shoot it out with the cops?"

"No, not the cops, but maybe the guys we ripped off."

"The Persians? What are *they* going to do? Squirt us with perfume?" Dante snickered.

Anthony couldn't help but laugh too.

Starla, partially wrapped in a towel, came in and sat on the couch next to Dante. "Just a minute," Dante told his brother. Eying the stash, Starla rubbed her foot on Dante's leg. "What makes you think they Persians know who got them?" Dante resumed his conversation, feeling cocky as he prepared Starla's lines.

"They know."

"Who told them?"

"I don't know. I spoke to Officer Hemming. They have friends too."

"He told me the same bullshit last night. I don't believe him."

"Maybe, but you better get your piece just in case."

"As soon as I can get it out of Starla's mouth."

"Don't say I didn't warn you."

"Are you coming tonight?"

"I don't think so. Roslyn made plans for us. Is everything set?"

"Double set."

"What do you mean?"

"We've got two bands showcasing. They've got to want at least one of them."

"We've got two bands playing at Max's tonight?" Anthony asked, actually impressed.

"Yeah, Nigel set it up for this punk he likes, but I got Freddy's band to go on first. They've got a much better chance at getting signed. They already have a song on the radio and people know them. This other guy, Cells, is just weird. And get this: he hurt his foot and can barely stand up!"

"At least Freddy will put on a good show. What time does he go on?"

"Midnight."

"Maybe I'll sneak out after we put the baby to bed."

"See you later." Dante hung up and took another hit. Laying back into the cushions, he moaned with the satisfaction as the drugs seeped into his system. It was the first time in years he felt like he had the upper hand on his brother. Leaning forward, he dialed Donny to brag, and Starla lit a cigarette. Donny didn't answer, so he left a rambling message. Starla snorted her lines while smoke from the cigarette they shared layered around them. Dante got up and went back to the bathroom. He pawed a few strokes through his greasy hair, admiring himself in the mirror. Starla came in and stood behind him, putting her arms around his torso with her palms to his chest. Dante reached back and grabbed her ass. "Tonight's my night, baby." He squeezed. "Why don't you do my hair and give me a makeup job? I may even brush my teeth."

"In a while." Starla slid one hand down Dante's front and sniffed the back of his neck. "Let's do a little more before we go out."

CHAPTER 59

Nigel got to the club at 9:00 and found Arnie at his usual table downstairs in the restaurant. He sat down across from him, not wanting to tell him about Bosco Dish, and hoping that he would be gone by the time they went on.

"How's it going, mate?" Arnie greeted him.

"Great, yourself?"

"You're looking sharp," Arnie said, noticing that Nigel was more dressed up than usual. "Got a full guest list?"

"Full list, full house, special guests."

"That's what I like to hear. Plenty of drinkers I hope. What's the surprise?"

"Can't tell you just yet. You'll find out tomorrow." Bluffing was all part of the game.

"Maybe I'll have to stick around and see for myself."

Nigel tried to sound excited. "You'll stay for the show?"

"I'll have to stay now. Don't want to miss your special guests."

Arnie surveyed the gathering crowd. "So, why is Donny D. calling me?"

Nigel chose to be coy. "He probably wants to make sure I put him on the list."

"He told my girl his band was playing here tonight." Arnie leveled his gaze and Nigel blinked. "You don't have to tell me; another one of Dante's genius moves?"

Nigel was relieved that Arnie wasn't angry. "Something like that."

"I know *you* wouldn't ask me to put those fools on. I have a reputation to uphold. My audience will tear them apart. This could be a scene."

"I owe you one, mate." Nigel fived him. "Why don't you come see me in a while. We've got some nose candy you won't believe."

"I've got some work to do. Maybe I'll catch you upstairs later."

Squeezing past the teetering confusion of amplifiers, speaker boxes, and cables that lined the narrow passageway out to the alley, Nigel got up and went toward the back, looking for Dennis and the roadies.

CHAPTER 60

Director Lawson sat in the back of an unmarked police van several blocks away from Max's Kansas City on 19th Street. It was 9:00 p.m., and his makeshift desk was stacked with an assortment of files that had been sorted through so many times that he couldn't remember exactly what was in each one. Numerous pictures of suspects, with handwritten notes scribbled on the bottom, were taped to one wall of the van, while guns, breathing masks, and other assault paraphernalia took up most of the other limited space. Trying to prepare himself, he rustled through internal FBI memos, partially blacked out CIA briefing pages, interagency contact information, and operational policy and procedure instructions from both NYPD and the FBI. It was more data than anyone could digest in one sitting. A case summary from the Customs Bureau, an FBI playbook with a diagram of the main characters and their relationship to one another, and a standard issue ATF Bureau bulletin detailing the safe way to handle dangerous chemical compounds were stapled together and stacked for distribution to the field teams that had reassembled. The information overload gave Lawson mental indigestion, and his policeman's intuition was dulled by the plethora of facts. He fidgeted with his communication switcher, fighting off a bad feeling in the pit of his stomach while Special Agent Farmer began distributing the packets to the teams who had met in front of the empty lot that had been designated as the staging area.

"Gillingham and Lowell," Farmer announced, holding up a packet. "You're back at the Old Medical Building.

"And our orders are?" Detective Gillingham asked.

"Besides you, we've got NYPD personnel in place to bust the Persians there. If everyone we want is in the same room, along with the evidence, it couldn't be more perfect. We'll give the go word when we're ready."

"So what are you doing *here*?"

"The Persians might not stay at their offices, and there's a good chance they might come here looking for their stolen merchandise. They probably already know who stole it by now, and we need to catch them with the evidence if they come to take it back. We're sure that some of their stuff is in Dante's possession."

"So we're using Dante as bait?"

"Yes. We've got backup watching the entrances and exits of their headquarters, but it's a complicated old building so we're not sure we have everything covered. You're out front on the point, so keep your radios on and let us know if you see anybody move. We'll let you know if we hear anything."

Detective Gillingham took the paperwork and led Ralph away. "What are we supposed to do?" Ralph asked, not understanding the strategy.

"Same as ever. Sit, watch, and wait," Detective Gillingham answered, as they neared the car.

"Falin and George," Agent Farmer continued, "You're outside, behind the club, where you requested. I hope, for all our sakes, your hunch is right this time Detective Falin."

"I've got a good feeling." Detective Falin assured him as he took his packet. "We'll keep an eye on the dressing rooms. That's where they usually break the stuff out."

"Detective Falin," Lawson interrupted. "Try to control your enthusiasm. This is an undercover operation, not a peep show. Keep your radio on silent, but check it."

Detectives Ailes and Ferguson were next in line. "You two are around the front of the club. There's an NYPD sticker for your car inside your packet," Agent Farmer said, making sure he gave them the right one. "Officer Casey and his team will back you up."

"Oh that's a comfort," Detective Ferguson mocked, elbowing his partner.

"Please try to stay serious for once in your life," Agent Farmer urged as they left.

"ATF? Where're Agents Arthur and Margaret?" Farmer called out.

"Right here," they answered in unison from ten feet away.

"You two are inside," Farmer said, looking down at his list. "My god! I never would have recognized you," he added, looking them over, impressed with their disguises.

"That's the whole idea." Agent Arthur primped his afro wig and swiped the packet from Agent Farmer with a flourish of his iridescent satin sleeve, spinning around for effect in skintight pants tucked into knee-high boots. Not to be outdone, Agent Margaret, in a leggy microskirt, platform heels, and a short white shag jacket that barely covered her skimpy top, slipped her arm through his as they stalked off together.

"Enjoy the show." A duty officer whistled.

"They *are* the show," another commented.

"Somebody keep an eye on them please," Lawson muttered to no one in particular.

Officer Casey helped Agent Farmer distribute the rest of the packets to the support personnel from NYPD, and when they were done, they joined Director Lawson inside the mobile command center.

"You sure we're not over-preparing?" Farmer probed.

"I don't think so," Director Lawson told him. "Detective Falin's got a long history of being right. You remember the Colorado bust a few years ago."

"Well, I hope he's right this time, because if he's not, this is going to be one giant waste of taxpayer money," Agent Farmer remarked, secretly hoping Rhamin had understood his message.

"Tell me again what you think is going to happen," Officer Casey, whose promotions were based more on loyalty than brainpower, asked.

"Same old crap," Director Lawson griped, shuffling through files. "We're just trying to catch the bad guys red-handed. We'll have to see who shows up where. Who's making the coffee run?"

CHAPTER 61

The Darius Trust breathed a collective sigh of relief as Homa revived from her spiritual encounter. As the only woman and the youngest participant, she was the object of everyone's attention, each in his own way. Bahram and Dr. Nouri were doting and sympathetic, concerning themselves with her physical comfort, while Mak's loyalty to the family skewed to a more pragmatic form of protection. Rhamin, who wore his heart on his sleeve, prepared a plate of chow mein for her like a servant offering sustenance to his master. Only Sattar saw her simply as an equal – albeit a less experienced one.

"Welcome back," Sattar greeted her as she reentered this world.

"How do you feel? Some food will settle your nerves." Rhamin proffered a plate.

Homa exhaled comfortably. "I feel fine. Wonderful in fact." Her eyes shone with the light of discovery and her smile eased the tensions in the room.

Sattar knew where she had been. "What did you see?"

"I met the Princess," Homa began the description of her experience with an uncharacteristically dreamy sigh. "She was much more beautiful than I imagined."

"Did she speak to you?"

"Yes, but not in words." Homa closed her eyes again, savoring the image in her mind.

"Did she show you anything?"

"Many things. Beautiful and terrible, but all was peaceful."

"Did she answer our prayers?"

"Yes. She showed me where they had hidden her Tears. It is a dark place with bad smells," she said, keeping her eyes closed, trying to preserve the memory.

"Were the seals broken?"

She opened her eyes and saw worry reflected in Sattar's face. "I only saw one bottle," she apologized.

"Two are missing." Sattar held her hand firmly and gave her instructions. "Close your eyes again, and tell us where to look."

Homa complied. Breathing deeply and concentrating, she searched her mind. But the only thing she saw behind her eyelids was Reggie. She opened her eyes and stared at him. Everyone else followed her gaze, and Reggie squirmed under their collective scrutiny. Mak instinctively moved closer to him as if to make sure he didn't react suddenly.

"I didn't do anything," Reggie claimed innocence. "It must have been Dante," he blurted out.

Getting the confirmation he was waiting for, Sattar rose from his seat and felt for the gun in his pocket. "Where does this Dante live?" he asked inimically.

Reggie deflected the pressure. "Not far from here."

"You must take me there," Sattar insisted.

"You want to go there now?" Reggie wasn't finished eating and gnawed on a rib bone to underscore his priorities.

"Now, Reggie. Or maybe...." A threatening darkness crept over Sattar's face.

"Now, Reggie," Mak repeated.

Refusing to be sweated, Reggie took his time putting the food container aside and wiping the grease from his mouth. "Okay, if that's what you really want." In spite of nearly two years as Dr. Nouri's driver, Reggie knew he wasn't really liked or trusted. Mak's hostility and Sattar's veiled threats helped convince him that there were better opportunities for a man with his skills. He started to think of a way he could get credit for to delivering Sattar to the cops.

Mak sensed trouble. "I will go with you," he volunteered.

"Good idea; you four stay here," Sattar commanded.

There was no disagreement. Dr. Nouri and Bahram had been through scares before, but this was Rhamin's first brush with immediate danger. He sat next to Homa to offer her comfort, but received more than he provided.

"Don't worry," she assured him. "The Princess has many friends."

Mak and Sattar flanked Reggie as they took the elevator to the basement and exited via the passage that connected to the parking garage of the building next door.

CHAPTER 62

Rebecca got back to her apartment after dark. Her roommates were both home, busying themselves with preparations for a night out on the town – and avoiding each other as much as possible. "Hello, I'm back," she called out as soon as she entered. The toaster oven timer was clicking off the seconds, and she could hear the water running, but no one answered her. She knocked on Monica's door.

"What is it?" Monica answered, annoyed.

"It's me, Rebecca."

Monica opened the door and came out, half dressed with her hair wrapped in a towel. "Oh hi. How was New Jersey?"

"Okay. How are things here?"

"Okay, I guess. Except Amy and I aren't speaking."

"Why not?"

An awkward silence passed between them as Monica realized that she couldn't tell Rebecca what the argument had been about. "Well, you know Amy. She gets so bossy."

"What was your fight about this time?"

Ameliah suddenly appeared. "Why don't you tell her the truth, Monica?"

Monica reddened, and a surge of tension jolted through the three of them. Ameliah folded her arms. "Are you going to tell her about your new boyfriend or do I have to?"

Monica looked at Rebecca apologetically. "I'm so sorry. It just happened." She touched Rebecca's shoulder as tears welled up in both of them.

"Maybe we've been livin' in a cracked house,
but that don't mean that it's goin' to fall." *20

"It's okay; I knew anyway," Rebecca whispered, forgiving her.
Monica was relieved. "You knew?"
"I could see it happening the other night. Men are such animals."
"I'll say, and thank God for that!" Ameliah butted in. "Now that you two are all made up, you want to come with me to see Freddy's big show tonight?"
"You're not still mad at me?" Monica questioned.
"I was, but if Becca forgives you, so do I."
"Why were you mad at her?" Rebecca asked.
"She violated the house rules. Jon slept over last night."
Hearing it said aloud, the news hit Rebecca in the pit of the stomach. She grimaced, trying to keep a new round of tears from escaping.
"I'm sorry." Monica apologized again. She tried to console her, but Rebecca turned away and burst out crying.
"Nice going, Amy," Monica scolded.
"It's not my fault. I wasn't the one who – "
"Stop it, both of you. You don't understand," Rebecca sobbed.
Ameliah was surprised. "We don't?"
"No, you don't. It's not Monica's fault. That's not why I'm upset."
Monica was confused. "What the matter then?"
"You had a fight with your parents?" Ameliah guessed.
"Nooo," Rebecca mewed painfully. "I can't really talk about it," she said, sniffling. "Where are you guys going tonight? I don't feel like being alone."

"Well, I'm going to Max's Kansas City to see Freddy," Ameliah said.

"That's funny, Jon is playing there tonight too," Monica added.

"Then I guess we're both heading to the same place."

"Is that okay with you, Becca?" Monica asked.

Rebecca thought for a moment. "I just want to be around other people."

"How soon can you be ready to go?" Ameliah asked, checking the clock.

Rebecca hadn't changed her clothes for two days and looked like it. "Well, I just got back, so I need some time to shower and get dressed. When did you want to leave?"

Monica was ready. "It's already 9:00, so we should go soon."

Rebecca eyed Ameliah's outfit. She had on tight white pants and black boots with silver trim. "Is that what you're wearing?"

"Yeah. I just got it this afternoon. You like it?" Her thin blousy top hung loosely and revealed some cleavage.

Monica's outfit was similarly provocative and Rebecca didn't feel up to the visual competition. "I don't know what to wear," she sighed.

"Just put on anything. You always look great," Monica encouraged her.

"Okay, give me a few minutes."

CHAPTER 63

It was already 9:00 p.m., and the two cups of instant coffee that usually helped Dante overcome his stupor were doing little to counteract the effects of the powerful narcotics. Starla was also woozy, but she was a few years younger than Dante and hadn't been abusing herself for as long. She was more coherent, and stumbling around the darkened apartment in her heels, she helped Dante get dressed by the light of the city outside their window. He held onto the sink for balance and watched in the mirror as she fixed his hair and used rouge on his pasty cheeks. Helping him into the bedroom, she found a collared shirt that hadn't been worn since it came back from the cleaners and guided his arms through the sleeves. He stood with his hands on her shoulders for support as she buttoned it and tucked it into his pants.

"What's that?" she asked, feeling something hard stuck in his waistband.

"That's just in case." He patted his gun.

"In case what?" She felt for his other weapon but it was limp.

"In case that one isn't working."

"Where's the stuff?" she asked, patting his pockets.

"I probably left it on the table by the TV."

Starla, who was already fully dressed, went to the living room. "Here it is," she called from the other room. "What should I bring?"

"Just fill my little bottle and put the rest in your bag."

Starla saw that Dante's vial was already full, so she grabbed it and put the baggie with the gray powder in the zippered part of her handbag. The blinking light from a sign outside sparkled on the glass bottles of Princess Tears.

"I'm all ready," Dante called. "Don't forget the stash."

"Coming." Starla caught a glimpse of the etching on one of the bottles. Mesmerized, she stared at the Princess' head, which seemed to be looking back at her. An unseen force guided her hand to the bottle that had been opened, and in one quick motion, she snugged the rubber stopper in and tucked the cylinder into the bottom of her purse. Slipping the long straps of her small snakeskin handbag over her shoulder, she headed for the door.

"You lock up," Dante, who was holding on to the banister halfway down the stairs, yelled up to her.

"Where are the keys?"

"I don't know, leave it open, just come on." Dante's voice trailed up from the next landing.

Starla couldn't find the keys so she left the door unlocked. "Coming." She caught up to him on the third floor landing.

Dante knocked on Nigel's door. Sonya was in there but didn't answer. "He must have left for the club already," Sonya heard Starla say as she helped Dante down the steps. The management office on the next floor was deserted, and only the perversely posed mannequins in the boutique window at street level saw them disable the alarm system and leave the building.

Reggie spotted them from across the street as they got into a cab. "There they go," he said, pointing to their taxi as it merged like a blob of yellow mercury with the rest of the cabs oozing down 7th Avenue. He also noticed the standard issue, undercover, dark blue Mercury pulling out behind Dante's cab – but he didn't mention that to Mak and Sattar.

Sattar chose the stationary target. "Is that their building?"

Reggie had been on all the floors. "That's where Dante lives."

Mak cast a wary eye on the four-story building. "Who's in there now?"

"How am I supposed to know?" Reggie snarked.

"Well, what goes on in there? How many people are *usually* there?" Sattar asked, calculating resistance.

"There's a couple of apartments on the third floor and Dante has the whole top one."

"What's on the second floor?"

"That's where their offices are."

Mak didn't see any lights on the second floor. "They're probably not open on Sunday night." The three men crossed the street and got closer. "Well, the store on the bottom is closed," Mak said, peering in through the window. "What kind of weird stuff do they sell in this place?" he added, shocked at the display.

Reggie had been a customer there. "I can get you a discount, old man," he needled.

Sattar was suspicious. "You know these people?"

"The girls here are real friendly. That's how I met Dante."

"Explain."

"No big deal. Some of the girls here do a little work upstairs for the management company."

"You've been to the offices upstairs?"

"I've been all over this building," Reggie bragged. "Who else lives here?"

"Like I said, Dante has the top floor. Real nice pad – or at least it was. Nigel, the British guy, has an apartment on the third floor, and the other apartment...." Reggie couldn't contain his guilty smile. "Oh, I've had some goood times in there!"

"We don't need to hear about your sex life, Reggie." Mak tried the front door and it was locked. "How do we get in this place?"

"We aint' gettin' in that way, island boy. Follow me." Reggie led them down the street to the next intersection.

"I hope you know where you're going," Mak said suspiciously, clutching the revolver hidden in his pocket as he passed Greenwich Village pedestrians dressed in strange street costumes.

Reggie turned down a side street and into the narrow slit between two buildings. He hoped they were being followed. "Not too fat to fit in here, big Mak?"

"Shut up, Reggie."

"Both of you keep quiet," Sattar shushed from behind as he wedged through the passageway and into the alley behind the row of buildings. They climbed over disassembled metal scaffolding, around rusted, broken, and discarded appliances, and through a clutter of fallen laundry and tossed garbage until they got to the bottom of the fire escape stairs on the back of the Pecorino's building.

Even with all his experience as a policeman, Mak was still amazed at where he wound up chasing criminals. "How did you find this place?" he asked.

"Never came in this way before." Reggie answered, gingerly picking his way closer. "I had a little problem one night, and the fellow I needed to speak to climbed down this fire escape. I just followed him," he said, touching the bottom of the iron ladder.

"How are we supposed to get up there?" Mak asked, trying to reach the metal rungs.

Sattar already had a plan. "Bring that water heater over here," he said, pointing.

Mak dislodged an ancient white cylinder from the dirt and rolled it underneath the bottom of the ladder. Steadying the appliance with wedges of debris, he stood on top and got hold of the bottom rung. It took a good strong yank to break through the rust and pull the ladder down low enough to grab the more. Energized, Mak hoisted himself onto the ladder and climbed to the second floor landing. Reggie and Sattar followed. Then they scaled the rickety iron steps to an unlocked window on the third floor, pried it open, and climbed into the stairwell. Seeing where they were, Reggie led them up to landing in front of Dante's door.

"You sure this is the place?" Sattar whispered as he drew his pistol. Reggie nodded and stood aside. Acting in accordance with police procedure, Mak positioned himself on the hinged side of the door with his gun drawn. Sattar tried the handle, and to his surprise, the door creaked open.

Dante's spacious pad, designed to be modern but suffering from neglect, was only lit with the borrowed lights of the city. Stale air, thick with smells of spent tobacco and organic mold, wafted out the top of the open door while the untainted atmosphere in the stairwell seeped in from the bottom. Sattar was the first one to enter, disturbing the palpable pall as if he were an agitator in an air-filled conjure pot. Both he and Mak were immune to the repulsive smells, but Reggie had to hold his sleeve over his mouth to filter out the suspended particulates. With wordless hand signals, Reggie led them toward the couch where he and Dante usually sat. They didn't see anyone around, but Sattar saw a cylinder of Princess Tears on the sofa table, twinkling in the refracted light of a neon sign across the street. Tightening his grip on his pistol, he quietly maneuvered in front of the vacant sofa and seized the bottle with a swipe of his other hand. Mak checked the perimeter for enemies.

Holding it up to the light, Sattar whispered, "It hasn't been opened," and tucked it into his overcoat pocket. "Where's the other one?" he asked, scanning the room.

Reggie only knew about the powder and had never seen any of the odd shaped bottles. "What is that stuff, moonshine?" he asked, cringing his nose.

"Never mind," Sattar answered waving his pistol. "You know this place; go see if anyone's here." Mak re-enforced the instruction with his own revolver and Reggie felt for his switchblade as he sneaked toward the bedroom. Sattar searched the sofa area and saw a mist of light gray powder covering the coffee table. He wiped it with his finger and tasted it, confirming his suspicions.

"In here," Reggie called from the bedroom. Mak and Sattar came quickly. They all recoiled as Reggie turned the lights on. Bedcovers and sheets were twisted halfway off the stained mattress of a platform bed with a rectangular wooden headboard. Dirty clothes, pillows, and shoes littered the floor, and empty glasses, plates, cutlery, and magazines crowded the surfaces of the black-painted, modern Danish furniture. Reggie held up a bag of Princess Powder in his hand like a trophy fish.

"Where'd you find that?" Mak asked suspiciously.

Reggie's pride gave him away. "I know where Dante keeps his stash."

Sattar took the packet from him and examined the unopened seal. "Where are the other ones?"

"What other ones?" Reggie feigned innocence.

"There were six," Sattar informed him sternly.

"Well, maybe I didn't see the other ones. I'll look again." Reggie went into the bathroom and a moment later came out with another bag. "That's all I could find." He handed it to Sattar.

Mak knew about crime scenes. "Show me where you found them."

"In here." Reggie opened a bathroom drawer filled to capacity with an assortment of packaged medicine, pill bottles, and drug store accessories. Mak took a long nail file and sorted through the jumble, knowing that this was not a stash drawer.

Sattar snooped around the bedroom while they were looking. "Where is the creature that lives here?" he asked with disdain. "We must find him."

Mak wasn't ready to leave. "You don't want to poke around here some more?"

"He'll tell us everything we want to know once we have him," Sattar seethed.

"Do you know where he went Reggie?" Mak asked.

Reggie had another packet in his pocket and was ready to go. "I don't know where he was going, but he sure ain't here."

"Let's go," Sattar said. "No use wasting any more time here."

"How do we get out of here without using the fire escape?" Mak asked.

"Beat's me; I always use the front door."

"Then I guess we will too," Sattar said decisively.

They left the lights on and the door open and took the stairs to the ground floor. Sonya heard their steps and looked through the peephole, thinking it might be Nigel. She recognized Reggie, and assuming he had brought some friends to do business with Dante, stayed in hiding. Once they made it to the ground floor, they opened the outside door and walked briskly down the sidewalk like innocent pedestrians in a hurry. As they reached the corner of the intersection with Bleecker Street, Reggie looked around, hoping someone was following them. No one was. Sattar hailed a cab and they returned to The Old Medical Building, going in the same way they had come out. The NYPD officer stationed in the basement behind the dumpster reported their re-entrance to Detective Gillingham.

"Who?" the Detective whispered to the lookout.

"I don't know. There were three of them."

"Copy. We saw them too."

CHAPTER 64

There was hardly any room to stand backstage at Max's Kansas City. Stacks of equipment lined the narrow hallway that still featured the wall scrawlings of the artists and poets who had created its mystique, and the legend was well protected by the limited access to the bathrooms, exit doors, and grungy cubicles that were designated as dressing rooms. Like most rock and roll venues, the club still advertised its connections to the past, but Andy Warhol, Lou Reed, and David Bowie hadn't been there for years, and the new breed of performers had distilled the cultural epiphanies of their predecessors into a toxic brew of irreverent alienation, usually delivered with earsplitting intensity. Roadies, band members, and hangers-on shared the insufficient space with managers, waitresses, and club employees, and everyone was more concerned with survival in the harsh punkish atmosphere than honoring history. Alcohol, tobacco, overcrowding, and illegal stimulants heightened the performers' excitement, and it was impossible to stand still in the constant ebb and flow of drinks, equipment, and people moving in and out of the random conflict.

The alleyway outside the back door served as an auxiliary waiting area, and physical contact with friends, enemies, and strangers was also unavoidable. Jon, Frankie, and Marco had gone there to check on their equipment and stayed, standing with their guitars until the preceding acts had vacated enough space inside for them to reposition closer to the stage. Cigarettes, joints, beer, and bluster bonded the determined throng outside together, and the waiting musicians barely acknowledged the roaring sound waves of the ongoing performance that beat against their fortitude every time the back door opened. Connections, costumes, and cleverness had gotten them this far, but at the stage door, the competition was more of an endurance contest than a talent show. Size mattered, and the bigger the retinue the greater the staying power. As just a three-piece, Jon's band needed all their tenacity to maintain their path to the stage.

Detective Falin, assigned to the backstage area, wasn't satisfied with doing the police work of monitoring the unfortunate mess of people outside. Determined to participate in the action, he had positioned near the dressing rooms where he could watch for illegal drug activity while ogling the backstage costume changes.

No one made room for the van that pulled up late with Cells' and Bosco Dish's equipment, so it double-parked across the mouth of the alleyway, blocking everyone else. Donny got out of the passenger side and wedged into the crowd like an icebreaker, using his muscular build to push the trapped musicians out of the way with stiff forearms and insincere apologies. Resistance, in the form of two beer-bellied bikers, built quickly into a shoving match that stopped his assault, and they sent Donny careening backwards, where he slammed against a mass of people that included Jon, Marco, and Frankie.

"Hey, man. What are you doing here?" Donny asked, almost thanking Jon for preventing his fall.

Jon pushed him away. "We're on at midnight."

"No you're not," Donny corrected him. "Freddy's got the midnight spot."

"Bosco Dish, playing here? I don't think so," Jon challenged him.

"Go check the list, punk." Donny challenged.

"I did," Marco, joining the disagreement, told Jon. "It says Boz Oz at 11:00, then Bosco Dish at 12:00, then us, and then someone else."

"Told you so." Donny said smugly.

"We don't have the midnight spot? That can't be!" Jon insisted. "Nigel promised us the midnight spot just a few hours ago. Where'd you see that?" he asked Marco.

"It's posted on the door," Marco reported, knowing it was not a good sign. "Maybe it's a mistake," he added.

"We're not on till 1:00 a.m.?" Frankie butted in. "What if the band before us goes over?

"Everyone will be gone by then," Marco voiced his fears of being bumped down the lineup.

Frankie was easily discouraged. "Yeah, our big showcase night. Thanks a lot, Nigel."

"Nice going, Cells. I knew this wouldn't work out," Marco added pessimistically. They all knew that the likelihood of keeping five bands on schedule was zero.

Donny riled them sarcastically. "Don't worry, guys, I'll be sure to get Freddy's band off at exactly 12:59."

Jon had heard enough. "You guys wait here with the instruments. I'm going to find Dennis and straighten this out," he said decisively, charging through the crowd.

Donny laughed at him. "Good luck."

Jon pushed his way to the stage door. When it opened to disgorge a line of sweaty musicians toting heavy amplifiers and holding pieces of a drum set over their heads, Jon slipped inside. Understanding the vital importance of musical equipment, the outside crowd moved aside to let the roadies pass as if they were EMTs making their way to an accident. As soon as they were through, roadies from the equipment van with Bosco Dish's and Cells' gear used the same considerate seam to maneuver their load inside.

CHAPTER 65

The short cab ride up to Max's was a longer journey than any of the three girls from New Jersey knew it would be. They sat quietly, three across, processing their apprehensions without looking for or giving friendly advice. Ameliah was the only one who spoke, but her banter lacked the enthusiasm of unlimited expectations. A few days of Freddy's impotent sexual conquests had left her unfulfilled, and she was already thinking about seeing Bradley at work on Monday. She had never been to Max's because of its low-life reputation, and wasn't looking forward to soiling her own. Fate was not on her side. Rebecca was too shaken by the news her father had shared to enjoy herself, regardless of where she was or what she was doing. Not wanting to be alone, a room full of noisy people – no matter what they were doing – seemed like a good way to drown out her fearful inner voices. She had never wanted a drink so badly, and was looking forward to letting go for a change. Her expectations would be surpassed. Monica was feeling guilty that she felt so good. Jon had called to say he was feeling much better, and her usual camaraderie with her friends had been supplanted by infatuation. Try as she might, she couldn't rid herself of a tingling excitement that started in her pants. She would never be able to reconcile her emotions. The girls got to the club a little after 10:00, paid their admission, and joined the alcohol-fueled circus already in progress.

CHAPTER 66

Reggie waved at the unmarked blue Mercury sedan parked near the corner before following Mak and Sattar through the door of the parking lot in building adjacent the Old Medical Building. He wasn't sure if anyone saw him, but he hoped they had.

Detective Gillingham called in his status report. "Suspect and two accomplices have re-entered the building."

Lawson was on the other end of the line. "Who's with him?"

"The doctor's assistant and the Laden warehouse manager."

"Where were they?"

"Unknown."

"Let us know if they go out again, and this time follow them."

"Understood." Detective Gillingham put down the receiver.

"What's going on?" Ralph asked him.

"Looks like we might actually earn our money tonight."

"What time do you think we'll be finished?" Ralph asked, yawning.

Detective Gillingham had already given up hoping that Ralph would be an asset, and answered with a soccer metaphor. "I don't know; that depends on if the Persian front line can score. The Italians usually have good goalies."

Ralph checked his watch and wondered if his wife and kid were home from New Jersey yet.

With part of his prize retrieved, Sattar had the energy of a bloodhound with a scent of his prey. His momentum carried Mak and Reggie through the subterranean passage and onto the service elevator. Once inside the confinement of the small space, the intensity of the hunt built a charge of static electricity that coursed through their bodies. Sattar mumbled to himself in a hoarse Persian whisper as the elevator ascended. Barely breathing, Mak hummed the conjure pot ritual through his nose. Feeling guilty and out of place, Reggie started to sweat. He plunged a hand into his pant's pocket, feeling for the evidence he had hidden there. Reggie's nervous fidgeting roused Mak's policeman's instinct, and fearing he might have a gun, Mak grabbed Reggie's arm as the door opened onto the tenth floor.

"What's in your hand, Reggie?" Mak asked abruptly, tightening his grip.

Reggie jerked his hand out of his pocket in self-defense, forgetting to let go of the packet. "Keep your filthy hands off me, island boy," he spat out, trying to conceal the bundle in his hand.

Mak grabbed his flailing arm as they exited the elevator, but Reggie wriggled free. "You want this?" Reggie taunted, pushing away and waving the purloined packet at Mak defiantly.

Sattar, who was a few steps ahead of them, turned to see what the commotion was about.

Reggie held the bag of Princess Powder in one hand and withdrew his switchblade with the other. He extended the blade and pointed it at Mak. "Get away from me or I'm gonna cut you," he threatened.

Mak drew his pistol and pointed it at him. "What do you think you're going to do with that fruit peeler, punk?"

Trumped, Reggie started to jump up and down and yell. "In here! Help! Police! Come and get them!"

"Put the knife down, you fool," Mak told him, coming closer.

Reggie slashed the air between them and continued yelling to attract attention. "Police! Help!"

Sattar drew his pistol and approached. "Quiet down," he ordered.

"In here; officer!" Reggie called out as if someone was watching. "I've got him for you. Come and get 'em." He waved the packed of powder over his head, bouncing on his toes as if here were on burning sand without shoes.

Sattar shot him in the thigh from ten feet away.

Reggie didn't feel it. "Missed me, you hairy freak! Police! Help!" he yelled, continuing his ruckus. The second shot hit him in the hand and the sting made him drop his knife. "Shit!" he cursed, twisting his hand in his shirt to stop the pain and bleeding.

Mak grabbed his other hand and wrested the bag of powder from him. He handed it to Sattar and put his gun to the base of Reggie's neck. Reggie tried to squirm away, but his leg started to throb and he realized he had been hit there too. Injured and hobbled, he succumbed to Mak's authority. Keeping Reggie's arm twisted behind his back, Mak picked up the knife and escorted his prisoner toward the laboratory suite. Sattar went ahead and opened the door.

Everyone had heard the gunshots, but the actual sight of bloody conflict was more graphic than they expected. Rhamin let go of Homa's hand and stood protectively between Homa and the trouble. Dr. Nouri and Bahram saw Mak holding Reggie prisoner and were baffled. Everyone looked to Sattar for an explanation.

"Reggie's got a problem," Sattar said dryly.

"You're the one's got the problem," Reggie corrected him.

Mak tightened his arm twist. "What's that supposed to mean?"

"Let go of me, you gorilla," Reggie squealed.

"Don't hurt him – yet," Sattar ordered. "What do you have to say for yourself, Reggie? Something you want to tell us?"

"I ain't gonna tell you nothing," Reggie mouthed off. "You can find out everything from the police when they get here."

"What business do you have with the police?" Sattar interrogated, sharing his concern with his partners.

Reggie finally shut his mouth. "I aint talkin'."

Mak forced him to sit down on a chair. "You think the police are going to help you before you bleed to death?" He glowered, pointing out the blood.

Dr. Nouri agreed with the diagnosis. "Let's get some bandages on those wounds."

"Good idea," Sattar said, bestowing his permission. "He's making a mess all over."

Homa picked up the bloody plastic bag with Princess Powder and looked at it curiously. She recognized the head on the wax seal. "Is this the cause of the problem?"

Rhamin put his hand on her shoulder and deferred to Sattar. A moment of indecision paused the wheels of time. No one wanted to answer her.

Reggie broke the spell. "What? She doesn't know?"

Dr. Nouri excused himself. "I'll go get some bandages,"

Reggie's mouth was on the move again. "Oh this is beautiful!" "Wait till you find out, sweetheart – "

Mak smacked him in the head before he could blurt anything else, then put his gun on Reggie's lips. "I suggest you shut that thing before I stick this in it and squeeze."

"It's okay, Mak." Homa said, coming closer. "I want to hear what he has to say."

"That's right, baby; uncle Reggie's going tell you where it's at." Reggie regained his swagger, but Mak tightened his grip and Reggie's tongue froze in pain.

"She knows what goes on around here, don't you, Miss Homa?" Mak interjected, trying to slow the pace of revelation. Dr. Nouri approached with medical supplies, and Mak held on to Reggie as the doctor cleaned and wrapped Reggie's hand. Then he knelt to inspect the thigh wound. Using a small scissors to slice Reggie's pants, he poked at the bloody flesh with a cotton-tipped stick.

Reggie constricted. "Ouch! That hurts!"

Dr. Nouri rose up, and while Mak held Reggie's arms, he put a dampened cloth over Reggie's mouth and nose. Reggie blinked helplessly and was unconscious in thirty seconds. Mak laid him on his back next to the wall. Dr. Nouri extracted the bullet from his thigh with tweezers and wrapped the wound with bandages.

Sattar noticed Rhamin looking out the window, toward the street. "What do you see out there?"

"Nothing, I'm not sure." Rhamin spoke without turning around. His father came closer to see.

"There's some cars parked in the middle of the street," Bahram reported, "and unless they're police cars, they're going to get tickets."

"Do you think someone heard the shots or Reggie yelling?" Rhamin asked.

"I don't know, the walls are pretty thick, and we're ten floors up."

Reggie's insinuations had unsettled Rhamin. "But what if they were waiting for a signal?"

"From who? Reggie?" Bahram hadn't considered it. "Is that possible?"

Sattar knew about treachery firsthand. "Anything's possible, and Reggie's definitely been up to something we don't know about," he noted, examining the bloodied bag of powder. "Homa, come and listen to Reggie's thoughts."

"How can I do that?" Homa asked.

"You cannot, but the Princess within you is strong. Come bring her closer."

Homa pulled her hood up and approached the unconscious traitor. "Let me see," she said, putting her hands on the top of Reggie's head and closing her eyes. The residual effects of smoking helped enter into a meditative trance. Her breathing grew slower and more deliberate. Visions of a chaotic crowd, pushing and falling in the darkness flickered in her mindscape. Loud voices, screeching roars, and random explosions rattled through her inner ear. The acrid smell of stale cigarettes and the noxious odors of the Laden warehouse suffocated her nasal memory. Homa's breathing became difficult as the sensory overload slowly built to a climax. Then, her vision suddenly separated into dissociated pieces and dissolved into nothingness. Sattar supported her torso as she slumped, spent. Her imagination's emptiness was soon replaced by the disembodied image of the Princess's head, which materialized from the ethers, still wearing the eerie plastic smile. Homa muttered unintelligibly to herself while everyone else looked on anxiously. Still rattled by the disturbances reverberating in her soul, she opened her eyes and removed her hands from Reggie's head.

"What did you see?" Sattar asked for all of them.

"I'm not sure, but the Princess came and made it all better – I think."

"Made what all better?"

"All the confusion, the people yelling, bad smells, the terrible noise and then...." Homa drifted back into reverie.

Reggie's gargled breathing slowed and he started to drool. Dr. Nouri placed his fingers on Reggie's limp neck muscles and felt his pulse. "We better get him upstairs." he said, more concerned with medicine than parapsychology. "I may need to operate."

Rhamin and his father helped Mak pick Reggie up and place him onto the wheeled gurney Dr. Nouri kept in the lab for naps and emergencies. They pushed the stretcher into the hallway and used the service elevator to bring Reggie to the medical offices on the fourteenth floor. After putting his old man overcoat back on, Sattar turned out the light, locked the door, and escorted Homa down the main stairwell.

It took the officer stationed in the basement too long to get permission to sneak up the back stairs to investigate the commotion he heard when Reggie got shot, and he got to the tenth floor a few minutes after everyone had gone. "All clear," the officer whispered into his police band receiver.

Detective Gillingham questioned him. "What's all clear?"

"Suspects are gone."

"Gone? Are you sure?"

The officer tried to open the door to the lab. "Pretty sure; the door is locked and the lights are out."

Detective Gillingham aimed his binoculars at the window and saw for himself. "Where'd they go? They were there a moment ago. Any signs of what that shouting was all about?"

The officer illuminated the dimly lit hallway with his flashlight. A spent bullet glinted in the darkness, and he noticed drops of moisture on the floor as he retrieved the shiny object. "I think I can confirm that what we heard were gunshots," he whispered, patting his own piece as he stood in the corner. "We have a crime scene up here. Better send a unit to investigate."

"Crime scene, copy. Please stand by." Detective Gillingham switched communication bands and called in his report to Director Lawson.

Ralph, who had heard the whole conversation, was energized by the activity. "Finally, something actually happened!" he said, savoring the taste of action and thinking about how the news would play out at home: his whole weekend would be justified; the story of police drama would become a family legend; his wife would forgive him; his son would respect him; and he wouldn't have to spend the rest of his career with the ignominy of "desk jockey" attached to his reputation.

But the night wasn't over, and while Ralph indulged his heroic fantasies, two hooded figures slipped out of the side door of the Old Medical Building and disappeared in the city shadows. Detective Gillingham's binoculars were still trained on the upper floor windows and he didn't see Homa and Sattar escape.

CHAPTER 67

Jon ran into Nigel in the crowded hallway outside the dressing rooms. The loud music made it almost impossible to carry on a conversation, so pointing and assumptions filled the comprehension gaps. "When do we go on?" Jon yelled at close range.

Nigel misunderstood the question. "They're almost done."

Jon was ready to resume his questioning but a full-bodied redhead pressed up against Nigel as she passed. Both men reeled from her overdose of patchouli and forgot what they were talking about. The music died down and sputtered to feedback stop. Jon was about to ask Nigel again, but was drowned out by the emcee shouting over the house PA, "Let's hear it for Wrong Orphan! Boz Oz is on next, so everybody stick around." House music amped up and the activity in the hallway elevated into an overcrowded shoving match as the frothing members of Wrong Orphan swelled toward the dressing rooms like a storm surge. Leading the charge, a guitar-wielding cretin in a torn and tie-dyed Tee-shirt parted the standers-by with the head of his guitar, whose array of randomly cut strings splayed from the tuning heads and menaced the eyeballs of anyone who didn't defend himself. Following in his wake, a black-booted goon with a shaved head and bruised arms covered in sweat and tattoos kicked unprotected shins out of his way, stepping on Jon's bad foot as he stomped past. Going the other way, the lead singer of Boz Oz, a short, fierce, performer with sturdy legs and battering elbows, stuck his sculptured beard and considerable girth into the oncoming human wave, slicing his way toward the stage with his band training behind him. Jon realized that he was about to be further injured in the riptide of cross purposes, gave up trying to talk to Nigel, and limped to the bar area.

He found Dennis at the bar, standing, and made unintentional contact with Agent Margaret as he edged into the non-space between her and Dennis. As Jon tried to get the bartender's attention, Agent Margaret, capably channeling her inner harlot, noticed something familiar about Jon. She didn't recognize him from the old photos she had been shown, and didn't connect her flirtation with him a few days ago in the magazine store, but her police instincts were keen enough to know that he was someone she should keep an eye on. Agent Arthur, positioned on her other side, also noticed Jon, but his afro wig had shifted precariously down his forehead, and he was more concerned with maintaining his disguise than vetting all the strange characters around him. Although the agents were struggling to stay on duty, their efforts to remain incognito were largely unnecessary, because the patrons of Max's believed that there was an unwritten agreement that suspended the laws of the city inside the club. There were just too many lawbreakers for a couple of agents to make any difference, so the party went on with their implied consent. The cinder-block walls that partially separated the bar from the stage area, along with the mass of bodies, diminished the din of boisterous chatter and pre-recorded music. Conversation was difficult, but possible. "There you are." Dennis welcomed Jon, moving aside to let him stand. "What are you drinking?"

"I'll have a Hiney," Jon ordered. Steadying himself on the bar, he inadvertently brushed against Agent Margaret, who felt a buzz of attraction pass between them. While re-crossing her legs, she not-so-accidentally bumped Jon back. Jon processed the energy as he tilted the bottle back, draining it in a few long series of gulps. A giant bottle of rum that had been made into a clock, with a second

473

hand in the shape of a banana, reminded Jon of his agenda. "Hey man. When are we on?" he asked Dennis, wiping the froth from his lips.

Dennis knew what had happened and tried to keep it simple. "Boz Oz at 11:00, Bosco Dish at 12:00, then Cells."

The confirmation that Freddy was on before him lit Jon's fuse. "I thought *we* were on at midnight?" he railed.

"So did I." There was nothing Dennis could do.

Jon was furious. "Bosco Dish? I can't believe it! They suck! How'd *they* ever get a gig here?" His imagination filled with retribution, and Halloween bats took to the air.

Trying to calm him, Dennis repeated the wisdom of the street. "Rock and roll with it. It's who you know, Joe."

Jon felt a bat shadow pass between him and the light. A foul odor, stronger than the smell of beer or cologne, gagged him. Dante appeared at the bar with bloodshot eyes, holding onto Starla for support.

"Double Jack straight up and two beers," Dante demanded, his words more slurred than usual. Agent Arthur recognized him and elbowed his partner. Dante leaned into Dennis' ear. "You see Donny?" he rasped.

"No," Dennis answered without turning around and exposing himself to the stench.

"Nigel?"

"He was over by the stage a while ago," Jon interjected, jerking his head in that direction.

Dante nodded, and the barmaid passed the drinks over to Starla. "My tab," Dennis told her, knowing how Dante operated.

Dante knocked his shot back in one gulp and intentionally dropped the empty glass on the floor. Swallowing the alcohol fire with satisfaction, he said "Now let's go find Nigel." With beers in hand, he and Starla moved toward the restaurant. Agent Arthur got up and followed them.

Standing with shoulders almost touching, the girls from New Jersey were grouped in a corner of the packed main room when Boz Oz took the stage. Two drinks into the evening, Rebecca found the offbeat antics of the kinetic frontman strangely entertaining. The guitarist stabbed the opening chords of their well known underground hit, "Queen of Lunch," whose chorus described workers' eagerness to catch a glimpse of the sexy female lunch truck driver that uses her looks to stimulate business. The crowd joined in the chorus and shouted *"Jim Jack Joe Johnny jump!"* performing the final directive in unison. Too shy to fully participate, Rebecca merely elevated on the balls of her feet when everyone else jumped, but it was far enough to temporarily lift the darkest burdens from the depths of her soles. Ever the showman, the vocalist, Simone LeFete, spotted her teetering on the edge of participation, locked her in his visual grip, and launched the opening set of lyrics of the next song at her with an accusatory finger. *"You strike me as a nice girl, don't strike me again."* She wasn't sure if he had singled her out, but the other patrons turned to see who he was pointing at while he sang *"give it to me."* With a mischievous nudge from her friends, Rebecca found herself in the thick of the excitement, drawn and propelled toward the stage by the unwritten laws of attraction. Bypassing her mental barriers, the Boz Oz frontman welcomed her proximity with pelvic twitches that communicated directly with Rebecca's baser instincts, releasing her into a full appreciation of magical musical frenzy.

The sight of the usually reserved Rebecca letting go and having a good time relieved some of Monica's guilt. She checked her watch, calculating how long it would be before Jon's band performed, and left Rebecca on the dance floor as she went looking for her own inspiration in the backstage area.

With Monica gone and Rebecca on the dance floor, Ameliah felt abandoned and retreated to a table in the corner. Her perfectly coiffed hairdo, new white pedal pushers, and expensive satin blouse made her feel overdressed and out of place, and she couldn't relate to what she saw as uncouth lowlifes performing erratic contortions and they had mistaken for dance moves. She wondered why Freddy would stoop to play at such a sleazy venue and seriously considered leaving before his band came on. Settling on a compromise, she sought refuge downstairs.

The two floors of Max's Kansas City offered customers valuable options. The restaurant downstairs was a place where they could go to soak up the alcohol in their systems with stale bread and overpriced burgers, and the racket from upstairs was muted enough that it was possible to carry on a conversation without damaging vocal chords. Customers who had not yet joined the fracas upstairs, and band members, gabbing and drinking themselves into readiness while waiting to play, congregated in the small room with seating for sixty. Waitresses plied the obstacle course with serving trays extended over their heads, and accidental food and beer showers caused by unsteady arms and unpredictable patrons were not uncommon.

To her complete surprise, Ameliah saw Bradley seated at a booth. He was sandwiched against the wall by an animated female with a short brown ponytail, opposite two other people she had never seen before. She tried to get his attention, but Jennifer's shrill cackle and air-jabbing hand gestures kept the focus of her table from wandering. There were too many people in the way for Ameliah to get closer, and she didn't know where else to stand, so she leaned against the wall looking lost and out of place. A server took her drink order, and while she was waiting for it to arrive, a handsome man, overdressed in mod attire with a poorly conceived afro wig, came and stood next to her.

Agent Arthur struck up a conversation. "Don't you love this place?"

Confused by the disconnect between his educated voice and foppish outfit, Ameliah couldn't tell whether he was serious. She decided to react to his voice rather than his appearance. "Not really."

Realizing that she hadn't fallen for his disguise, Agent Arthur changed tactics. "I hear the next band is supposed to be a little tamer," he sympathized.

"That's who I came to see."

"You're here for Bosco Dish?" Agent Arthur kept the conversation going. "I'm waiting to see the band that's on after them." His eyes wandered down Ameliah's outfit. "I hear they have an awesome set."

Ameliah basked in the attention, not realizing that Agent Arthur's flirtations were a cover for his true purpose, which was keeping an eye on Dante and his retinue, who were seated nearby. Ameliah had never met Dante, but when Donny entered the room and went straight to his table, both she and Agent Arthur took notice.

"Is that your friend?" Agent Arthur asked her.

"No, that's his manager."

"Who's the drunk guy at the table?" Agent Arthur asked, testing her.

"I don't know." Ameliah shrugged as her drink arrived.

Agent Arthur offered to pay, and flattered, she accepted. But as Agent Arthur undid his wallet, Freddy came up and put his arm around her. "Put your money away, man. She's not for sale," Freddy said, putting and arm her around the waist.

"She's all yours," Agent Arthur assured him. "I was just keeping her warm until you got back. Where you been, man?"

Freddy puffed up to rival Agent Arthur's gaudy appearance. "Getting ready for the show. My band's on next."

"Well all right! I'll be watching." Agent Arthur slapped him an insincere five. "See you later."

After he was gone, Ameliah vented her frustrations. "Where *have* you been?"

"There was a huge hassle out back with the equipment," Freddy groused. "I thought you were with your friends. Where are they?"

"I don't know, somewhere around here." "They left you by yourself?"

"I can take care of myself; I'm a big girl."

"Come on, let's get out of here." Freddy grabbed her hand and walked past Donny's table, receiving a folded bindle hidden in a handshake. Ameliah didn't notice, but Agent Arthur witnessed the exchange. Freddy and Ameliah took the stairs up to the main floor and found Nigel at the bar with Dennis and Jon. Monica had just left them to visit the ladies room with the coke bottle Jon had given her.

"Hello, Freddy." Nigel's greeting was polite but cold.

"Hey man, how you all doing?" Freddy greeted them cheerfully, oblivious to the fact that no one really liked him.

"Great," was all Dennis said.

"So, Cells," Freddy continued, trying to make friends, "you and I playing together again after all these years." He offered Jon a high five that wasn't accepted. Insulted, Freddy put him down. "He had the second best band in high school," Freddy explained to Ameliah.

Freddy's proximity brought out the worst in Jon. "Yeah, Flyshit and the Maggots had it all over us."

Nigel broke it up before it escalated. "No one wants to hear about your old high school rivalry. Aren't you on next, Freddy?"

"Yeah, we better get back there," he said, pulling Ameliah with him. "Donny said you were going to mix the house?" he asked Dennis.

"Whatever Nigel wants me to do."

Monica passed Freddy and Ameliah on her way back but didn't stop to talk. She wedged next to Jon at the bar and pushed the drug vial back into his hand under the counter, but the tiny bottle slipped through his fingers and fell on the floor, rolling under

Agent Margaret's barstool. Jon squatted quickly to retrieve it, but when he stood back up again the sudden change in his blood pressure triggered symptoms of the headache he had overcome earlier in the day. He held onto the bar, groping for support, and unintentionally put his hand on Margaret's leg. Margaret didn't realize he was dizzy and mistook his actions for a pass.

She addressed Monica and smiled coyly. "Better hang onto him, sweetheart, those wandering hands could get him into trouble."

"He's got all the trouble he can handle right here," Monica answered, putting Jon's arm around her waist to demonstrate her claim and help him stand.

Dennis could tell something was wrong. "You okay?"

"He looks a little flushed," Nigel agreed. "Better keep him off the juice for a while," he suggested to Monica.

A soft buzz filled Jon's head like a cotton fog. Monica's words appeared to be lip-synched and he couldn't understand anything she said. He knew he was among friends, so he let them guide him onto a barstool. Monica steadied him as he sipped tomato juice spiked with bitters and breathed through his nose, trying to regain his composure. A warm rush emanated from the base of his spine and spread into a high-pitched sizzle that was the sound of his brain frying. Jon's eyes teared from the internal pressure, and he wiped a newly formed layer of sweat from his forehead with the back of his sleeve. He tightened his back teeth, fighting off the nausea that he hoped wouldn't escalate back into a migraine.

Still seated next to him, Agent Margaret saw something was wrong. "Maybe he needs to see a doctor," she suggested, concerned.

"Oh, he'll be okay." Monica made light of the situation, not wanting to advertise their drug use. "He gets like this sometimes." Memories of what he did to her bedding were fresh in her mind.

"Just sit still," Nigel advised. "You don't go on for a while. We'll come and get you."

"I'll stay with him," Monica volunteered as Nigel and Dennis left the bar to set up Bosco Dish.

Conditions in the backstage alley had not improved. The spray-painted Wrong Orphan van was trying to get close to the load-out door by coaxing the human obstacles out of the way with its front bumper. The people trapped in its path, having nowhere to move, beat the sides of the vehicle with their fists, turning it into a booming steel drum loud enough to wake the dead in Jamaica. People were yelping in pain as the tires ran over feet, but before anyone was seriously injured, a husky roadie reached through the driver's window and began to throttle the insane skinhead driver responsible for the slow motion accident in progress. The van stopped as the driver thrashed in the roadie's grip, but, searching for traction, the driver's foot blindly pushed on the accelerator, lurching the van forward into the crowd. Several people were knocked down, and one unfortunate musician was pinned against the wall that had arrested the van's forward progress. Screams of the injured echoed off the alleyway walls and into the nearby streets. The driver was dragged out of the van through the window, and the same giant bearded roadies that had stopped Donny's obnoxious assault lifted the front bumper and rolled the vehicle back a few feet. The angry crowd turned its attention to beating the deranged driver, who tried to escape by crawling under the van. Detective Falin and Rudy heard the commotion and came to investigate, but were too late to understand what had happened and too far away to intervene.

CHAPTER 68

Sonya got Nigel's phone call at 10:00 p.m., just as she was getting ready to leave for the club. Her instructions were to stop by the apartment above the studio and retrieve the rest of the stash Nigel had left there before joining him. She caught a cab over to Heard Tracks and told the driver to wait outside while she went to fulfill her mission. Nigel had given her keys to the studio so that she could lock up for him on occasion, and their clandestine trysts in the apartment upstairs were a well-kept secret. An efficient covert operator, Sonya took the elevator up to the fourth floor, went into the studio's apartment, retrieved the small stash bottle from its usual hiding place, and exited within two minutes. The eerie feeling she had walking toward the elevator was confirmed by the sudden appearance of two hooded figures who emerged from the stairwell. They approached her menacingly and herded her into the open elevator with outstretched arms. The elevator doors closed, and Sattar pressed the stop button before it moved. Then he removed his head covering and showed his frightened prisoner the barrel of his pistol and his steely resolve. Sonya's involuntary urge to shriek was muffled by the touch of his hand to her mouth. Homa's deep, sympathetic eyes, peering from beneath her hood, mitigated Sonya's alarm, and the presence of another woman kept her worst fears from intensifying. The three stood in the creaky silence of the elevator shaft until Sattar felt it was safe to remove his hand from Sonya's mouth and speak.

"Who are you?" he asked.

Sonya was surprised it wasn't a nameless victim robbery attempt. "I'm Sonya, who are you?"

"Never mind that. What are you doing here?"

"I just came here to pick something up."

"What?"

"I don't live here."

"We know."

"How do you know?"

"That's our business. What did you come here for?"

"Something for the person who stays here."

"Dante?"

Sonya was shocked to hear his name. "No, do you know him?"

"You came for his drugs?"

Sonya couldn't understand how he guessed. "No. This isn't Dante's place."

"It isn't?" When it came to drugs, Sattar had well developed interrogation skills. "Whose drugs are they?" he asked, squeezing her forearm forcefully.

Sonya cracked under pressure. "Uh, they're not mine."

"Let me see them," Sattar insisted, brandished his weapon.

Shaken, Sonya took the vial from her pocket and handed it to him.

He gave it to Homa. "Open it and let me smell."

Homa unscrewed the cap and held the vial under her uncle's nose. The sight of his untamed beard and flared nostrils scared both women.

"As I thought," Sattar concluded. "It's ours." He nodded to Homa, who replaced the top and gave the vial back to her uncle. Sattar put it in his pocket and continued his interrogation. He stepped back slightly to get a good look at Sonya, who was dressed for a night out on the town in tight jeans, stylish boots, and a ruffled shirt. "Where are you going?"

The sudden turn of events had left her dumbfounded and out of her league. She pulled her jacket closed over her breasts. "I'm going to a club to see a band," she answered, unsure if the strange-looking people holding her hostage knew what she was talking about. "You know, musicians playing electric guitars, people drinking and dancing," she added innocently.

The mention of music playing, and Sonya's connection to Dante, struck a chord in Sattar's memory. Homa heard it too. She voiced their collective thought aloud. "Perhaps that's what the phone call to Rhamin was about."

"Perhaps. Where is this music club?"

"Not far from here, up on Park Avenue, around 19th Street. It's a very famous place." Sonya was relieved they weren't talking about hurting her and tried to make it sound like a legitimate destination.

The address confirmed their hunch. "We'll go there together," Sattar announced.

Sonya was shocked. She looked at Homa to see if he was joking or if he had something more nefarious in mind. "It's okay, we won't harm you," Homa assured her. "My uncle and I just want to get back what was stolen from us."

"I didn't steal anything."

"Yes, but your friends did."

"Nigel wouldn't steal anything," Sonya argued.

Sattar set her straight. "We don't know this Nigel, but he must have something to do with Dante Pecorino."

Sonya was unnerved they knew Dante's last name. "How well do you know Dante?" she asked, scared to imagine what else they might know.

"We know who he is and what he has done," Sattar said decisively.

Nigel had been complaining to Sonya about Dante for months, and she knew the misery Dante was capable of inflicting firsthand. "You want to find Dante?" she asked.

"You will help us?" Homa invited her defection.

Sensing an opportunity for escape and revenge, Sonya changed sides. "Dante is at the club I was going to when you stopped me. I hate him."

"You will show us where this club is?" Sattar asked, confirming his luck.

"You won't hurt Nigel?"

"If Nigel is your friend, he must be a good man," Homa said intuitively, coaxing cooperation.

Knowing her treachery would probably cost her her job, Sonya puffed a sigh of resolve. "I'll take you to where Dante is now."

Sattar pressed the first floor button and they descended as conspirators. The cab was still waiting and they slid in. At Sattar's instruction, the taxi stopped a few blocks away from their destination to let them out.

Detectives Ferguson and Ailes had redeployed to the Old Medical Building to investigate the reported gunshots, leaving the monitoring of the entrance to Max's Kansas City to Officer Casey and his New York City street cops. For them, it was just another night in front of a location that was an endless source of blotter filler. They weren't particularly motivated to follow the details of the case, so even though they had been prepped with photos, the two cops who had been left to monitor the front of the club were unable to identify the suspects.

As planned, Sonya and Homa went through the main door of the club, where Sonya's name on the guest list allowed them free entry. Sonya knew her way around, but Homa, who had never been to such a thoroughly American nightclub, was shocked to see how closely the licentious gathering resembled the poster collage in her room. She withdrew into the shapeless safety of her full-length robe, hiding the stitching she had used to weave her dichotomous personalities together. Club-goers, few of whom were naturally attractive, stalked and posed in sexually explicit attire that encouraged the wet kissing, groping, and public grinding they had come there to indulge in. Torn leather outfits, featuring open patches of tattooed skin and religiously themed decorative hardware, identified the repeat customers. Sonya was dressed like the rest of the girls who worked there, in crack-tracing jeans and a form-fitting top, with her hair tied snugly around the contour of her head. She greeted and small talked her way through the room, introducing Homa as her cousin from Puerto Rico. Homa stayed within Sonya's auric protection, and for the first time in her life, appreciated the modesty afforded by the modified burqa she was wearing. Her dull brown robe was so starkly different from the eye-popping display of twisted fashion fantasies that it was mistaken for a hip monk's costume, and the more brazenly clad were intrigued by the unexpressive mystery of Homa's appearance.

Sattar, who knew the police would be looking for him by now, walked a few blocks past the club and found the alley crowded with vans and people waiting to get in through the back door. Recognizing that his unkempt appearance wouldn't seem too far out of place, he tied his hair back and joined the muted madness outside the back of the club, pretending to be looking for a performer named Googoo. He was blending in with the pool of people eddying around the back door when Donny, clearing a path for, the keyboard player from Bosco Dish who never liked to come to gigs too early, moved him out of his way with a stiff forearm. "Out of the way, old man," Donny ordered.

"Be careful, son," Sattar warned. Too wound up to let the insult pass, he added, "You never know who you might be talking to."

"What's that supposed to mean grandpa?" Donny challenged him, shoving him dismissively into a wall. "Wanna make something of it?"

Sattar didn't want to risk revealing his pistol, so he unceremoniously shot Donny in the thigh without taking his hand from his pocket. Donny felt the sting and grabbed his leg in disbelief as Sattar moved beyond his reach into the crowd. Everyone who heard the loud pop thought it was the sound of the equipment truck engine backfiring, and Donny's yelp coincided with the curses of roadies who had just dropped a heavy anvil case. The first beats of Freddy's sound check boomed through the open back door, and Sattar surged into the backstage hallway with the next wave of performers, which included Marco and Frankie.

Detective Falin sent Rudy to investigate the new commotion in the alleyway, and in his push to the exit, Rudy unknowingly brushed right past Sattar, who was anonymously inching into the club with a line of people, like one more segment of a human caterpillar. Once outside, Rudy heard Donny's angry threat to kill the hairy freak who had just shot him, but didn't see any culprit to pursue. Inside, Detective Falin could not turn his head from the full-figured red headed woman in the semi-private dressing room responding to the Boz Oz frontman's attention to her breasts, and Sattar shuffled by him unnoticed.

The lure of the featured midnight act had packed the main room to suffocating capacity. Nigel stood off to the side with Jennifer who, despite standing directly in front of the blaring speakers with Bradley, still hadn't stopped talking. Her record company cohorts, Simon and Dave, stood nearby, tethered to her by the invisible leash of the stash bottle she had assumed control of, and with the aid of the unusually narcoleptic mixture, they all seemed to be enjoying the contrived pomposity of Freddy's band, who had begun their set. Nigel and Jennifer hyped each other in pre-deal foreplay by pointing out the positive signs of audience involvement. Bradley patted his thighs to the steady four-four time, grimacing joyously at the predictable pentatonic solos. As the second song, a midtempo ballad, ended, Starla and Dante joined them in the wings. Other patrons, who were not as high or entertained, suggested that the band play something a little faster, and Freddy obliged with an uptempo, twelve-bar blues rocker that put a spring in the feet of the dance happy. Gyrating to their own rhythm, Starla's hips caught the buzz and she bent forward, with her mouth open and arms flailing, adding a dose of wanton sexuality to the collective energy. Nearby dancers imitated her near-spastic movements, and the sight of Freddy's band winning over the crowd put the smirk of a winner on Dante's face. He nodded his satisfaction to Nigel and Jennifer, and broadcast his pride with a rotten-tooth grin at Simon and Dave. Unable to resist the excitement of the moment, Bradley pulled Starla onto the dance floor and engaged her in the simulated copulation that was accepted as the current dance craze. Dante noticed with satisfaction that the record execs were as entertained by Starla's antics as he was.

Sonya, with Homa in her trail, came upstairs and spotted Nigel and his friends in their business huddle. She navigated through the moving bodies to their position while Homa stayed on the perimeter, leaning against the wall with her arms crossed. Sonya's full frontal hug, which was supposed to have included the secret passing of the vial, produced a look of confusion on Nigel's face. She leaned into his ear and tried to explain, but the music was too loud for a long story. Neither of them wanted to make too much of a scene, so Sonya mouthed a silent, "I'll tell you later," and winked mysteriously.

Nigel had no idea what she was talking about – and didn't understand her curious head jerks in the direction of a far off corner. "It's okay," he mouthed back and stepped away, not wanting to reveal the depth of their intimacy.

Jennifer, who had come up through the ranks with Nigel and thought of him as a brother, could tell there was something going on between them. She was hoping it was drug related because her stash was running low. Nigel had told her he was expecting a delivery – and they both wanted to keep Simon and Dave tooted up until Cells played. But Jennifer didn't know what to do about Bradley. An infrequent drug user, Bradley was swooning over

Starla, enthused by the liberating feeling of his recent snorts and oblivious to Jennifer's embarrassment. She tried to get his attention but was overmatched by Starla's body parts.

Having lost most of his scruples, and forgotten all of his legal training, Bradley was dangling over the edge of decency when he caught sight of Ameliah. The shock of being seen by someone he worked with interrupted his euphoria, and he tried to winch himself back from the abyss as the song ended. Shocked by Bradley's behavior, and jealous of his infatuation with Starla, Ameliah moved to the edge of the stage, close enough to touch Freddy's cymbals. Hoping for both Bradley's and Freddy's attention but too sober to let it all hang out, Ameliah performed a dated pogo dance, imagining herself as part of the show. Still on her feet and dancing nearby, Rebecca imitated her hops, sharing the beat, and rediscovering friendship in the mindless joy of lively steps. Keeping an eye on Rebecca and Ameliah through the smoky stroboscopic darkness, Bradley danced closer, hoping to join their reverie, when an unexpected thrust of Starla's ass sent him stumbling into their midst. The butch woman in ripped tights and studded boots that he landed against pushed him back into Starla, setting off a minor shoving match. Ameliah tried to intervene, but the butch woman's dance partner, who had been waiting for an excuse to start a mosh pit, pushed her too. The tattooed thug from Wrong Orphan, who had been nursing a growing perversion for Starla from the sidelines, saw his opportunity to get his hands on her and joined the fray. He grabbed Starla's bosoms with both hands and squeezed them maniacally. Her screams brought Bradley to her defense, and she pounded her assailant on the back as Bradley choked him into letting go. A bouncer, strong enough to manhandle the drunken attacker, pushed the Wrong Orphan thug to the side before things got any further out of control.

Sensing the moment called for calm, Bosco Dish played a slow blues song that encouraged the grounding effect of full contact dancing. But deep inside Starla's purse the Princess began to cry. In the struggle to free herself from her attacker, the stopper on the bottle of Princess Tears had loosened, and a slow leak of concentrate dampened the leather insides of her shoulder bag, still hanging against her side. No one felt the effects of the potent fumes at first, but by the time Bosco Dish reprised their sappy love song that had been played on the radio, the dancers closest to Starla swayed as if they were smitten with the pop pabulum. Most of the truly deviant clubbers, who had stayed on the sidelines waiting for the rebellious moment they needed to justify their misdemeanor, booed and hissed Freddy's ariatic delivery. A protest of stomping boots from the perimeter built into a rhythmic fury as the slow song dragged on, until, unwilling to subject themselves further to the insult of Freddy's crooning, the standard bearers of punk impudence rushed the stage in an attempt to wrestle the instruments from the hands of the offenders. The musicians had to stop playing in order to defend themselves. Freddy fought off the attackers with jabs of his drumsticks, and a pitched battle between Bosco Dish and the crowd, full of verbal abuse, projectile spit, haymaker punches, and musical weaponry, escalated. Trying to minimize the chaos, Dennis, who was positioned opposite the stage behind the console, located the house lights and threw a blinding haze of fluorescent sobriety on the skirmish. Peacemakers, Agents Arthur and Margaret among them, helped separate the combatants, which allowed the band to dismantle their setup without being under attack. Dennis left the lights half lit so that the musicians could see what they were doing, and the discovery of two downed patrons refocused the room. A crowd gathered around the motionless bodies in the middle of the dance floor.

"Everybody please take a break," Dennis announced over the PA system. "Someone's sick. We'll be back in action in a moment."

"Amy?" Rebecca bent down to poke at her fallen friend.

"She's still breathing," someone noted.

Bradley was lying nearby. "So's he."

"What's the matter with them?"

"I can't tell."

"I don't see any blood."

"Who are they?"

Jennifer finally stopped jabbering when she realized her date was one of the victims. "Bradley?"

"Somebody call a doctor," Agent Arthur called out, staying in character as he felt for a pulse.

The call for help came into the nearby police station and Officer Casey was notified. He relayed the information to the FBI command center where Director Lawson was already trying to manage two reported shootings related to their investigation. Detective Falin, who was in the alley trying to deconstruct the alleged shooting there, answered the Director's communication on his handheld. At Lawson's instruction, he and Rudy came upstairs to assist Agents Arthur and Margaret. The lack of music and commotion from upstairs reduced the activity downstairs to a murmur. Most of the regulars, accustomed to incidents, just stayed put waiting for the distraction to be over, but news of injuries brought the curious upstairs.

The roadies from Cells were setting up when Donny, with a shirt tied tightly around his bleeding thigh, limped onto the stage looking for enemies. Blinded with anger, he didn't recognize Ameliah, who had partially awakened from her comatose state and was sitting up in the middle of the floor with Rebecca's assistance. Bradley was also conscious again, sitting on the sidelines where Jennifer had helped him move. Donny spotted Dante and Nigel at the edge of the room, and Starla was standing nearby, drifting in place like a flag in a light breeze.

Hidden in the shadows, Sattar saw Donny looking for him and stayed out of sight as he inched his way over to his niece. Homa hadn't moved since she got there. "Are you all right?" he asked, discretely.

"I'm okay, but what happened to them?" Homa recognized Rebecca kneeling over her friend. Monica had joined them.

"It could be the Princess." Sattar told her.

Homa didn't like the idea that the Princess would harm people – especially people she knew. "Where is she?" she asked, expecting a vision or sign. "I don't see her."

"Be patient. If the Princess is here, she will reveal herself."

Jennifer put her hand on Bradley's shoulder as he sat in a chair off to the side. "Feeling better?"

"I'm kind of dizzy."

"Just stay here. The medics are coming."

"I don't need a doctor. I'll be okay." He spied Ameliah sitting in the middle of the floor. "What happened to her?"

"I don't know. Maybe the same thing that happened to you." Jennifer was more concerned with how this might affect the showcase than Bradley's condition. She nodded to Simon and Dave who were ready for their next fix.

With no more casualties to gawk at, some of the crowd went back downstairs as the drummer of Cells began his noisy preparations. Foggy but determined, Jon strapped on his guitar and reviewed the set list with Marco on the side of the stage. Dennis restarted the house music and came on stage to help. The rest of the patrons resumed their dousing and the club tried to revive its spirit.

Monica, who had just come upstairs with Jon, helped Rebecca get Ameliah to a chair at the back of the room. Ameliah looked dazed. "What happened? Is she going to be okay?" Monica asked Rebecca.

Rebecca regained her motherly instincts and held Ameliah's hand. "I hope so. We were having such a good time, and then all these crazy people came rushing to stage and started fighting with the band. I couldn't see much, and when the lights went on, Amy was on the floor."

"Do you think she got pushed over? Maybe she hit her head?"

Rebecca looked for signs of trauma on her friend. Ameliah pushed her hand away. "Oh stop talking about me like I'm not here. I'm fine. I just felt a little dizzy but I'm all better now." She straightened her outfit and sat up. "I could use another drink."

"Maybe you've had too many."

"Maybe I have," Ameliah agreed, realizing that she didn't feel that well. "Are you guys ready to go?"

"You want to go home now?"

"I'm tired. Freddy's band is finished playing and I could use a good night's sleep in my own bed."

Monica was still buzzed. "Well, I came to see Jon's band, and he's on next, so I want to stay for that."

"I'd like to see him play too," Rebecca agreed. She was still feeling good and didn't want the night to end.

Everyone who needed a break went downstairs, and those that actually had somewhere to go on Monday morning left before Cells started playing. The exodus after the midnight show thinned the room, and the remaining customers, who appreciated the steady two-four drum parts of Billy Idol's promotional tape playing over the house speakers, developed a sense of conspiratorial intimacy.

But the Princess wasn't done crying about her captivity.

"Help!" Jennifer yelled loudly as she tried to hold Bradley up before he fell again. Starla grabbed his other arm, but the emanations from her purse weakened all of them. Nigel joined in the effort to keep them from falling, maneuvering the unsteady trio to some chairs. Dante came closer, but when he put his arm around Starla, he succumbed to the vapors, began to drool, and slumped against the speaker tower. Unsure of what she was supposed to do, Sonya kept her distance. The house lights dimmed, the background music faded, and the first crunch of Jon's electric guitar drowned out the cries of the mounting casualties. Simon and Dave, still far away enough from Nigel's toxic gathering to maintain their professional neutrality, shifted their attention to Jon's band.

The opening song was a raw, eight beat, driving diatribe delivered in authentic angst to the satisfaction of the terminally hip late night crowd that had nowhere else to go.

"Oh no, down on the corner
Pure love aint worth too much
I got a mental disorder
You can look but you cannot touch." *21

Rebecca and Monica left Ameliah at her seat, joining the irreverent fracas on the dance floor as the song built to the vamp.

"Don't touch.
Just look.
Don't stare.
I'm floating In air.
Come a come a come a come on." *22

Jon's long, raspy, blood-curdling screech capped the insanity-tinged climax of "Mental Disorder" with a mesmerizing urgency that unraveled in a frenzy of strangled lead notes, blistering bass runs, and piercing cymbal crashes, eventually ending in abrupt sonic seizure. The next song, "Chemical Reaction," with a sing-a-long chorus, gave the audience a much-needed backbeat, and the ska-influenced pocket drained the sidelines of able-bodied participants.

"What was in the air?
A chemical reaction.

I was made aware
Of a physical attraction
I would follow you right down
The only road I know.
Chemical reaction.
Physical attraction.
Only road I know." *23

Monica and Rebecca danced around together, holding hands like schoolchildren, and several others spontaneously joined their rotating circle. Already impressed with the effect Cells' performance was having on the audience, Simon and Dave came closer to Nigel and Jennifer, intending to indicate their satisfaction with the performance and willingness to make a deal. The sight of Jennifer slumped against the back of the speaker stack stopped them. They weren't sure if it was fatigue or drugs or if something else was wrong. Watching them from nearby, Sonya saw them hesitate and came closer, trying to keep their attention with flirtatious chitchat. Nigel, struggling to regain his equilibrium and claim his victory, smiled weakly as Simon and Dave stood by. Sonya put her arm in the crook of Nigel's elbow and tried to get him to engage the executives, but his proximity to the emanations from Starla's bag had sapped his concentration and his clumsy banter quickly degenerated into incoherence. Confused, Simon and Dave backed away.

The body count increased, as two strangers, seated near Starla, fell from their chairs, joining Dante, Bradley, and Jennifer on the dirty floor. Recognizing the signs of the mass poisoning they had been warned of, ATF agents Arthur and Margaret shed their pretenses, donned their breathing masks, and approached the stricken. The rest of the audience was oblivious, but as soon as Sattar saw the agents put on their masks, he knew what was going on. Agents Falin and Rudy abandoned their deception of fitting in and radioed FBI command from behind the speaker stack with the simple message that they hoped could be heard over the noise of the band. "Casualties, send medics," Detective Falin said, repeating the message twice before joining the ATF agents trying to establish a perimeter. But the breathing masks that the agents had been issued were designed to keep out dust and smoke, and the tightly woven fibers were unable to filter the invisible particles produced by the Princess Tears. Feeling dizzy, the agents were barely able to maintain a semicircle as they waited for help. Sonya also started to succumb to the odors, and among Dante's retinue, only Starla, whose habitual drug use had increased her tolerance, remained relatively unaffected. Lacking any medical training or real emotional connection to the afflicted, Starla allowed the agents to push her out of the way and onto the edge of the dance floor again. Stripped to her core qualities, in spiked heels, fishnet stockings, and a vinyl microskirt, her advertised sexuality was immediately consumed by an interracial, gender-crossed couple, who sandwiched her between them, grinding each other with the lower half of her body. Surprised and excited by the unorthodox foreplay, Starla coordinated her movements with theirs as Cells played the slack time song, "Love is a Thief."

> "Baby do, do you ever need it?
> Need it like, like I would feed it?"
> In a world where we were hungry
> Trippin' on the words that felt so right
> Love is a thief in the night." *24

Starla's braless nipples, barely covered by a thin nylon blouse, rubbed against her partners, hardening as they chafed. Her low-slung shoulder purse hung between her and the other female dancer, and they both pressed the cylindrical glass bottle against their groins. Sexually aroused, their gyrations rubbed the rubber stopper the rest of the way out, releasing more fluid. The Princess let

495

out a silent scream of satisfaction as the Tears drenched Starla's purse. Starla felt the rush of moisture leaking between her legs and didn't know if it was ejaculation or sweat, so when her partners melted off and crumpled to the floor, she put her hand to the wetness and smelled it. It was the last thing she remembered about being there.

"Get it out
Get it out in the open
Livin' lies
Livin' lies and now I'm hopin'
*Love is a thief in the night." *25*

The pile of bodies drew a crowd, but the toxic fumes quickly overcame those who got near enough to help or gawk at Starla's exposed red G-string. The disruptive activity on the dance floor allowed Sattar to pinpoint the location of the missing bottle, and he quickly applied the antidotal formula to two scarves he removed from his pocket. He gave one to Homa, and they tied the scarves around their mouths and noses like western bandits. Temporarily immune to the intoxicating effects of the Princess Tears, they snaked through the confused crowd. Sattar knelt at Starla's side as if to help her, looking for the bottle. He saw her shoulder strap and pulled it, like a fisherman checks his line for a catch, but Starla was lying on her purse. Rolling her onto her side to release the snag, he felt the distinctive shape of the bottle through the soft leather. Knowing its likely condition, Sattar angled the bottle up and snugged the stopper back in before separating the purse from its straps with a deft pull of his pocketknife.

What Monica saw was a creepy man with a bandana over his mouth, who looked like a knife-wielding robber, stealing the handbag from a motionless victim. "Thief!" she shrieked, just as the song ended.

496

"Thief!" the audience echoed as if she was complimenting the performance.

Jon saw her and waved. "Thank you, Monica," he said through the microphone. "That one is called 'Love is a Thief,' but I guess you already knew that."

"No! Thief!" Monica tried to get the crowd's help again, but they thought she was still cheering on her boyfriend. No one paid attention to the Sattar and Homa as they retreated back into the shadows. Monica's cries were drowned out as the next song began, and still in possession of most of her scruples, she was troubled that no one cared about the crime she had just witnessed. Rebecca couldn't understand why Monica was suddenly so upset, and tried to see where she was pointing. She noticed something familiar about the strange woman in a full length brown robe blending into the darkness, but couldn't make the connection. The woman turned and faced her, but Homa was unrecognizable in a hooded robe with her mouth and nose covered by a scarf. Only her eyes were exposed, and something in her deep stare activated the nerves Rebecca had successfully numbed for most of the evening. Frustrated and confused, she and Monica found Ameliah, seated glumly on the sidelines. The girls from New Jersey knew it was time to go.

But Max's Kansas City's reputation for partying out of bounds made the fallen seem like losers in the late night stamina contest, and, accustomed to the harsh realities of extreme behavior, the remaining audience lost the few concerns that had survived a long night of indulgence. They were content to let the men with the breathing masks move the bodies out of their way so they could resume their self-destructive frivolity, and to their delight, the band continued playing, despite the interruptions. The infectious beat of "Tappin Phones" afflicted their common sense as well as their sense of propriety, and the remaining contestants in the partying competition hopped and two stepped around the human obstacles strewn on the floor, assuming they were either too drunk to join them or had simply tired of the game.

"Tappin' phone lines information slips.
Dreamin' bout your mouth and hips.
Steam escaping through your lips.
I woke up shakin' and my body's achin'.
Hey what you trying to do – oh!
What you tryin' to do?
We're tappin' phone lines." *26

Upon word from Director Lawson and on Officer Casey's command, members of the NYPD sealed the front and back doors of the club. They found the club manager, and to the dismay of the occupants, had him turn on the all the lights in the first floor restaurant. Bar service came to a halt, and the stairs were cleared to make way for the ambulance personnel. Struggling with their own equilibrium, the Customs and ATF Agents upstairs were overmatched trying to manage twelve victims of aromatic poisoning in various states of consciousness. Feeding off the chaos and energy of the audience, Cells' performance morphed into a broken-play end-zone romp. Jon sang the synth line from the recorded version of "Tappin Phones" like a schoolyard teaser.

*"La da da **da**, da da **da da**, **daa**.*
Pho pho pho phone lines" *27

While he was singing, he looked over to the side where Nigel had been standing, fully expecting confirmation of a successful show. There were a few men with masks and some people slumped on chairs, but he didn't see anyone he knew. Frankie and Marco brought the rhythm section down to a moderate locomotive chug, expecting something – anything – that would signal their mastery of the moment, but Nigel and the record company executives were nowhere in sight. No one rushed the stage in adulation, and everyone who was still conscious was too distracted to notice the performance. The band stuttered to a stop like a baby carriage falling down a flight of stairs, and Jon faced his band mates with a sheepish shrug. Frankie and Marco were angry that their sweaty efforts had gone unappreciated, and as the numbing effects of the drugs were wearing off, Jon's injured foot began to throb again. He put his guitar down and used it as a cane to relieve the pressure. The house lights came up and revealed the extent of the disorder in front of him: All the dancing had stopped, and the floor was a confused mess of bleary-eyed revelers stumbling over fallen friends.

"Everybody please stay calm," an authoritative voice announced over the PA system. "Help is on the way." The beat officer who made the announcement had no experience talking to a post- midnight crowd at a rowdy nightclub, and his instructions had the opposite effect. The presence of mask-wearing officials and prone bodies, combined with the promise of "help" put a charge of panic in the remaining patrons who rushed the exits, hoping to escape scrutiny. Frankie beat his drums angrily as the audience dispersed and the mirage of triumph vanished.

Frustrated, Jon reprised his hoarse scream from "Mental Disorder" and yelled at the scattering crowd, "Aaahhh! Get out. Get out of here! All you fucking sheep!" Frankie beat his drums to imitate the sound of a machine gun and crashed his cymbals in explosive fury. Dennis cut off Jon's mic before he made any more enemies, but it didn't stop Jon's tirade. "I hate you. All of you stinking sheep! Fuck you! And you too, Nigel, wherever you are! You miserable teabag and all your too cool friends! All you record company pinheads, queers, and coke whores! You wouldn't know talent if it bit you in the neck. You all suck! All you fucking losers in your stupid costumes pretending to be so hip. I hate you – all of you!" He started to enjoy the sound of his diatribe, and even though the show was over, he picked up his guitar again and started to play. Insidiously, Frankie and Marco joined him in a warp speed version of Jon's invective "Don't Change Your Mind."

"With your plastic boots.
And your hula-hoops,
It's no substitute
For a gun that shoots.
And you're such a drag
With your pants that sag
And your leather bag
And your words that lag.
Don't change your mind!
It happens all the time
When you read between the lines
Time's up!" *28

White-coated EMTs brought stretchers to the dosed partygoers waking up from their narcotic naps. With the house lights up, Donny spotted Sattar hiding in the corner and used the cover of confusion to seek his revenge. He limped menacingly toward his trapped victim, pumping his powerful chest with simian vigor. But Sattar saw him coming, and as soon as Donny got close enough, Sattar rammed his small revolver against Donny's gut and pulled the trigger twice. The gunshots were muffled by flesh and drowned out by the drum sounds from the stage, and when Donny fell, he was just another body on the floor. Sattar moved his horrified niece away before the blood had time to leak out and be noticed. Cells continued to play, enjoying their unofficial role of providing the soundtrack for the unspooled sanity in front of them.

Unable to communicate with their command truck over the noise, Detective Falin tried to get the band to stop playing. He was wearing a facemask that he didn't want to remove, so he waved his arms in a universally understood crossing pattern in front of the band. Jon pretended that he didn't know what the detective wanted and turned up the volume knob on his guitar. Incensed, Detective Falin tried to grab the guitar out of Jon's hands, and they wrestled with the instrument for a few tugs until Jon, who had a better grip, smashed the solid end into the detective's head, knocking him back. Rudy saw his partner struggling and came to help, but Frankie came out from behind his drum set wielding his sticks, ready for a fight. Standing back, Detective Falin took out his gun and fired two loud shots at the ceiling. Startled, everyone stopped what they were doing. The shout of "Gunfire!" sent the last few stragglers running.

Sattar used the moment to sneak up behind an EMT and hold a Tears-soaked cloth to his face. The EMT crumbled immediately, and Sattar, pretending to try to hold him up, took his three quarter white coat as he fell. He put it on over his clothes, and, looking like he belonged, motioned to another medic for help with a fallen victim. The other medic, who was new to the profession, brought his empty gurney closer, and the two of them laid Homa, feigning illness, onto the wheeled cart. They carried her down the stairs and out to the waiting ambulances. Once outside, Sattar lined the gurney up with the other victims needing assistance and indicated that he would stay there while the EMT brought in another stretcher. When only the stricken would notice, Homa sat up, slid off the gurney, and allowed herself to be helped to the far side of an ambulance by her uncle. Out of view, Sattar threw Starla's empty purse in a trash bin and kicked his borrowed medic jacket under an ambulance. As the girls from New Jersey stood on Park Avenue trying to hail a cab, Rebecca noticed something familiar about the strangers walking across the street. She pointed them out to Monica just as they were disappearing down the subway stairs, but a taxi stopped in front of them and they were just glad to be on their way home.

EPILOG

Scraps of incriminating evidence littered the floors of the club, but it was impossible to know whom to arrest for what, so all the suspects who had been detained for questioning were released by dawn. With no one else to blame for anything that could be proven, Jon was the only one charged with an actual crime. Detective Falin had needed the help of four other officers to get him to the paddy wagon, and he was booked for resisting arrest, disturbing the peace, and assaulting an officer. There were so many bodies carried out to the ambulances that the police didn't realize that one of them, Donny, had been shot, until it was almost too late. Following his near death from peritoneal poisoning, Donny's life was saved by surgeons at a local hospital who re-plumbed his bile into a colostomy bag. Randi, who was still recovering in the same hospital, came to visit him the following day, but declined his invitation to join him in bed.

Dominic Pecorino got a call from his friends at the police station in the middle of the night. He called Anthony and told him to take care of it. Anthony drove over to the triage site near the club at 5:00 a.m. and transferred his brother and Starla from the back of a Medevac ambulance to his car. He drove them home, parked, and helped them up the stairs to Dante's apartment. Roslyn was up and waiting for him when he got home.

When Nigel regained his composure and freedom, he and Sonya went back to the apartment over the studio and screwed each other sober. Lying naked with his lover in his arms, Nigel smoked a cigarette and made promises to take her to England to meet his family.

The flashing lights from police reinforcements in the streets below had given the Darius Trust all the warning it needed to prepare for the staged assault on the Old Medical Building. Mak and Rhamin had used the service elevator to move Reggie into a second floor office that had been converted into a safe room. Dr. Nouri and Bahram had used a hidden entrance to access the laboratory and move the hookah behind the false wall they had built into the suite. While some officers were coming up in the main elevator and others were climbing the back stairs for their stealth assault, Bahram and Dr. Nouri took the service elevator, which could only be operated with a key, down to join Mak and Rhamin in the safe room. They stayed there until the police activity subsided, and just before dawn, they carried Reggie's unconscious body out of the building via the basement tunnel that connected to an adjacent building. Dr. Nouri's car was still parked a few blocks away and, after laying Reggie in the trunk, they took the side streets uptown to the Queensboro bridge. Reggie woke up the next day in unfamiliar surroundings, bandaged and drugged.

Detective Gillingham's 5:00 a.m. report to Director Lawson from Dr. Nouri's empty laboratory office came about the same time that Detective Falin showed up with Jon's arrest documents. Incredulous that the entire operation had only netted one rowdy musician, Director Lawson took an angry swipe at the papers on his desk that sent them flying all over the van. In the subsequent clean up, the record of Jon's misconduct was misplaced, and without the necessary paperwork, he was released from the overnight holding cell Monday afternoon.

The Customs Bureau Interdiction report that Detective Falin filled out characterized the operation as a success, based on the fact that the investigation had shut down the manufacture of the illegal substances, and he spun the facts to lobby for a promotion. Special Agent Farmer was the one who actually filled out the FBI case report, and he made sure that the Darius Trust was never mentioned by name. With no corroborating evidence recovered, Morris Draper's cooperation became the focus of the investigation into Laden Imports, which was recast as an IRS issue. Everything related to the Pecorinos was turned back over to their friends at the NYPD.

An exhausted Ralph Lowell finally made it home at 6:00 a.m. on Monday morning, but only had time to shower and change clothes before going into work. His wife made him coffee but didn't speak to him before she took Alfredo to school. Rudy was already at his desk, bragging to Melanie, when Ralph got to the office.

"Hey, Ralph, my man, some weekend!" he greeted Ralph enthusiastically as the receptionist went back to her station.

"Yeah, can't wait to do that again," Ralph yawned.

"Chalk one up for overtime!" Rudy marked their imaginary scorecard.

Ralph plunked down at his desk, absently staring out the window at the familiar brick building next door.

"Maybe this will cheer you up." Rudy said, handing him an overtime request form. The form was only a page long but had a lot of boxes to fill in. Most of the space on the back was left blank and asked for a detailed explanation. Ralph looked confused. "Just write the same thing as me," Rudy instructed, giving him his completed form to copy. "Don't worry about section two. You don't need to tell them everything that you did for the last two days. After you're done, I'll run them up to Detective Falin."

Ralph studied the document. "When do you think we'll get the money?" he asked.

"Detective Falin will sign them and they'll be submitted with the rest of his expenses. We should get paid in a couple of weeks if there's no problems."

"Okay, but what kind of problems could there be?"

"You never know with this kind of thing."

Ralph was alarmed. "What do mean?"

"Well, Detective Falin has to get his report approved by the FBI, and I hear they're not too happy with what happened, so it could take a while," Rudy admitted, "and there's always a chance...."

Ralph reached up in the air and erased Rudy's imaginary chalk mark.

Worried and exhausted, Homa called Asalah from the sofa where she had fallen asleep and asked her to open the office. With Homa absent, Asalah and Barbara spent most of the morning listening to Rita recount the juicy details of her Caribbean vacation with her new boyfriend. Rebecca showed up before lunch but was uncharacteristically quiet and disinterested. Her father called soon after she arrived, and she held the phone to her ear, staring blankly while he spoke in code. Mak called in, and hearing that Homa wasn't there, said he would be in later. Homa dozed on the couch until 11:00 a.m., fighting the inertia of fear, trying to imagine what she was going to tell her mother without making her more upset. When she finally sat up, resolved to face her mother's breakdown, she was surprised to see her in a good mood.

Homa couldn't believe her eyes. "Mother?"

Samani was dressed in white summer culottes, a bright floral top, and tennis shoes. "Good morning, princess," Samani giggled, smiling as she buzzed around the apartment, humming and dusting. "Did you sleep well?" she asked cheerfully.

Homa decided not to burden her with any details. "Not really."

"Well you might as well get up then. The sofa is never as comfortable as your own bed. You slept so late. You must be hungry." Samani chattered, feeling the lightheaded effects of black coffee and scented hankies.

"A little."

"Asalah called a while ago. She's minding the office and everything's fine. Shall we go out for lunch?" Samani suggested.

"Lunch sounds good." Homa sighed, relieved that her mother was okay, but uncertain about what was waiting for her at work. She went to her room, tied her hair back into a long ponytail, and put a shawl on over her jeans. They went outside into the warmth of a spring day and held hands as they strolled through Gramercy Park.

"How do you feel, mother?" Homa asked, looking for signs.

"I feel lucky. It's a beautiful day and I have my beautiful daughter with me." Samani glowed. "Your father is happy for us."

Homa looked up and saw the face of the Princess in a puffy cloud. After lunch they took a cab to the Laden warehouse. They chatted with Asalah and the office girls for a moment before retreating to Homa's private office. There was a message on the answering machine from Saeed, and they listened to it twice.

"Salaam, good morning, it is a lovely day here in Beirut. I'm missing you all so much but I have good news to share. We have contracted with cocoa suppliers in Nigeria and the first shipments will arrive soon. Please check the telex to make sure we receive everything that's been ordered. As you know, my brother Sattar will be here tomorrow and I am anxious to see him. Also, most importantly, we have been invited to Kurdistan for a very high level meeting. Our friendships in Kirkuk have never been stronger, and even though it's too soon to hope for any news of your father, we will make inquiries. Strength, dear Homa, the Princess is with you. Take care of your mother, and send my love to Asalah. Salaam."

Samani stood in front of the Princess head, touching its countenance as if it were alive. "You've seen the Princess?" she asked.

"Yes, mother, last night for the first time."

"And your Uncle Sattar, he was there?"

"Yes mother, Uncle Sattar was with me."

Samani thought for a moment. "But Saeed said Sattar was coming to Beirut. He was here for only a day?"

Homa decided to keep it simple. "Yes, he had some business to attend to and then he went back to Beirut."

"Dr. Nouri saw him?"

"Yes, Dr. Nouri will tell you all about it when you see him."

Mak tapped lightly on the office door. Homa opened it. "Come in, Mak," she said holding his gaze without blinking.

Mak understood Homa's silent request for discretion. "Good afternoon ladies. How nice to see you. So good of you to wake up and join us," he chided Homa playfully.

"Thank you, Mak. Is there something you need?"

"No, not really. I thought that you weren't here so I was just coming into your office to change a light bulb." He held up a small bulb and looked at the Princess head.

Homa understood. "Yes, thank you. She's been asleep for too long."

Jon got home from the police station Monday at dusk. He fell asleep immediately and didn't wake up until late Tuesday morning. Looking out his window, he thought about going in to work and making up a story to explain his absence the day before, but a police cruiser in the street heightened his worry that his arrest papers might have been relocated. Paranoid, he thought someone might have told his parole officer what happened, and the police would be waiting to re-arrest him for violating parole when he got to work. He didn't want to stay at his apartment in case they came looking for him there, so he decided to move out immediately. He didn't know where he could go or who he could tell, so he quickly threw his personal belongings in a duffle bag and packed up the recording equipment in his only suitcase. Still torn about leaving everything that seemed so right just two days before, he sneaked through the alley and hobbled to the lot in the East Village where he kept his van. Hoping it would be mistaken for a delivery vehicle, he double parked in front of his apartment building and left the blinkers on. Al wasn't around, and it only took him ten minutes to remove everything he owned. Unsure of where to go, he headed toward the river like a rogue sheep and dove off the radar – again.

Vaporized Characters

Agent Ralph Lowell – NY Customs Bureau
Agent Rudy George – NY Customs bureau
Ameliah – Jersey girl who works at law firm
Anthony Pecorino – Dante's brother
Arshan Zemmi – Homa's father
Bharam Darius – Monsouri cousin and partner
Dante Pecorino – family provocateur
Dennis Strider – Black Sheep manager
Detective Ailes – NYC Vice
Detective Ferguson – NYC Vice
Detective Monte Gillingham – NY Customs Bureau
Detective Todd Falin – NY Customs Bureau
Director Lawson – FBI Coordinator
Donny DiCalipari – Freddy's manager
Dr. Nouri – Old Medical Building owner, chemist
Freddy Wanamaker – Cells' rival
Herb Draper – accountant for Persians
Homa Monsouri Zemmi – Laden Imports manager
Jon Cells – aspiring musician
Mak (Colonel Mackenzie) – Laden warehouse manager
Monica – Jersey girl, dancer
Nigel Acton – studio manager, English
Rebecca Draper – Jersey girl, Herb's daughter
Reggie Whitehead – NY hustler, Dr. Nouri's driver
Rhamin Darius – Persian family business partner
Saeed Monsouri – Laden Import owner
Samani Monsouri Zemmi – Homa's mother
Sattar Monsouri – Laden Import owner
Starla – Dante's girlfriend

Vaporized Song Index